Romantic Tim

ELIZABETH
LOWELL

"It is not hard to see why Lowell's novels have enjoyed their superior success over the years."
—on *This Time Love*

"The masterful storytelling skills of perennial favorite Elizabeth Lowell place her in a rarefied class of authors who never disappoint."
—on *Running Scared*

"The powerful storytelling that is a hallmark of Elizabeth Lowell's work makes each of her books a riveting journey."
—on *Moving Target*

"An emotionally driven and sensually charged book that is vintage Lowell."
—on *Eden Burning*

"When it comes to delivering epic romance and suspense, Ms. Lowell is in a class by herself."
—on *Midnight in Ruby Bayou*

ELIZABETH
LOWELL

FIRE AND RAIN
& OUTLAW

HQN™

ISBN-13: 978-0-373-77253-7
ISBN-10:   0-373-77253-X

FIRE AND RAIN & OUTLAW

Printed in U.S.A.

CONTENTS

FIRE AND RAIN

CHAPTER ONE

WHAT IN HELL AM I DOING HERE?

Luke looked in the mirror, swiped a last bit of axle grease off his chin and had no fast answers for his silent question. In fact, he had no answer at all as to why he had stayed on at Cash McQueen's apartment knowing that Carla McQueen was coming to dinner.

It wasn't unusual for Luke to drive the long miles between his ranch in Four Corners country and the city of Boulder in order to visit his friend Cash. It wasn't unusual for the two of them to take on some kind of repair work on Cash's balky Jeep. It wasn't unusual for the two of them to split a pizza and a six-pack afterward and catch up on mutual news.

It was damned unusual that Carla would appear in the same room with Luke MacKenzie.

Is that why Cash dodged my question about who Carla is dating? Luke asked his reflection in the mirror. *Did she finally get over me and say yes to some nice city boy? And what business is it of mine if she did?*

Even as he tried to tell himself that it was only natural that he have a big-brotherly concern for the little sister of his best friend, Luke knew that was only part of the truth. The rest of the truth was a steel spur digging into his self-esteem: three years ago he had wanted Carla so badly that he had sent her running for her life from the Rocking M.

And him.

With an effort, Luke forced aside the image of Carla's wide blue-green eyes and trembling lips and the soft heat of her body flowing over his. That image had come to too many of his dreams, waking or sleeping. But that wasn't what he wanted from her. It sure as hell wasn't what he would take from her. What he wanted, all he would accept, was a return to the days when they had shared the kind of companionship Luke hadn't known was possible with a woman.

It's been three years. Surely Carla's forgotten the whole thing by now. Surely she and Cash and I can be an almost family again, the way we used to be.

God, I've missed the sound of her laughter and the way her smile used to light up the whole house.

"Hey, Luke, are you taking root in there?"

"I'm still trying to get your Jeep out from under my fingernails," Luke retorted to Cash. "You ought to trade that damn thing for a dog and shoot the dog."

The bathroom door opened. Cash's big body filled the frame with little left over.

"Give me your shirt," Cash said.

"Why?"

"The Jeep drooled all down your spine."

Luke made a sound of disgust that Cash didn't take seriously. But then, neither did Luke.

"The things I do for you," Luke muttered.

With quick, deft movements he rinsed his hands, stripped off the black shirt and fired it at Cash's head. Another shirt came flying back at the same speed. Luke pulled it on with a small smile; the shirt fit as well as one of his own. Cash was the only man Luke knew whose clothes he could wear without feeling as though he were in a straitjacket.

"Much better," Cash said. "Can't have you looking like something the cat dragged in and didn't eat. What would Carla think?"

"She's seen me looking worse."

"Not on her twenty-first birthday. Hurry up. I can't decorate a cake worth a damn."

"What makes you think I can?"

"Desperation."

Grinning, Luke tucked in the shirt and followed Cash to the kitchen, feeling very much at home. In many ways Carla and Cash were as close to a real family as Luke had ever come. His mother, like his grandmother and great-grandmother before her, had hated the Rocking M. Even worse, his mother had feared the land and the wind as though they were alive and hunting her. Finally she had had a nervous breakdown. Her parents had swept in from the East Coast, picked up the pieces of their daughter and removed her from the Rocking M. They had also taken Luke's seven-year-old sister, whom he loved as he hadn't permitted himself to love anything since. Neither mother nor sister had ever been heard from since that day.

At thirteen, Luke had been left alone with a silent, hard-drinking father and a ranch whose demands were as endless as the land itself was beautiful. At nineteen he had inherited the Rocking M. At twenty he had hired Cash to do a resources survey of the ranch. Six months later Cash had shown up for the summer with his half sister, a sad-eyed waif whose attempts at smiles had broken Luke's heart. Perhaps it was the memory of his own little sister, perhaps it was Carla's haunting eyes, perhaps it was only his own need to protect and care for something more gentle than himself. Whatever the reason, Carla had slipped past defenses Luke didn't even know he had.

One day while riding a distant corner of the ranch, he had found a sherd of ancient Anasazi pottery in September Canyon. He had given the piece of the past to Carla, trying to tell her that nothing is lost forever, that everyone is part of what came before and what will come after. Somehow she had understood all that he couldn't find words for, and she had cried for the first time since her parents had died. He had held her, feeling her trust as she gave herself to his strength and wept until she couldn't lift her head. And as he held her, he felt as though he himself were crying for all that he had lost when he had been about Carla's age.

"Yo, Luke," Cash said, snapping his fingers in front of the other man's whiskey-colored eyes. "Anybody home?"

Luke grunted. "Where's the cake?"

"Over there."

"I was afraid you were going to say that." Luke sighed as he looked at a lopsided chocolate heap that was charred on the sides and sticky in the middle. "Hope you made a bucket of icing."

"It's in the sink."

Luke glanced over at the sink. There was, indeed, a white substance in the sink. No bowl. Just sink.

"Tell you what," Luke drawled. "Why don't I bring the cake over, mess it around a bit and then turn on the garbage disposal?"

"I have candles," Cash said indignantly.

"Stick them in the ice cream."

"C'mon, *hombre*. Where's your sense of adventure? If we use the soup ladle for the icing, maybe we won't drip too much on the floor."

Luke was dumping the first load of icing on the cake when he heard Carla's voice call from the front door.

"Open up, big brother! My hands are full."

"Happy birthday, sis," Cash said, opening the door. "Look who's here. He just happened to—watch it!"

Luke had a glimpse of shocked, blue-green eyes, then Carla was grabbing frantically for the limp pizza box she had been in the process of handing over to Cash when she had spotted Luke.

"Nice catch, schoolgirl," Luke drawled, watching Carla with a masculine hunger he would never admit, because there was nothing he would permit himself to do to assuage that hunger.

Except look at her. He allowed himself to do that, his eyes cataloguing every feature. Sun-streaked chestnut hair, eyes like pieces of the sea, a body whose curves she never flaunted—but they were there just the same, a promise of heat that had made him ache since she was sixteen. With the ease of long practice, Luke shunted his thoughts aside, concentrating on seeing Carla as what she was: his best friend's kid sister.

"Pizza tastes better when you don't have to comb it out of the rug with your teeth," Luke pointed out.

"I'll take your word for it," Carla said, as though it had

been a day rather than almost a year since she had been this close to Luke. "I'm partial to plates and tables myself."

"You used to be more adventurous."

Luke saw the words slip past Carla's cool, tightly held surface and knew as clearly as if she had shouted it that she was remembering what had happened three years before, the night she had graduated from high school, stood in front of him and declared her love.

Most nights Luke might have been able to smile and send Carla on her way feeling no more than a little embarrassed for her sweet declaration. But it hadn't been most other nights. It had been one of the nights when his elemental hunger for Cash's little sister had driven Luke to the temporary relief of straight Scotch. Instead of turning away from her, he had come to his feet, grabbed her and kissed her with every bit of the wild hunger in him. When she had tried to slow him down, to talk to him, he had lashed out.

What did you think a man wanted from a woman who loves him, schoolgirl? And there's the problem, isn't it? You're a girl mouthing woman's words and I'm a man on fire. Run, schoolgirl. Run like hell and don't come back.

Carla had taken Luke at his word. She had run and she hadn't come back. And he had locked himself up in the barn with his tools, transforming his yearnings into gleaming shapes of wood—chair and dresser, headboard and footboard, beautiful furnishings for the dream that could not come true.

"Ah, well, live and learn," Carla said.

"What have you learned, sunshine?" Luke asked.

He saw the ripple of emotion in her clear eyes as he called her by the old nickname. But the emotion passed, and she was again watching him with the combination of distance and coolness that she had used on him whenever she couldn't avoid him.

"I've learned that being adventurous is another name for being a fool," she said.

Luke saw the tiny flinch she couldn't conceal and knew that he had hurt her. He hadn't really intended that. He had just wanted to see something besides aloofness and distance in her beautiful eyes.

"You've got no corner on being a fool," Luke said calmly. "Seems like all I do lately is chase stubborn cows and eat bad food." He yawned and stretched his arms over his head, flattening his palms on the ceiling in order to fully stretch his body.

"Get a cook," Carla said, walking past Luke to the kitchen.

As he lowered his arms, his fingertips accidentally brushed over her arm and her glossy, shoulder-length hair. The short-sleeved blouse she wore couldn't conceal the sudden ripple of goose bumps, helpless response to his touch.

"I've had six cooks in the past twenty months," Luke said. "Not a one of them could hold a candle to you. I've missed all those dinners when you and Cash and I would sit and talk about everything and nothing, and then Cash and I would fight over who got the biggest piece of whatever pie you'd made that day. Those were good times, sunshine."

Carla's hands gripped the pizza box too tightly. She slapped the box onto the counter and began transferring slices to a baking sheet.

"Bet you don't miss doing the dishes afterward," she said.

"The conversation was worth it," Luke said simply.

"Oh, no you don't," Cash said.

"I don't what?" Luke asked.

"You don't come sniffing around looking to make Carla

your cook for the summer, leaving me with a can opener for company."

Luke smiled slowly. "Hell of an idea, Cash. Sunshine, would you—"

"Nope," Carla said quickly, interrupting.

"Why not?"

Ignoring him, Carla bent over the open stove and positioned the limp pizza as though it were a gear in a Swiss watch.

"Why not?" Luke pressed.

"Cash would starve, that's why," she muttered.

"Slander! I can cook as well as the next man," Cash said.

"Sure," she retorted, "as long as the next man is Luke MacKenzie."

Before either man could speak, Carla spotted the brown-and-white mess at the end of the counter. Cautiously she dipped her finger in a thin white puddle that had formed on the tile next to the battered cake. Luke's eyes followed the tip of her tongue as she tasted the goo on her finger.

"Too sweet for gravy or paint," she said after a moment, giving Cash a teasing sideways glance. She stirred the puddle with her fingertip, noted that the white stuck to everything except the brown mound it had been poured over, and smiled. "I do believe my brother has invented a fairly tasty form of library paste."

Luke snickered.

"Slander," Cash said, trying not to smile. "Is that why you turned down my kind offer to cook and insisted on bringing pizza instead?"

"Bingo," Carla said.

"Which reminds me, how much do I owe you for the pizza?"

"A hundred dollars."

Carla's tone was so casual that it took a few instants for the amount to sink in.

Cash did a double take and asked, "What's on that pizza—beluga caviar?"

"Pepperoni and mushrooms. I included the birthday present I knew you'd be too busy chasing rocks to get for me."

"Oh. What did I get you?"

"A few more weeks with Fred."

"Fred?" Luke said before he could stop himself. "Who the hell is Fred?"

CHAPTER TWO

"FRED'S A WHAT," CARLA SAID.

"Huh?"

"Now you're getting the idea," she murmured.

Luke's eyes narrowed.

"Fred's her baby," Cash added unhelpfully.

"Do tell," Luke retorted. "And soon, I hope."

Carla fought against the smile she felt stealing over her lips, but couldn't stifle it any more than she could prevent the helpless yearning that went through her when Luke smiled approvingly at her in return. He hadn't changed. He was still tall, powerful, intense. His very dark brown hair set off his amber eyes, making them look gold in certain kinds of light. The trace of beard shadow beneath his high cheekbones perfectly suited his hard-jawed Slavic features.

For a moment it felt as though time had turned back upon itself, touching again the years before she had mistaken

Luke's affectionate tolerance for a very different kind of love. Longing swept through her, a futile wish that she had been different three years ago, or he had been; but she hadn't, and he hadn't, and the memories still shook her. She saw Luke as she had seen him that night, a huge, looming presence, his eyes a golden blaze of reflected firelight. The width of his shoulders had blocked out the world when he bent down and swept her up in an embrace.

The first instants had been pure bliss, the culmination of years and years of dreaming; and then his arms had tightened and tightened and tightened until she couldn't breathe. His mouth had become rough and demanding, forcing hers to open, giving her a kiss that was as hard and adult as the male body grinding intimately against hers. She had been confused, completely at a loss, and finally a little frightened. It wasn't how she had envisioned Luke's response to her declaration of love—where was the tenderness, the joy, the sweetness of knowing you loved and were loved in return?

With an effort, Carla banished the agonizing memories and answered Luke's question. "Fred is my truck."

"Tell him the truth," advised Cash. "Fred is a battered, bewildered, dwarf four-by-four that does its best to play with the big boys. I can't tell you how many times I've gotten a call and had to go and winch Carla out of some damned mud hole. Next time it happens I've got half a mind to make *you* go and get her, Luke. After all, it's all your fault that she's barreling all over the Four Corners chasing ancient shadows."

Luke's intent, golden eyes fixed on Cash. "It is?"

"Damned straight. If you hadn't given her that sherd of Anasazi pottery you found somewhere up in September Canyon, she never would have become interested in archaeology. If she weren't interested in archaeology, she wouldn't have been off running after old bones with her professors every summer and most vacations."

"I thought it was boys that girls chased," Luke said, fixing Carla with enigmatic golden eyes.

"I gave up chasing boys right after I graduated from high school," Carla said flatly. "And stop trying to change the subject," she continued, turning to Cash, changing the subject herself. "You owe me fourteen bucks for the pizza."

"And eighty-six bucks for truck repairs?"

She smiled slightly and shook her head. "No, but I wouldn't turn down a hug."

Cash engulfed Carla in a hug. Though she was five foot seven, the top of her head barely brushed Cash's chin. He lifted her and swung her around. When he set her down again, she was almost on Luke's feet. There was barely room for her to breathe. Luke was the same height as her brother, six foot three, and weighed within a pound or two of Cash's one ninety-six. That was probably one of the reasons the two men got along so well—they were built on the same scale. Big.

Without warning, Luke's long fingers tilted Carla's chin, forcing her to meet his eyes.

"Are you really all grown-up now, sunshine?"

The old nickname and the searching intensity of Luke's eyes took Carla's breath away, making speech impossible.

"Hey, that reminds me," Cash said. "It's been months since I've played killer poker."

"Not surprising," Luke retorted, releasing Carla with the speed of a man passing a hot potato on to its final destination. "It's been months since you've found an out-of-state sucker who doesn't know why Alexander McQueen is called 'Cash.'"

"Lucky at cards, unlucky at love."

Luke snorted. "I'll shuffle. Carla can deal. You open the champagne I brought."

"Champagne?" Carla asked, stunned.

She looked up into Luke's eyes. He was still standing close to her, so close that she could sense the heat of his big body. She hadn't sensed anyone's presence so acutely in years.

Three years, to be exact.

Luke's slow smile as he looked down at Carla made something stir and shimmer to life deep within her.

"Champagne," he confirmed, his voice deep. "You only turn twenty-one once. It should be special."

By the time the cards were shuffled, cut and dealt, Carla was sipping from a glass of golden champagne, which fizzed and sizzled softly over her lips and tongue. She hardly noticed the alcohol, for her blood was already sparkling from the memory of Luke's fingers on her skin.

Are you really all grown-up now?

The implications of that question scattered Carla's attention, making her lose at cards more rapidly than usual. Before Luke poured her a second glass of champagne, she had lost her original stake—six dollars. She handed over the last of her nickels without rancor, for it had been Cash rather than Luke who had won the lion's share of the pots. Long ago, Carla had decided that Cash must have made a deal with the devil in exchange for luck at cards.

By the time Luke poured Carla a third glass of champagne, the pizza was reduced to grease spots on the paper plates, and it had become clear to everyone that Cash's luck was running as high as ever. Luke was down to three dollars from his original six, and Carla had traded seven days' worth of home-cooked meals for fifty cents each and promptly had lost every penny.

Normally Carla would have stopped drinking halfway through her second glass of champagne, but nothing about her twenty-first birthday was normal—especially the presence of Luke MacKenzie. The champagne was a dancing delight that smelled as yeasty as the bread she loved to bake. Cash and Luke were in fine form, trading insults and laughter equally. When Luke poured a third glass of champagne for Carla, she was into Cash for a summer's worth of meals and Luke was down to seventy-five cents.

Carla rooted for Cash unabashedly, frankly enjoying seeing Luke on the losing end of something for a change. Luke took the "card lessons" in good humor, squeezing every bit of mileage from his shrinking pile of small change.

And then slowly, almost imperceptibly, Luke started winning. He rode the unexpected streak of luck aggressively, repeatedly betting everything he had and getting twice as much back from the pot. By the time the last drops from the magnum of champagne had been poured—by Carla into Luke's glass, in a blatant attempt to fuzz his mind—Cash was down to his last nickel. He tossed it into the pot philosophically, calling Luke's most recent raise.

Luke fanned out his cards to reveal a pair of sevens, nine high. Cash made a disgusted sound and threw in his hand without showing his cards.

"What?" Carla said in disbelief. She reached for Cash's abandoned cards, only to have her fingers lightly slapped by her brother.

"Bad dog, drop!" he teased. "You know the rules. It costs good money to see those cards and you're broke."

Carla withdrew her fingers and muttered, "I still don't believe that you couldn't crawl over a lousy pair of sevens."

"You forgot the nine," Luke said.

"It's easy to forget something that small," Carla shot back. She sighed. "Well, I guess this just wasn't your night, big brother. All you won was something you would have gotten anyway—a summer's worth of dinners cooked by yours truly."

"Sounds like a damned good deal to me," Luke said.

There was a moment of silence, followed by another. The silence stretched. Luke arched his dark eyebrows at Cash in silent query. Cash smiled.

"You'll have to throw in wages," Cash said.

"Same as I paid the last housekeeper. But she'll have to keep house, too. For that I'd bet everything on the table. One hand. Winner take all."

"What do you say, sis?" Cash asked, turning toward Carla. "Huh?"

"Luke has agreed to bet everything in the pot against your agreement to be the Rocking M's cook and housekeeper."

"You're out of school for the summer, right?" Luke asked.

She nodded, too off balance to tell him that she was out of school, period. She had crammed four years of studying in the three years since she had graduated from high school. It had been the perfect excuse not to spend summers on the Rocking M, as she had since she was fourteen.

"You can start next weekend and go until the end of August. A hundred days, give or take a few," Luke said casually, but his eyes had the predatory intensity of a bird of prey. "Room, board and wages, same as for any hired hand."

Carla stared at Cash. He smiled encouragingly. She tried to think of all the reasons she would be a raving idiot for taking the bet.

Her blood sizzled softly, champagne and something more.

"Do you have your toes crossed for luck?" Carla demanded of her brother.

"Yep."

She took a deep breath. "Go for it."

Cash turned to Luke. "Five cards, no discard, no draw, nothing wild. Best hand wins."

"Deal," Luke said.

Suddenly it was so quiet that the sound of the cards being shuffled was like muffled thunder. The slap of cards on the table was distinct, rhythmic. There was the ritual exchange of words, the discreet fanning and survey of five cards. Luke's expression was impossible to read as he laid his hand faceup on the table and said neutrally, "Ace high...and nothing else. Not a damned thing."

Cash swore and swiftly gathered all the cards together into an indistinguishable pile. "You're shot with luck tonight, Luke. All I had was a jack."

For an instant there was silence. Then Luke began laughing. When he turned and saw Carla's stunned face, his expression changed.

"When the isolation gets to you," Luke said carefully, "I'll let you welsh on the bet. No hard feelings and no regrets."

"What?"

"Women hate the Rocking M," Luke said simply. "I doubt that you'll last three weeks, much less three months. College has made a city slicker out of you. Two weekends without bright lights and you'll be whining and pining like all the other housekeepers and cooks did. You can make book on it."

Whining and pining.

The words echoed in Carla's mind, leaving a bright, irrational anger in their wake.

"You're on, cowboy," she said flatly. "What's more, you're going to eat every last one of your words. Raw."

"Doubt it."

"I don't. I'm going to be the one who feeds them to you."

Luke's slow smile doubled Carla's heart rate and set fire to her nerve endings. He laughed a soft, rough kind of laugh and gave her the only warning she would get.

"There's something to remember when you start feeding me, baby."

"What's that?"

"I bite."

CHAPTER THREE

WHAT IN GOD'S NAME AM I DOING here? Have I gone entirely crazy?

"Here" was on a dirt road winding and looping and climbing up to the Rocking M. All around Carla for mile upon uninhabited mile, the Four Corners countryside lay in unbridled magnificence. It wasn't the absence of people that was causing Carla to question her own sanity; she loved the rugged, wild land. It was the presence of people that was giving her stomach the ohmygod flutters. To be precise, it was the presence of one particular person—Luke MacKenzie, owner of a handsome chunk of the surrounding land.

And a handsome chunk himself.

In the back of her mind Carla kept hearing her brother's advice. *Chin up, Carla. You can do anything for a summer. Besides, you heard Luke. He won't be any harder on you than he is on any other ranch hand.*

"Thanks, big brother," Carla muttered as she remembered Cash's smiling send-off that morning. "Thanks all to hell."

Not that she was angry with Cash for being amused by her predicament. He had only been doing what big brothers always did, which was to treat their smaller sisters with a combination of mischief, indulgence and love. Nor was it Cash's fault that Carla found herself driving over a rough road to a live-in summer job with the man who had haunted her dreams for every one of the seven years since she had been fourteen. Cash wasn't at fault because he hadn't been the one to suggest the bet that he had ultimately lost.

However, he had neglected to mention that Luke would be part of her birthday celebration. When Carla walked in the front door and saw him, she had nearly dropped the pizza she was carrying. Luke had always had that effect on her. When he was nearby, her normal composure evaporated. She had made a fool of herself around him throughout her teenage years.

Well, not quite all of my teenage years, Carla told herself bracingly. *I was eighteen when I took the cure. Or rather, when Luke administered it.*

After that, she had stopped finding excuses to go out to the Rocking M and watch the man she loved. But she hadn't stopped soon enough. She hadn't stopped before she had told Luke that she loved him and begged him to look at her as a woman, not a girl.

The memory of that disastrous evening still had the ability to make Carla flush, go pale and then flush again with a volatile combination of emotions she had no desire to sort out or describe. The one emotion she had no trouble putting a name to was humiliation. She had been mortified to the soles of her feet. But she had learned something useful that night. She had learned that people didn't die of embarrassment.

They just wanted to.

So she had turned and run from the scene of her personal Waterloo. Driving recklessly, crying, putting as much distance as she could between herself and the man who was much too sophisticated for her, she had fled the ranch. All the way home she had told herself that she hated Luke. She hadn't believed it, but she had wanted to.

Since then, Carla had tried to put Luke MacKenzie out of her mind. She hadn't succeeded. Every time she went out on a date, she only missed Luke more. Not surprisingly, she didn't date much. The harder she tried to find other men attractive, the brighter Luke's image burned in her memory.

No man can be that special, Carla told herself fiercely. *My memory isn't reliable. If I were around Luke now, as a woman, he wouldn't be nearly so attractive to me. Familiarity breeds contempt. That's why I let all this happen. I wanted to get familiar enough to feel contempt.*

That, or outright insanity, was the only explanation for what had happened the evening of her twenty-first birthday, a celebration of the very date when she had legally become old enough to know better.

Look on the bright side. A summer on the Rocking M beats a summer as a gofer for the Department of Archaeology. If I have to check one more reference on one more footnote, I'll do something rash.

Get used to it. That's what being an archaeologist is all about.

While learning about vanished cultures and peoples fascinated Carla, she wasn't certain that a career as an archaeologist was what she wanted. She was certain that she was going to find out; she would begin work on her master's degree in the fall. But first she had to get through the summer. And Luke.

Carla's mind was still seething with silent questions when she drove into the Rocking M's ranch yard, got out slowly and stretched. She was presently just under three and one half hours from the bright lights of Cortez, assuming that the weather continued fair and clear. In bad weather, she was anywhere between six and sixty hours from "civilization."

The isolation didn't bother her. In fact, it was a positive lure; she had always felt drawn to the wide, wild sweep of the land. After she had turned seventeen, the only serious arguments she and her brother had ever had was over her tendency to go from camp with a canteen, a compass, and a backpack, and leave behind a note and an arrow made of pebbles to indicate the direction of her exploration. The fact that Cash did precisely the same thing didn't lessen his anger at Carla; in Cash's book, what was sauce for the goose was *not* sauce for the gander. When Carla had gone to Luke looking for sympathy, he had calmly told her that he didn't want her going alone anywhere on the ranch, including the pasture across the road from the big house.

Carla's mouth turned up slightly at the memory. She had been furious when the two men had ganged up against her. When she had started to point out that Luke was being unreasonable, he had told her that as long as she was on the Rocking M she would obey his orders. Period. End of discussion.

She hadn't argued. The next time she went into West Fork for supplies, she had started looking for work. That afternoon she got work as the cook and housekeeper for the OK Corral, a small motel-coffee shop at the edge of West Fork. The job included room and board. She had gone back to the Rocking M, unloaded the supplies, and started packing her clothes. When she was ready to leave, she went looking for Ten, Luke's ramrod. Ten had listened to her request, discovered where she was going to be working, and had gone to find Luke. Luke had flatly refused to let her use any of the ranch vehicles for any reason whatsoever, effectively imprisoning her on the Rocking M until Cash returned from his latest round of explorations.

Remembering the blowup that had followed made Carla's faint smile fade.

"Such a long face."

The sound of Luke's voice made Carla jump, for she had thought she was alone. She looked toward the long front porch of the ranch house. Luke was sitting in the shadows watching her. She couldn't help staring as he stood up, stepped off the porch and walked into the bright sunlight. It had been only a day since the card game in which she had lost her summer freedom, but she looked at Luke as though it had been a year since she had seen him.

Nothing about him had changed. Long-boned, hard, with a muscular grace that had always fascinated her, Luke overshadowed every other man she had ever known. He had haunted her, making boyfriends impossible. She could enjoy other students' company, pal around with them, go to shows or football games; but she simply couldn't take the boys seriously. When they wanted to go from friendship to something more intense, she gently, inevitably, withdrew.

Carla watched Luke walking toward her and prayed that her half-formed plan would work, that she would be able to get Luke out of her system, to cure herself of her futile longing for a man who didn't want her.

Not until Luke stood close enough for her to see that the sun had turned his eyes into clear, deep gold did Carla realize the true extent of her wager—and her risk. What if this didn't work? What if being close to Luke only increased her longing? What if this turned out to be as big a mistake as her job in West Fork had been?

"Already unhappy at being stuck in the sticks for a few months?" Luke continued, watching Carla closely.

"No. I was thinking about the summer I got a job at the OK Corral."

Luke's eyes narrowed and his mouth became a thin line. Carla winced.

"You got off easy," he said flatly. "If you'd been my sister, I would have nailed your backside to the barn for a stunt like that."

"Cash is brighter than that."

"Or dumber."

"Maybe he decided that teaching me wilderness skills was better than having me move out."

"Not just 'out,' schoolgirl. Into a no-tell motel."

"A what?"

"The OK Corral is the biggest hot-sheet operation this side of Cortez."

"Hot sheet?" she asked. Suddenly understanding dawned. "You don't mean...?"

"I sure as hell do."

"Oh...my...God."

Carla's blue-green eyes widened in comprehension. Amused by her own naïveté, she shook her head slowly, making light twist through her sun-streaked chestnut hair. Unable to hold back any longer, she let laughter bubble up. She finally understood why Luke had kept her a virtual prisoner on the ranch until Cash had come in from his geological explorations three days later.

As Luke watched Carla, his mouth gentled into a smile. Something that was both pain and pleasure expanded through him. It had been so good during the years when he and Cash had shared between them the radiant freshness that was Carla. She had a way of brightening everything she touched. Luke hadn't wanted to let Carla go out into the world any more than Cash had. The world could be brutal to a gentle young girl.

So we kept her and then I was the one to teach her how brutal the world can be.

The thought made Luke's expression harden. The memory of Carla's frightened, tear-streaked face, the broken sounds she had made as she fled into the night three years before; all of it haunted him.

"Lord, sunshine," Luke said in a deeper voice. "You were so innocent. No wonder Cash wanted to build a fence around you to keep out the wolves."

Carla's laughter died as she looked at Luke and knew that he was thinking of the night she had thrown herself at him. She felt herself going pale, then flushing beneath a rising tide of embarrassment. She hated the revealing color but knew there was nothing she could do to avoid or conceal it. So she ignored it, just as she tried to ignore Luke's comment about her innocence, his words like salt on the raw wound of her memories.

Yet if she were to survive this summer—and Luke—the past had to be put behind her. She was a woman now, not a stupid girl blinded by naive dreams of being loved by a man who was years too experienced for her.

"Fortunately, innocence is curable," Carla said. "Time works miracles. Where do you want me to put my stuff?"

For an instant she held her breath, silently willing Luke to accept the change of subject. She really couldn't bear reliving the lowest moment of her life all over again. Not in front of Luke, with his intense glance measuring every bright shade of her humiliation.

"Sunshine, that night you came and—"

"My name is Carla," she interrupted tightly, turning away, going to the tiny bed of the pickup truck. "Do you want me to park at the old house?"

"No. You'll be staying at the big house."

"But—"

"But nothing. I'm not having anything as innocent as you running loose after dark. One of my hands is no good around women, and none of them is any better than he has to be. When Cash is here, you can bunk in with him at the old house if you want. Otherwise, you're in the big house with me. It's hard to get men to work on a place as isolated as the Rocking M. I'd hate to have to drive one of my hands to the hospital because he was drinking and saw a light on in the old house and thought he'd try his luck."

"None of your men would—"

"Didn't you learn anything three years ago?" Luke cut in. "Men drink to forget, and one of the first things they forget is to keep their hands off an innocent girl like you."

"I'm not an inno—"

"Put that suitcase back," Luke said coldly, interrupting Carla again.

"What?" she asked, stopping in the act of taking a suitcase from the truck's small, open bed.

"I'm not going to spend the summer arguing with the hired help. If you can't take a simple order you can turn that toy truck around and get the hell off the Rocking M."

Carla stared in disbelief at Luke. Hurt and anger warred within her.

"Would you treat me like this if Cash were here?"

"If Cash were here, I wouldn't have to worry about protecting you from your own foolishness. He'd take care of it for me."

"I'm twenty-one, legally of age."

"Schoolgirl, when it comes to men and an isolated ranch like this, you aren't even out of kindergarten. Take your pick—the big house or the road to town."

Carla turned and began rummaging in the truck bed again. She hoped Luke couldn't see the tiny trembling of her hands at the thought of living in the same house with him, seeing him at all hours of light and darkness, fixing his food, making his bed, washing his clothes, folding them, caring for him. A thousand subtle intimacies, his whiskey-colored eyes watching her, no place to retreat, no place to hide.

Well, that's what I came here for, isn't it, to let familiarity breed contempt? And if the thought of that kind of closeness makes my knees turn to water, that's just tough. I'll get over him. I have to.

With all the coolness Carla could muster, she turned back to Luke. He said something harsh beneath his breath as he saw the pallor of her face and her wide, haunted eyes.

"Don't worry. I'm not going to jump your bones," he said savagely. "Hell, I wouldn't have touched you three years ago if I hadn't been drinking and you hadn't been offering. Look at you, all pale and trembling every time the subject comes up. You'd think I raped you, for God's sake."

"No," she said hoarsely. "No."

"Damn it, I'm not going to have you flinching and hiding every time I get three feet from you. Nothing happened that night!"

Hearing her declaration of love characterized as "nothing" stiffened Carla's knees. Her head came up and she asked in a low voice, "Do you want a cook and housekeeper for the summer?"

"Yes, but—"

She kept right on talking. "Then what happened the summer I graduated from high school is off-limits for conversation. It was the most excruciating, humiliating experience of my life. Thinking about it makes me—sick." Abruptly Carla stopped speaking and shook her head, making silky hair fly. "So unless you're trying to drive me off the ranch, you'll stop throwing that night in my face."

Being told that the memory of his touch sickened her did nothing to improve Luke's temper. He looked at Carla's tight, pale face and swore under his breath.

"It's too late to be hedging your bet," he said coldly. "I hired you for the summer. If you don't like what I talk about, get back in the truck and drive. You knew what I was like when you made the bet, so don't be trotting out excuses for welshing. And you will welsh, schoolgirl. After three solid weeks of the Rocking M, you'll be champing at the bit to see the bright lights just like the other females who came here."

"West Fork doesn't have any bright lights worth seeing."

"You should have hung around the OK Corral a little longer," Luke said sardonically.

Carla's temper frayed. She hated being reminded of how many times she had made a fool of herself around Luke.

"Did it ever occur to you it might have been the MacKenzie *men* rather than the Rocking M's isolation, that drove their wives into town?" Carla asked in a sugary voice.

"Don't bet on it. None of the MacKenzie men ever got any complaints in bed. It was being alone in the daytime that got to the women."

Carla set her jaw so hard her teeth ached. The thought of

Luke in bed literally took away her breath. Part of it was a virgin's fear of the unknown—but most of her breathlessness came from a very female curiosity about what it would be like to be Luke's lover, to feel his big body moving against hers, to hear his breath quicken at her touch and to taste again the warmth of his own breath.

"Which will it be?" he demanded. "The big house or the road?"

"The house."

No sooner were the words out of her mouth than Carla wondered if history were repeating itself and she was making a bad mistake because Luke's presence always muddled what few wits she had.

Before Carla could take back her words, Luke brushed past her and began unloading the truck.

"You brought enough stuff for the summer," he said, surprised.

"*Quelle* shock," Carla muttered. "The bet was for the summer, wasn't it?"

Luke gave her a sideways glance. "I said you could back out anytime. When I give my word, I keep it."

She took a deep breath and set fire to her last bridge to safety. "And I told you I wouldn't back out as long as I'm treated like any other hand. My word means just as much to me as yours means to you."

He searched her eyes for a long moment before he nodded. "All right, schoolgirl. I'll show you your room."

CHAPTER FOUR

LUKE SET THE LAST OF CARLA'S baggage just inside the door to the small upstairs suite that would be hers for the summer. Standing on tiptoe, staring over his back, Carla looked at the room and made a small sound of astonishment.

"What incredible furniture! Where did you get that headboard? And the dresser," she added, looking away from the queen-size bed. Without thinking, she crowded against Luke so that she could touch the satin surface of the wood. "The design is perfect, all curves, like running water or granite smoothed by rain. Where on earth did you find—"

"Leave your stuff for now," Luke said, all but pushing Carla out of the room and closing the door behind himself. The last thing he wanted to do was to talk about the furniture he had made three years ago in an effort to exorcise or appease the yearning within himself for the life and the girl he could not have. "I'll show you the kitchen next, then I've got to check on one of the mares."

Carla started to point out that she had seen the kitchen before, then shut her mouth. She had demanded to be treated like any other employee, and that's what Luke was doing. What she hadn't realized was that he would treat her like a stranger as well, refusing to answer even such relatively impersonal questions as where he had found the beautiful bedroom set.

Without a word Carla followed Luke down the stairs. The muscular ease of his walk fascinated her. Her glance lingered on the width of his shoulders beneath his blue work shirt and the powerful lines of his back as it tapered to a worn, wide leather belt encircling a lean waist. His jeans were faded in patterns determined by sun and sweat rather than by commercial acid washes. His boots were scarred by stirrups, spurs and brush.

The stairs ended in a hall whose floor was covered by earth-colored, unglazed Mexican tiles. Mentally Carla noted that a lot of that earth color might come off with a mop and a bucket of soapy water. The kitchen floor was of the same unglazed tiles.

Make that several buckets of soapy water.

With an inaudible sigh Carla noted the abundant signs of months of indifferent house cleaning. Windows were streaked where they weren't smeared. The counters, cupboards, drawers and appliances in the kitchen and adjoining laundry room had the dull shine of grease rather than the subtle shine of cleanliness.

Luke followed Carla's glance to the far corner of the kitchen, where chunks of spring mud still clung to the baseboard even though spring had passed. Tomato sauce or gravy—or both—made an uneven pattern down the bank of drawers to the right of the sink. On the floor, distinct paths crisscrossed from the back door to the sink to the stove and into the big dining room.

"The last four cooks weren't much on housekeeping," Luke muttered.

"Really? I thought it was just your wallpaper."

Luke glanced at the walls and grimaced. They were worse than the floor. He tried to remember the last time the walls had been scrubbed. He couldn't.

"I'll have one of the men wash them down."

"Don't bother, unless you plan to keep eating off them."

Unwillingly, Luke smiled. "It does look sort of like we've been serving dinner off the walls instead of the table, doesn't it?"

"Mmm," was the most tactful thing Carla could think of to say. "Do you want a late or early dinner?"

"Six and six."

"What?"

"Breakfast at six and dinner at six. The men who need a cold lunch packed for them will tell you at dinner the night before. Otherwise just see that the bunkhouse kitchen stays stocked with snacks and sandwich stuff."

Luke ran a finger lightly over the huge, six-burner gas stove and came up with a greasy fingertip for his trouble. He muttered something and wiped his hand on his jeans.

"What?" asked Carla.

"I've been so busy working on the ranch that I didn't realize the house had gone to hell."

"Nothing a little soap and water won't cure," Carla said with determined cheerfulness.

Or dynamite, she added silently, looking around. When she looked up again, Luke was studying her.

"If any of the hands bother you, let me know," he said.

"I don't mind them coming around and asking me to bake cookies for them," Carla answered, remembering other summers. "I could live without king snakes in the pantry, though."

Luke's lips twitched as he remembered the incident when an ambitious king snake had followed mice into the pantry. The snake had set up housekeeping among the sacks of rice and flour. At least, that was what each and every hand had solemnly sworn when Luke had heard Carla's scream and come running. He had caught the snake and taken it to the barn, where its predatory efforts would be more appreciated. Then he had begun questioning the hands very closely.

The shadow of a smile faded from Luke's mouth. "I wasn't worried about that kind of snake. It's the two-legged variety I had in mind. If one of my men makes you uncomfortable, let me know."

Carla looked perplexed. "I've never had any trouble with the hands before."

"The last time you spent a summer here, you looked more like a boy than a girl," Luke said bluntly. His gaze went from Carla's gold-streaked chestnut hair to her slender feet and back up again, silently cataloguing each lush curve. "No such luck this time. My men aren't blind. So if anyone crowds you, don't try to take care of it yourself. Come running to me or Ten and come fast. Got that?"

"I don't dress to catch a man's eye," Carla said matter-of-factly, indicating her summer uniform of jeans and one of her brother's old shirts with sleeves rolled up and trailing ends knotted to one side. "There shouldn't be any problem."

Luke's left eyebrow climbed as he followed Carla's

gesture. "Maybe. But if you swipe another one of my shirts, I'll take it out of your soft hide."

"This is my brother's shirt," she said indignantly, holding up a black shirttail in her hand.

Luke shook his head. "I got oil on it working on Cash's balky Jeep, so he loaned me a clean one for your birthday party."

"Figures," she muttered. "It's so comfortable I've been tempted to use it as a nightgown. Nylon is too cold or too hot. Your shirt was all soft and perfect."

Abruptly Carla's mouth went dry. The thought that the cloth draped so intimately around her body had once been wrapped just as intimately around Luke's sent an arrow of sensation glittering from her breastbone to the pit of her stomach. She swallowed and looked away from his clear, penetrating eyes.

"Don't worry," she said huskily. "I'll give it back to you as soon as it's washed."

"No hurry. I've still got Cash's shirt."

Silence stretched and then stretched some more, leaving Carla feeling breathless, uncertain. She looked back at Luke, only to find him watching her with unnerving intensity, as though he were measuring precisely where the disputed shirt fit her differently than it fit him.

"How do you want to arrange your time off?" he asked.

"What?"

Slowly Luke lifted his eyes to Carla's face.

"Your time off. Do you want to work six days and have one off, or do you want to work right through, or do you want to save up some days and take a little vacation?"

"I'll save them up," Carla said promptly.

"That's what the women all say at first, but after a few weeks they can't get to West Fork fast enough."

"Cash will be coming up in early August. I'll wait."

Luke's smile told Carla that he didn't believe it. He turned toward the back door. "If you need anything, holler. I'll be in the barn."

With a mixture of relief and disappointment, Carla watched Luke leave. The relief she understood; the disappointment she ignored. She looked around the kitchen, wondering where to begin. Everywhere she looked, a task cried out to be done. Fortunately she had the ability to organize her time. She didn't always use that ability, but she had it just the same.

"The cleaning will have to wait," Carla muttered, looking at the clock. "In two hours, twelve hungry hands will descend. Thirteen, counting Luke. Call it fourteen. Luke is big enough for two men. Then there's me. Dinner for fifteen, coming right up."

The number she had to feed seemed to echo in the silent kitchen. *Fifteen. My God. No wonder all the pots and pans are so big.*

The thought of feeding that many people was daunting. Carla had never cooked whole meals for more than herself, her brother and, when she was on the ranch, for Luke. The three of them had eaten in the old ranch house, whose small rooms were famous for mice, drafts and dust in equal measure.

Looking around, Carla gave each black sleeve another turn upward to make sure the cloth didn't get in the way. Then she went to the refrigerator and began taking a fast inventory of what was available.

The refrigerator held beer, apple juice, horseradish, ketchup, a chunk of butter, four eggs, a slab of unsliced bacon and an open package of baloney that had quietly curled up and died. The big freezer opposite the stove was more rewarding. It held enough meat, mostly beef, to feed half the state of Colorado. As long as the propane held out, they wouldn't starve. All she had to do was thaw a few roasts in the microwave.

"Oops," Carla said, glancing around. "No microwave. Not enough time to cook frozen roasts, either."

She went to the pantry, hoping for inspiration. "Canned stew, canned chili, canned chicken...yuck. No wonder Luke is short-tempered. Eating out of cans is enough to sour the disposition of a saint." The other side of the pantry was no better. She was confronted by a solid wall of cans as big as buckets—tomatoes, peas, green beans, corn, pitted cherries and coffee. There were also half-empty fifty-pound sacks of flour, sugar, rice, cornmeal and dried apples. The bread bin held four wizened crusts.

"So much for hamburgers," she said unhappily, "and I doubt if anyone delivers pizza this far out."

A burlap bag bulged with potatoes. Another bag was full of onions. Pinto beans dribbled out of a third bag. She grabbed that bag with both hands and lifted. It weighed at least ten pounds. That was enough beans to make real chili or *frijoles refritos* or any number of dishes. She could feed an army—but not in the next two hours.

Behind the bag of beans Carla spotted a cardboard box that had been shoved aside and forgotten. Inside the box was package after package of spaghetti. Each package held two pounds of the slender, dried pasta. The fragile sticks had been broken but were perfectly edible otherwise.

"I sense a spaghetti dinner on the horizon," Carla said.

She grabbed two packages, hesitated, and grabbed two more. When she cooked for Cash and herself, a pound of dried pasta fed both of them with enough left over for several of her lunches. But then, she always served fresh salad, garlic bread and dessert with the spaghetti. Bread and salad were out of the question, so she grabbed an extra package of pasta, bringing the total to ten pounds.

"My God, it will take an army to eat this much. I'll be making cold spaghetti sandwiches for weeks and the hands will riot and Luke will tear a strip off me big enough to cover the south pasture."

Carla frowned at the last package of pasta, then decided she could always take the leftovers to the bunkhouse for the hands who wanted a midnight snack. Arms bulging with packages of spaghetti, she went back into the kitchen. There she dumped the pasta on the counter and went back to the freezer. The hamburger came in five-pound freezer packages that were frozen as solid as a stone.

She unwrapped a brick of ground meat and dropped it into a cast-iron frying pan that was so big and heavy it took both hands for her to lift it up onto the stove. A box of wooden matches sat on the stove itself. She lit the burner beneath the frozen meat, covered the pan and went to work on the sauce. Several forays to the pantry resulted in a can of tomato sauce the size of a bathroom sink, an equally intimidating can of whole tomatoes, and ten fat onions.

After rummaging in the cupboards near the stove, Carla found a kettle the size of a laundry tub. She set it aside for cooking the noodles and found a slightly smaller cousin to hold the sauce. She nearly had to turn the kitchen inside out to find a hand-held can opener that worked. As she wrestled with the awkward can and poured a river of tomato sauce into a big pot—too quickly—she discovered how the kitchen walls had gotten their splatter patterns. She wiped up what she could reach, lit the burner under the sauce and went to work peeling and chopping onions. Between bouts of crying she prodded the hamburger, prying off bits of meat as the frozen block slowly loosened.

By the time the hamburger had thawed and was browning with the onions in the huge pan, nearly an hour had passed. A determined search of the kitchen had turned up no oregano and no whole garlic. A geriatric bottle of garlic granules was available, but she had to hammer the plastic container on the counter to knock loose a little of the contents.

"What on earth have the cooks been feeding everyone?" Carla asked in exasperation. "No herbs, no spices, no—" The clock caught her eye. "Uh-oh. I'd better get dessert going or there won't be any of that, either."

Carla ran up to her bedroom suite, tore through four boxes until she found her cookbooks, and raced back downstairs. The recipe for cherry cobbler said it fed eight. She doubled it, spread it into the smallest baking pan she could find—which was half the size of a card table—and discovered that the pan was way too big for the contents.

"Oh well, men always like dessert. I'll put it in their lunch along with the cold spaghetti sandwiches."

She mixed up two more double batches of cobbler, poured them into the pan with the first batch and lit the oven. Even after doing six times the normal recipe of cobbler, she still had half of the huge can of cherries left over. She set it aside, saw that time was getting away from her and went back to the spaghetti sauce.

The meat and onions were browned and the pot of tomato sauce and chopped tomatoes was finally coming to a boil. The size and weight of the frying pan made draining the meat and onions an awkward process—especially using a kitchen towel as a pot holder—but she finally managed it. Next she had to dump the meat and onions into the pot of sauce. In doing so, she discovered another way to decorate the walls. Muttering, she mopped up and told herself that she would have to learn to manhandle a heavy pot and a gallon or two of sauce without making a mess.

"Speaking of gallons, I'd better get the spaghetti water on," she muttered, pushing back her hair with her elbow because her fingers were only slightly less messy than the walls.

By the time Carla filled a huge pot with water and lugged it to the stove, she finally understood why men rather than women chose careers as chefs; you had to be a weight lifter to handle the kitchen equipment. She turned the fire on high and mopped up the floor where she had spilled water on the way to the stove. The places she left behind were relatively clean, making the rest of the floor look much worse by comparison.

For a moment Carla was tempted to slop a little tomato sauce on the sort-of-clean spots to even things up, thereby delaying the hour of reckoning when she had to clean the floor. She loved to cook but hated housework. She knew her own weakness so well that she worked twice as hard at cleaning, making up for her own dislike of the job.

But it would look really nice with a few dollops of tomato sauce. Nobody would even notice.

Carla managed to avoid the temptation only because she remembered the green beans, which should have been on the stove ten minutes ago. Another trip to the pantry yielded a gallon can of green beans. While they heated, she sliced bacon, fried it and sliced more onions to sauté in the bacon fat. From time to time she checked the spaghetti water.

"I know a watched pot never boils, but this is ridiculous," she said beneath her breath, lifting the lid and testing the water with her fingertip.

Dead cold.

From the barn, corral and bunkhouse came the sounds of men wrapping up tasks in preparation for dinner. Two pickups came in from opposite directions, pulling horse trailers behind. Four men got out and stretched, tired and hungry from a long day of checking cattle on land leased from the federal government. The horses being unloaded from trailers neighed to the horses that were already rubbed down and had begun to tear great mouthfuls of hay from the corral feeding rack.

The men would be just as hungry.

Anxiously Carla listened as the bunkhouse door slammed repeatedly, telling her that the men were going in to wash up for dinner. Laughter and catcalls greeted a cowboy whose jeans showed clear signs of his having landed butt-first in the mud. He gave back as good as he got, reminding the other men of the time one of them had slipped in a fresh cow flop and another had been bucked off into a corral trough.

Carla couldn't help smiling as bits of conversation drifted through the open window. For the first time she realized that she hadn't heard a human voice since Luke had vanished into the barn. The thought went as quickly as it had come, pushed aside by the fact that the spaghetti water was barely lukewarm. At this rate dinner would be at least half an hour late and Luke would be thinking he had gotten the bad end of the bet.

Hurriedly Carla tasted the tomato sauce, added more garlic and checked the spaghetti water again. Nothing doing. The outside door into the dining room squeaked open and then closed. The room, which adjoined the kitchen, was more like a mess hall than a formal dining room. There were two long tables, each of which could seat ten comfortably and fourteen in a pinch, twenty chairs, a wall of floor-to-ceiling cupboards and not much else.

It occurred to Carla that the tables were bare of plates, cups, utensils and napkins, not to mention salt, pepper, ketchup, steak sauce, sugar and all the other condiments beloved by ranch hands. Groaning at her forgetfulness, she dumped the half-cooked onions and bacon into the pot of green beans and frantically began opening cupboards, searching for plates. She was so busy that she didn't hear the door between the kitchen and dining room open.

"Smells good in here. What's for supper?"

"Spaghetti," Carla said without turning toward the male voice.

"Smells more like cherry pie."

"Ohmygod, *dessert*."

She raced past the man who had walked into the kitchen. A fast look in the oven assured her that the cobbler had survived her neglect. All she had to do was maneuver the big pan out of the oven to let the cobbler cool. The kitchen towel wouldn't stretch to do the job of handling the pan.

"Pot holders," she muttered, straightening from bending over the oven.

"Looks like cobbler from here."

The voice came from about a foot away from Carla's ear. Her head snapped around and she looked at the man for the first time.

Long, lean and deceptively lazy-looking, Tennessee Blackthorn was watching Carla with an odd smile on his face.

"Ten! Is it really you?" Carla asked, delighted. "The last time I heard, you had a phone call in the middle of the night, went into Cortez and never came back."

"Never is a long time." Smoke-colored eyes swept appreciatively from Carla's oven-flushed cheeks to her ankles and back up. "Guess we can't call you *niña* anymore. You finally grew into those long legs and bedroom eyes."

She laughed. "I love hungry men. They'll flatter the cook shamelessly in hopes of an early dinner. You're out of luck, though. The watched pot isn't boiling."

"He's out of luck, period," Luke said from the back door, his voice cold.

CHAPTER FIVE

CARLA DIDN'T REALIZE HOW MUCH her expression changed when she turned toward Luke, but little escaped Ten's eyes. He measured the complex mixture of yearning and distance, hope and hunger in her look, and he knew that nothing had changed.

"Still chasing moonlight over black water, aren't you?" he asked softly.

If either Carla or Luke heard, neither answered. They were looking at each other as though it had been years, not hours, since their last meeting.

"The pot holders are over there," Luke said in a clipped voice, gesturing toward a drawer near the stove, never looking away from Carla's vivid blue-green eyes.

"Pot holders," Carla repeated, absorbed by the arching line of Luke's eyebrows, the clean curves of his mouth, the shadow of beard lying beneath his tanned skin.

"Pot holders," repeated Luke.

"Still smells and looks like cobbler to me," Ten said to no one in particular.

"Don't you have something to do?" Luke asked pointedly, finally looking away from Carla.

"Nope. But if you give me a cup of coffee I'll find something."

Luke eyed the man who was both his friend and the ramrod of the Rocking M. Ten returned him stare for stare...and smiled. Luke barely controlled his anger. He knew he had no reason to be angry with Ten; of all the ranch hands, the ramrod would be the least likely to hustle Carla into bed. But hearing Ten talk about Carla's *long legs and bedroom eyes* had made Luke savagely angry. The fact that his anger was irrational, and he knew it, only made him more angry.

"Coffee?" Carla asked, feeling a sinking in her stomach. "I forgot to make coffee!"

"How the hell can you forget coffee?" Luke demanded, turning on Carla, glad to find a rational outlet for his anger. "Any ranch cook worth the powder to blow her straight to hell knows that the first thing you make in the morning is coffee and the last thing you clean at night is the coffeepot!"

"Well," drawled Ten, "I guess that sure settles that. Carla isn't a ranch cook and we're going to starve to death opening cans with our pocketknives. Sure you wouldn't like to think it over, boss? Wouldn't want you to go off half-cocked and shoot yourself in the foot."

Luke said something under his breath that made Carla wince. She turned away and began searching through cupboards with hands that shook. All she found was peanut butter, jelly and a jar of pickled jalapeño peppers. She grabbed the jar and shoved it into Luke's hand.

"Here. Suck on one of those. It will cool you off."

Ten's laughter filled the kitchen. Luke slammed the jar back onto the shelf and gave Carla a narrow-eyed look.

"Listen, schoolgirl. This is the real world where men work hard and get hungry. I said dinner at six and I meant it. If you're too immature to get the job done I'll find a woman who can."

Luke turned and left the kitchen before Carla could answer. Not that she had anything to say; she hadn't heard Luke so cold and cutting since the night three years ago when he had told her that she wasn't woman enough to love a man.

"Hey," Ten said gently, "don't take the boss seriously. He's just upset about that black mare of his. She's going downhill fast and the vet can't figure out why."

Carla made a neutral sound and kept on searching the cupboards. She found nothing useful. Part of the problem was that she was fighting against tears. The rest of the problem was that she wanted to throw things.

"Is that big pot boiling yet?" she asked tightly.

Ten lifted the lid. "Nope."

"Close?"

"Nope. I'll tell the men to take their time washing up."

"Thanks."

Carla finally found the pot holders, retrieved the cobbler and set it aside to cool. While looking for the pot holders she also found the coffeepot. Like everything else in the kitchen, the pot was oversize. It quite literally made gallons of coffee at a time. She filled everything, putting in twice the coffee any sane person would have wanted, and thumped the pot onto the stove to perk.

By the time she lit the burner under the coffee, the spaghetti water was showing vague signs of life. With a heartfelt prayer she slammed the lid back in place and resumed searching the cupboards for plates.

"What are you looking for?" Ten asked from the doorway.

"Plates," Carla said despairingly, shutting another cupboard door with more force than necessary.

"They're in the mess hall, along with knives, forks, spoons and all the rest."

She flashed him a grateful smile. "Thanks."

Ten shook his head as Carla rushed past him, all but running. "Slow down, *niña*. The men won't starve if they have to wait a bit for chow."

"Tell Luke."

"All right."

Carla grabbed Ten's arm as he headed through the kitchen toward Luke's office at the other end of the house.

"I was just kidding," she said quickly.

"I wasn't." Ten looked down at Carla's unhappy face and shook his head. "You haven't been here two hours and already you look like somebody rode you hard and put you away wet. Have you tried telling Luke how you feel?"

"The first day on a job is always tough."

Ten made an impatient sound. "That's not what I meant. Have you told Luke that you're in love with him?"

For an instant Carla felt as though the floor had dropped from beneath her feet. She tried to speak. No words came. Red flooded her face.

Ten sighed. "Hell, Carla. There isn't a man on this place who doesn't know it, except maybe Luke. Don't you think it's time you told him?"

Her lips trembled as she thought about a night three years ago. She licked her dry lips and said carefully, "He knows."

Ten said something harsh beneath his breath, took off his

hat and raked his fingers through his black hair. After a moment he sighed and said, "It's none of my business, but damn it, I hate seeing anything as gentle as you get hurt. Chasing something that doesn't want to be caught can be real painful."

"That's not…" Carla's voice faded. "That's not why I'm here. I came to cure myself of loving…of my childish infatuation…" She swallowed twice and tried again, holding her voice steady with an effort. "I think Luke must have guessed why I'm here, so he's doing everything he can to help the process along."

It was Ten's turn to be speechless. He shook his head and turned away, swearing softly. As an afterthought he added, "I'll set the table."

"Thank you, Ten. I'll be more together tomorrow, I promise." Silently Carla added, *I've got to be. I can't spend the summer holding my breath, feeling my heart beat like a wild bird in a net, listening, listening, listening for Luke's footsteps, his voice, his laughter.*

The rattle of the lid against the pot of spaghetti water jarred Carla from her unhappy reverie. The water was boiling energetically. She added salt and oil and began ripping apart packages of pasta. By the time the last package went in, the water was back to lying motionless in the pot. Anxiously she looked at the big kitchen clock. Six-twenty.

At least the vegetable part of the meal was ready. It was only canned green beans, but the bacon and onion gave the limp beans a whiff of flavor. Carla would have felt better if she had had a few loaves of garlic bread to put out on the table as well, but there was no help for it. Pasta, meat sauce, green beans and cobbler were all that was available. And she didn't even have that. Not yet.

Worst of all, the coffee water was barely warm.

Stifling a groan, Carla rushed into the dining room and began helping Ten distribute cutlery around the tables, which had been pushed together to make a single large rectangle. The surface of the table itself dismayed her; it was no cleaner than the kitchen counters or walls. Whoever had wiped the table in the past had rearranged rather than removed the grease.

"Wait," Carla said to Ten. "The table needs cleaning."

"You start cleaning now and we won't eat until midnight."

She bit her lip. Ten was right.

"Where does Luke keep the tablecloths?" she asked.

"The what?"

She groaned, then had an inspiration. "Newspapers. Where does Luke keep the old newspapers?"

"In the wood box in the living room."

A few minutes later Carla ran back to the dining room carrying a three-inch stack of newspapers. Soon the big table was covered by old news and advertisements for cattle feed and quarter-horse stud service. By the time she and Ten had finished laying out silverware, the hands were beginning to mill hopefully in the yard beyond the dining room. One of the braver men—an old hand called Cosy—stuck his head in the back door. Before he could open his mouth, Ten started talking.

"I said I'd call when chow was on." The ramrod's cold gray eyes measured Cosy. "You getting hard of hearing or are you just senile?"

"No sir," Cosy said, backing out hastily. "I'm just fine. Planning on staying that way, too."

Ten grunted. Cosy vanished. The door thumped shut behind him.

"They must be starving," Carla said, looking as guilty as she felt.

"Nope. They still remember the cookies you used to bake.

When Luke told the men you'd be cooking for a few days, they started drooling."

"Tell them to relax. I'll be here all summer, not just for a few days."

Ten shrugged. "The last woman who stayed here more than three weeks was ugly as a rotten stump and drank to boot, but what really got her sent down the road was that she couldn't cook worth a fart in a windstorm."

Carla fought not to smile. She failed.

The left corner of Ten's mouth turned up. "Finally we took up a collection to buy her a bus ticket to Nome."

"Alaska?" asked Carla.

"Yeah. She got a job scaring grizzlies away from salmon nets."

Feminine laughter bubbled up. Soon Ten was laughing, too. Neither one of them noticed the big man who had come to the kitchen through the living room and was now leaning against the corner counter, his thumbs hooked in his belt and his mouth a bleak downward curve. He glanced at the clock. Six-forty. He glanced at the stove. Everything looked hot and ready to go. Whiskey-colored eyes cut back to the laughing couple in the dining room.

Just when Luke had opened his mouth to say something savage on the subject of cooks who couldn't get dinner ready on time, Carla grabbed Ten's wrist and looked at his watch.

"The pasta should be done by now, if the hands don't mind it al dente."

"What?"

"Chewy," she said succinctly.

"Hell, after a day on the range, we'll eat whatever we can get, any way we can get it, including raw."

Carla grimaced. "Yuck. Pasta sticks to your teeth that way."

Laughing, shaking his head, Ten leaned forward and tugged gently on a shining strand of Carla's hair. "I'm glad you're back. You bring sunlight with you."

Almost shyly, Carla said, "Thanks, Ten. It's good to be back. I love this place."

"The place or the owner?"

The question was so soft that Carla could pretend not to have heard it at all. So she smiled at Ten and turned toward the kitchen without answering, not knowing how much her sad smile revealed of her thoughts. As soon as she was through the door she spotted Luke leaning against the counter, impatience and anger in every hard line of his body.

"I was wondering when you'd remember that you were hired to cook, not to flirt with my ramrod."

"I wasn't flir—"

"Like hell you weren't," Luke said curtly, interrupting Carla. "Watch it, schoolgirl. Ten smiles and is handsome as sin, but that soft-drawling SOB has broken more hearts than any twelve men I know. He's not the marrying kind, but he's plenty human. If you throw yourself at him hard enough, he might just reach out and grab what's being offered. And we both know how good you are at throwing yourself."

Carla went pale and turned away.

Luke swore harshly beneath his breath, furious with her and Ten and himself and everything else that came to mind. He watched with narrowed, glittering eyes while Carla grabbed two pot holders and went to the kitchen range. By the time he realized that she was reaching for the wildly boiling kettle of spaghetti and water, it was too late. She was already struggling with the huge kettle, her whole body straining as she lifted at arm's length the weight of five gallons of water and ten pounds of pasta.

Just as Carla realized that she couldn't handle the kettle—and hadn't the strength to lower it without splashing boiling water down her front—Luke's arms shot around her body. He covered her hands with his own and lifted, taking the weight of the kettle from her quivering arms. Together they gently set the heavy pot on the back burner once more. For a few moments neither one moved, shaken by the realization of how close Carla had come to a painful accident.

Luke bent his head, brushing his cheek so lightly against Carla's hair that she couldn't feel it. When he took a breath he smelled flowers. The scent was dizzying, for it carried with it a promise of womanly warmth, a promise that was repeated in Carla's curving hips pressed against his body. She was trembling, breathing with soft, tearing sounds.

Desire turned like an unsheathed knife in Luke's guts, hardening him with shocking speed. He lifted his hands and stepped back as though he had been burned. And he had, but by something hotter than boiling water.

"My God, schoolgirl!" Luke exploded. "Don't you know better than to try to lift five gallons of boiling water off the back of this stove?"

Carla shook her head and said nothing. Nor did she turn around.

"Are you all right?" Luke demanded.

Slowly she nodded.

The line of her neck and shoulders tugged at Luke's emotions, reminding him of how vulnerable she was, how close she had come to hurting herself. The thought of boiling water scoring her soft skin made him feel as though he himself had been burned.

"Sunshine?" Luke said softly. "Are you sure you didn't burn yourself?"

The unexpected gentleness made tears burn beneath Carla's eyelids. She blinked fiercely, not wanting to cry in front of Luke, who already thought her a child. *Schoolgirl.*

"I'm fine," she said, her voice husky.

Carla took a steadying breath and inhaled the scent of Luke, a compound of leather and male heat and the clean fragrance of soap. She longed to turn and put her arms around him, to feel his arms around her, to hold and be held and never let go.

But she hadn't come to the Rocking M for that. She had come to let go of something she had never held.

"Thank you for saving dinner," Carla said, closing her eyes, trying not to breathe, for with each inhalation she took in the warmth and male scent of Luke.

"Dinner?" he asked.

"The spaghetti."

Gently Luke turned Carla around and brought her chin up until he could see her eyes. His breath came in hard, bringing with it the promise of flowers and warmth.

"You could have dumped that spaghetti all over the floor and I wouldn't have given a damn, so long as you weren't burned."

He examined her face intently, then unclenched her fingers and examined them for damage. Gently he traced the backs of her hands and arms until he reached the barrier of rolled-up black sleeves. His sleeves, his shirt, her wide blue-green eyes watching him. He traced her smooth, fine-grained skin one more time and felt desire roll through him like thunder through a narrow canyon, a force that made even stone tremble. He dropped her hands and turned away abruptly.

"Not a mark. You were lucky, schoolgirl. Next time you better think before you grab something too big for you. I might not be around to bail you out."

The change in Luke from tender to abrupt was disorienting to Carla. Before she could stop herself, she said, "I'm not a schoolgirl."

"Last time I checked, the University of Colorado was a school. What do you want me to do with that damned kettle?"

There were several tempting options, but Carla limited herself to the most practical one.

"Pour off the water in the sink."

Luke handled the heavy, awkward kettle with an ease that made Carla flatly envious.

"Now I know why cavewomen put up with cavemen," she muttered to herself, thinking Luke couldn't hear.

But he could. He glanced over his shoulder, saw the compound of admiration and desire in Carla's eyes as she watched him, and didn't know whether to smile or swear at the renewed leap of his blood. As he poured gallons of steaming water into the sink, he couldn't decide whether having Carla around for the summer was the worst idea he had ever had—or the best.

By the time Carla had the spaghetti loaded into a serving dish, the ranch hands were seated around the table in hushed expectancy. As she carried the fragrant, steaming mound of pasta into the dining room, she felt like a lion tamer carrying a single lamb chop into a cage full of big, hungry cats.

"Start on this round," she said. "I'll be back with the sauce in a minute."

The pot with the sauce in it wasn't as awkward as the kettle of boiling water had been, but Luke had taken care of the job anyway. The sauce was now in a soup tureen. A ladle that was twenty inches long stuck out of the rich red sauce.

"Thank you," Carla said, smiling briefly at Luke as she

grabbed the tureen. "Go sit down and eat. I can handle the rest."

Without a word Luke lifted the big tureen from Carla's hands and walked into the dining room. She found a big crockery bowl and filled it with green beans. She hurried out to the men.

"Here you are. All I have to do is find a spoon."

An assortment of mumbles greeted her. She didn't hear. She stood rooted to the floor, staring in horrified fascination as the spaghetti bowl made the rounds of the table. Each man heaped his plate with pasta, piling it high and wide, cramming aboard every bit possible and then some. By the time each man had been served, not so much as a single limp strand was left in the huge bowl.

Cosy, who had been the last to be served, took the green beans from Carla and gave her the empty pasta bowl in return.

"If you hurry back with more, you may be able to have a bite yourself before we dig in for seconds," Cosy said, grinning.

The hands who had already buried their pasta in sauce and had begun eating paused long enough to chorus Cosy's remarks. A lot of compliments for her cooking were thrown in, as well.

Carla smiled and tried to acknowledge the praise, but her heart wasn't in it. She was thinking desperately of the gallons and gallons of boiling water that had just gone down the kitchen drain. It would be impossible to cook more spaghetti in time to get it on the table for a second serving. And even if it were possible, at the rate the sauce was disappearing, there wouldn't be anything to put on the pasta but salt, pepper and a splash of ketchup.

Maybe Cosy's just teasing me. Surely no man could eat one of those huge servings and come back for more.

Carla looked toward Ten, who had been the first man to be served. He was better than halfway through his plate and showed not one sign of slowing down.

My God. Even Cash doesn't eat that much, except when we're camping and he's been tramping all over getting rock samples.

Realization hit. A day's work out on the open range was certainly the equivalent of Cash's geological explorations. The hands were definitely going to be coming back for seconds.

The bowl of green beans thumped onto the table. Carla turned and headed back for the kitchen.

"Aren't you going to eat?" Luke asked as he reached for the rapidly vanishing sauce.

"I'm not hungry."

Carla hurried into the kitchen and began opening can after can of chili.

CHAPTER SIX

THE MEMORY OF THAT FIRST NIGHT as the Rocking M's cook still had the power to raise color in Carla's cheeks a month later. The ranch hands had ribbed her mercilessly but not unkindly; Luke had muttered something about cooking for men instead of schoolboys; and Ten had gotten his head handed to him for pointing out that the food was four times as good as anything they had eaten in years, so why complain over short rations?

In fact, Ten had gotten his head handed to him on a regular basis since Carla had come to the ranch. From the look on Luke's face at the moment, Ten was about to get another full serving of his boss's temper. Hurriedly Carla tried to take the scrub brush from Ten's hand.

"Thanks for the help, but Luke is right. He didn't hire you to clean walls."

"You've been working longer hours than any hand since

you got here," Ten said calmly, hanging on to the brush. "This is my day off, and if I want to scrub kitchen walls, I'll damned well scrub kitchen walls."

Luke looked at Carla's drawn, unhappy face and felt his temper rise even higher. Ten was right; Carla had been working twelve-hour days since she had come to the ranch. Every floor in the ranch house was clean enough to eat from. The kitchen counters and cupboards gleamed with cleanliness, as did the beaten-up wooden tables in the dining room. Thanks to Carla's detailed shopping lists, the pantry and cupboards were packed with various foods, the refrigerator was bursting with fresh fruits and vegetables, and a menu was posted in the dining room so that the men would know just what the coming week held in the way of meals.

Even as Luke stood glaring at Ten and Carla, the kitchen was fragrant with the smell of chocolate chip cookies baking in the range's huge oven. Apple, cherry and blueberry pies had become staple items at the dinner table. Homemade baking powder biscuits and bread helped to fill in the cracks. Waffles and pancakes were common breakfast fare. Fresh brownies appeared in lunch bags with gratifying regularity.

And Carla looked as though she hadn't eaten a bit of any of the bounty. Luke suspected she had lost weight since she had come to the ranch. He was certain that she smiled less frequently than ever in his memory. He was also certain that he was the cause of her unhappiness. Each time he told himself that he wouldn't lose his temper with her again, he would see her looking up at Ten with wide eyes and laughter trembling on her lips; and then Luke would feel anger racing through his blood, driving out the desire that was so much a part of him these days that he barely noticed it.

Luke tried to tell himself he was grateful that Carla no

longer followed him around like a lost puppy, but he didn't believe it. Slowly, painfully, he had come to the realization that he had wanted Carla at the ranch for the summer because of her transparent feelings for him, not despite them.

For the past four weeks he had thought often of other summers when he had been the sun in her sky…and she had been the sun in his. At some deep, hidden level of his mind, he had wanted to know again that feeling of being special to someone. It was a heady sensation, one he had never before known, for his father had been too busy working the ranch to pay much attention to his son; and his mother had had nothing left over from fighting her own interior devils.

Damn it all to hell, Luke fumed silently. *Why did Carla have to grow up and spoil everything?*

There was no answer for Luke's angry question, unless the insistent beat of his own blood was a kind of answer. Maybe Carla hadn't spoiled anything after all. Maybe she had grown up enough not to run away in fear if he held her against his rigid, hungry body and tasted the honey of her mouth once more.

Not a chance. She's just a schoolgirl.

She's twenty-one. A lot of women have kids by the time they're that age—and they didn't get them by running away from a man's kiss, either.

Luke knew his reasoning was true as far as it went. But there was another truth, one that came a lot closer to home, a truth that lay beneath Luke's hair-trigger temper.

There are two men I call friends. She's the kid sister of one of those men.

Yeah. And she's going to break her heart on the other one if I don't stop it.

That's Ten's problem. And Cash's.

But it wasn't, and Luke knew it. He wanted Carla. He wanted to take the clothes from her body and look at her, touch her, taste her, sheathe himself in her until there was nothing but her passionate heat bathing him and ecstasy bursting through both of them. He wanted that until he woke up sweating, shaking, wild.

She is Cash's sister, for God's sake! Have you forgotten that?

No. That's why I waited until she turned twenty-one, old enough to do whatever she damn well pleases.

Silent questions, answers, questions, retorts, questions; and finally the question that had no answer but silence and rage.

Are you going to ask her to marry you?

It was an impossible situation. Luke had vowed long ago that he would never ask a woman to be his wife unless she were ranch-born and ranch-raised, able to accept the hard work and isolation that was part and parcel of the Rocking M's rugged life.

But Luke had found no ranch girl who could reach down past his harsh exterior and touch his soul. He had found no ranch girl who could make his body leap into readiness with a look, a smile, the clean scent of her skin. That was what Carla did. She made the raw lightning of desire run like liquid fire in his veins.

Gradually Luke realized that Carla was watching him with shadowed, unhappy eyes; and Ten was watching everything with an infuriating smile on his handsome face.

"Counting to a hundred, boss man?" Ten asked in mock sympathy. "You know, you never did have the temper of a saint or a martyr, but lately you could have taught Satan himself a trick or two."

Ten's drawl was as mocking as his smile. Luke felt his hold on his temper slipping. The only thing that made him hang on to his self-control was the certainty that Ten wanted him to lose it.

"Keep pushing, Tennessee. You'll get there."

"I'll take that as a promise."

"Carla, why don't you go check on those kittens in the barn," Luke said, never looking away from Ten's calm, handsome face. "Make sure none of them get lost."

"The cookies will—"

"I'll take care of them," Luke interrupted, his voice soft. Too soft.

Carla looked from one man to the other with wide, worried eyes. She started to speak, only to have her mouth go dry when Luke looked at her. Without another word she turned away. The taut silence was broken by the light sound of Carla's retreating footsteps. The back screen door squeaked open and banged shut.

Luke waited for a long count of fifteen before he spoke.

"All right, Ten. Let's have it."

"You do know how to tempt a man," muttered Ten, watching Luke with narrow gray eyes.

"So do you. Why are you trying to pick a fight with me?"

Ten didn't bother to deny it. "Just thought I'd give you something as mean as yourself to take out your temper on."

"Meaning?"

"You've been riding Carla hard since she got here. No matter what she does, you tear a strip off her."

"Maybe. And maybe I think my cook has better things to do than chase my ramrod."

"Yeah, I kind of thought that might be the burr under your saddle." Ten's mocking smile faded. "You don't have a kind word to say to Carla, yet when someone else does, you jump real salty. You never used to be a dog in the manger, but the way you're acting lately, a man might think if you can't have Carla you don't want anyone to have her."

"She's too young to talk about having."

"Bull, boss man. She's a woman all the way to the soles of her feet." Ten saw the shift in Luke's expression, the flash of hunger and anger. The ramrod nodded, satisfied with what he saw. "She's fully of age. If she wants a man, she's entitled."

"Leave her alone, Ten."

"Why? You've made it real clear you don't want her. Hell, it's not like she was a kid anymore. The men in Boulder aren't blind. By now, one of them has probably taught her why women are soft and men are hard."

"Drop it."

Ten sighed, lifted his hat and raked his fingers through his black hair. "You're being a damned fool," he said calmly. "The way I see it, Carla has loved you for years and you've pushed her away for years. Finally you made it stick. She went off to college and found men who didn't push her away. She grew up. Then she came back to see how you stacked up against her memories and her new experiences with men."

"Carla isn't the type to sleep around," Luke said tightly.

"Who said anything about sleeping around?" Ten retorted. "I was talking about a young girl who was sent out of here with her pride in shreds. Seems to me she could be forgiven for finding a nice boy or two who wanted to kiss all the wounds and make her feel like a woman instead of a 'schoolgirl.'"

Luke said not one word, but the thought of Carla being touched by another man shook him. The thought of her being taken by anyone sent a killing rage through Luke's veins. He had been so sure, so unspeakably certain, that she would never allow anyone to touch her but him.

Ten measured the barely contained rage in Luke's expression and shrugged. "Suit yourself, boss man. But you should know one thing. Carla told me she came here this summer to get over you. You keep riding roughshod over her feelings and she'll walk out of here at the end of the summer and never look back. Then where will you be? You may not be her first man, but so what? You're the one who was given first call and you turned her down flat. Your fault, not hers. You'll never find another woman with half what she has to offer and you know it."

There was a long, taut silence while Luke measured Ten with the cold yellow eyes of a cornered mountain lion.

"I wasn't cut out to live in a city," Luke said finally.

"Did she ask you to?"

"No, but sooner or later she would. The Rocking M is hell on women. I'd rather not marry at all than have a woman walk out on her kids and her husband, or hit the bottle or go crazy staying on the ranch and make everyone's life a living hell."

"Carla wouldn't—"

"Like flaming hell she wouldn't," Luke said savagely. "Do you think my mother or my aunts *wanted* to betray their children and husbands? Do you think my father or my uncles deliberately picked weak women to marry? Do you think I want to watch Carla get thin and sullen grieving for a way of life she can't have if she's my wife? Or maybe you think I should be like some college kid and just take what she's offering and not worry about marriage, is that it?"

Ten swore beneath his breath, the words all the more violent for the softness of his voice.

"Now you're beginning to understand," Luke said. "Stay away from her, Ten. This is the only warning you'll get."

"What if I'm thinking of marriage?"

Luke closed his eyes for an instant. When they opened there was no emotion showing; not anger, not fear, not desire, nothing but an icy emptiness.

"Are you thinking of marriage?" he asked softly.

"She's the kind of woman that makes a man think of hearth fires and long winter nights and babies teething on your knuckles," Ten said. Then he sighed, raked his fingers through his hair again and added, "But that's all it will ever be for this cowboy. Thinking. Dreaming. I'm piss-poor husband material and no one knows it better than I do." He jerked his hat into place and met Luke's eyes. "Ease off on the spurs, Luke. Carla has a real tender hide where you're concerned."

"And if I don't?" Luke asked, more curious than angry.

"I'll get to feeling protective and you'll jump salty one too many times and we'll have hell's own fight. Then you'll be short one ramrod and the ranch will be short one boss." Ten smiled wolfishly. "You're bigger than I am, but you'd start out fighting fair. I wouldn't. Be quite a brawl while it lasted."

Unwillingly Luke smiled in return, then laughed. After a moment his face settled into grim lines once more.

"Hell of a mess, isn't it?" Luke said quietly.

"It'll do," agreed Ten. "Why in God's name did you let Carla come to the ranch this summer if you knew it was going to drive you crazy?"

"I…" Luke closed his eyes and shook his head. "It seemed like a good idea at the time. She didn't have a summer job. The Rocking M didn't have a cook. The men were going to rebel if they had to keep eating slop that hogs wouldn't touch. Carla is a fine cook. Some of the best meals I ever had were ones she fixed for Cash and me over in the old house."

Luke rubbed the back of his neck and grimaced. "Like I said. It seemed like a good idea at the time. Besides, I expected her to cry uncle by now."

"Carla?"

"It's been four weeks. She must be dying to see a movie or get her hair fixed or whatever it is that women do in town. I promised her before she ever came back here that all she had to do was say the word and the bet was off, no hard feelings and no regrets."

"You don't know her very well, do you?"

It was an observation, not a question, but Luke answered anyway.

"What do you mean?"

"Carla never backed up an inch for anyone, including that hardheaded brother of hers. She made a deal with you. She'll keep it or die trying." Realization hit Ten. "That's why you're riding her so hard—you think you can goad her into quitting."

Luke looked uncomfortable but said nothing.

"Not one chance in hell, buddy," Ten said succinctly. "Carla may be pretty to look at and have a smile as soft as a rose petal, but that's one determined girl. Think about that the next time you start in on her. You're beating a hog-tied pony. She can't escape."

Luke's breath came in harshly. He hadn't thought about Carla in that way, as a person of pride and determination. He had seen her either as a girl too young for him or as one more woman who would be ground up by the Rocking M's isolation and demands. His breath hissed out in an explosive curse.

Ten smiled sympathetically. "You've got your tail in a real tight crack. It's pretty hard on a man when he's damned if he does and damned if he doesn't."

"Do us both a favor, Ten," Luke said, giving the other man a hard look.

"Sure."

"Stop trying to run interference for Carla. Every time you start hovering over her like a mother hen, I get to thinking about how good stewed chicken would taste."

There was an instant's silence before Ten threw back his head and laughed. He was still laughing when Luke set out for the barn with angry, long-legged strides.

CHAPTER SEVEN

"Did you find that ghost stud yet?" Ten asked Luke.

The ramrod's voice had no inflection but his smoke-gray eyes were lit with a combination of sympathy and laughter. Ten knew that Luke had spent long hours out on the range in order to avoid being close to Carla, not to find the near-mythical black stallion that inhabited the narrow red canyons and rugged breaks of the extreme southeastern portion of the Rocking M.

"No, but I saw his tracks a time or two," Luke retorted, piling a huge helping of roast beef, browned potatoes and gravy on his plate.

He glanced up as Carla put a bowl of crisp, fresh green beans next to his plate. With difficulty he forced himself to watch his dinner instead of Carla. She was more beautiful to him each time he looked at her. The thought that he had driven her into the arms of some college boy had tormented

Luke. His days had become longer and longer, but even half-dead from overwork, he had only to look at Carla to feel hot claws of desire sinking into him.

Finally Luke's thoughts had driven him to stay away from the ranch house entirely. He had spent five days roaming the Rocking M, sleeping out, waking with his whole body hot, clenched, burning with passion. During the day he had chased his thoughts as though they were cloud shadows flying over the face of the land.

At the end of five days, Luke still hadn't decided which was worse, the thought that Carla had had another man, or the realization that her virginity would no longer be a barrier holding them apart. They wanted each other. They were both of age. They could take each other, work the passion out of their systems, and then they could go on with life the only way that made any sense.

Separately.

She came here to cure herself of me. Why the hell hold back? Why not take what we both want so bad that we can't look at each other without shaking?

"Thanks," Luke said to Carla, his voice harsher than he had meant it to be.

Carla's smile was soft and hesitant, for Luke's expression was forbidding. He had been out on the range for the past five days; even before that he had been distant. Ever since he and Ten had argued almost four weeks ago. If they had argued. Ten had refused to talk about it. In any case, there certainly seemed to be no anger between the two men now.

For a few unguarded moments, Carla's luminous blue-green eyes watched Luke with transparent hunger, measuring the changes five days had made. His beard stubble had become a thick darkness from cheek to jaw, making his rare smiles flash by comparison. He looked tired, drawn, as though he had been sleeping as badly as she had.

Forcing herself not to linger at the table with Luke, Carla went back to the kitchen. She had already done the dinner dishes and was in the process of mixing up a quadruple batch of cookies. No matter how many cookies she made, they disappeared in a matter of hours. There were times when she thought the men were feeding them to the cows.

"Got any more of that coffee?" called Luke from the dining room.

"About a gallon. How's the gravy holding out?"

"You could bring a quart of that, too."

Carla smiled to herself as she filled another gravy boat, grabbed two hot pads and wrapped them around the thin wire handle of the coffeepot. When she got to the dining room, Ten was gone.

"Where's Ten?"

Luke grimaced at Carla's mention of the other man. "In the bunkhouse, I imagine. Why? You need something?"

"No. I was just wondering how Cosy's hand is doing."

Luke took the gravy boat and began drowning potatoes. "What did Cosy do this time?"

"He cut himself and wouldn't go to the doctor. I sewed it up as best I could, but I'm no surgeon."

Gravy slopped heavily from the boat and ran down onto the clean table as Luke's head snapped toward Carla.

"You *what?*" he asked.

"I sewed Cosy up with the curved needle and silk thread I have in my camping kit. Cash taught me how to do it years ago. He's forever cutting his hands when he's out prospecting. Most of the time a butterfly bandage will get the job done, but Cosy wouldn't hear of anything that fancy. He said a plain old needle and thread was all he wanted. When I was finished he doused everything in the gentian violet solution I've been putting on the calf that cut itself on wire." She glanced aside at Luke's plate. "Your gravy is getting away."

Luke looked down, scooped up runaway gravy on his finger and licked it off. He had to repeat the process several times before the problem was taken care of. At the same time he watched Carla while she set down the coffeepot, shifted the hot pads so that both hands were protected and poured him a mug of coffee. She maneuvered the awkward pot with unexpected grace. Nearly two months of working on the ranch had taught her how to handle the heavy kitchen equipment.

"You do that real slick," Luke said.

Carla looked up, startled. "What?"

For a moment Luke forgot what he had been saying. Carla's eyes were close, clear, like blue-green river pools lit from within. Her lips were full and pink, their soft curves a silent invitation to a man's hungry mouth.

"The coffeepot," Luke said, his voice deep. "You handle it like you've been doing it all your life."

"Pain is a great teacher," Carla said dryly. "You don't have to get burned more than two or three times before you figure out that there's no future in hurting."

Luke's eyes narrowed to glittering amber slits as her words sliced through him like razors. *Pain is a great teacher. There's no future in hurting.* He wondered if Ten had been right, if Carla had come back to the Rocking M to cure herself of the pain of wanting a man who didn't want her.

But Luke did want her. He wanted her until he welcomed pain as a diversion from the agony gnawing in his guts whenever he looked at her and saw what he should not have. Even if she weren't innocent, she was still his best friend's kid sister; and even if she had been a complete stranger, there was still the grim truth about the Rocking M and women. The two didn't mix, as every MacKenzie man but one had found to his grief.

And yet there Carla stood, watching Luke with hungry, haunted, haunting eyes, making his body harden in a single wild rush, forcing him to bite back a curse and a groan.

Stop looking at me, he railed at Carla silently. *Stop wanting me. Can't you feel what you're doing to me? Is this revenge for what I did to you three years ago?*

The words went no farther than Luke's mind, for he had just discovered that the protective layer of anger he had wrapped around himself since Carla had arrived was gone, worn out by nearly eight weeks of use. Nothing came to him in his need except a bone-deep weariness and the understanding that Ten had been half-right—Luke had been beating a hog-tied pony.

But the pony was himself, not Carla.

Wearily Luke rubbed his neck with his right hand, trying to loosen his muscles. It wasn't the endless days of hard driving and hard riding that had tied him in knots; it was that he had run and run and run—and then looked up only to find himself in the same place where he had started, reflected in the eyes of Cash's kid sister.

"Did the big storm catch you on the wrong side of Picture Wash?"

Carla's soft question sank slowly into Luke's churning thoughts. All that hadn't been said sank in, as well—her hesitation even to speak to him, her concern that he had been out in the open when thunder rolled down from the peaks and the earth shuddered, and her yearning simply to hear his voice answering her own.

Luke knew just how painful that yearning was, for he had been haunted in exactly the same way. He had heard Carla's voice on the wind, in the darkness, in the silver veils of rain sliding over ancient cliffs. More than once he had awakened in the night, certain that he had only to reach out to feel her softness and warmth curled alongside his body; but his seeking hands had found only darkness and the cold, rust-colored earth of the remote canyon where he had camped.

"No," Luke said softly. "I was back in one of those side canyons where the cliffs make an overhang that keeps out the rain."

"Like September Canyon?"

"Yes. Did Cash tell you about that place?"

"No. You did, when I was fourteen and you gave me a fragment of Anasazi pottery you had found along September Creek. I still have the sherd. It's my...talisman, I guess. It reminds me of all that once was and all that might yet be."

Carla looked past Luke and the ranch house walls, seeing the canyon whose existence had haunted her almost as much as Luke. Both the canyon and the man were aloof, distant, compelling. Both of them fascinated her.

Luke's breath came in and stayed, for there was such yearning in Carla's voice and face that it made his throat close.

"Cash promised to take me to September Canyon when he comes in August," she continued. "I'll taste the rain winds and hear water rushing over stone, and I'll see in every shadow a culture that was old before Columbus set sail for India and found the New World."

"I never found any ruins," Luke said finally. "I know they're there, probably way up September Creek or Picture Wash or maybe even Black Springs..." His eyes took on a faraway look in the moments before he shrugged and returned to eating. "The ranch takes too much time for me to have much left over for chasing legends."

"I'm surprised Cash hasn't found any Indian ruins. He must have crawled over every square inch of the Rocking M."

Luke shook his head. "Not a chance. There are parts of this ranch that no one has ever walked, white or Indian. Besides, Cash has been poking around hard rock country. He's a granite and quartz man. Most ruins are found way up washes or creeks that wind between sandstone walls. No gold to be found there. Beautiful country, though. Wild as an eagle and damned near as hard to get to."

"The Anasazi and their natural fortresses..." Carla focused on Luke with intense, blue-green eyes, grateful to have found a neutral subject that interested both of them. "Have you ever wondered what frightened the Anasazi so much that they withdrew to those isolated canyons?"

"Other men, what else? You don't go to all the trouble of building your towns halfway up the face of a sheer cliff, risking the life of every man, woman and child as they climb up and down to tend the crops or draw water, for any animal less dangerous than man."

"In the end running and hiding didn't do the Anasazi any good. The ruins remain. The people are long gone."

"Maybe," Luke said softly. "And maybe it's like mourning the passing of the Celts. They didn't die so much as they became something else. I think some of the Anasazi came down out of their fortresses and changed into something else. I'll bet Anasazi blood flows in Ute and Apache, Navajo and Zuni and Hopi. Especially the Hopi."

Carla looked at Luke curiously. "You sound like you've studied the Anasazi."

"Self-defense." He looked up at her and grinned. "You

asked me so many questions after I gave you that piece of pottery, I had to dig pretty deep for answers. Cash must have mailed me most of the university library."

She laughed, then shook her head. "Poor Luke. I must have pestered you half to death. You were incredibly patient with me."

"I didn't mind the questions. When it was too dark or wet or frozen to work, I'd sit and thumb through those books, looking for answers and finding more questions than even you had."

Luke's long fingers caressed his coffee cup absently as he remembered the long, quiet evenings. Carla watched his hand with unconscious longing.

"When the snow piled up in the canyons," he continued, "I'd sit and think about people who lived and died speaking a language I've never heard and never will, worshipping unknown gods, building stone fortresses with such care that no mortar was needed, block after block of raw stone resting seamlessly next to its mates. However else the Anasazi succeeded or failed as a people, they were crafts-men of the kind this earth seldom sees. That's a good thing to be remembered by."

Luke lifted his coffee cup in a silent salute to Carla. "So you see, your curiosity about that little piece of pottery I gave you opened up a whole new piece of history for me. I call it a fair trade."

"More than fair," she said, her voice husky with memories. "You gave me a world at the very time my own had been jerked out from under my feet."

Luke frowned, remembering the unhappy, fragile fourteen-year-old whose eyes had held more darkness than light. Not for the first time, he cursed the fate that took from a girl her mother and her father in one single instant along an icy mountain road.

"Cash gave you the world," Luke said quietly. "I just sort of came along for the ride."

Carla shook her head slowly but said nothing. She had already embarrassed herself once telling Luke of her love for him; there was no need to repeat the painful lesson. She had been only fourteen when she had looked into his tawny eyes and had seen her future.

It had taken her seven years to realize that she hadn't seen his future, as well.

"Sit down and have some coffee," Luke said. "You look...tired."

Carla hesitated, then smiled. "All right. I'd like that. I'll get a mug."

"We can share mine," he said carelessly. "I'll even put up with cream and sugar, if you like."

"No need. I taught myself to like coffee black."

What Carla didn't say was that she had learned to like black coffee because that was the way Luke drank it. Even after the disaster three years before, she had sat in her college apartment sipping the bitter brew and pretending Luke was sitting across from her, drinking coffee and talking about the Rocking M, the mountains and the men, the cottonwood-lined washes and stands of piñon and juniper, and the sleek, stubborn cattle.

When Carla put her hand on the back of a chair that was several seats away from Luke's, he stood and pulled out the chair next to his. After only an instant of hesitation, she went and sat in the chair he had chosen for her.

"Thank you," she said in a low voice.

Behind Carla, Luke's nostrils flared as he once again drank

in the scent of her, flowers and warmth and elemental promises she shouldn't keep. Not with him.

Yet he wanted her the way he wanted life itself, and he had no more anger with which to keep her at bay. He had only the truth, more bitter than the blackest coffee. With a downward curl to his mouth, he poured more of the black brew into his mug and handed it to her.

"Settle in, sunshine. I think it's time you learned the history of the Rocking M."

CHAPTER EIGHT

"THIS LAND WASN'T SETTLED AS fast as the flatlands of Texas or the High Plains of Wyoming," Luke said. "Too much of the Four Corners country stands on end. Hard on men, harder on cattle and hell on women. The Indians were no bargain, either. The Navajo were peaceable enough, but roving Ute bands kept things real lively for whites and other Indians. It wasn't until Black Hawk was finished off after the Civil War that whites came here to stay, and most of them weren't what you would call fine, upstanding citizens."

Carla smiled over the rim of the coffee mug. "Didn't the Outlaw Trail run through here?"

"Close enough," admitted Luke. "One of my great-great-greats supposedly was riding through at a hell of a pace, saw the land, liked it and came back as soon as he shook off the folks who were following him."

"Folks? As in posse?"

"Depends on who you talk to. If you talk to the MacKenzie wing of the family, they say Case MacKenzie was just trying to return that gold to its rightful owner. If you talk to other folks, they swear that Case MacKenzie was the one who cleaned out a bank and hit the trail with sixty pounds of gold in his saddlebags, a full-blooded Virginia horse under him and a posse red hot on his trail."

"Who do you believe?"

"Well, I leaned toward the outlaw theory until I showed your brother the MacKenzie gold."

"You still have it?"

"About a handful. Enough that Cash could see right away that it wasn't placer gold. He went back and checked old newspapers. Seems the bank had been taking deposits from the Hard Luck, Shin Splint and Moss Creek strikes. Placer gold, all of it. Smoothed off by water into nuggets or ground down to dust in granite streambeds. The gold my ancestor carried was sharp, bright, running through quartz like sunlight through springwater. Your brother took one look at it and started hunting for Mad Jack's mine."

"Cash never told me about that."

"I asked him not to tell anyone, even you. Last thing I need is a bunch of weekend warriors digging holes in my land."

"You're serious, aren't you? The gold you have really came from Mad Jack's mythical mine?"

"The mine might or might not be myth," Luke said dryly. "The gold was real, and so was old Mad Jack Turner."

"What makes Cash think the gold came from your ranch?"

"The gold that was passed down through the family looks a lot like the gold from other mines in the area—same proportion of tin or silver or lead or copper or whatever. And then there's our family history backing up the assay. Case had a brother who married a girl he'd found running wild in mustang country. She was Mad Jack's friend. The country she ran in was just south of here. Since Mad Jack went everywhere on foot, it stands to reason that his mine is somewhere nearby. At least, that's what Cash figured seven years ago. He's been hunting that mine ever since, every chance he gets."

Luke leaned forward and took the coffee mug from Carla's fingers. He told himself that he hadn't meant to brush his hand over hers as he freed the mug, but he didn't believe it. He also told himself that he couldn't taste her on the mug's thick rim, and he didn't believe that, either. He took a sip, looked at her and smiled a slow, lazy kind of smile.

"You've been snitching chocolate chips from the cookie batter, haven't you?"

Carla made a startled sound, then flushed, realizing that somehow she had left a taste of chocolate on the mug.

"I'm sorry. I'll get my own cup."

"No," Luke said softly, holding Carla's chair in place with his boot, making it impossible for her to push away from the table and stand. "I like the taste of…chocolate."

He watched the sudden intake of her breath and the leap of the pulse in her neck. When he looked at her mouth, the pink lips were slightly parted, surprise or invitation or both. Her eyes were wide and her pupils had dilated with sudden sensual awareness.

Luke drank, watching her over the rim, putting his mouth where hers had been and savoring the coffee all the more because of it. When he put the mug back in her fingers, he turned it so that when she lifted the mug to drink, her mouth would touch the same part of the rim his had.

"Drink," Luke said softly, "and I'll pour some more."

Unable to look away from him, Carla brought the mug to

her mouth. When the warm rim brushed her lips it was as though Luke had kissed her. Carla's fingers trembled suddenly, forcing her to hold the mug with both hands as she sipped. The betraying tremor didn't escape the tawny eyes that were watching her so intently. When she lowered the mug and licked her lips, she heard the soft, tearing sound of Luke's quickly drawn breath. He took the mug from her again, poured coffee, sipped and then returned the mug to her.

"Case MacKenzie liked more than the land around here. He found a girl whose daddy hadn't been fast enough with a gun or lucky enough with a miner's pick. Mariah Turner had inherited water rights to Echo Canyon Creek, Wild Horse Springs and Ten Sentinels Seep, and mineral rights to a lot more country. She also had every outlaw in the whole damned territory camped on her doorstep."

Carla closed her eyes and relaxed slowly as she listened to Luke's deep voice talk about people who had lived more than a century ago, people to whom the Four Corners country was a landscape both intimately encountered and nearly unknown, a wild place where white history was nonexistent and Indian history was so old that most of it had been long forgotten.

"I've seen pictures of Mariah," Luke said. "I know why the outlaws were circling around howling at the moon. She was all woman. But she had more than a good body and a pretty face. She had the kind of guts that make a man want to catch moonlight and bring it to her in his cupped hands like water, just to see her smile."

Luke sipped coffee while Carla watched, her breath held, tasting in her mind the coffee that was sliding over his tongue, wishing she could be that close to him just once before she died. Watching her, sensing what she was thinking, Luke handed the mug back to her and continued speaking.

"Mariah held on to the land and played outlaws off against one another like a nineteenth-century Queen Elizabeth, letting no man get the upper hand in her life. For two years the outlaws fought for her favors—and made sure that no man got close to her without being killed—and then her worst fears came true. An outlaw who was better with a gun than any of the others rode into her valley. The other outlaws couldn't take the man head-on and he was too quick and too wary to take by ambush."

"What happened?"

"Mariah was lucky. The man was Case MacKenzie."

"The one with the saddlebags full of gold?"

"The same." Luke smiled. "He didn't plan to get married. He didn't even plan to fall in love. Yet before long he was writing notes to himself, talking about hair that was the color of dark mountain honey and sunlight all mixed together." Tawny, intent eyes moved over Carla's hair. "Like your hair. Your eyes are like Mariah's, too, clear and direct. And your mouth is like hers. The kind of mouth that makes a man want…"

Luke let his voice die away. He took the mug and sipped again, forcing himself not to say any more. The hint of chocolate left by Carla was sweeter than any kiss he had ever tasted.

"Maybe you've got Turner blood in you, sunshine. The more I look at you, the more you remind me of Mariah." Luke sighed and rubbed his neck with his right hand, cursing the luck that had him living with a woman he wanted and must not take. "Mariah was the woman Case had been looking for in more ways than one. He had been trying to find Mad Jack Turner's son, to give him his share of his father's gold. Well, it was too late for Johnny Turner, but not for his daughter, Mariah. The gold was just what she needed to improve the Rocking M's beef stock, hire honest hands and make the place a real ranch instead of an outlaw roost."

Luke laughed softly, remembering his father and grandfather telling the same story to him years ago. "And while Mariah was at it, she improved the human stock, too. She had eight children by the man no one could kill, the husband she called her 'beloved outlaw.' One of the kids was Matthew Case MacKenzie, my grandfather's father. Then came Lucas Tyrell MacKenzie, then my father, Samuel Matthew MacKenzie, and then me, Lucas Case MacKenzie. And the Rocking M came with the MacKenzie name, passed on to whichever son had the sand to make a go of ranching in this country."

Carla looked at Luke's face, burned by wind and sun, dark from days without shaving, marked by fine lines radiating out from the corners of his eyes, lines left by a lifetime of looking into long distances and sunlight undimmed by city smoke. In his faded blue chambray shirt, worn jeans and scarred cowboy boots, Luke could have easily stepped out of the pages of his own family history.

"I'll bet you look like him," Carla said softly.

"My father?"

"No. The beloved outlaw. Case."

Something in Carla's voice made desire leap fiercely within Luke, but it was unlike any desire he had ever known. It was not only her sweet body and soft mouth he wanted; he also felt an almost overpowering need to hold her and be held by her in return, to hear her whisper that he was her beloved outlaw, the one man whom she had been born to love.

The one man she must not love, for he could not give her the life she deserved.

"I envy Mariah," Carla continued slowly. "She gave her outlaw everything a woman wants to give her man, and in doing so she became a part of the land every bit as much as the ancient ruins or the Indians who drew on Picture Cliff and then disappeared. Everyone always talks of the West as though it only belonged to cowboys and Indians and outlaws. It belonged to the women, too. In their own way, they fought just as fiercely for the land as any man ever did. I would like to have been a part of that."

"Don't kid yourself, schoolgirl," Luke said sardonically. "No matter how they start out, women end up hating this land, and with good reason. The country grinds them up like they were corn rubbed between two rocks."

"It didn't grind up Mariah Turner MacKenzie."

Luke shrugged and drank coffee. "She was one in a million. I've never envied any man anything, but I envy Case MacKenzie Mariah's love. He found a woman with enough sheer grit to take on this brutal, beautiful land and never cry for mama or silk sheets or the company of other women. Hell, I take it back—Mariah was one in *ten* million."

"A lot of women lived in the West," Carla said evenly. "More than a fifth of the homestead claims were taken out by women who were alone."

Luke's eyebrows came up. "I didn't know that."

"Of course not. Men write history."

He smiled slightly, a flash of white against the dark beard stubble. Then the smile faded and he pinned Carla with his eyes. There was no desire in his glance now, no fire, nothing but the cold sheen of hammered metal.

"Case's son wasn't lucky. Matthew MacKenzie married a Denver girl. She was the youngest of a big family and she spent the first ten years of the marriage having babies and crying herself sick for mama. Two of her kids survived. By the time they were in their teens, she was back in Denver."

Luke took a sip of coffee and rotated the mug absently on the tabletop. Carla watched, afraid to speak, sensing that he was trying to tell her something but he didn't quite know how to go about it.

"Divorce was out of the question in those days. The two of them simply lived separately—he was on the ranch, she in the city. The boy, Lucas Tyrell MacKenzie, grew up and inherited the Rocking M," Luke continued. "He was my grandfather. He married the daughter of a local rancher. She had three kids and was pregnant with a fourth when her horse threw her. By the time he got her to a doctor, she and the baby were both dead. Eight years later my grandfather married again. Grandmother Alice hated the Rocking M. As soon as my father was old enough to run the place, my grandparents moved to Boulder."

Carla listened without moving, hearing echoes of old anger and fresh despair in Luke's voice; and worst of all, the silent, unflinching monotone of a man who knew he could not have what he most wanted in life.

"Dad and his two brothers lived on the ranch. One after another they went to Korea. One after another they came home, married to women they had met, where they took their military training."

Luke lifted the coffee mug again, realized it was empty and set it aside. He didn't need it. The rest of the MacKenzie story wouldn't take long to tell.

"It was a disaster," he said calmly. "It had been hard enough to find a woman who would tolerate life on an isolated cattle ranch even in horse-and-buggy days. In the days of suburbia and flower children and moon shots, it was impossible. One of my uncles moved off the ranch and into town; his wife quit drinking and he started up. My other uncle refused to move to town. His wife made his life a living hell. My two cousins and I used to sleep in the barn to get away from the arguments. One night my aunt couldn't take it anymore. My uncle had hidden the car keys, so she set out on foot for town. It was February. She didn't make it."

Luke's lips twisted down in a hard curve. "In any case, she got her wish. She never saw the sun set behind the Fire Mountains again."

A chill moved over Carla's skin. She had heard enough bits and pieces about Luke's past to guess what was coming next. "Luke, you don't have to tell—"

"No," he interrupted, watching Carla with bleak yellow eyes. "I'm almost done. My mother hated the Rocking M from the moment she set foot on it. But she loved my father. She tried to make a go of it. She simply wasn't tough enough. At first we didn't even have a phone for her to talk to her family or friends. No women lived nearby. Nothing but kids and the kind of work that has broken stronger women than my mother ever was, even on her best day.

"One night the wind started screaming around the peaks and she started screaming right along with it. A week later her parents came for her. They took her, my sister and my cousins—both girls—and they went back east, saying the Rocking M wasn't a fit place for females. I never saw my sister again. She was seven. All I have of her is some old pictures and the doll I was mending for her. When they took her away I was out chasing strays. I didn't even get the chance to say goodbye. Afterward Dad set out to drink himself to death. He was a big man. It took him years, but he finally made it."

"What about your mother?" Carla asked unhappily.

"I hear she remarried. I never saw her again."

Carla looked into Luke's bleak amber eyes and felt her own heart turn over with a need to hold him, comfort him, give him some warmth to offset his cold memories.

"Luke," she whispered.

Without thinking Carla pushed back from the table and went to Luke, taking his face in her hands, feeling the beard-roughened warmth of his cheeks against her palms. He sat motionless, but his eyes blazed within his silence. He made no effort either to pursue or to withdraw from her touch.

"Luke, I…"

Carla's voice died because she didn't know what to say.

"Luke," Carla breathed, bending down to his mouth, almost touching it with her own, trembling.

She had little experience to guide her, only her own need to know the heat and textures and taste of this one man. She could feel the rush of his breath over her lips, smell the coffee he had recently drunk, sense the warmth that waited for her finally within her reach. With aching slowness she lowered her head until her mouth brushed over his. She repeated the caress again, another brushing motion, and then again and again, and each time she lingered longer, pressed against his mouth a bit more, until finally she could feel the hardness of his teeth behind the warm resilience of his lips.

It was good, so very good, but it wasn't enough. Carla remembered how it had been to taste Luke. Hot, wildly exciting, transforming her in the few seconds before the kiss had become too adult, too hard, demanding more of her than she had dreamed at eighteen; but she had dreamed many, many times since then, and running through her dreams like streamers of fire had been the memory of his taste, the electric intimacy of his tongue caressing her own, the hard length of his body imprinted on her own softness.

Remembering how it had been three years ago, Carla slowly opened her mouth until she could touch Luke's lips with just the tip of her tongue. She felt the shock wave of sensation that went through him at the caress, making his powerful body tremble. A small whimper escaped from the back of her throat when she tried to breathe and found she couldn't; she was held in the vise of the sensual instant, wholly focused on the sensations spreading from the tip of her tongue throughout her body.

The sound of surprise and discovery that Carla made sent another shock wave moving through Luke, shaking him.

"Sunshine," he whispered, "oh, baby, don't…"

He had no breath to finish, for she had taken it from him with another gliding caress of her tongue. The sound he made then was not unlike hers when she discovered she couldn't breathe. She trembled and moved her mouth again, instinctively fitting it more closely to his, touching his lips with her tongue, finding warmth, seeking the greater warmth she knew lay within.

Luke tried not to lift his arms, tried not to close them around Carla, tried not to turn and ease his legs between hers, tried not to pull her down until the soft weight of her was astride his thighs. But it happened anyway, the catching and the holding, the turning and the pulling down. It all happened in sweet, slow motion despite his desperate reluctance to allow any part of it to happen at all. His body simply ignored the commands of his mind, for the shy gliding of her tongue had taken away his ability to remember yesterday and foresee tomorrow.

There was enough self-control in Luke not to frighten Carla as he had three years ago, but not enough to turn her away as he knew he must. Like a mountain lying in wait for dawn, poised in the instants between darkness and light, Luke let Carla come to him—first the faint hint of warmth, then the delicate pressure of sunshine sliding down his body to rest in his lap, sending heat radiating through him. He whispered her name again, a word more felt than heard, for it was breathed from his mouth into hers.

The piercing sweetness of hearing him say her name was greater than anything Carla had dreamed, making her shiver and cry out, a cry that went no farther than the dark warmth of Luke's mouth. Moments later he felt the gentle scalding of her tears against his lips and was racked by emotion himself. To be wanted like that was more than he had believed possible, even in his hottest dreams.

Trembling, pressing closer and closer to the heat and power of Luke's body, Carla touched his tongue with her own, wanting the taste of him to fill her mouth as it had once before. She felt the sudden, fierce clenching of his thighs as she settled more fully onto his lap, pressing lightly against him with her breasts and hips and belly. And still the kiss stayed gentle, almost fragile, balanced on the blazing edge of fire.

She wanted to tell him that it was all right, that this time she wouldn't turn and run if he kissed her back, kissed her hard, kissed her as though he were dying of thirst and she was a clear spring for his taking. But she said nothing, for in order to speak she would have had to end the kiss...and that she could not do. She had dreamed of this too long, too completely, dreaming all the way down to her soul.

So Carla kissed Luke as she wanted to be kissed, tasting him deeply, feeling the sweet abrasion of beard stubble at the edges of his lips and beneath her palms, pressing closely, sinking into him, trembling, feeling him tremble in return. His mouth opened as he both allowed her greater freedom and took her own mouth in return. His tongue slid between her teeth, tasted her in wild silence, found every hidden softness of her mouth and then slowly, slowly began an intimate rhythm of penetration and retreat.

The languid stroking was repeated by his big hands smoothing up and down her back, her legs, easing her closer, shifting her hips with gentle pressures, lifting her body into more perfect balance with his; and all the while he continued the complete seduction of her mouth, making it wholly his. Her tongue moved in rhythm with his, she tasted of him, her breath tore as his did, and the small sounds of passion he drew from the back of her throat were the essence of his own desire.

Luke's hands clenched and his short nails raked with sensuous precision down Carla's spine. He felt the breaking of her breath, the wild shudder of her body, the involuntary arching of her hips into his. He tried to bite back a cry of pleasure-pain as she rocked softly against his aroused flesh, but a groan escaped his control; and she drank the passionate sound as he had drunk her own small cries.

The warmth of Luke's hands followed the slow unbuttoning of Carla's blouse, and as each button came undone his teeth sank gently into her tongue, distracting her. She would have let him undress her anyway, distraction or no, for her skin was on fire and her clothes were stifling her and she wanted to be as naked as her tongue sweetly tangling with his.

Luke had just enough self-control left to know if he unhooked Carla's bra, he wouldn't stop undressing her until she was wholly nude, her body open to him, and he was naked within her. With hands that shook, he pushed aside the soft folds of cotton blouse and smoothed his palms over her breasts once, lightly.

He might as well have taken a whip of fire to her. She shivered, transfixed, and her nipples hardened to his soft touch.

Knowing he shouldn't, helpless to prevent himself, Luke slid a long finger beneath each bra strap and slowly caressed the hollow of Carla's collarbone to the warm slope of her breasts. He hesitated, groaned almost soundlessly and eased his fingers farther down, beneath the warm lace, stroking slowly, savoring the rise of warm, firm flesh, the satin areola, the velvet of her nipples. Sweetly, in the same rhythm as his tongue mating with hers, he flicked back and forth over the tight peaks beneath the lace until they were as hard as the male flesh thrusting hungrily between his thighs.

A soft, ragged moan was torn from Carla's lips, a sound Luke took into his own mouth, devouring it as he wanted to devour her. For long, rasping seconds he plucked her velvet nipples until she quivered wildly and her hips rocked in silent pleading against his hard flesh. He freed one hand and let it slide over her belly, tracing the zipper of her jeans without opening it, sliding down and down until he could feel her humid heat resting in the palm of his hand. He moved slowly, rocking with her, wanting her until it was like dying not to take her.

With a sound of anguish Luke ended the kiss, freeing his mouth without freeing Carla's body from his caressing hands. She trembled violently, breathing as raggedly as he was, her eyes dark with the first passion she had ever known.

"I want you," Luke said harshly, flexing his hand into Carla's secret warmth, shuddering when she moaned. "But that's all it will ever be," he continued through clenched teeth, understanding finally the dimensions of his own personal hell. "Wanting. No rings and vows, no babies and color snapshots and scrapbooks to put in with the old albums. No happily ever after. I'll grind no modern woman into bits on the Rocking M. I'll leave no more children to be raised without mothers. The MacKenzie line will end with me."

Shocked, trembling, trying not to cry, Carla felt Luke's pain more deeply than her own.

"But I want you to know this," he continued, his voice savage, his eyes blazing with all he would never know, never do, never be. "No matter who you marry or how many lovers you take, no matter how long you live, no man will ever want you the way I do."

With a swift, powerful movement Luke stood, lifting Carla and setting her aside in the same motion.

"Stay away from me, sunshine. If you come to me again like this I'm afraid I won't have the strength to say no. Then I would take you and hate you and myself and the ranch that's as much a part of me as my soul."

CHAPTER NINE

"Cosy just left," Luke said, answering Carla's question and watching her intently despite the activity around the corral. "Why? Did you want to go to town with him?"

Carla shook her head, making a shaft of sunlight tangle and run through her hair. "I've got a recipe I want to try and it needs a particular spice. By the time I realized it, it was too late to put it on the list."

Luke snapped his leather work gloves impatiently against his thigh. "Hell, schoolgirl, this is a ranch, not a fancy city restaurant. West Fork never heard of most of the junk you want to put in the food."

Carla's chin came up as belligerently as Luke's. "Listen, cowboy, the only complaint I've ever had from the men about my cooking is that their horses are threatening to go on strike over all the extra poundage they have to haul around these days."

A corner of Luke's mouth turned up. "Heard rumors of that myself. Even Ten ordered a new pair of jeans, and that old boy was nothing but rawhide and hard times before he started putting away your food like there was no tomorrow. First thing you know he'll be as fat as I am."

"You? Fat?" Carla looked Luke over from the brim of his cowboy hat to the toes of his boots. "Pull my other leg. There's not an extra ounce on you anywhere. You and Ten are enough to make me yank my hair out. The more I feed you, the better you look, and Lord knows neither one of you was exactly ugly to begin with."

Luke laughed despite the stabbing pleasure Carla's frank admiration sent through him. He had tried to keep her at arm's length since she had come to him in the blazing silence of the dining room and taught him just how much a man could want a woman and still survive not having her. He had twenty-three more days of hell to endure until her stint as cook and housekeeper was over.

Twenty-three days. He wondered if he could make it. Keeping Carla at a distance had proven to be impossible. The anger he had turned against her earlier in the summer was simply gone, burned up in the far hotter fires of his passion for her. He was edgy, he slept badly, he was short-tempered— but not with Carla. No matter how much easier it would have been to be angry with her, he simply could not feel rage toward the girl who had come to him, offering her body and her soul to him with a single shattering kiss.

One kiss, but no more. Carla had heeded Luke's pain, if not his warning. She continued to serve Luke hot food when he came in long after the other hands had eaten. She poured coffee for him, joined him if he asked her to, listened with transparent pleasure when he talked about what he had done that day. She cleaned every inch of the house, washed and mended everything in his closet and drawers. She joked with all the men equally, giving no man any encouragement to become personal, and did it all so diplomatically that Luke was reminded of Mariah Turner's deft handling of the courting outlaws.

In all, Carla had done nothing to earn Luke's displeasure and everything to fulfill the terms of the bet. He could hardly blame her if sometimes he turned around unexpectedly and saw her watching him with desire and wonder mingling in her beautiful eyes. He watched her in the same way, was caught in the same way, and walked off in the same way.

Alone.

Nothing was said. No excuse was given. None was needed. Luke and Carla could not have understood each other better if they had been connected to the same central nervous system.

And time after time, late at night, when thunder and lightning stalked the wild land, Luke heard Carla pacing her room, then tiptoeing down the hall to the kitchen. A few minutes later he would hear the faint scrape of a dining room chair being moved; and he would lie awake, his body clenched with savage need, and picture how she must look at that instant, sitting and sipping hot lemon water, wearing nothing but the black shirt he had left with Cash…the shirt Carla had chosen to use as a nightgown, wearing nothing beneath it but her fragrant skin.

Sometimes it was Luke who awakened, paced and went to the kitchen for something warm and soothing. Sometimes it was Luke who scraped a dining room chair over linoleum and sat shirtless, his jeans half-buttoned, with nothing under the jeans but his rigid, intractable hunger for his best friend's kid sister.

"I'd better do the breakfast dishes," Carla said.

She turned away, unable to bear the intensity of Luke's eyes a moment longer. Yet even with her back turned, she felt him watching her as she went to the house. The thought of leaving tomorrow with Cash for September Canyon was all that kept her from throwing back her head and screaming in a combination of frustration and…frustration. She had thought there could be no worse punishment than loving a man who didn't love her.

She had been wrong. Wanting a man who wanted but refused to take her was worse. Much worse. She felt his unhappiness as acutely as her own.

Do you feel my pain, Luke? Is that why your eyes follow me, watching every step, every breath, every gesture?

Don't do that. Don't watch me. Don't look at my mouth and remember how it felt to kiss me so deeply that we tasted of each other long after the kiss ended. Stop torturing yourself. Stop torturing me.

Twenty-three more days. God, how can I do it? And how can I not?

Forcing herself not to think about it, Carla went to the kitchen and frowned over the recipe she wanted to make that night for the men. It was a French recipe for beef stew that had a long, elegant name. But she lacked one of the pungent herbs she needed. She reread the ingredient list again, went to the cupboard and sighed. The closest she could come was sage, which was already in the recipe.

"If only it were pine nuts," she muttered, flipping pages, looking for another recipe, "there would be no problem. I'd just go up the trail to MacKenzie Ridge and shake down some ripe piñon cones and spend the next three days getting the sap out of my hair."

Remembering, Carla laughed. But it had been worth it to see the look on the men's faces when they asked what the tasty crunchy things in the green beans were. She only wished Luke had been there to share the joke, but it had been during the time he had spent days camping out, scouring the ranch for something he never named.

Suddenly Carla remembered the juniper branch that Luke had brought to her yesterday, saying he thought she might like the smell of it in her room. The deep green of the needles had been studded with the small, powdery silver blue of the hard berries. Flipping quickly to the index of the cookbook, Carla looked up juniper, found a recipe in which it was used and discovered that a very few berries went a long way in flavoring any stew. She closed the book, ran upstairs to her room and returned with several pungent berries in her hand. Singing softly to herself, she began assembling the ingredients for *boeuf à la campagne*.

By dinnertime the smells emanating from the ranch house were enough to make a hungry man weak. As usual when Luke wasn't around at dinnertime, Ten was the first man in the door by a good forty minutes. He looked at the stove, noted that she was using the big pot again and crossed the kitchen quickly.

"I'll take care of that," he said.

"Thanks, but I can—"

"Want to get me fired?" Ten interrupted, taking the heavy pot from Carla's hands, pot holders and all.

"Of course not!"

"Then make real sure I do the heavy lifting when Luke isn't around or he'll have my butt for a saddle blanket. He was very particular about not having you wrestle with gallons of boiling stuff."

The realization that Luke had told Ten to help her made emotions shiver invisibly through Carla.

"Thank you," she said huskily. "I have to admit I've been thinking of rigging a block and tackle for the stove."

Ten smiled as he set the pot full of stew on the worn counter. "Smells like heaven."

She gave him a sideways look. "I'd have guessed you were more familiar with *un*heavenly smells."

He laughed and began filling two huge serving dishes with stew, using a ladle the size of a soup plate. Smiling, Carla turned back to her other dinner preparations, grateful for Ten's quiet help...and at the same time unable to keep from wishing that it were Luke's hands lifting the heavy pots, Luke's arms flexing with casual strength, Luke's broad shoulders making the kitchen seem small.

"Is Luke coming in for dinner?" Carla asked two seconds after telling herself she wouldn't.

"Nope."

"Is he...camping again?"

"Not this time. Some fool cow took a notion to tangle with barbed wire. Luke will walk her to the barn after he sews her up a bit." Ten looked up at the clock. "Be a few hours yet."

"Ladle some of that into the small pot, would you?" Carla asked. "I'll keep it warm for him."

"You're spoiling him shamefully."

She shrugged. "Just doing my job."

"None of the other cooks ever kept food warm for the man who worked through dinner."

"From what I've heard, none of them cooked anything worth keeping warm," Carla said dryly.

Ten bent over the ladle and inhaled. "Damn, but that smells really fine. What's in it?"

"You wouldn't believe me."

"Sure I would."

"The usual things, plus bourbon and juniper berries."

Ten blinked. He sniffed again. "Juniper berries?"

"Think of them as Rocking M peppercorns."

"You think of them. I'm going to eat before you tell me something I don't want to know."

Cosy's voice called plaintively from the next room. "Hey, ramrod, you planning on sharing any of that with the men what do the real work or are you going to keep it all for yourself?"

"Don't get your water hot," Ten retorted. "If we fed you on the basis of work, you'd have starved to death long before now."

Carla just managed to remove the smile from her face before she walked into the dining room carrying a tray of steaming biscuits and a pot of dark mountain honey. Ten followed with the big bowls of stew. The food vanished shortly after it was put on the table.

The speed with which Carla's cooking disappeared no longer appalled her, for she had become accustomed to thinking in terms of feeding men who routinely burned three and four thousand calories a day. During roundup, branding, calving and other seasonally demanding kinds of work, the men would work sixteen-hour days, during which they would eat a minimum of four big meals and all the "snacks" they could cram into their pockets, saddlebags or the glove compartments of their pickup trucks.

Before Carla sat down to eat, she went back to the kitchen with the stew bowls, filling them again from the much-reduced volume of the cooking pot. After bringing the new bowls of stew, plus coffee refills, two more trays of biscuits and a new pot of honey, she sat down and ate her own dinner.

She didn't lack for company; the men who weren't polishing off second helpings were working their way through a third plate. By the time she had eaten her first—and only—serving, the men were through eating. It was the part of the meal Carla enjoyed most, for the full, satisfied men tended to sharpen their wits on one another while she brought in dessert.

Sometimes it was Carla who came in for her share of ribbing, but she enjoyed even that. It reminded her of the good-natured give-and-take she and Cash shared—and Luke, too, until that disastrous summer.

"What's this I hear about you running off tomorrow and leaving us to starve?" Cosy asked as he mopped up the last of the savory gravy with a biscuit.

"True," Carla said cheerfully. "I've saved up some days off."

"And you're going to run off to the city and never think of the brokenhearted boys you left behind."

"Actually," Carla said, standing up and gathering dirty plates, "I'm running off to September Canyon."

"Same difference," mumbled Cosy.

"It is?"

"Sure. We'll starve just the same."

"You can live off the fat of the land," Ten pointed out to Cosy.

"Speak for yourself, boy. I'm trim as a rattlesnake and twice as mean."

"Three times as ugly, too," called Jones from the end of the table. As the other men laughed, Jones kicked back and lit up a cigarette, sending a streamer of smoke across the table. "But that's still one hard-hearted woman," he added, gesturing toward Carla with a burned match. "Leaving us to starve and not turning a hair over it."

"Hate to disappoint you boys," Carla said, pausing in

the doorway with her arms loaded with dishes, "but I doubled up on everything I made this week and froze half. You won't starve."

Shaking his head, Jones rocked back from the table and blew out another stream of smoke. When Carla returned and began passing out dessert, Jones watched her closely and said as though no time had passed, "It's not the same a'tall. Nothing's as good as fresh." He gave Carla a thorough, up-and-down look and took another drag on his cigarette. "'Course, I might forgive you if you gave me a big kiss before you leave."

"Nope," Carla said instantly, hearing Ten's chair creak as he turned toward the brash young hand.

"You sure about that?" Jones asked, blowing out smoke again, looking at her with open appraisal. "Bet I could change your mind, little darling."

"Not a chance. Nothing personal, but kissing you would be like licking an ashtray."

The men laughed loudly. After a moment, Jones shook his head and laughed, too. Ten's smile flickered very briefly, but there was a look in his eyes that told Carla a ranch hand called Jones would be hearing the rough edge of his ramrod's tongue. And, she admitted to herself, it might be just as well; during the past few weeks she had become increasingly aware of Jones. Of all the hands, he was the only one she took care not to be alone with. It was nothing he had said or done; she simply didn't like the way he looked at her.

Ten lingered while, one by one, the other men finished dessert. The hands had taken to carrying their dirty dishes into the kitchen after a meal, which saved Carla a lot of running back and forth. There was usually some more good-humored joking as the hands grabbed a final cup of coffee before going to the bunkhouse for a night of cards, TV, VCR movies or a few rounds on the battered old pool table.

Ten rolled up his sleeves and began scraping dishes. While he did it, he kept an eye on the men who came and went from the kitchen. Especially Jones. The hands sensed their ramrod's displeasure. No one lingered tonight. They carried in dishes, grabbed a cup of coffee and vanished.

Carla waited until everyone had left before she turned to Ten and said neutrally, "The way you're snarling, not one of those hands is going to so much as say good-night to me from now on."

Ten smiled slowly. "The men understand. They can go so far and no farther."

"Fine," Carla said, irritated by the feeling of being protected beyond any reasonable need. "But what would happen if I wanted to get to know one of the men better?"

For an instant there was silence. Then, "Do you?"

She threw up her hands. "That's not the point."

"Sure it is."

"But—"

"Think of it this way," Ten said, interrupting calmly. "If you did want to get to know one of the hands better, you'd be doing him a real favor if you left the Rocking M and took him with you. Otherwise, he'd be a mighty sorry puppy about the time Luke turned up and started hammering out postholes with him. You don't want some nice, stupid boy on your conscience, do you?"

"Is it so awful just to want to have fun with somebody?"

"Try Luke."

"I'd love to," Carla shot back. Hearing the stark emotion in her own voice made her wince. "Never mind, Ten. Guess

I'm just—" she shrugged "—ragged. I'm looking forward to my time off."

"Yeah, I'll bet cooking for this bunch of wolves can get real wearing."

She shook her head. "Cooking, no. Cleaning? Amen."

The outside door to the kitchen slammed behind Luke. "Then stick with cooking, schoolgirl. We're not having a fancy dress ball or white glove inspection here anytime soon," he said, tossing his hat onto the counter. "If you wax the closet floor once more I'll break my neck reaching for shirts." He threw Ten a cool look. "Working late?"

"Just following orders."

Luke went wholly still. "Who's crowding her?"

"Jones," Ten said.

"No," Carla said quickly. "It's not like that. He hasn't done anything."

Luke looked at Ten.

The ramrod shook his head, disagreeing with Carla.

Luke nodded abruptly and said to Ten, "I'll draw his pay. Have him off the Rocking M by noon tomorrow."

"Luke," Carla said urgently, "you can't fire a ranch hand just because he made a joke about kissing me."

"Like hell I can't." He glared down at Carla with narrow golden eyes. "Jones has a bad reputation with women."

"So does Ten, according to you," Carla pointed out tightly.

"Not like Jones. Ten never took anything that wasn't offered. Jones did, and maybe more than once. He got off easy because the gal wasn't exactly a virgin to begin with, but that doesn't change what happened. Even a prostitute has the right to say no to a man."

Carla started to speak but was too shocked.

"I hired Jones because there aren't any women on the

Rocking M and he's a top hand when he isn't drinking and trying to prove he's God's gift to girls. Then you came here. Jones swore to me he wouldn't drink and he wouldn't so much as look at you. I haven't caught him looking, but I'm not so sure about the booze."

Luke glanced at Ten, who nodded.

"Thought I smelled it on him yesterday in the pasture," Luke muttered, rubbing his neck angrily. "Damn it to *hell.* Tell Cosy to drive Jones into West Fork tonight. Tell Jones not to come back. Ever."

"He'll want to hear it from you," Ten said.

"You really think he's that stupid?" Luke asked hopefully, watching Ten with the eyes of a cougar.

The ramrod's smile was slow and savage. "Probably not. Too bad. You've been spoiling for a fight. Couldn't happen to a nicer guy than Jones."

"Yeah. I should have fired that SOB the second I knew Carla was coming here. Females and the Rocking M. Nothing but trouble."

"And good cooking," Ten added. "Don't forget that. Carla's got more of those chocolate chip cookies you favor stashed in the freezer. Nothing like a good woman to spoil a man, is there?"

"While it lasts, no. But when she's gone—and she always goes—it just makes the hard times harder."

CHAPTER TEN

THE KITCHEN DOOR SNAPPED SHUT behind Ten, leaving Carla and Luke alone in the taut silence. Silently she watched while Luke went to the sink, rolled up his sleeves and began washing up. He rinsed dust off his face, soaped all the way up his muscular forearms to his elbows and used a nailbrush on his hands. That was one of the things Carla had always noticed about Luke; no matter how hard he had worked or how tired he was, he always came to her table with clean hands.

And such handsome hands they were, almost elegant despite their large size. Long, lean fingers and neatly trimmed nails. A hand deft enough to pick a tiny flower without bruising it and strong enough to lift a saddle one-handed and lower it onto a cow pony's back. Luke's hands fascinated her. Warm, hard, capable of trembling with desire and yet still touching her with restraint, sensitive enough to measure and savor all the textures of her breasts, caressing her nipples from softness to velvet pebbles.

"Did I miss some dirt?"

Carla's head snapped up to meet Luke's eyes. "What?"

"You were staring at my hands."

"I…" Carla's voice died. She closed her eyes, unable to bear the exquisite torture of looking at Luke's hands any longer and remembering how it had felt to be touched by him, if only for a few moments. "I'll see if your dinner is still warm."

"You mean the wolves left some scraps for me?"

"I stood over the stew with a shotgun."

He smiled. "Did you eat?"

"A little."

He hesitated, then said slowly, as though against his better judgment, "Keep me company and I'll help you finish off the dishes."

"Sold," Carla said instantly. Her blue-green eyes appreciated Luke's smile and noted the signs of a long day's work in his face. "But you don't have to do my job, too. You look like you've been working so hard that you're too tired to sleep properly."

Luke's eyes narrowed. He wondered if Carla had heard him prowling the kitchen for the past three nights. When he was awake he could banish the memory of her body pressed to his, but when he slept, it was different. In his dreams he sat half-clothed in the dining room and she came to him, laughter and sunshine and sensual heat that bathed him in passion until he cried out; and then he awakened alone, sweating, his breath a tearing sound in the darkness.

"Sit down," Carla said. "I'll bring dinner to you. You must be starved."

Luke barely kept himself from saying he would rather

have Carla than any dinner on earth; and he would rather have her in the dining room, sitting astride his lap, her head thrown back, her nipples taut and glistening from his mouth, her body sheathing him, bringing him relief from the torment of wanting her.

"Whatever you give me always tastes good," Luke said finally, trying not to watch Carla's mouth too hungrily.

The look in his golden eyes made her breath catch. A delicate, invisible shiver went from her breastbone to the pit of her stomach.

At that instant Carla realized that she should put Luke's dinner on the table, return immediately to the kitchen and finish the dishes, leaving him to eat alone. Then she should go put one of the Rocking M's movie cassettes on the VCR and watch it. Alone. Or she should read one of her own or Luke's many books on archaeology and the history of the West, or she should make more casseroles and cookies for the men to eat while she was camping in September Canyon, or...anything but sit in aching silence watching Luke eat, envying the very food that touched his lips.

"Go sit down," Carla said huskily. "I'll bring you dinner."

She brought Luke's food to him, sat down with him, watched him eat and envied the food that touched his lips. The silence was both electric and oddly companionable. Not until Luke had had time to appease the worst of his hunger did Carla begin asking him about his day.

"Did you see more cougar tracks around the Wildfire Canyon seep?"

He nodded and smiled to himself. "Looks like she has herself at least one cub, maybe two."

"You aren't going to hunt her," Carla said, reading Luke's expression and the nuances of his voice.

It was a statement rather than a question, but Luke answered Carla anyway, thinking aloud as he had become accustomed to doing with her in the quiet hours after the long day's work was done.

"The cat's in pretty close to the ranch buildings," Luke said slowly. Then he shrugged. "I'll probably regret it, but I won't touch her unless she starts living off calves instead of deer. There's a big part of me that likes knowing cougars have come back to the lower canyons to live the way they did when Case MacKenzie rode into the country."

"Like the wild black stallion?" Carla asked.

"Well," Luke drawled, rubbing his cheek, "you can't prove by me that that old stud is alive in anything but Ten's mind. Cougars, now…I've seen cougars."

Luke sipped coffee, then leaned back in his chair, relaxing and enjoying the peaceful moment. "I think cougars must be the prettiest cat God ever made. Quick, quiet, moving smooth as water, with eyes that remind men we aren't the only life worth caring about on earth. There were wild animals a long time before there were cities. And if we don't screw it up, there will be wild animals a long time after humans get smart and plow the cities under."

Carla smiled softly at Luke. "Do you suppose the Anasazi sat inside their stone apartment buildings and listened to cougars scream?"

"Wouldn't surprise me, especially in the higher canyons. But I'm sure the Anasazi heard coyotes wherever they built." Luke looked up from his coffee and caught Carla watching him with blue-green eyes full of longing. "Did you hear them last night, crying to the moon?"

"Yes. I stood by the window and listened for a long time."

"So did I."

Carla looked into Luke's tawny eyes and felt delicate splinters of sensation quiver through her. In her mind she saw Luke standing by his bedroom window, his body bare of all but moonlight, his eyes reflecting the limitless, elemental night; and all around him, surrounding him, was the mysterious song of coyotes. In her mind she was standing there with him, sharing his warmth, wearing only cool moonlight on her skin…moonlight and the memory of what it had been like to feel Luke's caress. Without knowing it, she shivered.

Luke's hand tightened around his fork until his knuckles showed white. It was a physical effort for him not to reach out and pull Carla onto his lap once more, kissing her once more, caressing her breasts once more; but this time he would remove her jeans and know her soft heat for the first time, nothing between his hunger and the wild, sweet melting of her body at his touch.

"So damned beautiful," he whispered. "And so damned impossible to have."

Carla blinked and focused on the present instead of on her timeless sensual dreams. "What?"

For an instant Luke didn't respond. When he spoke it was only half the truth, for the other half was too painful to speak aloud.

"The night," he said huskily. "It's beautiful. It could be yesterday or tomorrow or a thousand years ago. Some things never change. Like mountains and moonlight."

And man and woman. You and me.

The words rang so clearly in Carla's mind that she was afraid she had spoken them aloud. But Luke's expression didn't change. He continued to watch her with eyes like a cougar's—tawny, intent, deep with things that were impossible to name or speak aloud. Yet like the mountain lion stalking eternity in the rippling canyon shadows, Luke was connected to the intangible, indescribable, indestructible reality of the land itself.

"And like the canyons steeped in sunlight and sage," Luke continued slowly. "Like ancient trails snaking up steep rock walls, wild maize watered by thunderstorms, stone canyons older than human memory. Things that last, all of them. Things with staying power. The land demands it. That's why most people live in cities and look for cheap thrills. It's easier. No staying power required. But they'll never know what it's like to stand and look out over a canyon and feel yourself deeply rooted in the past, with the sunlight of ten thousand days locked in your body and your life branching into the future like the land itself."

Although Luke said nothing more, Carla knew he was thinking of his mother and his aunts and his grandmother, women whom the land had ground to dust and blown away on the relentless canyon winds. She wanted to touch him, to hold him, to tell him that the land lived in her soul as it did in his.

"Luke—"

"This is good stew," he said simultaneously, talking over Carla. "I suppose it has a fancy French name."

For a few seconds she fought against the change of subject. Then she looked at Luke's empty plate, freeing herself from the golden intensity of his eyes.

"*Boeuf à la campagne*," she admitted.

"Country beef, huh? Stew by any other name is still beef and gravy."

Carla blinked at Luke's accurate translation before she remembered that he had a fine arts degree from the University of Colorado. He also had a library of literature and history books that provided him with entertainment more often than the TV programs dragged from the sky by the Rocking M's satellite dish. Yet his western drawl and easy use of cowboy idioms had fooled more than one prospective beef buyer into believing that Luke had the intelligence and sophistication of a panfried steak.

"You and Ten are complete frauds, you know," she said. "Cowboys, my foot."

"Why, whatever do you mean, little bit?" Luke drawled, then spoiled it by laughing.

He settled more deeply against the back of the dining room chair, realizing as he did that evenings had become his favorite part of the day, especially when he worked late and had Carla all to himself. He enjoyed her quickness of mind and easy silences and her laughter when he told her fragments of the Rocking M's humorous lore—the dance hall girls and the Sisters of Sobriety watching one another from the corners of their eyes while a half-drunk pet pig sat outside the church, waiting for its completely drunk master to finish wrestling the devil and go home.

"*Boeuf à la campagne,*" Luke repeated, shaking his head, smiling. "Hell of a thing to serve to a cowboy." Then he paused, remembering what had happened that morning. "Isn't that what you wanted to make but didn't have the ingredients for?"

"I did a little creative substituting."

"Yeah? What did you use?"

"Juniper berries and bourbon."

Luke blinked. "Really?"

"Jest as shore as God made l'il green apples," she drawled broadly. "Rightly speaking, I cain't call it *boeuf à la campagne* no more. More like Rocking M stew. Better 'n possum, an' thet's God's own truth."

Luke's smile widened and then he laughed without restraint. So did Carla. For a few moments he felt as though he had been transported back to the time when he and Carla and Cash had sat around the old house's rickety table long after dinner, talking and teasing and just enjoying one another's company. It was as close to feeling part of a loving family as Luke had ever come.

Then he had ruined it by falling on Carla like a starving cougar on a rabbit. The fact that she had offered herself to him with her eyes full of girlish dreams only made his actions worse. He should have told her gently that he was honored, but it was impossible. He should have sent her on her way with her pride intact, if not her dreams. But he hadn't. He had kissed her too hard and then had shredded her with a few savage words when she panicked.

So she had avoided him for the past three years and had come back to him this summer only to exorcise the girlish dreams of the past. And him. He didn't blame her for wanting to cut him out of her life, but he would spend the rest of his life wishing he had handled her differently. Then he could at least have continued to enjoy the undemanding companionship she brought to him, a sharing of thoughts and experiences that he had never come close to having with another woman.

Sex he could have from any number of females. Peace was something he had known only with Carla.

Sunshine.

Luke didn't know he had said the word aloud until he saw the sudden expansion of Carla's pupils as she watched him questioningly. He stood up with a controlled violence that hinted at the turbulence beneath his impassive exterior.

Who are you trying to kid, cowboy? Luke asked himself derisively. *You want more than conversation and good cooking from Carla. You want everything she has to give to a man, and you want it as hard and as hot and as deep as possible.*

Yes. And that's why I'll stay the hell away from her. I've gone this long without having her. I can go the rest of my life. What I couldn't survive would be watching the light in her eyes killed by the one thing in life that I love—this savage land.

She loves the ranch. She's said so more than once.

Sure. For a few weeks every summer. Big deal.

She's been here a lot longer than a few weeks. Not once has she whined about not having anything to do or anyone to talk to or anything else. Hell, she's not even planning on going into town on her days off. She's going camping with Cash.

Wait until winter. Wait until the weather closes down and there's no way in hell to get off the Rocking M.

Luke's inner argument ended as though cut off by a knife. The horrifying harmony of his mother's screams rising and falling with the wind still echoed through his nightmares. He would never subject someone he cared about to that kind of torment.

Never.

CHAPTER ELEVEN

THERE WAS NO ONE ABOUT, NO ONE near, no one in the world but Luke bending down to Carla, enveloping her in his warmth. His arms closed around her and she trembled even as she locked her arms around him. There was nothing under her feet, nothing over her head; she was spinning slowly, slowly, and he was spinning with her, holding her close, moving against her with sweet friction while around them a campfire burned in the slow rhythms of consummation, setting fire to the world, tongues of fire everywhere, everything burning and spinning and burning, she was burning—

Carla's eyes opened and her hands clenched the sheets as the aftermath of the dream twisted through her body. Her breath was broken, her skin hot, her body aching everywhere Luke had touched her weeks ago, touching her for only a few moments before setting her aside and telling her never to offer herself to him again.

I'm afraid I won't have the strength to say no. Then I would take you and hate you...

Beyond the window, dawn spread down MacKenzie Ridge's black slopes, bathing the shadowed land in the colors of life. Restlessly Carla threw back the covers and got up. She was reaching for her clothes when she remembered that today was the beginning of her time off. Smoothing Luke's black shirt around her hips, she went back to bed.

Sleep was impossible. She had slept little last night, and if the sounds Luke made as he paced from bedroom to living room to kitchen and back again were any indication, he had slept no better than she had.

Trying not to think, trembling as the aftermath of her burning dream rippled through her, Carla lay and listened to the sounds in the ranch house. The upper story was quiet, which meant that Luke had already showered and gone downstairs. The smell of coffee permeated the house, which meant that someone—probably Luke—had made coffee. The back door into the kitchen snapped shut, and then she heard male voices. The words were not distinguishable, but she knew that Ten had arrived and was ribbing Luke about something.

The door to the dining room had a distinctive squeak. Carla heard it many times in the next hour as she turned restlessly in bed, first to one side and then the other, back to front to side to back, but never comfortable for long. She told herself that the smell of ham and eggs and hot cereal was making her too hungry to sleep, but she knew better. She was straining to hear Luke's voice, wondering if he were any less withdrawn this morning than he had been last night, when he had stood up abruptly and left the table.

Carla still couldn't believe her small joke about cowboys and drawls had offended Luke. He had laughed harder than she had. Then he had looked at her with an intensity that had made her weak. Before she could reach out to him, before she could do so much as blink, he had stood up and walked out of the room.

Oh, Luke, don't you see how good we could be together? I can talk to you better than I can to anyone, even Cash. I can laugh and listen and you can do the same with me. We don't even have to be in the same room to enjoy being together. Just sitting and reading in the same house with you is better than going out with men I don't care about.

Don't turn away from me, Luke. Let me show you that I'm more like Mariah MacKenzie than I am like your mother.

The words ran over and over through Carla's mind in a litany of pain.

"Stop it, Carla McQueen," she finally told herself aloud. "Just stop it. You can't make someone love you, and if you aren't old enough to know it, you should be!"

The hissed ferocity of her own words joined the unhappy thoughts that were turning in Carla's mind. She had come here to exorcise Luke so that she would be able to get on with her life, to date and fall in love like other girls.

But cutting Luke from her heart and mind had proven to be impossible. Each shared moment of laughter, each smile, each conversation, each gentle silence, each day she spent close to Luke embedded him more deeply in her soul. Last night it had taken a frightening amount of self-control not to run after him. She didn't know if she had the strength to hold back her emotions any longer, yet she couldn't bear a repetition of what had happened three years ago, when she had declared her love and had been told she wasn't old enough to know how to love a man.

Schoolgirl.

Slowly Carla realized that it had been many minutes since she had heard anyone moving around the house. The hands must have finished breakfast and gone about their work. She turned to the table next to her bed. The small travel clock told her that Cash was still several hours away from the Rocking M. Even worse, she had nothing to do to make the time pass faster. She had been packed and ready to go to September Canyon for three days. All she needed was her brother's arrival.

With a sound of impatience Carla pushed off the bed covers and got up. She paced the room aimlessly for a few minutes before she paused in front of the dresser. She ran her fingers caressingly over the wood's finely polished surface. After a moment, her hand went to the small carved ebony box that traveled with her everywhere. Smooth, graceful, elegant in its curving lines, the box had been a gift from Luke on her sixteenth birthday. Though he had said nothing, she suspected he had made it for her, just as he had made Cash a miniature display cabinet for gold nuggets.

Carla used the box to hold her most valued possession. Not jewelry, but a simple sherd of pottery, another gift from Luke. She had been fourteen and recently orphaned when he had given the odd gift to her. She had never forgotten that moment or the tawny depths of his eyes or his deep, gentle voice trying to reach past her terrible loss and give her what comfort he could.

I found this in September Canyon and thought of you. You can look at this bit of clay and know that a long time ago a woman shaped a pot, decorated it, fed her family from it, maybe even passed it on to her children or her children's children. One day the pot broke and another pot was made and another family was fed until that pot broke and another was made in a cycle as old as life. It's hard, but it isn't cruel. It's simply the way life is. Whatever is made is eventually unmade and then remade again.

The sherd nestled into Carla's palm like an angular shadow. The black finish of the pottery was set off by white lines. The geometries looked random now, but the whole pot would have revealed patterns that were only hinted at in the sherd.

And that, too, was what Luke had told Carla. Then he had held her while she wept and finally accepted that her parents were gone and would never come back again.

For a moment, echoes of past tears ached in Carla's throat. Very carefully she replaced the sherd in its velvet-lined nest. Looking back, she knew it had begun then, the years of incoherent longings that had condensed into puppy love, first love, a girl's stumbling progress toward womanhood; it had begun with the ancient pot sherd and culminated in an emotion that was as much a part of Carla as breath itself.

As the truth sank into Carla, she measured the depth of the mistake she had made in coming back to the Rocking M; there was no schoolgirl infatuation to be exorcised by a summer's proximity to the everyday reality of Luke MacKenzie. She loved Luke with a woman's timeless, unbounded love. She could more easily sever her right hand from her wrist than she could cut Luke from her soul.

With trembling fingers Carla set the small box back onto the dresser. Just as she turned away, the downstairs telephone rang. She grabbed her robe and raced out of the bedroom.

"Hello?"

"Caught you sleeping, didn't I?" Cash asked.

"Nope. I've become a card-carrying member of the Dawn Brigade since I came to the Rocking M."

Cash laughed. "Well, go back to bed, little sister. I won't be out to pick you up until late afternoon."

"Why?"

"The Jeep is on strike."

"What happened?"

"Who knows?"

"You needn't sound so cheerful about it."

"Sorry, sis. I'll do my best to get out there by four o'clock."

"But it will be too late to go to September Canyon by then and rain showers are predicted tonight and if we aren't on the other side of Picture Wash before it fills it may be days before we can cross!"

"I'm sorry, Carla. Look, maybe I can borrow a truck and—"

"No," she interrupted, feeling guilty for jumping on Cash for something that was beyond his control. "It's all right. I've just been looking forward to seeing September Canyon after all these years of hearing about it."

"Why don't you get Luke to drive you over? He needs a few days off."

The thought of having Luke to herself within the cliff-rimmed silence of the canyon was enough to make Carla's pulse ragged. Yet in the next instant her heartbeat settled to normal, because she knew Luke would refuse to go with her. She had asked him several times to take her to September Canyon; each time he had said no, it was too far to go for just an hour or two of looking around.

"Luke is pretty busy," Carla said neutrally. "If nothing else works out, I'll just drive on ahead. Luke has told me that the canyon isn't hard to find, it's just remote. You can catch up with me when you get your malevolent Jeep straightened out."

There was a silence during which Carla sensed her

brother's reluctance to agree to her going to September Canyon without him.

"Promise you won't try rock climbing alone?" he asked at last.

"Of course not. I won't sleep in dry washes during a thunderstorm, either," she added sardonically.

"And if you find any ruins, you won't poke around in them unless someone else is with you?"

"Cash—" she began.

"Promise me, Carla. From what I've heard, some of the floors in those ruins are damned risky."

She sighed. "Cash, I'm twenty-one. I won't do anything foolish, but I won't be hamstrung, either. I've wanted to see September Canyon for seven years. I've worked for weeks and weeks with only a handful of days off in order to save up time. I'm going camping with or without you. If that upsets you, I'm sorry. You'll simply have to trust me."

"What if the Jeep can't be fixed or the rains come and you're stranded in the canyon for a week?"

"I have enough supplies for me for two weeks, remember? I'm carrying your food, too."

"What if it snows?"

"In *August?*" Carla laughed. "C'mon, big brother, you can do better than that. At this time of year I'm far more likely to get sunstroke than frostbite and you know it."

Unwillingly, Cash chuckled. "All right, all right. Let me put it this way, sis. My head knows you're old enough and smart enough to take care of yourself. My gut keeps telling me to protect you."

"Give your gut a rest. Your head did a fine job of teaching me how to camp in wild places."

"Won't you be afraid to be alone?"

"Would you?" she asked quickly.

Cash sighed. There was silence for a moment before he said softly, "Okay. I'll catch up with you as soon as I can."

"Thanks, Cash."

"For what?" he muttered. "You would have gone anyway, whether I liked it or not."

"Yes, but thanks for trusting me anyway."

"You're a big girl, Carla. It just takes a little getting used to. Give yourself a hug for me."

"You, too."

Smiling, Carla hung up the phone. The smile faded as she acknowledged to herself the real reason she was going on to September Canyon alone; she was afraid if she stayed at the ranch house one more night, she would say something she would spend the rest of her life regretting.

Something like *I love you, Luke.*

Thirty minutes later Carla had washed, dressed, eaten breakfast and was looking for a good place to leave her note explaining what had happened to Cash's perverse Jeep. Finally she taped the note to the kitchen faucet, knowing that the first thing Luke did at the end of a day was to wash up for dinner.

"I'M COMING, DAMN IT!" Luke muttered to the imperiously ringing phone.

Luke told himself that he had come back to the ranch house early to see if Carla had made coffee before she and Cash left, but he knew it was a lie. He was coming in to see Carla before she left—and he was too late, or the damned phone wouldn't be ringing. The kitchen's screen door slammed behind Luke as he strode angrily across the room toward the phone, which had been ringing relentlessly. Fourteen times, by last count.

The lack of savory odors and edible tidbits struck Luke forcefully as he reached for the phone. Without Carla, the kitchen was about as welcoming as the corral trough on a winter morning.

Get used to it, cowboy, he advised himself. *And not for the few days she's camping. A few weeks from now the bet ends.*

Angrily Luke picked up the receiver and snarled, "What!"

Cash whistled softly. "Who bucked you off into the manure pile?"

"Cash? What the hell are you doing near a phone?" Luke demanded. "You and Carla are supposed to be hammering down stakes in September Canyon about now."

"Tell it to my psychotic Jeep."

"Hell," sighed Luke. "How far did you get?"

"Boulder."

"Told you to trade that damned Jeep for a dog and shoot the dog, didn't I?"

"Many times."

Luke laughed shortly. "I'll bet Carla's happy. You've given her a perfect excuse to take off for the bright lights."

"I did?"

"Sure. She's going to see you," Luke said, feeling disappointed that Carla had gone to the city after all.

"She is?"

"Of course she is. She hasn't admitted it to anyone, but I know she's dying to get her hair fixed or her nails done or shop for makeup or whatever it is that women do in big cities."

"We must have a bad connection," Cash said dryly. "Would it help if I banged the receiver on the table?"

"What in hell are you talking about?"

"Funny, I was going to ask you the same question. Let's start all over again. You remember Carla, my kid sister, the one who's been cooking for you and that bunch of starving cowboys since June?"

Luke made a rough sound, but before he could get a word in, Cash kept on going, answering his own question.

"I thought you might. Now Carla—my kid sister, remember?—has been saving up days off so she can go camping in September Canyon. You with me so far?"

"Cash, what the hell—"

"Good," Cash interrupted. "You're still with me. Now hang on tight, cowboy, this is where you got bucked off last time. I am in Boulder. Carla is not. She's not coming here, either. She's on her way to September Canyon."

"*Alone?*"

"Yes."

"For the love of God, why did you let her do a damn fool thing like that!"

"Yo, Luke!" Cash said loudly. "I think you've been bucked off into the fresh stuff again. Carla, my kid sister—you *do* remember her, don't you?"

Luke swore.

"Yeah, I thought you did," Cash continued. "Well, she's twenty-one. Even if I were at the ranch—which I'm not, remember?—I wouldn't have stopped Carla. She may be my kid sister, but she's not a kid anymore. She's old enough to do what she wants."

Luke started to speak, but Cash wasn't finished talking yet.

"You got that, Luke? Carla's only a girl in our memories, and that's not fair to her or to us. Now, are you still with me or are you sitting on your butt in a pile of road apples wondering what hit you?"

There was silence while Luke absorbed his friend's message. "You're a fool, Cash McQueen," he said softly.

"No. I'm a gambler, which is a different thing entirely. Even so, I'd prefer not to have Carla spending too much time alone in the kind of country she's headed for."

"How long do you think it will take you to get your damned Jeep fixed?" Luke asked tightly.

"I'm having a part flown in from L.A. Soon as that comes I'll be up and running."

"Cash, damn it—"

"Have a nice trip, Luke."

For a long minute Luke stared at the dead phone. Then he slammed the receiver into the cradle and went looking for his ramrod.

CHAPTER TWELVE

CARLA'S SMALL PICKUP TRUCK bounced and slithered through one of the countless small washes that crossed the ragged dirt road. When she came to what could have been another ranch crossroad or simply one more "shortcut" leading to nowhere in particular, she stopped the truck and checked the map. Only the dashed, meandering line of the ranch road showed. No crossroads, no spurs, nothing but the single road heading generally southeast across the national forest land where the Rocking M had leased grazing rights. The tongue of national forest ended at the edge of a long line of broken cliffs that zigzagged over the countryside for mile after mile. The line of cliffs was deeply eroded by finger canyons and a few larger canyons where water flowed year-round.

One of those many creases in the countryside was September Canyon.

A swift check of the compass assured Carla that she was still heading in the right general direction. Out here, that was as good as it got; road signs simply didn't exist. She got out of the pickup, stretched and assessed the weather. Scattered showers had been predicted for the Four Corners country, with a good chance of a real rain by sundown. At the moment clouds were sailing in fat armadas through the radiant sapphire sky. The clouds themselves ranged from brilliantly white to a brooding slate blue that spoke silently of coming rain.

The high peaks off to the north were already swathed in clouds as solitary rainstorms paid court to mountaintops rarely reached by man. To the south, cloud shadows swept over land broken by canyons and rocky ridges. Random, isolated thundershowers showed as thick columns of gray that were embedded in the earth at one end and crowned by seething white billows on the other.

Even as Carla appreciated the splendor of rainbows glittering among the racing storm cells, she was relieved to see that none of the isolated thundershowers had ganged up and settled in anywhere for a good cry. She had driven dirt roads long enough to know that she didn't want to drive through mud if she could help it. Nor was she enthusiastic about the idea of fording washes that were hub-deep in roiling water. Fortunately it was only a few more miles to Picture Wash, and from there it was just under three miles to the mouth of September Canyon. Even if she had to walk, she would have no trouble making it before sunset.

Smiling at the excitement she felt rising in herself at the knowledge that she was finally within reach of the canyon that had haunted her for seven years, Carla got back in her little pickup and drove down the road, trailing a modest plume of dust behind.

The dust Luke raised heading for September Canyon could in no way be called modest. A great rooster tail of grit and small pebbles boiled up in the wake of his full-size pickup truck. He drove hard and fast, but never dangerously. He knew each rut, pothole and outcropping of rock in the road. Close to the ranch house he drove between barbed wire fences marking off pastures. Farther from the house he came to the open grazing land.

There was no gate to the open area. There was only a cattle guard made of parallel rows of pipes sunk into the road at a right angle. The pipes were spaced so that a cow would shy back from walking on them for fear of getting a hoof caught in the open spaces between the bars. The cattle guard offered no deterrent to vehicles beyond the startling noise caused by tires rattling and clattering over pipes.

Luke occupied his mind with the condition of the road or the look of the cattle grazing nearby or the number and kind of plants growing in roadside ditches. The road needed grading. The fences could have used tightening in a few places. The cattle were sleek and serene, grazing in good forage or lying beneath scattered trees to ruminate. The roadside plants were lush with water from a recent storm that had raced by, grooming the land with a wet, lightning-spiked tongue.

More rain threatened. Luke had outrun one thunder-storm, dodged another by taking a shortcut and had plowed through a third. The clouds overhead suggested that evasive maneuvers wouldn't work much longer. He assessed the state of the sky with an anger he didn't examine and pushed harder on the accelerator, picking up speed. If it kept raining off to the southwest, water would be running in Picture Wash before sunset and Carla might become isolated on the other side. There were no other roads into September Canyon. The only trail was one he had discovered seven years before, when he had been combing the Rocking M's most distant canyons on horseback, looking for strays. In good weather the trail was harsh enough; in bad weather it would be hell.

I'll take the trail, if it comes to that. Carla shouldn't be out there by herself.

Why not? asked a sardonic corner of Luke's mind. *She's safer out there alone than she is with me and I damned well know it.*

Surely I can keep my hands off her until Cash gets here.

Yeah, that's what he was gambling on, wasn't it? And that's why I called him a fool.

Luke's mouth flattened into a grim line as the truck began to descend in a long series of switchbacks that would eventually lead to the lower elevations where Rocking M cattle grazed in winter and cottonwoods grew year-round, shading sand-bottom creeks with massive elegance.

Usually the creeks ran clear, as transparent as the raindrops that had spawned them. But by the time Luke reached Picture Wash, the water was a churning swath of brown. He stopped the truck, got out and guessed the height of the water over the dirt road by how much of the streamside vegetation was underwater. There was no doubt that Carla had crossed here—the narrow tires of her baby pickup had left a trail right into the water. The fact that she hadn't bogged down proved that she had crossed earlier, before Picture Wash had filled with runoff water. The stream was double its normal volume now but still could be forded by a vehicle with four-wheel drive, good axle clearance and a skilled driver. But if Luke had been an hour later, he would have spent the night camped on the wrong side of the wash.

Luke drove the truck through the muddy water and accelerated up the rise on the far side. A passing thunderstorm had dampened the road enough to show tracks clearly but not enough to make driving tricky. The sight of the tread marks left by Carla's ridiculous pickup acted as both goad and lure to Luke. He didn't even pause to look at the outcropping of smooth, rust-colored rock that had given the wash its name. Ancient tribes and not-so-ancient cowboys had inscribed their marks in ageless stone, leaving behind stylized pictographs or impenetrable scrawls.

The road bent off to the right, following the base of the cliffs that paralleled Picture Wash. A few miles farther up, the road turned off into one of the many side canyons that emptied into the wide, sandy wash. There was nothing to mark this canyon as different from any other except the new tire tracks overlying a vague hint of older tracks—that and a discreetly placed cairn of stones telling anyone who could read trail signs to turn left there.

It was barely half an hour to sundown when Luke drove up next to Carla's toy pickup and parked. He got out, took one look at the sky and pulled on a knee-length yellow slicker that was slit up the back to permit riding a horse. Within moments he was headed for the spot where a bend in September Creek had undercut the stone cliff. The creek had long since changed course, cutting a new bed on the far side of the canyon, a hundred yards away and thirty feet lower in elevation. The ancient streambed was now high and dry, protected by an overhang of massive stone that shed rain in long silver veils. Beneath the overhang it was dry except for a single, moss-lined seep no bigger than a hat. The water from the seep was clean and cool and sweet, as heady to a thirsty hiker as wine.

Like the experienced camper she was, Carla had set everything out before she went exploring. Two sleeping bags were stretched over individual strips of foam mattress. A campfire was laid out, ready to ignite with a single match. Cooking gear and firewood were stacked nearby. Someone who came in cold, wet and tired could be comfortable within a few minutes.

Luke turned his back on the overhang and went looking for Carla. Beyond the protection of the slanting stone, her tracks showed clearly against the countless dimples raindrops had left in the dust. Even though her tracks were obvious, Carla had left a small pile of stones that indicated the direction she had taken. Luke followed quickly, knowing that she would mark any changes in direction by another pile of stones.

Ten minutes later he climbed up the shoulder of a tongue of land that poked out into September Canyon. From where he stood, he couldn't see the overhang where Carla had set up camp, but he could see three miles down the creek itself to the point where it joined Picture Wash. The view was wild, untouched, unchanged since man had first come to walk the land thousands upon thousands of years ago. Indigo storm clouds seethed in slow motion, impaled on shafts of pure light thrown off by the setting sun. Red cliffs wept streams of silver tears, fragile waterfalls whose lifespan could be measured in hours. There was no wind, no rain, no sound but that of silence itself, an immensity that embraced sky and untamed land alike.

And watching it all was Carla, standing at the very edge of the rise, a smile on her lips and serenity in every line of her body.

Slowly Luke walked toward Carla, watching her watch the land, hungry for her in ways he couldn't name, savoring the fact that she so obviously loved the untouched vista of stone and sunlight, silence and cloud. She had had every excuse in the world to drive into Boulder's concrete excitements and enticements, but instead she had headed even deeper into the uninhabited land.

But only for a few days, Luke told himself savagely. *Remember that. She just came here for a few days of vacation. That's a hell of a long way from being able to take a lifetime of isolation. No woman wants that, and no man has the right to ask for that kind of sacrifice.*

And no matter how beautiful the Rocking M might be, it was isolated. There was no doubt about it, no finessing it, no forgetting it.

"You're damn lucky it's me rather than some stranger following your tracks up here," Luke said roughly.

Carla spun around, her eyes wide with surprise. "Luke! My God, you scared me sneaking up like that!"

"Sneaking?" Luke looked at his cowboy boots. "Schoolgirl, I couldn't sneak up on a corpse wearing these."

"Maybe not, but you crept up on me just fine. What are you doing here?"

"You took the words right out of my mouth."

"I'm taking a vacation, just like I planned."

"Not quite," Luke said tightly. "Last I heard, Cash was still in Boulder."

"Only until the Jeep gets fixed."

"And meanwhile you expected me to let you stay out here alone?"

"Why not? You do several times a year. Cash has more than once."

"That's different."

"It sure is," Carla agreed. "Neither one of you can cook

worth a damn. It's a wonder you haven't starved to death. I won't have that problem. I can cook."

"Carla, damn it—" Luke took off his hat and raked his fingers through his hair in frustration.

"What?" she asked calmly.

He hung on to his temper. Barely. "Listen, schoolgirl, this may be a joke to you but it isn't to me. What would you do if you got injured while you were all alone up here?"

"The same thing you or Cash would," Carla said matter-of-factly. "I'd treat myself as best I could and then drive out. If I couldn't drive, I'd make the best shelter I could and wait for someone to miss me, follow my trail markers and help me."

"What if we weren't in time?"

"What if there were a blizzard and I froze to death?" she countered.

"In *August?*"

Carla laughed. "That's exactly what I said to Cash when he dragged up a blizzard as an excuse for me not to come here alone."

Luke snapped his Stetson against his thigh in taut anger. He closed the distance between himself and Carla, not stopping until he was only inches from her.

"What if some man found you here alone?" Luke demanded in a low, hard voice.

"That's less likely to be a problem here than in so-called civilization," Carla pointed out, warily measuring Luke's anger. "In cities women are mugged, beaten or worse. Having other people around is no guarantee a woman is safe from a man."

The sudden wariness in Carla's eyes cost Luke what small hold he had on his tongue. For an instant all he could see was the Carla of three years ago, a girl scared and trembling as his fingers bit into her resilient hips, pulling her close, dragging her up against his hardened body.

"Don't get scared and bolt, schoolgirl," he said coldly. "I won't attack you."

Carla's head came up proudly. "I never thought you would."

"You must have thought it once," he shot back, "because you ran like hell and stayed away for three years."

With a tight motion of her body, Carla turned away, looking back over the land once more.

"That was humiliation, not fear," she said finally. "I was naive enough to believe I had something to offer you. You pointed out my foolishness in very unmistakable terms. I was mortified, but you had every right to say what you did and I knew it. That's why I was so ashamed."

Luke looked at Carla for a long moment. His mouth flattened in a line of anger and pain. When he spoke, his voice was resonant with restrained emotion.

"I've regretted that night like I've regretted nothing else in my life."

Carla turned back toward Luke, a wondering kind of surprise showing clearly in her blue-green eyes. He was looking at the sky, not at her.

"Rain coming on," he said, replacing his Stetson with a smooth motion. "We'd better get back to camp."

Her thoughts in turmoil, Carla followed Luke back to camp. There was little conversation while she cooked dinner and even less talk while Luke helped her wash dishes. She poured coffee while he added wood to the campfire, increasing the delicate, searing dance of flames. When she handed him a cup of coffee, he thanked her with a nod and then turned his back to the fire and to her, concentrating on the view of September Canyon.

During supper, the last of the red light had drained from the sky, leaving a luminous indigo twilight. Isolated clouds had expanded, flowed outward and joined with others of their kind in a slow embrace. In the darkness soft rain began to condense.

There was no dazzling flare of nearby lightning or fanfare of thunder, simply the gentle persistence of water drops materializing from the night and free-falling through darkness until they caressed the rugged body of the land. Gradually the vast silence became alive with the whispers and sighs and fragmented murmurings of tiny waterfalls gliding over massive stone cliffs.

Carla sat cross-legged near the campfire, looking across the flames at Luke. His yellow slicker had been cast aside beneath the protective overhang. His open-necked shirt, worn jeans and boots were first revealed and then concealed by the languid rise and fall of flames. The metal camp cup he held in his large hand gleamed like quicksilver. He reminded her of the land itself, enduring and powerful, full of unexpected beauty and deep silences.

Luke didn't notice the intensity of Carla's regard. Standing with his back to the flames, he watched the veils of raindrops glittering with reflected fire against the limitless backdrop of night. From time to time he sipped coffee from his cup. Other than that, he made no movement. He neither spoke to nor looked at Carla, yet the silence wasn't uncomfortable, merely an extension of the shared silences they often enjoyed while he ate a late dinner or helped her clean the big coffeepot and measure out coffee for the following morning.

"Why?" Carla asked without warning, as though only seconds had intervened since Luke had stood with her and looked out over the late afternoon on the promontory half a mile up September Canyon.

Not turning around, Luke answered in the same way. "Why did I grab you three years ago?" He laughed roughly. "Hell, schoolgirl, you're not *that* naive."

"And I'm not a schoolgirl anymore. Didn't Cash tell you? I went to college year-round so I could graduate in three years."

Luke said nothing.

Carla persisted, unable to help herself, needing to know about the night that had changed her life, the night that apparently had scarred Luke, too. "Why do you regret what happened so much?"

For a long time there was only silence and the sinuous dance of fire and rain.

"It was the sweetest offer I've ever had," Luke said finally. "You deserved better for it than I gave you. You deserved slow dancing and candlelight kisses and candy wrapped in fancy foil. You deserved a gentle refusal or a gentle lover, and you got…me."

Carla was too surprised to speak. She watched Luke's shoulders move in what could have been a shrug or the unconscious motion of a man readjusting a heavy burden.

"There was nothing gentle or civilized in me that night. I wanted you until I shook with it. I'd wanted you like that for years. When you seemed to want me, I lost my head."

Luke turned, snapped his wrist and sent the dregs of his coffee hissing into the fire.

"It's just as well," he continued. "Once I was sober I'd have hated myself for taking you. You were so damned innocent. It was better that some other man got to be your first lover. At least he didn't hurt you."

"What?"

Again Luke laughed roughly as he bent over the coffeepot, refilling his cup while he talked. "If your lover had hurt you, it would have made the front pages—'Cash McQueen Avenges Kid Sister.' But there weren't any headlines."

"Not surprising. There wasn't any lover, either."

Luke's head snapped up. For the first time since they had come to camp he looked directly at Carla. Firelight outlined his shocked expression.

"Are you saying that you're...that you haven't...?"

"You needn't look at me like I just fell out of a passing UFO," Carla said uncomfortably. "Has it ever occurred to you that all the studies saying half or two-thirds of girls have lovers before they're married also means that between one-third and one-half of the girls *don't?* What's so shocking about that?"

"One-third of you are saving yourselves for marriage, is that it?" Luke asked as he set aside the coffeepot and straightened up again.

Carla shrugged, but Luke didn't notice. He had turned his back to the fire again—and to her.

"I don't know what their reason for waiting is," Carla said. "I only know mine."

Silence, a sip of coffee, then Luke asked slowly, "What's your reason?"

"The flame isn't worth the candle."

"What?"

"More pain than gain," Carla said succinctly. "You see, the older I get, the more I realize that I don't like men being close to me. Not like that. Breathing their breath. Tasting them. Not able to move without touching them. *Close.*"

Slowly, as though pulled against his will, Luke turned around to face Carla again. He looked at her for a long, taut moment before he said, "You had a funny way of showing it that night in the dining room when you gave me the sweetest dessert a man ever had."

The memory of those few, incredible moments in Luke's arms went through Carla like lightning. She tried to speak but was afraid to trust her voice. She licked her lips, looked away from him and tried again to talk.

"It's different with you," she said huskily. "It always has been. I can't...help it. That's just how it is."

Although Carla tried to speak casually, her voice trembled. The honesty of her words hadn't come without cost; but then, neither had Luke's confession that it had been desire rather than contempt for her that had driven him three years ago.

Abruptly Luke turned away and began prowling the perimeter of the overhang as though he were a cougar measuring the dimensions of its captivity. Half a creature of fire, half a creature of night, wrapped in the elemental rhythms of rain, Luke was a figure born from Carla's dreams. Unable to look away from his lithe, powerful, restless movements, she simply sat and watched him with a soul-deep hunger she couldn't disguise.

And then he turned and looked at her with a hunger as deep as her own.

CHAPTER THIRTEEN

SLOWLY CARLA CAME TO HER FEET. Without looking away
from Luke she skirted the fire, scarcely aware of the flames,
for it was the golden blaze of Luke's eyes that consumed her.
Motionless, waiting, every muscle taut with his inner
struggle, he watched her slow approach. He knew he should
turn away from her, walk out into the rain and keep on
walking until the heavy running of his blood slowed. He
shouldn't stay rooted to the land while she came closer to
him. He shouldn't watch with eyes narrowed against the pain
of wanting and his whole body rigid from battling his endless
hunger for the girl who could arouse him with a word, a
look, a breath.

The girl he had promised himself he would never take.

Carla stopped only inches away from Luke. She looked
into his eyes until she could bear no more. She leaned
forward, speaking his name in a voice as murmurous as the

rain. When there was no answer, she raised a trembling hand to his cheek. The gentle touch of her fingers made him shudder as though he had been brushed by lightning. She felt the violent currents of restraint and passion coursing through him as though they were her own. She knew if she touched him again there would be no more turning back for either of them, no more frustrated desire, nothing but the sweeping reality of a man's hunger and a woman's answering love.

Where once the depth of Luke's passion had frightened Carla, it now sent wild splinters of sensation through her. She had never felt the sweet violence of her own sensuality with any other man. She doubted that she ever would—not like this, her body shaking as she reached toward the man she had loved before she understood what a man needed from a woman who loved him.

Delicate fingertips traced Luke's dark eyebrows, the blunt Slavic thrust of his cheekbones, the knife straightness of his nose, the heavy bone of his jaw, caressing him as she had a thousand times in her dreams. When she touched his mouth he made a raw sound and she trembled. That, too, had been part of her dream, his wanting her until he would feel the same tearing pain at not having her that she felt at being separate from him.

"Love me," Carla breathed against Luke's mouth. "Teach me how to love you."

"Baby," Luke said hoarsely, shuddering, unable to force himself to step back from her. "Don't do this to me. I've wanted you too long."

"Please, Luke. Oh, please, don't turn away. I've dreamed of you for so many years."

Luke looked down at Carla's haunted eyes and trembling lips and suddenly knew that he could no more turn away from her now than he could walk out of his own skin. With that bittersweet realization an odd calm swept through him, a feeling of potency and certainty combined. In no longer battling himself he had redoubled his own strength. That was good. He wanted that extra control. For Carla, not for himself. For Carla he wanted to be the kind of lover he had never been with any woman.

A small movement of Luke's wrist sent his coffee cup in an arc that ended out in the rain. Slowly his big hands came up and framed Carla's face with a tenderness that stopped her breath. Only in that instant did she admit to herself that she had been expecting a passionate onslaught from Luke of the kind that had frightened her three years ago.

"I've dreamed, too," Luke said, his voice deep, watching Carla with eyes that reflected the warmth and heat of flames. "I've filled so many empty hours dreaming of living that night all over again, of having you stand in front of me again, offering yourself, looking at me and trembling with hope and desire. And now you're standing in front of me again, and you're trembling… Is it fear, sunshine? Tell me it isn't fear."

"I don't know why you make me shake," Carla said, trying to laugh, making only an odd, ragged sound. "But I know it isn't fear."

Luke's slow, essentially male smile made Carla's heart turn over with desire. The leashed hunger in his eyes stopped her breath. Gently he turned her until her back was no longer to the fire. Without moving, hardly even breathing, he looked for a long time at the silken curves of her hair, the elegant arch of her eyebrows and the silent dance of flames reflected in her eyes. And then he began looking at her all over again.

She didn't understand why he had turned her profile to the fire, why he made no move to touch her now. "L-Luke?"

"I want to see you," he said simply. "I want you to see me."

The warmth of his hands enveloped Carla in a gentle vise. His lips traced the graceful margin between her hair and her face, smoothed her eyebrows, breathed warmth against her eyelids, outlined the hollow of her cheeks, whispered along her chin. She stood enthralled, unable to move even if she had wanted to, unable even to breathe, suspended between fire and rain and the unexpected, exquisite tenderness of Luke's passion. When his lips finally brushed her mouth, her pent breath came out in a moan.

Luke froze, lifted his head and saw the glitter of tears caught in Carla's long lashes.

"Does my kiss really mean that much to you?" he asked, his voice strained.

She opened her eyes and looked at him, unable to speak.

"My God," he whispered, shaken.

He bent down to her mouth once more, murmuring the nickname he had given to her the first time he had seen her smile so many years ago. The sound of his voice mixed with the fluid murmur of water sliding over stone in the darkness beyond the fire. He brushed her mouth once, twice, then again and again, touching her with the tip of his tongue each time, taking tiny sips of her until her lips parted helplessly, hungrily, and the tip of her tongue touched his.

"Yes," Luke said huskily, encouraging her. "Do you want that, too? Do you want to taste me the way you did in the dining room?"

Blindly Carla turned her face to follow Luke's teasing, gentle, maddening mouth, lips that kissed and lifted, kissed and lifted, never giving her what she suddenly, wildly needed. She made a sound of frustration and need that was too ragged to be a word.

"I hope yes is what you're trying to say, sunshine," he murmured, flexing his hands, pulling her closer to his body. "I hope you liked the taste and feel of me, because remembering that kiss has kept me awake too damned many nights since then."

Carla's eyes opened in surprise. "You, too? I would lie in bed and remember kissing you."

She didn't understand what it did to Luke to hear that hunger for him had left her sleepless. She only knew that the powerful hands framing her face trembled for an instant. He breathed a word that could have been prayer or curse or both hotly mingled.

"Show me the kind of kiss you wanted when you lay awake," Luke said against Carla's lips. "Show me your dreams. Let me make them come true."

Her arms slid up around Luke's neck as she pulled herself up on tiptoe, balancing against his big body. His palms slid from her face to her shoulders and then around her waist, holding her close, but not so close that she would be frightened by the hard bulge of flesh beneath his jeans. Softly her lips brushed his and her tongue glided along his lower lip. He shuddered but made no move to take her mouth. Her arms tightened more and she trembled.

"Please," Carla whispered against his lips. "Please, Luke. In my dreams I tasted you."

Luke's lips opened on a low sound of pleasure-pain and suddenly there was no barrier to the kind of kiss Carla had both remembered and dreamed. Her tongue sought and found his for a wild, hungry tasting; and then his arms closed harshly around her, arching her into his body in helpless response to the naked, innocent demands of her kiss. Instantly he tried to pull back, cursing his own loss of control.

But Luke found he couldn't pull back. An unexpected, fiercely feminine strength held him close, for Carla was placing no leash on her own response, her own dreams. She was kissing him as she had dreamed of being kissed, hunger and trembling, heat and sensual fire; and something more, something she couldn't name but knew waited for her within this one man's arms.

Luke bent down, arching Carla's supple body more deeply, bending her into the curve of his own body, satisfying her instinctive urgency to match a woman's soft heat with a man's hard need. His arms tightened even more as he slowly lifted her until she had no support but his strength, no place to rest but against his hard flesh, nothing but his heat and hunger surrounding her. She was spinning languidly, turning, folded in hot darkness, sweetly consumed by fire, and Luke was spinning with her, the taste of him spreading through her, his arms locked around her, a dream coming true, wrapping her in ribbons of fire.

A long time passed before Carla felt herself being lowered slowly to the ground, still held so close as Luke eased her down his body that she could feel each ripple of his muscles, the snaps of his shirt, the blunt metal of his belt buckle and the much blunter ridge of his arousal pressing against her. When her feet touched the ground she stumbled, taken unaware by the weakness of her knees. Instantly his arms tightened, supporting her. She felt the rock hardness of his thighs and then he groaned, locking her hips against his as he moved in the primal rhythms that had once frightened her and now sent an incandescent heat cascading through her, echoing the movement of his hips.

Groaning, Luke tore his mouth away from Carla's and forced himself to loosen his hold on her. He was breathing roughly, all but out of control. His mouth felt empty, violently hungry for the sultry completion it had so recently known. He closed his eyes, caught between frustration and surprise.

"Luke?" Carla asked shakily. "What is it? Did I do something wrong?"

His eyes opened. Her breath stopped as she looked at the twin pools of molten gold. His smile was like his eyes, hot and restrained, bemused and very hungry.

"It's all right," Luke said. "I just thought I knew all that mattered about men and women and sex. I was wrong."

"What do you mean?"

"I can't put it in words, but I know it's true just the same. Give me your mouth again, sunshine. I've never enjoyed just kissing anyone so much in my life."

"But I'm not—not that experienced," Carla said, perplexed and pleased at once, her thoughts vaporizing at the heat of his eyes, her hands clinging to his arms because she was thoroughly off balance.

Luke's eyelids lowered in reflexive pleasure as he ran his thumb over Carla's flushed lips. She followed his caresses with the tip of her tongue, caressing him in turn.

"You're so damned honest," he said huskily. "Your words, your responses. I didn't know a woman could be that passionately honest. It's making things harder than I expected. Kiss me, baby."

"What things?" Carla said shakily, letting Luke take the weight of her body as she reached up to give him the kiss he had requested. Then she heard her own words and buried her face against his neck, realizing anew precisely what that hard ridge of flesh was beneath his jeans—and aware, too, that his arousal made her feel proud and restless and more than a little curious all at once. "Er, besides the obvious, that is."

"It's obvious, all right." Luke laughed softly, realizing that his changed body didn't frighten Carla as it had three years ago. He tilted her face up and saw the mixture of feminine pride and virginal curiosity in her expression. Amusement and passion warred for control of his body. Both won. "God, I wish I could stop time and keep you locked away forever. My own very private supply of sunshine," he said against her lips.

When Carla started to answer, Luke took her mouth with a hunger that shook both of them. She felt vividly the velvet penetration of his tongue, the power and hardness of his arms lifting her, the world turning and dipping, ribbons of fire wrapping around them once more. When the ground came up softly to meet her, she realized that she was lying on one of the sleeping bags with Luke beside her, urging her closer and closer to himself. She trembled even as she pressed more intimately against his big body.

"Are you all right?" he asked.

"Yes."

"You're trembling."

"So are you."

"I know. I barely had the strength to lift you."

Carla's eyes widened and her hands tightened on Luke's muscular shoulders, silently pointing out the inherent power of his body.

"Yeah, being weak came as a surprise to me, too," he said, his voice uneven with desire and laughter. He whispered her name and bent down to her mouth once more. "I ache, Carla. Want to kiss me and make it all better?"

The passionate whimsy of Luke's question made her smile. She was still smiling when his mouth came down on hers in a slow, complete mating that drew a moan from deep within her. He drank the small sound and thirsted for more.

Luke's hands smoothed over Carla's body, seeking her breasts, caressing them in hot silence. Her cotton shirt and sheer bra didn't conceal her immediate response. He caught the hardened nipple between his fingers and plucked rhythmically, hearing her shattered moan, tasting it, feeling it, demanding it with the deep seduction of his kiss and the hunger of his hands.

When Carla's breasts were hot and swollen, their tips hard and aching for more of Luke's caresses, his right hand slid down her body. Stroking, probing, smoothing, inciting, he savored the curve of her waist and belly. She arched against his hand, burning and shivering, needing something more, unable to tell him what she wanted because her mouth was wholly his, caught in a slow mating she didn't want to end.

Luke's palm caressed her hips and thighs repeatedly, pressing against her, moving her in the rhythms of his tongue deep within her sweet mouth. Gently, inevitably, his hand eased higher and higher between her thighs until he could go no farther. His fingers curved around her and his palm began to move slowly, insistently, rhythmically; and the sultry heat that blossomed at his touch made him groan.

His hands and mouth became harder, more demanding, dragging a broken sound from Carla, a sound that incited Luke unbearably. He wanted to hear more such cries ripple from her, wanted to coax them from her in a fiery, unending cascade, wanted to discover and savor and taste each of her responses. He wanted to consume her and find hot consummation in an unbridled intimacy he had neither sought nor desired with any woman but her, and he wanted it until he died.

The broken whimpers Carla was making finally penetrated Luke's passion. He tore his mouth away from hers and dragged his hands free of her rich, alluring softness.

"Luke—please—I—"

In the moment before control came back to Luke, he shuddered like a man in torment.

"Sorry," he said hoarsely, smoothing the hair away from Carla's face. "I'm sorry, sunshine. I didn't mean to frighten you."

"That's not—" Carla's voice broke. "I didn't mean—"

She tried to bring herself under control but couldn't. She made a ragged sound and captured one of Luke's hands, kissed his palm, then closed her teeth on it in helpless response to the baffling, conflicting feelings raging within her, wanting to caress and savage him at the same time.

"Oh, baby," Luke said, closing his eyes, his whole body clenched in violent response. "You're killing me and you don't even know it."

"I'm sorry," Carla said shakily, shocked by her own actions. "I don't know why I did that. I just—just—"

He didn't wait for her to finish her sentence. "I'll forgive you if you do it again."

"What?"

"You heard me. Only harder, baby. Harder."

Luke's body tightened as Carla sank her teeth into the pad of flesh at the base of his thumb. Her barely restrained violence told Luke that her frustration equaled his own, and she didn't even know what she was missing. The thought of giving her what she needed sent a searing rush of blood through his body that nearly undid him.

Watching Carla, feeling as though he were going to lose control with the next breath or the one after, Luke lifted his hand, licked the small marks she had left on his skin and saw her tremble. His fingers closed on his collar and he pulled sharply. The shirt came undone with a rippling sound as metal snaps gave way, revealing a dark pelt of hair and muscles gleaming with firelight and desire. His hand shot out and wrapped around her head, pulling her against his naked chest.

"Again," Luke whispered.

Uncertain, Carla brushed her mouth over Luke's chest, raked him lightly with her teeth, tasted the salt of his passion and the fierceness of his restraint, inhaled the exciting smell of skin and soap and male heat. Slowly she put her mouth against Luke again, tasted him again, felt the unbridled sensuality of his response. A soft, fragmented sound came from her lips as urgency rushed through her, twisting her, making her ache. Her hands clenched against his chest.

"Harder," Luke said, watching Carla with burning golden eyes. "Go ahead. Bite me. That's what you want. You're shaking and tied up in knots and you know I'm the cause of it and you want it to stop but you want it to go on forever, too. You're frustrated and on fire and confused and you want to take it out on me. Do it, baby. *Do it.*"

With a small, wild cry, Carla did what Luke urged, what she wanted, what she needed. Her teeth sank sensually into the flexed muscles of his chest, testing his strength and her own restraint at the same time. He made a hoarse sound of pleasure and encouragement. Her fingers worked through the wedge of springy, silky hair, pulling and kneading, her nails biting into his hard flesh even as her teeth did.

Luke laughed and urged Carla on while he undressed her. His words were dark and hot, punctuated by the ragged rush of her breathing and his own. The scoring of her nails down his chest was like wild, hot rain, and the primitive caress of her teeth was stroke after stroke of lightning scorching through him, setting him on fire. He didn't know how much longer he could endure the sweet torment, but he knew he was going to find out. The thought of denying himself one fiery instant of Carla's passion was worse than any frustration he might feel at the moment.

With a hoarse groan Luke finally pulled Carla's mouth up to his own and devoured her in a ravenous kiss that would have frightened her only minutes before; but now she needed that fierce claiming more than breath itself. She put her arms around his neck, tangled her fingers deeply in his hair and gave back the kiss with an unleashed passion that matched his.

The world spun again as Luke's hands moved over Carla like hard, warm rain, dissolving everything away, leaving her naked and shivering in his arms. He held her, felt her shaking, heard her broken breaths and remembered all the years he had spent dreaming of having her offer herself to him again and his own vow that he would be gentle if she ever did. Cursing his own nearly overwhelming need, aching, burning alive, he fought for self-control.

Carla called his name, her voice breaking.

"It's all right," Luke said tightly. "I won't hurt you, sunshine. You're so wild that I forgot you're not used to this."

She forced herself to breathe. "C-can you get used to this?"

"Being naked?"

She shook her head. He saw the helpless shivering of her body and waited, but she said nothing more.

"What?" he urged softly.

Carla made an odd sound and dug her nails into Luke's chest in an unconscious gesture of sheer frustration.

"Wanting," she said, her voice aching. "And not having. Wanting and wanting and *wanting*."

Before she had finished speaking, Luke turned away and began stripping off his own clothes, throwing them aside. When he turned back to Carla and lay on his side again, she was sitting up, looking at him. All of him. He froze, motionless, regretting his haste and the fact that she had never seen a naked, aroused man before; and he had never been more aroused. He saw the change in her expression, the heedless passion suddenly checked, as though the blunt reality of his hunger had shocked her.

"Still want me?" Luke asked, his voice rough with restraint.

Carla's only answer was the glide of her fingernails over Luke's chest, down the center line of his body, below his navel to the thatch of dark hair. There she hesitated for a moment before she touched the evidence of his desire with curious fingertips. When he jerked reflexively, she looked up into his blazing golden eyes.

"I don't know which is more exciting," he said thickly, "seeing your sweet curiosity or feeling it."

"You don't...mind?"

Slowly Luke shook his head, then caught his breath as Carla's soft fingertips found each irregularity in his hot flesh and lovingly traced it. He had never known such a fragile, tender, consuming exploration. He had never guessed that he could be so aroused without losing control, but he refused to consider letting go, because even in sexual release he had never known such wild pleasure as he was discovering right now.

"Will you mind?" Luke asked, running his hand caressingly along Carla's calf, her knee, her inner thigh.

"What?"

"When I touch you the way you're touching me."

Before Carla could answer, his fingers had discovered the

soft, swollen, sultry flesh at the apex of her thighs. She made a startled sound and reflexively closed her legs around his hand.

"Is that yes or no?" Luke asked, rubbing gently, finding and stroking the nub hidden within her soft folds.

Carla's breath broke as pleasure showered through her, a wild, unexpected cascade of sensation that made her shudder. He felt the sudden, small melting, saw mist bloom beneath the firelight on her skin and wanted to lower himself over her, sink into her, filling her, bathing his aching flesh in her passionate response. Eyes closed, back arched, moving helplessly against his touch, she shivered again, melted again, searing him with her heat.

"Sunshine?" Luke whispered, caressing Carla with tiny motions, tearing a moan from her lips. "Look at me."

Carla's eyes opened, dazed by passion. His hand moved again, sliding over her, gilding her with the sultry rain of her own response. He wanted more, much more of her, but he didn't want to take it. He wanted her to give herself to him while she looked at him, knowing every bit of what was happening.

"Don't hide, baby," he said softly. "Open for me."

For a moment Carla looked at Luke; then his fingertips moved gently and pleasure shimmered and burst inside her. With a small moan she shifted her legs, allowing him greater intimacy, wanting it as much as he did.

"That's it," he said, his low voice both praising and encouraging her. "Brace yourself on your hands and relax those beautiful legs for me."

As Carla leaned back, Luke's fingers moved coaxingly, skimming her flushed skin, teasing her, asking silently for what she had given no other man.

"L-Luke?"

"It's all right," he said, his voice deep. "Just a little more.

Open just a little more. Let me—" His voice broke as Carla obeyed, allowing him into her softness. "Oh, baby, you're like honey."

He shuddered even as she did, pleasure rushing wildly between them at the slow glide of his caress, penetration and retreat, a silken measuring of her ability to receive the gift of his body. Slowly he rose over her, kneeling between her legs, redoubling and deepening his presence within her softness. When his thumb found and teased the velvet focus of her passion, she sank back onto the sleeping bag with a hoarse cry.

Luke froze, afraid that he had hurt Carla despite all his care.

"Don't stop," she pleaded brokenly, looking at him, moving helplessly against his hand, caught up in an urgency that stripped away everything but her incandescent need. "Oh, Luke, if you stop I'll die."

"Sunshine," he said, "baby, are you sure?"

Carla's body answered for her, bathing Luke in sweet fire, burning away all his questions. Slowly he lowered himself over her. The teasing of his fingertips was replaced by the hard flesh she had so recently explored. The satin caress sent ripples of pleasure through her, expanding rings of sensation that burst sweetly, melting her in rhythmic waves. Gently Luke rode the waves of her passion, letting them ease his way, merging with her gradually, lovingly.

The slow consummation wrung a low moan from Carla. She had never felt anything so exquisite as the merging of flesh with flesh, the elemental fire of her lover's body blending with her own equally elemental rain. A lightning stroke of pain flashed through her, but it swirled away and was lost in the glittering, gathering storm that was consuming her—Luke's mouth on her neck, her throat, her eyelids, and his fiery words licking over her. She arched upward again and again in the primal rhythm of the union. His body enfolded her, surged deeply within her, a part of her. She tried to tell him that she could take no more, the pleasure was too great, she was dying; but the only word she could say was his name. A glittering darkness swept over her, followed by a wild shimmering of her body that shook her to her soul, hurling her into ecstasy.

Luke heard his own name called again and again, a passionate litany that echoed the rhythmic tightening of Carla's body beneath him, around him, demanding all that he had withheld, all that he was, all that he had. Her name was a hoarse cry torn from his throat as passion exploded into a release that was unlike any he had ever known, violent and tender at once, ecstasy convulsing him savagely, softly, endlessly, as he gave himself to the woman he had sworn never to take.

CHAPTER FOURTEEN

CARLA STIRRED AND REACHED OUT for the muscular warmth she had become accustomed to during the night. When her hands found nothing but cool air and emptiness rather than Luke's big body, her eyes opened. An instant later she saw him. Wearing only jeans, he was standing at the edge of the overhang, sipping coffee, watching a land swept clean by rain. As though he sensed that she had awakened, he turned around. The hot cascade of sunlight pouring in behind him made it impossible for her to see the expression on his face.

Without a word Luke came and sat on his heels next to Carla's sleeping bag. Light illuminated half his face, leaving the other half in darkness. For long moments he watched Carla with tawny, enigmatic eyes. Cradled between his hands, the metal camp cup sent fragrant steam into the air.

"Are you all right?" he asked finally.

She nodded and slid her hand from the sleeping bag's warmth to touch the smoothness of Luke's freshly shaved cheek.

He closed his eyes. "Are you sure?"

"Luke, what's wrong?"

"When I washed this morning…" His voice faded. "You bled last night."

"It didn't hurt then. Or now."

Luke said something rough underneath his breath and stood up with an abrupt surge of power. "*You were a virgin.*"

"You knew that before you—before we—" Carla stammered. "Luke, I told you. You knew!"

"Yes," he said savagely. "I knew. But I didn't really *know* until I saw your blood on my body this morning. Then it all became real. Too real." He raked his fingers through his hair. "God, what a mess!"

Carla felt as though she had been struck. Stunned, she said nothing.

Without looking at her, Luke stalked back to the overhang and stared broodingly out over the uninhabited land.

"Well, schoolgirl, you got what you wanted," Luke said after a moment, sending the dregs of his coffee arcing into the sunshine with a brutal snap of his wrist. "I hope to hell it was worth the price."

"I don't—don't understand."

"No, I don't suppose you do. That's what being young is all about. Doing and not understanding. But I understand. I should have walked away from you. I knew it the same way I know fire is hot and rain is wet." Memories tightened Luke's body, echoes of a passionate night he would never forget. "But I didn't have the strength to walk away from you."

Carla felt cold seeping into her flesh, settling in an icy lump at the pit of her stomach as she remembered what Luke had told her weeks before: *Stay away from me, sunshine. I'm afraid I won't have the strength to say no. Then I would take you and hate you...*

"Get up, Carla. I've got water warmed for you. After you wash we'll go into town and make a bigger mistake than we made last night. But there's no help for that, either."

There was no inflection in Luke's voice, nothing to tell Carla what he was thinking.

"What will we be doing in town?" she asked warily.

"Can't you guess, schoolgirl? This is your lucky day. You're getting married."

There was a long silence while Carla measured the hard features of the man she loved.

"Why?" she asked.

Luke made a savage, impatient gesture. "Last night, that's why, and you damned well know it. You came to September Canyon a virgin. No man worth the name would take that from you and give nothing in return."

A slow, complex anger blossomed in Carla. She had dreamed of marriage to Luke, but never under these circumstances—duty and honor, not love.

He didn't love me years ago. He didn't love me last night. He doesn't love me now.

Nothing has changed.

Then Carla realized that something had changed; she wasn't a child to run from Luke's anger anymore. Nor was she childish enough to cross her fingers, marry a man who didn't love her and hope that it would all work out.

"The rest of your life seems an excessive price for a fast toss," Carla said evenly.

Luke gave her a sharp look but saw only a feminine reflection of his own lack of expression. That surprised him.

He had become accustomed to watching moods and emotions move across Carla's face.

"I knew the stakes when I took cards in the game," Luke said curtly, looking away from the elegant feminine curves rising above the sleeping bag's dark green material. "Hurry up and get dressed. If we don't get out of here quick, we might not get out for days. It's already raining in the highlands. Won't be long before it gets wet here."

"Don't let me keep you."

"Your baby pickup won't get one hundred yards the way the road is now. You'll have to come with me. We'll get your truck later."

"No."

"What?"

"No," Carla repeated coolly. "N-O. A word signifying refusal. A negative. The opposite of yes." Each syllable was clipped, unflinching. "I'm not going with you in your truck. I'm not going into town with you. I'm not marrying you. I came to September Canyon for a vacation. I'm going to have that vacation. If you don't like it, you're free to leave."

Luke's head snapped around. He had never heard that precise tone from Carla, smooth and remote and utterly controlled, telling him that he had no right to order her around.

But she was as wrong as she was naive. He knew what had to be done. "Listen, schoolgirl—"

"I've listened," Carla interrupted, "which is more than you have. One. I'm not a schoolgirl. Two. You've made it very clear that you don't want to marry me. Three. There will be no marriage."

"Four," he shot back. "You might be pregnant. Ever think of that, schoolgirl? Or are you on the pill?"

"N.Y.P., cowboy," she said with a calmness she didn't feel.

"What does that mean?"

"Not Your Problem."

"What the hell are you talking about? Of course it's my problem! Or didn't you know that it takes two to make a baby?"

"And only one to carry it. Guess which one of us that is? N.Y.P., cowboy."

Luke glared at Carla. She didn't back up one inch, giving back a stare as level as his own. He measured her determination and realized that the deep well of passion he had discovered in Carla wasn't limited to making love. The girl who had fled from his passion three years ago had become a woman with cool blue-green eyes and hot flags of anger flying in her cheeks. The combination was...exciting.

Angrily Luke felt his body respond as it had always responded to Carla. His lack of control over himself made him furious.

"What are you planning on telling Cash when you start losing your waistline and your breakfast?" Luke asked coldly.

"*If* that happens—and it is by no means a certainty—I'll tell Cash that he'll be an uncle along about May of next year."

Luke's breath came in swiftly. An odd feeling twisted through him at the thought of Carla having his child.

"After you tell him, Cash will do his best to kill me," Luke pointed out. "Is that what you want? Revenge?"

"Don't worry. I'll make it very clear that I turned down your generous offer of marriage."

"That won't be good enough. He'll want to know why. So try out your so-called reasoning on me. Why won't you marry me?"

"Unlike you, Cash is bright enough to figure out all by

himself that I don't want to spend the rest of my life as your jailer."

Luke's breath came in sharply. "Funny you should put it that way. I sure as hell don't want to spend my life as your jailer, either. And that's how you would come to look at the Rocking M—as a jail."

"You're wrong. I love the ranch."

"For a few weeks. In the summer. What about in the winter, Carla? What about the day I come back from breaking ice in the watering troughs and find my children sobbing and terrified because their mother is screaming in god-awful harmony with the wind? What then?"

The past haunted Luke's topaz eyes and his deep voice. The sight of his pain took away Carla's anger, leaving only her love. She ached to take the darkness from him, healing him, giving him hope for the future; but she couldn't change the past and she didn't know how to make him believe in their future. In her.

"I'm sorry, Luke. I'm so sorry." Carla's voice thinned with the effort of controlling her tears. "Please believe me. I'd give anything to be able to change your past. Except last night. I wouldn't trade last night, Luke. I have a whole life to live. I want to live it knowing that once, just once, I touched the sun."

Thunder belled through September Canyon, following invisible lightning. The scent of fresh rain drifted beneath the overhang. There was a random pattering, like an orchestra warming up, and then the raindrops gathered and began falling in a gentle, consuming rhythm.

Luke heard the sound and knew it was too late to go into town; but then, it had been too late the instant he had heard her describe the night she had first felt him within her body.

I touched the sun.

The knowledge that being his lover had meant so much to Carla disarmed Luke. He had taken something from her that she could give only once, yet she had no recriminations, no harsh words, no hints of the raw truth: he had been experienced, she had not. He had known where the kisses would inevitably end. She had not. He should have controlled himself.

He had not.

Gently Luke pulled Carla from the folds of the sleeping bag and into his arms. He wanted to tell her that knowing he had pleased her made him feel proud and powerful and oddly humble, but he had no words, nothing to give her in return, nothing to remake the unchangeable instant when elemental need had transformed her, taking virginity and bringing ecstasy in return.

"I'm glad I brought you pleasure," Luke said huskily. "I would take back every instant if I could, but not that. It's so rare, sunshine. So damned rare."

The feel of Carla's warm, bare skin against his body as she put her arms around him made Luke ache with more than sexual need. He held her close, rocking very slowly, smoothing her hair with the palm of his hand, knowing with a combination of sweetness and sadness that she had touched him in a way no other woman had, taking him to the sun, sharing the burning center of life itself with him.

And he could not have her again.

He must not. For her sake, and for his own. He was all wrong for her. She was all wrong for him, a modern woman on a ranch where time stood still, imprisoning women, breaking them. Carla was far too generous and beautiful to be destroyed like that. She deserved more than he had given her. She deserved to be cherished, protected, revered... sunshine in a world that knew too much darkness.

Luke touched Carla's lips with a single brushing kiss before he loosened his arms and led her the few steps to the fire. Without a word he poured part of a bucket of warm water into a washpan, swirled a cloth around, soaped it and handed it to her.

"If you're shy about washing in front of me, I'll take a walk," he said quietly.

Carla's hand was shaking so much the slippery cloth eluded her fingers. Luke caught the warm, soapy cloth and looked questioningly at her.

"Are you sure you're all right?"

"I'm s-sorry," she said, trying to control her voice.

But Carla did no better steadying her voice than she had her hands. She ducked her head, hiding her eyes as she tried to take the cloth from Luke's hand. He didn't let go. Instead he put his other hand beneath her chin so that she had to meet his eyes.

"Sunshine, what's wrong?"

"Don't you know?"

Helplessly Carla looked at the tempting masculine pelt curling down until it narrowed and vanished beneath the jeans he had pulled on without bothering to button them more than halfway. As she saw the faint crescents and scratches on his skin, memories of last night swept over her. He had been so perfect as a lover and she had been so eager, so breathless, so *inexperienced*. No wonder he wasn't doing handsprings at having her naked in his arms again. She had clawed him like a cat, left marks on him, bitten him, demanding him, all of him.

Carla sucked in her breath, closing her eyes, unable to face Luke with the memory of her own wantonness burning in her mind.

"No, I guess you don't know," Carla said, her tone ashamed and almost bitter. "Why should you? I don't affect you the same way you affect me."

"Look at me," Luke said, his voice deep, gentle, soothing. "Tell me what's wrong."

Carla's eyes opened. She looked through Luke rather than at him.

"In case you hadn't noticed," she said tightly, "I'm stark naked and you're nearly so, and you can make me tremble when you're fully clothed and clear across the room. It was bad enough before last night, but now it's worse. I want you. *I still want you.* And you don't...you don't want..." Her voice frayed.

Blood hammered explosively through Luke, wrenching at his self-control.

"Sweet God," Luke said harshly. "You do know how to push a man, don't you? I promised myself I wouldn't touch you that way again and there you stand naked and shaking. And then you tell me you want me! How the hell am I supposed to say no?"

"I didn't ask you to say no, did I?" Carla laughed unhappily and made a grab for the washcloth. "Never mind, Luke. I don't blame you. In your shoes I don't suppose I'd be dying for another round of amateur hour, either."

The savage word he said made her wince.

"That's not what I meant and you know it," Luke said between clenched teeth. "Damn it, Carla, *help me*. I'm trying not to ruin your life!"

"Of course," she said, her voice sad and empty and utterly disbelieving.

The unhappiness in Carla's face and tone affected Luke as deeply as the passion that was making her tremble.

"Baby, please…don't do this to me."

The yearning, husky timbre of Luke's voice made Carla bite back tears. Automatically she reached out to him in pain and sympathy and a need that transcended even the desire she felt for him. When her fingers touched his chest a visible shudder of response went through him.

"Luke, I—"

"Too late," he interrupted heavily. "It always seems to be too late with you. All you have to do is touch me and I burn. I should say no to you. I know it. But I can't. Give me your mouth, baby. It's a lifetime since I kissed you."

Luke's free hand threaded into the silky curls of Carla's hair, seeking the warmth of her scalp, pulling her head back as he lowered his mouth over hers. His tongue probed her lips until she sighed and he slid into her eager warmth. The kiss was deep, heavy, drenched with the sensuality Luke had spent years trying to control around Carla.

But no longer. The past was as cold as the future would be, but the present was here, now, and it seethed with fire.

When Luke finally ended the kiss, separating himself from Carla, she whimpered softly, wanting more. The sweet sound made him smile, but he didn't take up the flushed invitation of her lips. Keeping his hands off her was impossible, but he would at least control the way he touched her. A few more kisses like that and he would lose his head as he had last night, taking her without protecting her.

"I didn't tell you what it was like for me last night," Luke said, slowly rubbing the soapy cloth over Carla's shoulders, her neck, her arms. "I don't know if I can tell you. I'm damned sure I shouldn't even try, but shouldn't doesn't seem to cut much ice when it comes to you, sunshine."

Luke's crooked smile tugged at Carla's heart, making her

want to smile and cry in return. She started to speak but the words wedged in her throat when the warm cloth moved over her breasts and they tightened in a wild, aching rush.

The sound of the cloth being rinsed out blended with the gently seething rain. After a few moments Luke laid aside the cloth and soaped up his hands instead.

"I barely touched you last night," Luke said. He smiled at Carla's look of shocked disbelief. "It's true, baby. I should have made it last forever. I wanted to, but you made me lose my head. You're making shreds of my control now. Look."

He held up his soapy hands, revealing their fine tremor.

"But I didn't mean to," she said. "I don't even know how to. It's just that when you touch me—"

The words became a moan as his hands found her taut breasts and began smoothing over them in warm, soapy caresses.

"I love hearing your breath break when I touch you," Luke murmured. "I love feeling your breasts rise to meet my hands. I love feeling your nipples harden. I love knowing that your heart is beating faster and your breath—"

Carla tried to speak, but all that came out was a husky sound of pleasure when his fingers teased her, making her nipples harden even more.

"—your breath is coming faster," he whispered. "I love that, too. I love knowing you're as helpless to control your body when I touch you as I am when you touch me."

The gentle, irresistible tugging of Luke's fingers made a wild shiver course visibly through Carla's body. His eyes narrowed into glittering topaz slits as he felt an answering thrill race through his own flesh. An odd, consuming curiosity bloomed in him as he dipped his hands in warm water and rubbed up a mound of lather before turning back to her.

"Baby?" Luke whispered against Carla's mouth, finding her nipples, tugging at them. "What does it feel like when I do this to you?"

"Like—" She made a breathless sound and lifted herself into his touch, twisting slowly, increasing the pressure of his caress.

"Tell me," he coaxed.

"Fire," she whispered. "A glittering kind of fire going all the way to my knees."

Strong hands followed Carla's words, moving slowly, caressing and bathing her in consuming intimacy. His fingers slid delicately between her legs, bringing pleasure even as they gently washed away all signs that she had given herself to a man for the first time only a handful of hours ago.

For long, wild moments there was only the sound of Carla's ragged moans and Luke's hands gliding over her body and the rain outside softly sliding over hard stone. When Luke knew his control could take no more, he reluctantly turned away, grabbed the washrag with fingers that insisted on trembling, and rinsed the cloth thoroughly. He rinsed Carla just as thoroughly, bringing the clear water to her skin again and again, touching her as impersonally as he could until not a bit of soap remained; and still he rinsed her, for it was his only excuse to touch her.

"Luke?" Carla asked finally, not understanding.

She could see by the tension of his face and the occasional tremor in his hands that he was aroused, yet nothing caressed her except warm water and the soft cloth.

"Hold still, sunshine. I'm almost done."

His voice was deep, husky with the pounding of his blood.

"Does that mean I get to bathe you next?"

The thought of Carla's hands touching him as intimately as he had touched her made Luke groan and swear at the same time. After a final, unnecessary passage of the washcloth over the dark, damp triangle at the apex of Carla's thighs, Luke very delicately ran his fingertip between her legs, smiling and aching at her response.

"Bathing me would be a bad idea," he said hoarsely.

"Why? Wouldn't you like it?"

"I'd like it too much. I'd lose control."

Carla's eyes widened.

"It's always been that way with you," Luke said simply. "I was afraid if I ever touched you, I'd have to fight myself to let you go. The first time I touched you, you ran. If you hadn't, I'd have laid you down in front of the fireplace and taken you. The second time I touched you, you didn't run. I had a hell of a battle with myself, sunshine. Since that night I've dreamed of having you in my lap again, only this time your body would fit me like a hot satin glove…"

Luke's voice frayed. For a few moments there was silence while he visibly fought for self-control.

"So I didn't touch you after that night in the dining room," Luke continued roughly. "Until last night."

"But I wanted you to touch me," Carla whispered. "I wanted it so much I would wake up in the middle of the night and ache. For you, Luke. *For you.*"

The words sent a hammer blow of need through Luke that brought him to his knees. He put his forehead against Carla and fought for control.

"I'm aching so much now," she said huskily. "I hurt. Make the ache go away, Luke."

"Baby…oh, God…don't…"

"Please," Carla whispered, shivering. "Please, Luke. Love me."

Luke's fingers bit painfully into the resilient curves of

Carla's hips. He shuddered once, a whiplash of violent need and restraint. Then the grip of his fingers eased and he began smoothing up and down the back of her legs, her hips, her waist. He kissed the scented valley between her breasts, moving his face slowly from side to side, caressing her with his hair, his cheeks, his lips. The lazy, sensual savoring made her tremble.

Luke turned his face once more and Carla felt the unexpected, velvet rasp of his mouth across the tip of her breast. Her breath fragmented into a moan of surprise and pleasure.

"I wanted to do this last night," Luke said, punctuating each word with teasing licks and tiny bites, "but I was too hungry for you."

Slowly he nuzzled the resilient, scented flesh, tasting Carla, tracing the line where smooth skin became textured velvet nipple. Sensations splintered through her as his tongue teased and tempted and shaped her. She sank her fingers into his hair and held him close, wanting to give herself to him, afraid that he would stop caressing her and turn away.

Luke's big hands smoothed down Carla's legs, then back up again. His long fingers flexed into her thighs, her hips, the graceful length of her back, kneading her with a slow, consuming sensuality that matched the rhythm of his mouth transforming her breasts into burning centers of sensation. After a long, long time he lifted his head and admired the flushed, glistening peaks.

"So beautiful," Luke murmured.

"Don't stop," Carla pleaded.

"Not a chance," he said, smiling with bittersweet acceptance. "I've hardly even begun."

He let the warmth of his breath rush over one sensitized breast. The tip of his tongue touched the hard nipple and then circled her in a tender caress that made her tremble. His tongue tasted her again, delicately, before his teeth closed on her with exquisite care. The whimper that came from her lips owed nothing to pain, everything to the pleasure that was licking over her in shimmering cascades of fire.

"I've wanted to do this since I saw you run in from a rain shower with your shirt sticking to you and your nipples standing up so proud and hard," Luke said huskily, turning to Carla's other breast, taking its peak into his warm mouth.

"Why didn't you?" She shivered with pleasure. "I wouldn't have minded."

"You were barely sixteen."

Carla's body stiffened in shock. "You wanted me that long ago?"

"Yes," he whispered, burying his face in her breasts, turning his head caressingly from side to side. "I wanted you until I could have screamed with it. But I shoved it down, buried it, ignored it, because I wanted something else even more."

"My brother's friendship?" Carla guessed.

"And yours." Luke kissed the swollen pink tip of first one breast, then the other. "When you and Cash were on the Rocking M, it was as close to a real family as I ever came. I needed that more than I needed sex."

"You can have both now."

"It doesn't work that way, sunshine," Luke whispered, his eyes narrowed against memories. "Not on the Rocking M."

Before Carla could ask Luke what he meant, one lean hand slid between her legs, seeking the softness that was concealed by dark curls. Her thoughts scattered as she felt again the gentle, probing caress of his fingertips. When he tested her silken depths, his name rushed between her parted lips in a startled cry as her knees gave way.

A few instants later Carla found herself back on the sleeping bag with Luke smiling down at her.

"You look surprised," he murmured. "Didn't anyone ever warn you that your knees can give way?"

"I didn't believe them," she admitted huskily. "I do now. You turn my bones to honey."

Luke's eyes closed and his breath came in with a swift, husky sound as he bent over Carla and whispered, "Turn to honey for me. Let me taste your sweetness."

He kissed the sensitive curves of her ears, of her lips, of her breasts. Her navel fascinated him. He returned to the shadowed dimple again and again, probing with the sleek tip of his tongue, biting gently, making her moan with the unexpected sensations radiating out from her core. His caresses were like raindrops, a brushing of his mouth over her skin and then another brush and another until sensations overlapped and ran together, no beginning and no end, just heat gathering and rippling over her body, making her twist in slow motion as pleasure gathered, filling her until she moaned.

The touch of his tongue and the edge of his teeth on her legs came as a surprise and a very sharp pleasure. The warm pressure of his palms parting her thighs was another kind of caress, another kind of pleasure. When he pressed harder in silent request, asking that she open herself to him, she gave herself with a graceful abandon that nearly undid him. Slowly he bent down, tasting her with an intimate caress that made her cry out in surprise and passion.

"It's all right," Luke murmured, brushing the sensitive inner surface of Carla's thighs with his cheeks, gentling her even as his teeth took tiny, tiny bites of her softness. "You're all honey," he breathed against her. "So sweet. Don't fight me, sunshine. Let me have you this way. No risk, no pain, just…this."

The melting caress Luke gave Carla tore a wild, low cry from her throat. He traced her softness very lightly, silently coaxing and reassuring her. Then his caresses changed, urging her rather than seducing, demanding rather than gentling, consuming her in a shattering intimacy that brought her to ecstasy again and again, his dark words and her rippling cries blending with the falling rain, until finally she lay spent and trembling in the aftermath of wild ecstasy.

Only then did Luke lay beside Carla, hold her, gently kiss the tears from her eyelashes.

"Don't do this to me again, sunshine," Luke whispered, not knowing if Carla heard. *"Please. Don't."*

CHAPTER FIFTEEN

EVEN WEEKS LATER, THE MEMORY of that morning in September Canyon made Carla's breath catch. Luke had given her so much and had taken nothing for himself. Nor had he allowed her to give him anything in return. When she had calmed enough to draw a breath without having it break into fragments, he had stood up and walked out into the rain, leaving her alone with the echoes of his whispered plea.

Don't do this to me again, sunshine. Please. Don't.

Luke had done everything possible to make certain neither one of them was tempted into revisiting the passionate landscape of their dreams. He worked long days out on the range, getting up before dawn and rarely returning to the big house before ten o'clock. At meals he spoke to Carla when courtesy or necessity required it. Beyond that he said nothing to her.

And he walked across the room to avoid touching her.

At first Carla had thought that Luke's deliberate distancing of himself from her would pass, that he would allow himself to talk to her, to touch her, to be touched by her in more than physical ways. But hours had become days and days had become weeks. Luke hadn't relented. If anything, he had become more accomplished at evading even the remote chance of being alone with her. Day after day he eluded her until all her days on the Rocking M were gone.

Even today, the last one she was supposed to spend on the ranch. Tomorrow Carla was scheduled to leave the Rocking M. Tomorrow she was supposed to turn her back on a lifetime of dreams and the man she loved.

Why won't Luke even talk to me? Doesn't he know I love him? Doesn't he know I'm not like his mother or his aunts? Why won't he even give us a chance?

Tonight I've got to talk to him. Somehow I've got to make him understand. I can't leave tomorrow with this polite distance between us, as though September Canyon were only a dream and now I'm awake, aching...

The sound of something boiling over on the stove brought Carla out of her unhappy thoughts. She turned the gravy off and began mopping up. The burner hissed angrily at the touch of the cloth while she worked. Just as she finished, the back door slammed and the sound of booted feet rang in the silence.

Carla spun around with a hope she couldn't wholly conceal, any more than she could hide her disappointment that it was Ten rather than Luke. Even so, she smiled in greeting, putting aside her unhappiness as she always did when other people were around. But she was slower to conceal her feelings today, and her smile wasn't quite steady.

"Hi," Carla said. "There's nothing heavy to lift off the stove tonight."

"Then I'll just steal a cup of coffee," he said, watching her intently.

"Is something wrong?" she asked.

"I was just going to ask you the same question."

"Everything's fine. Dinner will be on time and big enough to feed an army."

"That isn't what I meant." Ten hesitated, swore under his breath and said bluntly, "You look unhappy."

"I'm always unhappy to be leaving the Rocking M," Carla said, her voice as matter-of-fact as she could make it. "Don't you remember? I used to pitch a regular fit when it was time to go back to Boulder."

"You were going back to school, then. What are you going back to now?"

"Actually, I'm going to help Cash wrestle with his doctoral thesis. He's a whiz at cards and hard rock mining, but type-writers frustrate him."

Ten started to say something, thought better of it and shrugged. "We're sure going to miss you."

"Thanks." Unshed tears scorched Carla's eyelids. Impulsively she gave Ten a hug. "I'll miss you, too."

Ten wrapped his arms around Carla, lifting her off the floor in a bear hug just as the back door slammed again.

"Put her down."

The tone of Luke's voice made Carla stiffen. Automatically she moved to end the hug. Ten's arms tightened, holding her captive. With a taunting lack of speed, Ten lowered Carla's feet to the floor, released her and turned to confront Luke.

"Something wrong, boss?"

Carla winced. She had learned that Ten only used the word "boss" when he thought Luke was out of line.

"Dinner is ready," she said quickly to Luke. "I'll set an extra plate. I wasn't expecting you."

"I figured that out right away," Luke drawled coolly, "when I walked in and found you practicing your newfound techniques on my ramrod. Let me give you a bit of advice, schoolgirl. Ten doesn't like being tripped and beaten to the floor any more than I do."

The sardonic words caught Carla completely unprepared. Luke had been so polite to her since September Canyon, so proper and distant. Not by so much as a word or a look had he alluded to what had passed between them; and now he was all but saying she had thrown herself at him and he had been unhappy at the result.

"Speak for yourself, boss man," Ten drawled, his voice every bit as cool as Luke's. "If Carla is in the mood to trip me, I'll fall to the floor any way she wants me."

"I didn't mean the hug that way," she said unhappily, watching both men, her face pale.

"Hell, I know that, honey," Ten said without looking away from Luke. "It's the boss who's a little thick between the ears where you're concerned."

"Don't kid yourself, ramrod. She may look as innocent as—"

"If you say any more," Ten interrupted curtly, "you'll regret it."

"Oh? And I suppose you're going to make me all regretful?" Luke asked.

"I won't have to. You'll look in the mirror and your stomach will turn over."

Ten's quiet certainty was more effective than a blow. Luke closed his eyes for a long count of three. When his eyes opened again they were no longer a savage, glittering gold.

They were nearly opaque, full of shadows, as dull as gold could be. Ten muttered something sad and savage under his breath, but before either man could say anything more, the sound of the ranch hands gathering in the yard came through the open door.

"Find somebody else to give you the beating you think you deserve, Luke," Ten said softly. "I like you too well to enjoy hammering on you." He turned to Carla. "Go wash your face, honey, or you'll be answering a lot of questions about those tears."

Carla fled without a word.

When she came back, dinner was on the table and Luke was nowhere in sight. Ten looked up and smiled encouragingly at her.

"Told you she was just slicking up to impress us," he drawled to the table at large. "Nice job, honey. You look good enough to eat."

"Then it's a good thing for me you're already working on seconds, isn't it?" she said, smiling in return.

Only Ten noticed that Carla's smile hovered on the brink of turning upside down, and he wasn't going to point it out. He stood, pulled out her chair and seated her with easy grace.

"Thank you," Carla said, glancing up into his gray eyes as he bent over her. Quietly she added, "You're a good man, Ten. I don't know why some woman hasn't snaffled you off."

"One did," Ten murmured as he sat down again next to Carla. "It was a lesson to both of us."

"Hey, ramrod," Cosy said, jerking his thumb toward Luke's place. "The boss came in early today. Should I drag him out of the barn to eat?"

"Depends on how lucky you feel."

Cosy hesitated. "Uh-oh. You mean he's in the shop?"

"Yeah."

"Turning big hunks of wood into little bitty shavings?"

"Yeah."

"Is the door locked?"

"Yeah."

Cosy settled more deeply into his chair. "You gonna keep those potatoes for yourself or are you gonna share them with the hands what do the real work?"

Smiling thinly, Ten passed the potatoes.

"What are you two talking about?" Carla asked Ten.

The ramrod hesitated, then shrugged. "When things get to grinding too hard on Luke, he goes to his wood shop in the barn and locks the door behind him. You know that bed and dresser and table in your room?"

"I've been trying to figure a way to spirit the bedroom set out of the house when I leave," she admitted. "I've never seen any furniture one-tenth so beautiful."

"Luke made each piece three years ago. He worked all summer, way into the night, night after night, and then put in long days of ranch work every day, as well. After a few weeks of that he looked like hell, so I decided to talk some sense into him." Ten shook his head ruefully. "That's a mistake I won't make twice. I'd as soon take on a cornered cougar with a licorice whip as tackle Luke when he's holed up in his workshop."

Carla's uncertain appetite faded entirely as she digested Ten's words. Three years ago she had offered herself to Luke with unhappy results for both of them: *I've regretted that night like I've never regretted anything in my life.* So he had locked himself in his workshop and dealt with his emotions by creating an extraordinary bedroom set and putting it into a room no one used. Three weeks ago she had offered herself to Luke once more…and when it was over, he had whispered, *Please don't do this to me again.*

Now Luke had locked himself away once more, and he wasn't going to come out. Not while Carla was still on the Rocking M. She was sure of it. She was also certain she couldn't let that happen. She loved Luke too much to walk away and pretend that nothing had occurred between them except a one-night stand that never should have happened.

"Don't do it, honey," Ten said too softly for anyone but Carla to hear. "Don't be the one to give Luke the fight he's looking for. You'll both regret it."

Carla's head snapped up. She stared at Ten, startled by his accuracy in reading her thoughts.

"But I love him," she whispered.

"That just makes you more vulnerable."

"Luke came in early today. Maybe he wanted to talk to me. Maybe he…" Carla's voice frayed over the hope she couldn't put into words.

Maybe he wanted to ask me to stay.

The rest of the meal was a blur to Carla. She pretended to eat but only rearranged food on her plate. She looked attentive, but her thoughts went frantically around and around, trying to find a way past Luke's refusal to talk to her.

Afterward, when the table was clean and the kitchen was spotless and Luke still hadn't come back to the house, Carla went up to her room and began the unhappy task of packing. In the hope of luring him out of the barn, she carried out her luggage and boxes and loaded everything noisily into her little truck. It was a tight fit; because rain threatened, she was stuffing everything into the passenger side of the tiny cab.

No one came out of the barn while Carla arranged and rearranged boxes in the truck's small space. The men who poked their heads out of the bunkhouse and offered to help her were politely refused. She made many unnecessary trips, taking up as much time as possible, but finally she had no more excuses to linger around the yard and cast hopeful, sideways glances at the barn.

Carla went upstairs and washed her hair during a leisurely shower, hoping if she weren't downstairs, Luke would feel free to come into the house. The instant she stepped out of the bathroom, she knew that Luke hadn't come in from the barn. There were no small sounds of someone stirring around the kitchen warming food or pouring coffee or washing up. There was simply silence and darkness and the distant flare of lightning dancing over MacKenzie Ridge.

Luke, don't send me away like this, not a word, nothing but silence. Talk to me. Give me a chance.

Nothing came in answer to Carla's plea but summer thunder, a reverberation more felt than heard.

Carla went to the dresser, opened the box Luke had carved for her and picked up the pottery fragment within. It was cool and hard and smooth, as though time itself had condensed in her palm. For long, long minutes she stood motionless, infusing ancient clay with the living warmth of her own body, holding the sherd as though it were a talisman against her deepest fears. Finally, gently, she replaced the sherd and packed the box into the overnight case that was her only remaining bit of luggage.

The sheets were as cool as the Anasazi fragment had been. Carla lay between them and waited to hear Luke's footsteps coming up the stairs.

The storm came first, a sudden, sweeping tumult riding on the back of a wild wind. Carla listened to all the voices of the storm, the high keening of the wind and the bass response of thunder, the sudden crackle of lightning and the liquid drumroll of rain. In between she heard the sound of Luke's footsteps coming up the stairs. He passed her door without a pause. The noise of the bathroom shower blended seamlessly with the falling rain—long and hard and relentless. Both shower and rain stopped with no warning. In the silent spaces between peals of retreating thunder, random creakings of the floorboards told Carla that Luke was prowling the confines of bedroom and bath, bedroom and bath and back again, ceaselessly.

Carla lay and listened, her hands clenched at her sides, her whole mind caught up in a single, silent plea: *Come to me, Luke. Once, just once, can't you come to me?*

The footsteps came down the hall and passed her bedroom door after a hesitation so small she couldn't be sure she hadn't imagined it. The stairs creaked, telling her that he was walking toward the kitchen.

Walking away from her.

Carla waited and waited, but the footsteps didn't return. Anger came to her as suddenly as the rainstorm had come to the land. With a sweeping motion of her arm, she threw the bedcovers aside and stood trembling, flooded with adrenaline and determination.

I'll make him listen to me.

Wearing only the black shirt Luke had left with Cash and she had never returned, Carla went down the hall on soundless bare feet. The only light on in the house came from the kitchen, but it was enough to illuminate the stairs. She took them in a rush.

Luke wasn't in the kitchen as Carla had expected. He was in the dining room, his chair turned away from the table, his elbows on his knees, a cup of forgotten coffee cooling on the table beside him. He was barefoot, wearing half-fastened jeans with nothing beneath but the desire that had made sleep impossible.

When Luke's eyes met hers, Carla felt as though she had touched bare electrical wire. His eyes had the feral blaze of a cornered cougar.

"Go back to bed, schoolgirl. Go now."

"We have to talk."

"Why? Are you pregnant?" he demanded, giving voice to the thought that had haunted him, his baby growing inside Carla's body, the sad history of the Rocking M repeating itself all over again after he had vowed that it would end with him.

Yet he wanted that baby with a yearning that was as deep as his need for Carla. Being torn between what he wanted and what he knew he must not have was making him wild. He could take no more—especially when she stood in front of him, wearing his shirt, her eyes luminous and her body etched in fire on his senses.

"It's not that," Carla said impatiently, determined not to be distracted from the main issue, which was Luke's determination not to face what was between them. "It's your refusal to—"

Luke's temper flashed at Carla's casual dismissal of the very pregnancy that had haunted him. He cut off her words with the same kind of attack that had once driven her away from the Rocking M and him. But not far enough. Not long enough.

This time he had to make it stick.

"Then why are you here?" he asked coldly. "You want more sex? Forget it. I was damn lucky not to get you pregnant in September Canyon. I'm not a fool to fall into the same trap twice. Sex isn't worth it."

But Carla was no longer a girl to flee from a man's anger.

She held her ground despite the pain of his words twisting through her.

"That wasn't sex," she said. "It was love."

"It was sex," Luke countered savagely. "That's all men and women feel for each other. Plain old lust, schoolgirl."

"Some men. Some women," Carla agreed. She walked slowly toward him, fingers shaking slightly as she undid the top button of the black shirt, then a second, then a third. Her whole body was trembling with an urgency that was the other face of desire. She had to make him understand. She simply had to. "But not everyone is like that. I love you, Luke."

"Do you? Then button up and leave me in peace."

"But you won't be in peace. You'll be aching. You want me. You can't deny it, Luke. The evidence is right in front of you for both of us to see."

He said a single, harsh word.

She smiled sadly. "That's the general idea, but in our case it's called making love."

"I don't love you."

Carla's step faltered but didn't stop. She gathered her courage and continued to stalk her cornered cougar.

"I don't believe you," she said.

When her fingers undid the final button, the shirt parted to reveal the very feminine curves beneath. Luke's breath came in swiftly as her body was revealed and then concealed with each motion of the long, open shirt. He tried to look away, but couldn't. She was his own dream walking toward him, calling to him, her voice as much a part of him as his soul.

"Don't do this, baby."

"You're a big, strong man," Carla said, kneeling between Luke's long legs. "If you don't love me, prove it. *Stop me.*"

Her challenge was as unexpected to Luke as the feeling of

his jeans coming suddenly undone, revealing the hard proof of his desire. He grabbed her wrists and dragged her hands upward, away from his hungry body.

It was a mistake. Even as her fingers tested the power of his clenched chest muscles, her hair fell across his hot, erect flesh in a silken caress. Before he had recovered from the shock, he felt the tip of her tongue in a soft, incendiary touch.

If he hadn't already been sitting down, the savage torrent of his own response would have brought him to his knees. A harsh sound was ripped from his throat as every muscle in his big body clenched with the violence of his passion. He held her wrists with bruising force, but neither he nor she knew it. They knew only that the world was ablaze and they were the burning center of fire.

Between each sleek caress, each glide of velvet tongue against satin skin, Carla whispered her love to Luke; and somewhere between initial refusal and final acceptance, his hands released her wrists and his fingers threaded into her hair, caressing and holding and teaching her with the same aching motions. Every breath he took was her name, every heartbeat a hammering demand, his body hot, shimmering with leashed passion until he groaned harshly and could take no more. He lifted her, fitted her over himself and gave her what she had demanded, burying his hungry flesh in her, filling her with the sultry pulse of his ecstasy until the wild, shuddering release was finally spent and he could breathe once more.

"Think about this when I'm gone," Carla said, kissing Luke's eyelids, his cheeks, tasting the salt of passion glistening on his skin. "Think about this and remember what it was like to be loved by me. Then come to me, Luke. I'll be waiting for you, loving you."

CHAPTER SIXTEEN

"WHEN ARE YOU GOING TO STOP this foolishness and call him?" Cash demanded from the hallway of Carla's apartment. His tone was divided between exasperation and concern, as was the look he gave her.

Carla glanced from the enigmatic sherd of pottery lying in her palm to the dresser where the telephone sat in a silence that hadn't been broken for ten weeks. Slowly she looked at the twilight-blue color of Cash's eyes as he walked into her bedroom. His usual easy smile was absent and his jawline looked frankly belligerent. His sun-streaked, chestnut hair was awry, making its indomitable natural wave all the more pronounced.

"Call who?" she asked.

"Santa Claus," Cash retorted.

"It's a bit early for Christmas lists."

"It's nearly Thanksgiving and you've been home since the end of August."

Carla's slender fingers curled protectively around the pot sherd. She said nothing. She could count as well as her brother could. Better. She knew to the day when she had become pregnant: the last day on the Rocking M, when she had risked everything on one last throw of the dice.

And lost.

"Well?" demanded Cash.

"Well what?"

"When are you going to call Luke?"

Very gently Carla replaced the sherd in its hand-carved nest, closed the lid and put the box on the dresser.

"I'm not."

"What?" Cash said.

"I'm not going to call Luke. I've chased the poor man for seven years. Don't you think it's time I left him in peace?"

Uneasily Cash assessed his sister's expression. Carla had grown up since the beginning of summer. Though she had said nothing specific, the sadness underlying her smiles told Cash that the summer hadn't worked out the way he had expected. What he didn't know was why.

"Luke has been fascinated by you for years, but you were too young," Cash said with his customary bluntness. "By the time you were old enough, he had made a habit of pushing you away. To make it worse, he has this fool idea that the Rocking M destroys women, and he loves that ranch the way most men love a woman. So I threw in a set of winning hands and sent you off for a summer of cooking on the Rocking M, where Luke could see for himself that you weren't going to fold up and cry just because you couldn't get your nails done every two weeks."

Surprise replaced sadness in Carla's face. "You set me up with that card game?"

"You bet I did. I thought the summer would give you two a chance to get acquainted with each other as adults, without me around to remind either of you about the years when you were a young girl in braids with a massive crush on a man who was old enough and decent enough to keep his hands in his pockets!"

"It worked," Carla said neutrally. "You weren't around to remind us."

"Like hell it worked. We're back to where we were three years ago, with Luke meeting me in West Fork for cards and beer and asking sideways questions about how you are and if you're dating and do I like any of the men you bring home."

Carla closed her eyes so that Cash wouldn't see the wild flare of hope his words had given to her. The hope was as unreasonable as her seven years of longing for a man who didn't love her had been.

"Luke is just making polite conversation," Carla said, her voice soft in an effort to hide her pain. "If he really wanted to know about me, he would pick up a phone and ask me himself."

"That's what I told him the last time he asked."

She smiled sadly. "And the phone hasn't rung, has it?"

"So make it ring. Call him."

"No."

The word was soft, final.

"Then I will."

"Please, Cash. Don't."

"Give me one good reason why I shouldn't."

"I don't want you to."

"That's emotion, not reason. Give me a reason, Carla. I'm

fed up with watching the two people I love walking around half-alive. I was looking forward to a wedding at the end of summer, not a damned funeral!"

A single look at Cash's face told Carla that she wasn't going to win this argument. Her brother's easy smile and warm laughter concealed a steel core that was as deep and as hard as Luke MacKenzie's.

"Would you settle for being an uncle?" she asked softly.

"What?"

"I'm pregnant."

A shuttered look settled over Cash's face as he absorbed Carla's words. "Are you sure?"

"Yes."

"Does Luke know?"

"No."

Cash grunted. "I didn't think so. If he knew, I'd have a brother-in-law damned quick, wouldn't I?"

"No."

There was a long silence while Cash waited for Carla to explain. She said nothing.

"Talk to me," Cash said curtly. "I trusted Luke. Tell me why I shouldn't go out to the Rocking M and beat that son of a bitch within an inch of his life."

"It wasn't Luke's fault."

"That's bull, Carla! He's old enough to keep his hands in his pockets, and he damn well knows how babies are made or not made! Any man who seduces a virgin should have the decency—"

"He didn't seduce me," Carla said, cutting across her brother's angry words. "I seduced him."

"*What?*"

"I seduced Luke MacKenzie!" Carla yelled, letting go of

her pride and her temper in the same instant. "I came up on his blind side, took off my clothes and made him an offer he couldn't refuse!" She took a deep, sawing breath and said more calmly, "So if you feel you have to beat somebody for a breach of trust, beat me."

Cash opened his mouth. No words came out. He cleared his throat and asked carefully, "And afterward?"

"Luke felt obliged to get married. I refused."

"Why?"

It was Carla's turn to be shocked into silence. It passed quickly, driven out by the same unflinching determination that had kept her from picking up the phone and calling Luke.

"I'll tell you why, brother dear. I'll go trout fishing in hell before I marry a man who doesn't love me."

"Don't be ridiculous. Luke loves you. Hell, he's loved you for years."

Tears came suddenly to Carla's eyes. She tried to speak but was able only to shake her head slowly while she fought for self-control.

"Lust," she said finally, her throat so tight she could barely squeeze the word out. "Not the same, Cash. Not the same at all."

"I don't believe you," Cash said flatly.

He reached past her for the telephone. Both of her hands clutched his wrist in a contest of strength that she couldn't possibly win.

"Then believe this," she said, her voice shaking. "If you tell Luke I'm pregnant I'll get in my truck and drive and keep on driving until I'm sure neither one of you will ever find me!"

"But, honey, you're pregnant. Be reasonable."

"I am. I'm not a charity case. I don't need a mercy marriage."

Cash flinched.

Too late, Carla remembered her brother's brief, unhappy marriage to a girl pregnant with another man's child.

"I'm sorry. I didn't mean that as a slap at Linda. She did what she believed she had to do." Carla put her arms around Cash and hugged him. "And your taking me in after Mom and Dad died ruined any chance you and Linda had. It also taught me that a man's sense of honor and decency is no substitute for love in a marriage. If Luke loved me, he would have called by now. He hasn't. Now it's up to me to pick up the pieces of my life. It's not Luke's problem, Cash. It's mine."

Cash kissed Carla's forehead, hugged her in return and said softly, "Honey, I'm as sure that Luke loves you as I am that I love you."

"Don't," she whispered, her voice aching with suppressed emotion. "You'll just make me cry. I miss him so much. It's like dying to know that he—he doesn't—doesn't—"

The shudder that racked Carla's body was transmitted instantly to her brother. His arms tightened around her.

"Go ahead and cry, honey," Cash whispered, closing his eyes, putting his cheek against Carla's hair, holding her. "Cry for both of us. And for Luke. Cry for him most of all, because he lost the most."

For a long time Cash held his sister, stroking her hair slowly, letting her cry out all the years of dreams that hadn't come true. When she had finally calmed, he kissed her cheek and released her.

"I'm not sure what I'm going to do about this," Cash said, pulling a handkerchief from his pocket and wiping away Carla's tears. "But I know what I'm *not* going to do. I'm not going to pick up the phone today and tell Luke you're pregnant. I interfered once with the two of you, and it blew up in everyone's face."

Cash put the handkerchief in Carla's hand and wrapped her fingers around it.

"But, honey, once you start showing, someone's sure to mention it to Luke. Then there will be blazing red hell to pay." Cash hesitated, then added softly, "If you don't tell him by Christmas, I'll have to do it for you."

What Cash didn't put into words was his belief and fervent prayer that Luke surely would have called Carla by then.

CHAPTER SEVENTEEN

A COLD WIND HOWLED DOWN FROM MacKenzie Peak, a wind tipped with the promise of sleet or snow. A gust caught Ten halfway between the bunkhouse and the barn. He ducked his head, pulled up the collar of his shearling jacket and went in the side entrance to the barn. The room he headed for had once held harness for the Rocking M's wagon horses. Now the room held woodworking tools—and a man who wielded them the way a wizard wields incantations against vicious demons.

The door had been locked since the evening Carla McQueen had driven off the Rocking M. After Luke had spent a long day working on the ranch, he would spend the evening and too much of the night locked inside the room, where the scream of a power saw biting into wood filled the spaces between the cries of the winter wind.

Ten was the only man who dared to disturb Luke in his

lair. Lately, even Ten was thinking the matter over three or four times before he raised his fist and rattled the door on its hinges, praying that a small bit of Christmas spirit had sunk into Luke's hard head.

"Telephone, Luke!"

"Take a message."

"I did."

"Well?"

"Cash wants to know if you've seen Carla."

The scream of the power saw ended abruptly.

"What?"

"You heard me."

"What makes him th—"

"How the hell should I know?" interrupted Ten. "You have questions, go ask Cash yourself. I'm damn tired of standing around in a cold barn yelling at a man who's too blind to find his butt with both hands and a mirror the size of a full moon!"

Luke yanked opened the door and gave Ten a hard look. Ten returned it with interest.

"Give it to me again, slowly," Luke said.

"Lord, how you tempt a man," Ten muttered. "Listen up, boss. Cash McQueen is on the phone. Carla is missing. He seems to think she came here."

"On the day before Christmas?"

"Maybe she has some Christmas cookies for the hands."

Luke gave Ten a disbelieving look.

"Well, she brought us cookies a few years ago," Ten said blandly. "Maybe she decided to do it again. What other reason could she have for coming all the way out here?"

Luke stepped out of the room, slammed the door behind him, locked it, pocketed the key and stalked into the house. The kitchen phone was off the hook, waiting for him.

"Cash, what the hell is going on?"

"I hoped you could tell me. I had to overnight in New Mexico. When I got back, I found a note from Carla saying she had something to do at the Rocking M. So I called, but Ten says she isn't around."

"When did she leave?"

"She should have been at the ranch house hours ago," Cash said bluntly.

"Maybe she decided to go somewhere else."

"She would have called and left a message on my answering machine."

Luke sensed the presence of Ten behind him. He turned and shoved the phone into his ramrod's hand.

"Talk to Cash," Luke said curtly.

"Where are you going?"

"To check the south road for tread marks left by a baby pickup truck. If I'm not back in ten minutes, you'll know I found tracks and kept going."

"To where?"

"September Canyon."

MUDDY WATER SHOT UP and out from the big pickup's tires as Luke forded Picture Wash with unusual velocity. He told himself he was pushing so hard because he was worried about Carla being alone in the desolate canyon with a storm coming on. But he didn't believe the rational lie. He drove like hell on fire because he was afraid she would have come and gone before he got there.

What's the hurry, cowboy? he asked himself sardonically. *Nothing has changed. Nothing can change. You can't have both Carla and the Rocking M. Beginning and end of story.*

There was no answer but the power of Luke's hands

holding the big truck to the rutted road at a speed that was just short of reckless. The turnoff into September Canyon was taken in a controlled skid that made the truck shudder.

Relief coursed through Luke when he saw Carla's tiny pickup parked near a clump of piñon. He stopped nearby, pulled on his jacket and began walking quickly toward the overhang. The rich golden light of late afternoon slanted deeply across the canyon, heightening every small crevice in the cliffs and every tiny disturbance of the soil, making the land look as though it had been freshly created.

There was no sign that Carla had been beneath the overhang since August. There were no fresh ashes in the fire ring, no new tracks near the seep's clean water, no sleeping bag stretched out and waiting for the night that would soon descend.

I was right. She isn't planning to stick around.

The realization sent a cold razor of fear slicing through Luke. The feeling was irrational, yet it couldn't be denied.

I could so easily have missed her. Why didn't she tell me she was coming? Why did she drive all the way out to the Rocking M and not even say hello?

No sooner had the questions formed than their answers came, echoes of a summer and a passion that never should have been, Carla's voice calling endlessly to him, haunting even his dreams: *Remember what it was like to be loved by me. Then come to me, Luke. I'll be waiting for you, loving you.*

But he hadn't gone to her. He had gone instead to the old harness room. There he had transformed his yearning, his pain and his futile dreams into gleaming curves of wood, pieces of furniture to grace the family life he would never have.

Wind curled down through the canyon, wind cold with distance and winter, wind wailing with its passage over the empty land. The overhang took the wind, muffled it, smoothed it, transformed it into voices speaking at the edge of hearing and dreams, a man and a woman intertwined, suspended between fire and rain, their cries of fulfillment glittering in the darkness.

Abruptly Luke knew why Carla hadn't set up camp beneath the overhang. She could no more bear its seething not-quite-silence than he could.

It took only a few moments for Luke to find the tracks Carla had left when she headed up the canyon. Her footprints followed the trail markers she had left in August. All other signs of her previous visit had been washed away by rain. Luke walked quickly, fighting the impulse to run, to overtake the girl who had left nothing more of herself in September Canyon than a fragile line of tracks that wouldn't outlive the next winter storm.

Filled with an anxiety that he neither understood nor could control, Luke scrambled up the narrow tongue of rock and debris that looked out over the canyon. There was no one waiting at the top, no girl with blue-green eyes and a smile that set a man to dreaming of marrying one special woman, having a family with her, watching their children grow to meet the challenges of the beautiful, unflinching land.

"Carla?"

No answer came back but the haunted wind.

Luke looked around quickly for Carla's tracks but found none. Where the surface wasn't gravel it was solid rock. He glanced up the canyon, then down, then up again. No one was in sight. He scrambled down the far side of the promontory. There were no rocks piled to mark the way, nothing to indicate which direction Carla had taken. If she had left tracks, the rich sidelight of the descending sun would have made them stand out like flags.

"Damn it, Carla," he muttered, scanning the view impatiently, "you know better than to take off without leaving any markers to—"

The angry words stopped when Luke's breath came in fast and hard and stayed there. His head snapped around and he looked up the canyon again. This time he saw nothing but rock, piñon, sunlight and shadow. Yet there had been something there before, a glimpse of right angles and rectangular shadows that were at odds with his expectations. Nature's geometry was circular, curve after curve flowing through unimaginable time. Man's geometry was angular, line after line marching through carefully divided time. He had seen a hint of man, not canyon.

Carefully he turned his head again. There, just at the corner of his vision, Luke glimpsed right angles and rectangular shadows tucked away amid September Canyon's graceful curves. Only the unusual angle of the sunlight allowed him to see the cliff house, for it was screened by trees and nestled in one of September Canyon's many side canyons. A chill moved over Luke as he realized that he was looking at the ruins of a cliff house that had been old when Columbus set sail for India and found the New World instead.

And within those stone ruins a hidden fire burned, sending a thin veil of smoke toward the cloud-swept sky.

As Carla had before him, Luke walked toward the ruins. Even knowing they were there, and having the richly slanting light as an aid, he found it difficult to locate the ruins once he looked away. He stopped, took his bearings from the canyon itself and walked toward the ruins with the confidence of a man accustomed to finding his own way over a wild land. He didn't call out to Carla; wind and silence were the only voices suited to hidden canyons.

Luke found Carla at the very edge of the ruins, sitting in an ancient room that had no ceiling. Enough of the walls remained to give shelter from the keening wind. The small fire she had built burned like a tiny piece of the sun caught amid the twilight of the ruins. She was staring into the heart of the fire, her right hand curled into a fist. Tears shone like silver rain on her cheeks, a slow welling of sadness that made Luke's own throat ache.

"There's a storm coming on," he said, his voice husky with emotions he couldn't name. "You shouldn't camp here. There's not enough shelter. Why don't you come back with me?"

Carla turned and looked at the man whose child was growing within her body, the man she loved.

The man who didn't want her love.

"No, thank you," she said politely. "I don't want to impose on you."

A coolness moved over Luke's skin that had nothing to do with the swirling wind.

"That's ridiculous," he said. "You know you're always welcome on the Rocking M."

"Don't."

"Don't what?"

"Lie. I'm not welcome on the Rocking M and we both know it. You were relieved to wake up and find me gone."

"Carla—"

Luke's throat closed and the silence stretched while Carla watched him with blue-green eyes that were darker than he remembered. Then her lips curved in a small smile that was sadder than any tears he had ever seen.

"Don't worry, Luke. I'm not going to throw myself at you again. I've finally grown up. I'm as tired of being pushed away by you as you are of having to push me."

She laughed suddenly. The soft, broken sound made Luke flinch, but she didn't see it. She had opened her right hand and was staring at the fragment of ancient pottery that rested on her palm. Luke endured the silence as long as he could, then asked the only question he would allow himself.

"Did you find that here?"

A brief shudder went over Carla, but that was her only acknowledgment that she was no longer alone. Just when Luke began to wonder if she would answer, she spoke in a flat, colorless voice.

"You gave this to me seven years ago. I brought it back to the place where it belongs. Full circle."

Luke felt as though the world had dropped away from beneath his feet. Always in the past he had known with unspeakable, absolute certainty that Carla would come back to the Rocking M, to him, bringing sunshine and laughter and peace with her. He had come to count on that, hoarding memories of her like a miser counting jewels, knowing that one day he would look up and she would be there again, watching him with a love she had never been able to hide.

The realization of what had happened sank into Luke like a blade of ice, slicing through him even as it froze him, teaching him that he had never known pain until that moment. Carla had come back, but not to him. She would leave again.

And she would never come back.

"I'm selling the ranch."

Shocked by Luke's words, Carla looked up, facing him again. The pain she saw in his golden eyes made her feel as though she were being torn apart.

"But—why?"

"You know why."

With a small, anguished sound, Carla turned back to the fire, knowing that there was no more hope. All her dreams, all her love, everything was destroyed.

"Cash shouldn't have called you," she said hoarsely. "He promised me until Christmas."

Carla's fingers clenched around the pottery sherd. The pain of it reminded her of why she had come to September Canyon. She drew back her arm to hurl the ancient sherd back into the fire.

"No!" Luke said.

He moved with shocking speed, closing his much bigger hand around her fist, forcing her to hold on to his gift. Slowly he knelt in front of her, bringing her right hand to his lips despite her struggles.

"Don't leave me, sunshine," Luke said, kissing Carla's slender fingers. "Stay with me. Love me."

The words pierced Carla's last defenses, teaching her how little she had understood of pain until that moment. She couldn't breathe, couldn't speak; she could only be torn apart by the knowledge that it had all been for nothing, all the pain, all the loneliness, all the years of yearning.

And now he was pressing his lips against her fingers, pleading with her to stay, to give him the love he had always pushed away in the past. Now, when Cash had told Luke she was pregnant.

Now, when love was impossible.

Duty. Decency. Honor. Obligation. The words were colder than the wind, more massive than September Canyon's stone ramparts. The words were crushing her. She couldn't live a lifetime with Luke, knowing every time that she wasn't loved. She couldn't even live another instant that way.

"Let me go, Luke," Carla said, her voice breaking. "I

can't bear being your obligation. I can't bear knowing the only reason you came to me at all is that Cash told you I'm pregnant."

"*Pregnant!*"

The dark center of Luke's golden eyes dilated with a shock that was unmistakable. With quick motions he unbuttoned her jacket.

"Didn't he—" Carla's voice broke as Luke's big hands went from her throat to her hips, discovering every change four months of pregnancy had made in her body.

"My God," Luke said again and then again, his voice ragged.

Slowly his hands moved over her, touching her in wondering silence because he could not speak.

"Cash didn't tell you?" Carla whispered, sensing the answer yet unable to help the words. She had to know. She had to be certain.

Luke shook his head.

"Then why—why did you come here?" she asked.

He took a deep, shuddering breath and said simply, "I had to."

Carla watched Luke with uncertain eyes, afraid to think, to hope. "I don't understand."

With a gentleness that made Carla tremble, Luke brushed his lips over the shining trails her tears had made on her cheeks. It was the first time he had ever kissed her without being asked; the realization was as devastating to Carla as the tenderness of his caresses. Without thinking, she raised her hand to push him away, unable to bear being hurt again.

"Don't," Luke said hoarsely. "Please don't push me away, sunshine. I know I deserve it, but I can't—oh, God, I can't bear losing you. When Cash told me you had come to the Rocking M, I went crazy. I knew you had come to September Canyon but I didn't know why. I hoped—I hoped so much you were coming back to me.

"And then you told me you were going to leave my gift here and never come back. *Full circle*. That's what you mean, isn't it? Leaving and never coming back to me again?"

Slowly Carla nodded.

Luke closed his eyes and fought to control the emotions clawing at him. "Until a few seconds ago," he said finally, "I thought I'd accepted the fact that I could have a family or I could have the Rocking M. I've realized it for years, since before I even knew you and Cash. I tried not to care, because I love this ranch more than I ever wanted any woman." Luke bent his head a bit more, tasted the tears shining on Carla's lips and felt his own eyes burn. "Then one day I looked at you and saw a woman I wanted to have children with…"

His voice went from husky to hoarse as emotion closed his throat. For long, sweet seconds he moved his hands gently over Carla's womb as though to caress the life within.

"I'd sworn never to sacrifice my woman and children to the Rocking M," he said. "I knew what this land did to women. I had heard about it, seen it, almost been destroyed by it when I was young."

Luke drew a quick, broken breath and fought for control. "Every time I looked at you, I was reminded of the truth," he whispered. "I could have the ranch or I could sell it and have you. So I pushed you away and hungered for you to come back, because as long as you came back I could have both you and the Rocking M. Do you understand?"

Carla tried to speak but all that came out was Luke's name, a ragged sound as painful as his voice.

"Don't cry," he whispered, kissing her gently, repeatedly, as though he could drink all the sadness from her with his lips, leaving her free of pain. "It's all right. When I realized you would never come to me again, the choice was easy. I can live without the Rocking M but I can't live with knowing I hurt you."

Luke tilted Carla's chin up until he could see her eyes. "Where do you want to live after we're married?"

"On the Rocking M."

Pain and a wild, flaring hope tightened Luke's features in the instant before he shook his head. "I'll never ask that of you."

"Do you believe I love you?"

"There could be no other reason for what you've done, giving me so much, asking for so little and getting even less. I'm sorry for that, baby. I'm so damned sorry. You deserved so much more from me."

Carla pulled Luke's head closer, returning the gentle kisses he had given her, loving him so much it was a sweet kind of pain.

"The Rocking M is part of you," she whispered between kisses. "If I hadn't loved the ranch, I couldn't have loved you. Not really. I could have had a schoolgirl crush on you. I could have been infatuated with you. I could have been fascinated by you. I could have been everything except in love with you. But I love the ranch, and I love you." Carla smiled suddenly, making the tears in her eyes sparkle like crystal in sunlight. "In fact, you should be worried that I'm marrying you *for* the Rocking M, not in spite of it."

"Sunshine," Luke said, his voice catching, "I want you to be happy. Are you sure?"

"As sure as I am pregnant."

He closed his eyes. "Are you happy about that?"

"Being pregnant?"

Luke's eyes opened. "Yes."

"Oh, yes," Carla murmured, covering his hands with her own, cradling him against the new life growing within her body. "Are you?"

"I can't—I don't—have words." Luke bent down and kissed her hands, then sought the warmer flesh beneath that sheltered his baby. "When you left, I shut myself in the barn and made a cradle and a crib and a rocking horse for the child I would never have. And then I made a—rocking chair so that you—could—" His voice broke. He tried to speak, but all that came out was a raw whisper. "I looked at the chair—and dreamed of you nursing our child—and knew it would never—never—"

Carla felt the shudders that ripped through Luke's control, felt the scalding heat of his tears against her skin and held him until she ached. For long minutes there was only the sound of his broken breathing and her own whispered words of love. Finally he stood up, carrying her with him, holding her as close as the beating of his own heart.

Then Luke looked down in Carla's clear eyes. He felt something shimmer through him like sunrise, transforming him, freeing him from the darkness of the past, giving him a vision of a future more beautiful than his hungry dream. He wanted to tell Carla all that he saw—a girl with dark hair and golden eyes and her mother's flashing smile, a boy with gentle hands and blue-green eyes and his father's easy strength, a man and a woman sharing and building and creating together, giving back to life the gift it had given them.

The vision was so clear to Luke, so real, beyond question or doubt. He wanted to share it with Carla, to tell her that neither one of them would ever be lonely again. Yet of all the gifts that had come to him, of all the truths yet to be given and received, only one came to his lips when he bent down to her, for it was the only truth that mattered.

"I love you, sunshine."

OUTLAW

CHAPTER ONE

DIANA SAXTON DROVE INTO the Rocking M's dusty ranch yard and shut off the car's engine. The first thing she saw was a cowboy as big as a barn door standing on the front porch. Unconsciously her hands clenched on the wheel, betraying her instant unease in the presence of men in general and big, well-built men in particular.

The ranch house's front door opened and closed. When another equally big, hard-looking man in boots and jeans came out of the house and began walking toward Diana, carrying a geologist's hammer. Over toward the corral, a third cowboy was climbing onto a horse. The man was so big that he made the horse look like a kid's pony.

My God, Diana thought, *don't they have any normal-size men out here?* Crowding that thought came another. *I can't spend a summer close to these men! But then, I won't have to. I'll be at the September Canyon site.*

Someone called out from the house. Diana recognized Carla MacKenzie's voice and let out a soundless sigh of relief as the first big man turned immediately and went back inside at the sound of his name. Luke MacKenzie, Carla's husband.

As a bit of Diana's uneasiness faded, she recognized the second man. Cash McQueen, Carla's half brother. He was coming toward Diana, slipping the hammer into a loop on his leather belt as he walked. Hastily she got out of her car. She had learned in the past few years not to show her distrust of men—especially big men—yet she still couldn't force herself to be close to any man in a confined space, particularly a car.

Before Cash got to Diana, another call from the house stopped him. He waved to her, said something she couldn't understand and went back into the ranch house.

A sudden burst of activity outside the corral caught Diana's attention. A horse had its head down between its forelegs, its back was steeply arched and its body was uncoiling like a released spring. A few spectacular bucks later, the horse's beefy rider lost his grip on the saddle. He hit the ground, rolled to his hands and knees and came up onto his feet with a lunge. He grabbed the bridle close to the bit and began beating the horse with a heavy quirt. The horse screamed and tried to escape but was helpless against the cruel grip on the bridle.

Without stopping to think, Diana started toward the terrified horse, yelling at the man to stop. Before she had taken three steps, a man in a light blue shirt vaulted the corral fence and landed like a cat, running toward the brutal cowboy, gaining speed with every stride. The running man was smaller and unarmed, hardly a fair match against the huge, beefy man wielding a whip.

Behind Diana, the ranch house door slammed and men came running. Another man ran out of the barn, saw what was happening and yelled, "Careful, ramrod! Baker's quirt has lead shot in it!"

Baker wheeled to face Tennessee Blackthorn, the Rocking M's ramrod. Baker flipped the quirt over in his hand, wielding the thick leather stock as a club rather than using the whip end against Ten. When his thick arm lifted, Diana screamed and men shouted. Only Ten was silent. He closed the last few feet between himself and Baker as the lead-weighted quirt came smashing down.

Ten didn't flail with his fists or duck away from the blow. The edge of his left hand connected with Baker's wrist. The quirt went spinning up and away, flying end over end through the air. Simultaneously the ramrod's right fist delivered a short, chopping blow to Baker's heart. Ten pivoted, slammed an elbow into Baker's diaphragm and sent another chopping blow to his neck as the big man bent over, folding up, all fight gone. Before the quirt even hit the ground, Baker was stretched out full length facedown in the dirt, unmoving.

Torn between disbelief and shock, Diana came to a stop, staring at the Rocking M's ramrod. She shook her head, trying to understand how a man who was six inches shorter and sixty pounds lighter than his adversary had begun and ended a fight before the bigger man could land a blow. As though at a distance she heard Cash and Luke go by her, moving more slowly now.

"Nice work, Ten," Luke said.

"Amen," said Cash. Then, to Luke, "Remind me never to pick a fight with your ramrod. Somebody taught that boy how to play hardball."

Ten said nothing, for he was more interested in calming

the frightened horse than in talking about the brief fight. "Easy, girl. Easy now. No one's going to hurt you. Easy... easy."

As he spoke, he approached the sweating, trembling mare. When he saw streaks of blood mixed with the horse's lather, he swore, but the soothing tone of his voice never changed despite the scalding nature of his words. Slowly he closed his hands around the reins and began checking over the mare.

As Ten's hands moved over the animal, it began to calm down. Not once did the ramrod look toward the motionless Baker. Ten knew precisely how much damage he had done to the brutal cowboy; what Ten wanted to know was how badly the horse had been hurt.

Cash sat on his heels next to Baker and checked for visible injuries. There was nothing obvious. After a few moments Cash stood and said, "Out cold, but still breathing."

Luke grunted. "Any permanent damage?"

"Not that I can see."

"He won't be swinging a quirt for a while," Ten said without looking up from the mare. "Not with his right hand, anyway. I broke his wrist."

"Too bad it wasn't his neck," Luke said. "You warned him last week about beating a horse." Luke turned to Cosy, who had yelled the warning about the quirt to Ten. "Bring the truck around. You're on garbage detail tonight."

"Where to?" asked Cosy.

"West Fork."

"Forty miles out and forty miles back, damn near all of it on dirt roads," Cosy grumbled. "In the old days we'd have dumped his carcass on the ranch boundary and let him walk to town."

"Not on the Rocking M," Luke said, stretching lazily.

"My great-granddaddy Case MacKenzie once killed a man for beating a horse."

Slowly Diana retreated, walking backward for a few steps before turning and moving quickly toward her car. Though she was a student of human history—Anasazi history, to be precise—she wasn't accustomed to having her history lessons served to her raw. She didn't like having it pointed out that the veneer of civilization was quite thin, even in modern times, and it was especially thin in men.

I shouldn't be shocked. I know better than most women what men are like underneath their shirts and ties, shaving lotions and smiles. Savages and outlaws. All of them. Outlaws who use their strength against those who are weaker.

A vivid picture came to Diana's mind—the man called Ten coming over the fence, attacking the big cowboy, reducing the larger man to unconsciousness with a few violent blows. She shuddered.

"Diana? What happened?"

She looked up and saw Carla standing on the front porch, holding a tiny baby in her arms.

"One of the men was beating a horse," Diana said.

"Baker." Carla's mouth flattened from its usual generous curve. "Ten warned him."

"He did more than that. He beat him unconscious."

"Ten? That doesn't sound like him. I've never seen him lose his temper."

"Is he your ramrod?"

Carla nodded. "Yes, he's the Rocking M's foreman."

"Light blue shirt, black hair, small?"

"Small?" she asked, surprised. "I don't think of Ten as small."

"He's a lot smaller than Baker."

"Oh, well, even Luke and Cash are smaller than Baker. But Ten's at least six feet tall. A bit more, I think." Carla stood on tiptoe and looked out toward the corral. "Is he all right?"

"His wrist is broken."

"Ten's hurt? Oh my God, I've got to—"

"Not Ten," Diana interrupted quickly. "Baker is the one with a broken wrist."

"Oh." Relief changed Carla's face from strained to pretty. "Then Ten will take care of it. He's had medic training." She looked closely at Diana. "You're pale. Are you all right?"

Diana closed her eyes. "I'm fine. It was a long drive out and the road was rough. Now I know why. I was going back in time as well as miles."

Laughing, shaking her head, Carla shifted the sleeping baby and held out her hand to Diana. "Come in and have some coffee. French roast, Colombian beans, with just enough Java beans blended in to give the coffee finesse as well as strength."

Diana's eyelids snapped open. The dark blue of her eyes was vivid against her still-pale face. "I'm hallucinating. They didn't have French roast in the Old West, did they?"

"I don't know, but this isn't the Old West."

"You could have fooled me," Diana said, thinking about outlaws and brawls and a man with the lethal quickness of a cat. But despite her thoughts, she allowed Carla to lead her across the porch and into the cool ranch house. "Your ramrod would have made one hell of an outlaw."

"In the old days, a lot of good men were outlaws. They had no choice. There wasn't any law to be *in*side of." Carla laughed at the expression on Diana's face. "But don't worry. The bad old days are gone. Look in our side yard. There's a satellite dish out there sucking up all kinds of exotic signals from space. We have television, a VCR, radios, CD players, personal computers, a dishwasher, microwave, washer-dryer—the whole tortilla."

"And cowboys swinging quirts full of lead shot," Diana muttered.

"Is that what Baker did?"

Diana nodded.

"My God. No wonder Ten lost his temper."

"What temper? He looked about as angry as a man chopping wood."

Carla shook her head unhappily. "Poor Ten. He's had a tough time ramrodding this crew in the past year."

"'Poor Ten' looked like he could handle it," Diana said beneath her breath.

"The ranch is so remote it's hard to get good men to stay. I don't know how we'd manage without Ten. And now that we've found museum-quality Anasazi artifacts in September Canyon, the pothunters are descending in hordes. Someone has to stay at the site all the time. Cash has been doing it, but he has to leave tomorrow for the Andes. We're going to be more shorthanded than ever."

"The Andes, huh? Great. Everybody deserves a vacation," Diana said, cheered by the thought that there would be one less big man on the Rocking M.

"Cash isn't exactly going on a vacation. One of his colleagues thinks there's a mother lode back up on the flanks of one of those nameless granite peaks. That's the one thing Cash can't resist."

"Nameless peaks?"

"Hard rock and gold. Ten calls Cash the Granite Man but swears it's because of Cash's hard head, not his love of hard-rock mining."

Carla tucked the baby into an old-fashioned cradle that was next to the kitchen table. The baby stirred, opened sleepy turquoise eyes and slid back into sleep once more as Carla slowly rocked the cradle.

"How's the little man doing?" Diana asked softly, bending over the baby until her short, golden brown hair blended with the honey finish of the cradle.

"Growing like a weed in the sun. Logan's going to be at least as big as his daddy."

Diana looked at the soft-cheeked, six-week-old baby and tried to imagine it fully grown, as big as Luke, beard stubbled and powerful. "You'd better start domesticating this little outlaw real soon or you'll never have a chance."

Carla laughed in the instant before she realized that Diana was serious. She looked at the older woman for a moment, remembering the class she had taken from Dr. Diana Saxton, artist and archaeologist, a woman who was reputed not to think much of men. At the time Carla had dismissed the comments as gossip; now she wasn't sure.

"You make it sound like I'm going to need a whip and a chair," Carla said.

"Those are the customary tools for dealing with wild animals, and men are definitely in that category. What a pity that it takes one to make a baby."

"Not all men are like Baker."

Diana made a sound that could have been agreement or disbelief as she began stroking the baby's cheek with a gentle fingertip, careful not to awaken him. She admired the perfect, tiny eyelashes, the snub nose, the flushed lips, the miniature fingers curled in relaxation on the pale cradle blanket. Gradually she noticed more of the cradle itself, how the grain of the wood had been perfectly matched to the curves of the cradle, how the pieces had been fitted without nails, how the wood itself had been polished to a gentle satin luster.

"What a beautiful cradle," Diana said softly, running her fingertips over the wood. "It's a work of art. Where did you get it?"

"Luke made it. He has wonderful hands, strong and gentle."

Diana looked at the cradle once more and the baby lying securely within. She tried not to think how much she would like to have a child of her own. Sex was a necessary step toward conception. For sex, a woman had to trust a man not to hurt her—a man who was bigger, stronger and basically more savage than a woman. Years ago, Diana had abandoned the idea of sex. The thought of a baby, however, still haunted her.

"If Luke is gentle with you and little Logan," Diana said quietly, touching the pale blanket with her fingertips, "you're a lucky woman. You have one man in a million."

Before Carla could say anything more, Diana stood and turned away from the cradle.

"I think I'll take a rain check on that coffee. I want to get my stuff unloaded before dinner."

"Of course. We're putting you in the old ranch house where all the artifacts from the site are being kept. Just follow the road out beyond the barn. When the road forks, go to the right. The old house is only about a hundred yards from the barn. Dinner is at six. Don't bother to knock. Just come in the back way. The dining room is just off the kitchen and both rooms have outside doors. We all eat together during the week. Sundays the hands fend for themselves. You'll eat with us."

Diana looked at the long, narrow room just off the

kitchen. Two rectangular tables pushed together all but filled the room. She tried to imagine what it would be like to eat surrounded by big male bodies. The thought was daunting. She took a slow breath, told herself that she would be spending nearly all of her time at the site in September Canyon, and turned back to Carla.

"Thanks," Diana said. "I'll be back at six, whip in one hand and chair in the other."

CHAPTER TWO

THE ALARM ON DIANA'S DIGITAL watch cheeped annoyingly, breaking her concentration. She set aside the stack of numbered site photos, reset her watch for a short time later, stretched and heard her stomach rumble in anticipation of dinner. Despite her hunger, she was reluctant to leave the hushed solitude of the old house and the silent companionship of the ancient artifacts lining the shelves of the workroom.

Slanting yellow light came through the north window, deepening the textures of stone and sandal fragments, potsherds and glue pots, making everything appear to be infused with a mystic glow. Diana couldn't wait until tomorrow, when she would drive to September Canyon. Photos, artifacts and essays, no matter how precise and scholarly, couldn't convey the complexity of the interlocking mystery of the Anasazi, the land and time.

Her mind more on the past than the present, Diana

walked slowly into the bathroom. The slanting light coming through the small, high window made the gold in her hair incandescent and gave the darker strands a rich satin luster. Her eyes became indigo in shadow, vivid sapphire in direct light. The natural pink in her smooth cheeks and lips contrasted with the dark brown of her eyebrows and the dense fringe of her eyelashes.

Once Diana would have noticed her own understated beauty and heightened it with mascara and blusher, lipstick and haunting perfumes. Once, but no longer. Never again would she be accused by a man of using snares and lures to attract members of the opposite sex, then teasing and maddening them with what she had no intention of giving. Never again would she put herself in a position where a man felt entitled to take what he wanted in the belief that it had been offered—and if it hadn't, it should have been.

Soap, water, unscented lotion and a few strokes with a hairbrush through her short, gamine hairstyle and Diana was ready for dinner. She thought longingly of the four-inch heels she wore when she was teaching to add to her own five feet three inches of frankly curved female body, but wearing a cotton pullover sweater big enough for a man and faded jeans with four-inch heels would be ludicrous. Besides, the scarred, rough-country hiking boots she wore most of the time added at least two inches to her height.

And she was going to need every inch of confidence she could get.

"Mmmrreoooow."

Diana's head snapped toward the window at the unexpected sound. A lean, tiger-striped cat with one chewed ear was standing outside on the tree limb that brushed against the bathroom window. The cat's forepaw was batting hopefully at the bottom of the window, which was open a crack.

"Hello," Diana said, smiling. "Do you live here?"

The paw, claws politely sheathed, patted again beneath the length of the opening.

"I get the message."

She pushed up the window enough for the cat to come in. It leaped from windowsill to the edge of the sink with an effortless grace that reminded her of the Rocking M's ramrod vaulting the corral fence and landing running.

The cat sniffed Diana's meager toiletries, nosed the peppermint toothpaste, sneezed, *yeowed* softly and stropped itself against her midriff. She ran her palm down the cat's spine, enjoying the supple arch of the animal's body as it rubbed against her in turn. Soon the vibrations of an uninhibited purr were rippling from the cat.

"You're a sweetheart," Diana said. "Would you let me hold you?"

The cat would. In fact, it insisted.

"Goodness, you're heavy! Not fat, though. You must be all muscle."

The purring redoubled.

Laughing softly, Diana smoothed her cheeks and chin against the vibrant bundle of fur. The cat moved sinuously in return, twisting against her in slow motion, relishing the physical contact. And shedding, of course.

Diana looked at the gray and black hairs sticking to the navy cotton sweater she was wearing. She shrugged. Maybe some of the men would be allergic to cats. The thought had a definite appeal.

"C'mon, cat. Let's see if they allow felines in the dining room."

The cat burrowed more tightly into Diana's arms, clinging with just a hint of claws while she closed the bathroom window. Cradling the purring animal, Diana made a quick circuit of the old house, making sure that everything was buttoned up in case the thunderstorm that had been threatening for the past hour actually got down to work. The bedroom was in order—windows shut, clothes put away, sheet turned down on the double bed with its antique headboard and blessedly new mattress set. The window over the kitchen sink was closed. The workroom with its two long tables and countless bins and cubbyholes and shelves was as orderly as it was ever likely to be.

Absently Diana ran her fingertips over the smooth surface of a cabinet, wondering if Luke had made this furniture as well as the cradle. She suspected he had. There was a quality of craftsmanship and care that was rare in modern furniture.

Her stomach growled. She eased her wrist out from under the cat and looked at her watch. Twenty minutes to six. Her alarm would be going off again soon, telling her she had to be where she very much didn't want to be—in a room full of strange men.

Maybe if I get there early, I can grab a plate of food and a seat at the corner of the table. That way I won't be completely surrounded by savages.

Men, not savages, she reminded herself automatically, trying to be fair.

The part of herself that didn't care about fair shot back: *Men or savages. Same difference.*

Diana remembered the fine-grained, carefully wrought cradle and mentally placed a question mark beside Luke's name. It was just possible that he wasn't a savage or an outlaw beyond the pale of gentle society. For Carla's sake,

Diana hoped so. Carla had been one of her favorite students—bright, quick, eager, fascinated by the Anasazi's complex, enigmatic past.

The watch alarm cheeped again. The cat's tail whipped in annoyance.

"I agree, cat, but it's the only way I remember to be anywhere. Once I start working over potsherds or sketchbooks, everything else just goes away."

The cat made a disgruntled sound and resettled itself more comfortably in her arms.

Diana shut the front door and looked down the narrow path that led from the old ranch house to the bigger, more modern one. Reluctant to confront the Rocking M's oversize men, she lingered for a moment on the front step of the old house. The grove of dark evergreens that surrounded the original ranch house was alive with rain-scented wind. Clouds were seething overhead, their billows set off by spears of brassy gold light that made the wild bowl of the sky appear to be supported by shafts of pure light. Distant thunder rumbled, telling tales of invisible lightning.

She took a deep breath and felt excitement uncurl along her nerves as the taste of the storm wind swept through her. She had been cooped up in classrooms too long, earning money so that she could explore the Anasazi homeland during the long summer break. The boundless, ancient land of the Four Corners called to her, singing of people and cultures long vanished, mysteries whispering among shadow, shattered artifacts waiting to be made whole. That was what she had come to the Rocking M for—the undiscovered past.

Caressing the cat absently with her chin, Diana walked the short distance to the big house. When the wind shifted, the smell of food beckoned to her, making her aware of the fact that she had missed lunch.

The outside door into the dining room was open. Diana looked in, but nobody was inside yet. From the bunkhouse beyond the corral came the sound of men calling to one another, talking about the day's work or the impending storm or the savory smell of dinner on the wind. Quietly Diana walked the length of the dining room toward the door leading into the kitchen. She had just begun to hope that she would be able to grab a plate and eat alone when she stepped into the kitchen and stopped as though her feet had been nailed to the floor.

There was a man standing with his back to her, a stranger with wide shoulders stretching against the black fabric of his shirt. The suggestion of male power was emphasized by the line of his back tapering down to lean hips, the muscular ease of his stance and the utter confidence of his posture as he stood motionless in black jeans and black boots that were polished by use.

My God, he's as tall and straight and hard as a stone cliff. No wonder he's confident. All he has to do is stand there and he dominates everything.

Reflexively Diana backed up but succeeded only in giving away her presence by bumping into a counter.

"Carla?" the man said, turning around slowly. His voice was deep, slightly rough, a ragged kind of velvet that was as dark as his clothes. His head was bent over something he was holding. His hair was intensely black, subtly curly, thick. "Can you give me a hand?"

Diana opened her mouth to say that she wasn't Carla but was so surprised by what she saw that no words came out.

A tiger-striped kitten lay cupped in the man's lean, callused hands. The contrast between the man's strength and the kitten's soft body was as shocking as the clarity of the man's ice-gray eyes looking at her. Abruptly she realized that she had seen him once before, under very different circumstances.

"Y-you're the ramrod," she said without thinking.

"Most people call me Ten. Short for Tennessee."

"You—Baker—the horse—"

Ten looked more closely at the woman who stood before him, her unease as badly concealed as the alluring curves of her body beneath her loose cotton sweater.

"Don't worry," Ten said. "He won't be back. Have you seen Carla?"

Diana shook her head, making light twist through her short, silky hair. Ten's nostrils flared slightly as he smelled the freshness of soap and sunshine and female skin.

"Think you could put Pounce down long enough to help me with Nosy?"

"Pounce?" Diana asked, wondering if she had lost her mind.

"That sly renegade who's grinning and purring in your arms."

"Oh…the cat." Diana looked down. "Pounce, huh?"

Ten made a sound of agreement that was suspiciously like a purr. "Best mouser on the Rocking M. Usually he's standoff-ish, but he can sense a particular kind of soft touch three miles away. From the smug look on his face, he was right about you."

The kitten stirred as though it wanted to be free. Long fingers closed gently, restraining the tiny animal without hurting or frightening it.

"Easy there, Nosy. That wound has to be cleaned up or you're going to be dead or three-legged, which amounts to the same thing out here. And that would be a shame. You're the best-looking kitten that ugly old mouser has sired."

Bemused by the picture man and kitten made, Diana opened her arms. Pounce took the hint, leaped gracefully to the floor and vanished into the house. Drawn against her will by the kitten's need, Diana bent over Ten's hands.

"What's wrong with it?" she asked.

"She was just living up to her name. Nosy. Either one of the chickens pecked her, or a hawk made a pass at her and she got free, or one of the bunkhouse dogs bit her, or…" Ten shrugged. "Lots of things can happen to a newly weaned kitten on a ranch."

"Poor little thing," Diana murmured, stroking the kitten with a fingertip, noticing for the first time that the fur on the animal's left haunch was rucked up over a knot of swollen flesh. "What do you want me to do?"

"Hold her while I clean her up. Normally her mother would take care of it, but she went hunting a week ago and didn't come back."

Diana looked up for an instant and received a vivid impression of diamond-clear eyes framed by thick black eyelashes that any woman would have envied. The eyelashes were the only suggestion of softness about Ten, but it reassured Diana in an odd way.

"Show me what to do."

The left corner of Ten's mouth tipped upward approvingly. "Hold your hands out. That's it. Now hold Nosy here, and here, so I can get to the haunch. Hold on a little harder. You won't hurt her. She's still at the age where she's all rubber bands and curiosity."

The description made Diana smile at the same instant that warm, hard fingers pressed over her own, showing her how much restraint to use on the kitten.

"That's good. Now hold tight."

In the silence that came while Ten gently examined the kitten, Diana could hear her own heartbeat and feel the subtle warmth of Ten's breath as he bent over the furry scrap of life she held in her hands.

"Damn. I was afraid of that."

"What?" she asked.

"I'll have to open it up."

Ten reached toward the counter with a long arm. For the first time Diana noticed the open first aid kit. The sound of the wrapper being removed from the sterile, disposable scalpel seemed as loud to her as thunder.

Gray eyes assessed Diana, missing nothing of her distress.

"I'll get Carla," he said.

"No," Diana said quickly. "I'm not squeamish. Well, not horribly squeamish. Everyone who works at remote sites has to go through first aid training. It's just…the kitten is so small."

"Close your eyes. It will make it easier on all of us."

Diana closed her eyes and held her breath, expecting to hear a cry of distress from the kitten when Ten went to work. Other than a slight twitch, the animal showed no reaction. Diana was equally still, so still that she sensed the tiny currents of air made when Ten's hands moved over the small patient. The words he spoke to Nosy were like the purring of a mama cat, sound without meaning except the most basic meaning of all—reassurance.

There was the sharp smell of disinfectant, the thin rasp of paper wrappings being torn away and a sense of light pressure as Ten swabbed the wound clean.

"Okay. You can open your eyes now."

Diana looked down. The kitten's haunch was wet, marred only by a tiny cut. Most of the swelling was gone, removed when Ten lanced the boil that had formed over the wound.

"Thorn," Ten said, holding up a wicked, vaguely curved fragment. "Wild rose from the looks of it."

"Will Nosy be all right now?"

"Should be."

Long fingers slid beneath the kitten, moving over Diana's skin almost caressingly as Ten lifted the animal from her hands. Her breath froze, but Ten never so much as glanced at her.

"C'mon, Nosy," he said, cradling the kitten against his neck with his left hand. "You've taken up enough of the lady's time. What you need now is a little sleep and TLC."

"TLC? Is that a medicine?"

The corner of Ten's mouth curved up again. "Best one in the world. Tender Loving Care."

As he spoke, Ten stroked Nosy's face with a fingertip that was as gentle as a whisper. After a few strokes the kitten looked bemused and altogether content. Within moments Nosy's eyelids lowered over round amber eyes. There was a little yawn, the delicate curl of a tiny pink tongue, and the kitten was asleep.

With a feeling of unreality, Diana looked at the ramrod's hard hand curled protectively around the sleeping kitten and remembered that same hand breaking a man's wrist and then slamming him into unconsciousness before he could even cry out in pain.

Ramrod. The name suits him.

But so did the sleeping kitten.

CHAPTER THREE

DINNER WAS ON THE TABLE AT SIX o'clock, straight up. By long-standing custom, no one waited for latecomers. That included Luke, who was still on the phone talking to the sheriff. No one took Luke's place at the head of the table, but formality ended there. Cash and Carla sat facing Diana and Ten across the table. Diana had managed to secure a seat just to the left of the head of the table, ensuring that she would have only one person seated next to her. Even so, she felt crowded, because that one person was Ten.

To Diana's eyes, the long dining table was supporting enough food for at least twenty people. Five cowhands sat at the other end of the table. There was room for five more men and seven men in a squeeze, but the Rocking M was shorthanded. Only nine people were seated at the moment. Then the outside door banged and a new cowhand called Jervis rushed in and snagged the platter of pork chops before he had even sat down.

"Where's Cosy?" Jervis asked as he slid into a chair and began forking pork chops onto his plate.

"Garbage run," Ten said.

Jervis hesitated, looked around the table and said to Ten, "Baker, huh?"

Ten grunted.

"Who gave him the good word?"

"I did."

"How'd he take it?"

"I didn't hear any complaints."

Cash half strangled on laughter and coffee.

"Something funny?" asked Jervis.

"Ten had Baker laid out cold in six seconds flat," Cash said casually, reaching for the gravy. "He's probably still wondering what hit him."

"Can't say as I'm sorry," Jervis said. He dished a mountain of potatoes onto his plate before he turned and looked Ten over. "Not a mark on you. You must be as much an outlaw as Cosy said you were. That Baker did a lot of bragging about what a fighter he was. Talked about men he'd busted up so bad they pi—er, passed blood for months."

Ten glanced at Diana before he gave the cowhand an icy look. "Jervis, why don't you just shovel food and leave the dinner conversation to Carla. Miss Saxton isn't used to anything less polished than a faculty tea."

"Sorry, ma'am," Jervis said to Diana.

"Don't apologize on my account," she quickly. "Life at remote archaeological sites isn't as polished as Mr., er—"

"Blackthorn," Ten said politely.

"—Blackthorn seems to think," Diana finished. "I don't cringe at a few rough edges."

"Uh, sure," Jervis said, trying and failing not to stare at

the noticeable gap that had opened up between Diana's chair and Ten's.

The other cowhands followed Jervis's look. Snickers went around the table like distant lightning, but not one man was going to call down their ramrod's ire by being so rude as to point out that the university woman was politely lying through her pretty white teeth.

Diana didn't notice the looks she received, for she was grimly concentrating on her single pork chop, scant helping of potatoes and no gravy. Despite her usually healthy appetite, her empty stomach and the savory nature of Carla's cooking, Diana was having trouble swallowing. Even though none of the other men at the table were as big as Cash—and Luke wasn't even in the dining room—she felt suffocated by looming, uncivilized, unpredictable males.

"Miss Saxton," Ten continued, "will be here for the summer, working at the September Canyon site." He glanced at the woman, who was at the moment subtly hitching her chair even farther away from him, and drawled, "It *is* Miss, isn't it?"

Carla gave Ten a quick glance, caught by the unusual edge in his normally smooth voice. Then she noticed what the cowhands had already seen—the gap that had slowly opened up between Diana's chair and the ramrod's.

"Actually," Diana said, "my students call me Dr. Saxton and my friends call me Di."

"What does your husband call you?" Ten asked blandly.

"I'm not married."

Ten would have been surprised by any other answer, a fact that he didn't bother to conceal.

"Dr. Diana Saxton," Ten continued, "will be spending most of her time at the September Canyon digs. In between, she'll be living at the old house, which means that you boys better clean up your act. Voices carry real well from the bunkhouse to the old house. Anybody who embarrasses the lady will hear from me."

"And from me," Luke said, pulling out his chair and sitting down. "Pass the pork chops, please." He looked at Diana, saw the gap between her chair and Ten's and gave the ramrod a look that was both amused and questioning. "Didn't you have time to shower before dinner?"

The left corner of Ten's mouth lifted in wry acknowledgment, but he said nothing.

"When are you leaving?" Carla asked quickly, turning toward her brother, Cash. She didn't know why Diana kept edging farther away from Ten but guessed that she would be embarrassed if it were pointed out. By and large the cowhands were kind men, but their humor was both blunt and unrelenting.

"Right after we play poker tonight," Cash said.

"Poker?" Carla groaned.

"Sure. I thought I'd introduce Dr. Saxton to the joys of seven-card stud."

Smiling politely, Diana looked up from her plate. "Thanks, but I'm really tired. Maybe some other time."

The cowhands laughed as though she had made a joke.

"Guess they teach more than stones and bones at that university," Jervis said when the laughter ended. "Must teach some common sense, too."

Diana looked at Carla, who smiled.

"My brother is, er, well…" Carla's voice faded.

"Cash is damned lucky at cards," Ten said succinctly. "He'll clean you down to the lint in your pockets."

"It's true," said Carla. "His real name is Alexander, but anyone who has ever played cards with him calls him Cash."

"In fact," Luke said, pouring gravy over mounds of food, "I'm one of the few men in living memory ever to beat Cash at poker."

Cash smiled slightly and examined his dinner as though he expected it to get up and walk off the plate.

"Of course," Luke continued, "Cash cheated."

Cash's head snapped up.

"He wanted Carla to spend the summer on the Rocking M," Luke said matter-of-factly. "So he suckered her into betting a summer's worth of cooking. Cash won, of course. Then he turned around and carefully lost his sister's whole summer to me." Luke ran his fingertip from Carla's cheekbone to the corner of her smile before he turned to Cash and said quietly, "I never thanked you for giving Carla to me, but not a day goes by that I don't thank God."

Diana looked at the two big men and the woman who sat wholly at ease between them, smiling, her love for her husband and her brother as vivid as the blue-green of her eyes. The men's love for her was equally obvious, almost tangible. An odd aching closed Diana's throat, making an already difficult dinner impossible to swallow.

"I hope you know how lucky you are," she said to Carla. Without warning, Diana pushed back from the table and stood. "I'm afraid I'm too tired to eat. If you'll excuse me, I'll make it an early night."

"Of course," Carla said. "If you're hungry later, just come in the back way and eat whatever looks good. Ten does it all the time."

"Thanks," Diana said, already turning away, eager to be gone from the room full of men.

Nobody said a word until Diana had been gone long enough to be well beyond range of their voices. Then Luke turned, raised his eyebrows questioningly and looked straight at Ten.

"Are you the burr under her saddle?" Luke asked.

There was absolute silence as all the cowhands leaned forward to hear the answer to the question none of them had the nerve to ask their ramrod.

"She saw me take down Baker," Ten said. "Shocked her, I guess. Then I made her hold Nosy while I cut that boil. Now she thinks I'm a cross between Attila the Hun and Jack the Ripper."

Luke grunted. "Nice work, by the way. Baker, I mean. Nosy, too, I suppose. Carla was worried about that fool kitten. Me, I think we have too darn many cats as it is."

Luke caught the light, slow-motion blow Carla aimed at his shoulder. He brushed a kiss over her captive hand and said, "Honey, from now on put Diana next to you at the table. If the pretty professor moves her chair any farther away from Ten, we'll have to serve her food in the kitchen."

The cowhands burst out laughing. For a few minutes more the talk centered around the overly shy professor with the striking blue eyes and very nicely rounded body. Then food began to disappear in earnest and conversation slowed. After dessert vanished as well, so did the cowhands. Cash went upstairs to pack, leaving Ten, Luke and Carla alone to enjoy a final cup of coffee before the evening's work of kitchen cleanup and bookkeeping began.

Ten rubbed his jaw thoughtfully and was rewarded by the rasp of beard stubble. Undoubtedly that, too, had counted against him with the wary professor. Which was too bad— it had been a long time since a woman had interested him quite as much as the one with the frightened eyes and a body that would tempt a saint.

"How do you want to divide up Baker's work?" Luke asked Ten.

"I can take the leased grazing lands over on the divide, but that leaves the Wildfire Canyon springs without a hand."

"I'll take the grazing lands and have Jervis camp over at Wildfire Canyon during the week and weekends at September Canyon."

"That will make for long days for you," Ten said, glancing quickly at Carla. He knew that Luke had been trying to spend as much time as possible with his wife and new son.

"Your days will be even longer," Luke said. "Starting tomorrow, you're ramrodding the dig at September Canyon."

"Jervis can do it. He gets along with the university types real well. You'd never know it to listen to him, but he taught math in Oregon before he took up ranch work."

"You'd never know it to listen to you, either," retorted Luke, "but I happen to know a certain ramrod who speaks three languages and who still gets calls in the middle of the night from official types who want advice on how to get sticky jobs unstuck."

Ten said nothing.

"But they're just going to have to wait in line," Luke continued. "I've got all the trouble you can handle right in September Canyon."

Without moving, Ten became fully alert. Luke saw the change and smiled thinly.

"You expecting some kind of trouble at the site?" Ten asked.

Luke looked at Carla. "Don't I hear Logan crying?" he asked.

"Why don't you go and check?" Carla offered.

The look Luke gave Carla plainly said he wished she weren't listening to what he was saying to Ten. She looked right back, plainly telling Luke that she wasn't leaving without a good reason. Reluctantly he smiled, but when he turned to Ten the smile faded.

"The sheriff called," Luke said. "There's a ring of pothunters working the Four Corners. They dig during the week and avoid the weekends when there are more people in the backcountry. They're professional and they're tough."

"How tough?"

"They roughed up some folks over in Utah. The Park Service isn't making any noise about it, but the backcountry rangers are going armed these days. So are the pothunters."

"Want me to leave now for the site?" Ten asked.

"No. One of the sheriff's men is camping out that way, unofficially. But he's got to be back on the road early tomorrow."

Into the dining room came the clear sound of an unhappy baby. Carla put her hand on Luke's shoulder and pressed down, silently telling him not to get up.

"I'll leave before dawn," Ten said, watching Carla hurry from the room.

"The professor won't like that."

"I'll be quiet," Ten said dryly.

"Don't bother. She's going with you. That little Japanese rice burner of hers wouldn't get four miles up the pasture road, much less across Picture Wash to September Canyon."

Ten smiled rather wolfishly. "She's not going to like being trapped in a truck with me. Or are you sending Carla to ride shotgun?"

"Nope," Luke said cheerfully. "She's got two full-time jobs riding herd on me and the baby."

"That's the problem. We've all got too damn many full-time jobs and not enough hands."

"I put the word out at every ranch for three hundred

miles," Luke said, stretching his long arms over his head. "All we can do is wait. Jason Ironcloud promised he'd start breaking horses as soon as his sister's husband is out of jail. Until then, he's got to take care of her ranch."

"What's the husband in for—the usual?" Ten asked.

"Drunk and disorderly."

"The usual."

Luke grunted agreement.

Ten rubbed his raspy chin thoughtfully. "Nevada called. He's pulling out of Afghanistan. He'll be home in a few weeks."

Luke glanced sideways at Ten. "Is he still a renegade?"

"All the Blackthorns are wild. It's the Highland Scots blood."

"Yeah. Outlaws to the bone. Like you. You don't make any noise about it, but you go your own way and to hell with what the rest of the world thinks."

Ten said only, "A few years of guerrilla warfare tends to settle down even the wildest kid."

"You should know."

"Yes. I should know."

Luke nodded and said softly, "Hire him."

Ten looked at Luke. "Thanks. I owe you one."

"No way, *compadre*. I should have been the man to shake the kinks out of Baker, not you."

A slight smile crossed the ramrod's face. "My pleasure."

Luke looked thoughtful. "Does Nevada fight the same way you do?"

"Wouldn't surprise me. He was taught by the same people."

"Good. He can trade off guarding September Canyon with you." Luke sighed and rubbed his neck wearily. "You know, there are days I wish Carla had never found those damn ruins. It's costing us thousands of dollars a year in manpower alone just to keep pothunters out."

"We could do what some of the other ranchers have done."

"What's that?"

"Sell some of the artifacts to pay for protecting the ruins."

"The September Canyon ruins are on your part of the ranch," Luke said, his face expressionless. "Is that what you want to do?"

Ten shook his head. "I'll give the land back to you before I sell off artifacts. Or I'll give the land back to the government if neither one of us can afford to protect the ruins. My head knows that ninety-eight percent of those artifacts aren't unique—universities and museums are full of Anasazi stuff as good or better. Once the excavation has been carefully done, there's no good reason not to get back the cost of the digging by selling off some of the stuff."

"But?" Luke asked.

Ten shrugged. "But my gut keeps telling me that those artifacts belong in the place where they were made and used and broken and mended and used again. It's pure foolishness but that's how I feel about it, and as long as I can afford it, I plan on keeping my foolish ways."

Luke looked at Ten and said quietly, "If my drunken daddy had sold pieces of the Rocking M to anybody but you, I would have been in a world of hurt with no place to call home."

Ten stood and clapped Luke on the shoulder. "It was an even trade, *compadre*. Back then, I was in a world of hurt and looking for a home."

"You've got the home. What about the hurt? Still have that?"

"I got over it a long time ago."

"Then why haven't you married again?"

"A smart dog doesn't have to be taught the same lesson twice," Ten said sardonically. "I'm a hell of a lot smarter than a dog."

"She must have been something."

"Who?"

"Your ex-wife."

Ten shrugged. "She was honest. That's better than most. When the sex wore off she wanted out. By then I was more than willing. Next time I was smarter. I didn't marry just because my blood was running hot. After a few weeks the same thing happened, only this time the girl didn't want to admit it. I shipped out the first chance I got."

"That was a long time ago. You were a wild kid chasing girls who were no better than they had to be. You're different now."

Ten shook his head, "You got lucky, Luke. I didn't. You learned one thing about women and marriage. I learned another."

Without giving Luke a chance to speak, Ten left the room. Behind him, Luke sat motionless, listening to the sound of Ten's fading footsteps and the soft thump of a closing door.

CHAPTER FOUR

AS THE DIRT ROAD ZIGZAGGED across national forest lease lands and down the steep side of the high, mountainous plateau where the Rocking M ranch buildings were located, the land became more dry and the earth more intensely colored. Gullies became deeper, rocky cliffs more common, and the creeks and rivers widened into broad, often dry washes winding among spectacular stone-walled canyons. Juniper and piñon mixed with sagebrush, giving the air a clean, pungent smell. In deep, protected clefts where tiny springs welled forth, a handful of true pine trees grew next to cottonwoods. Along the canyon bottoms the brush thinned to clumps. Depending on altitude or exposure, juniper, piñon, cedar and big sage grew.

Diana watched the changing landscape intently, seeking the plants that were the hallmark and foundation of Anasazi culture—yucca and piñon, bee plant and goosefoot. On the higher flatlands she also looked for stands of big sage, which grew where the earth had been disturbed and then abandoned by man. Each time another nameless canyon or gully opened up along the rough dirt road, she looked at the unexplored land with a yearning she couldn't disguise.

"Stop it," Ten said finally. "You're making me feel like the Marquis de Sade."

Startled, Diana turned toward him. "What?"

"Don't worry. I'm not talking about the way you hug the door handle as though it were your last hope of safety," Ten drawled, giving her a sideways glance.

A flush crawled up Diana's cheeks. She looked down and saw that she was all but sitting on the door handle in order to get as much distance as possible between herself and Ten.

"I—it's nothing personal," she said, her voice strained.

"Like hell it isn't," Ten said calmly. "But that's not what made me feel like a sadist. It's the way you look at all those canyons that's getting to me. It's the way a starving man looks at food, or a thirsty man looks at water, or Luke looks at Carla when they all sit in the rocking chair while she nurses Logan. If it will make you feel any better, we can stop and get closer to whatever it is you love so much."

Ten's perceptivity startled Diana. It was unexpected in a man. But then, Ten had been unexpected from the first moment she saw him. The longer she was around him, the more unexpected he became.

"That's—that's very kind of you, Mr. Blackthorn, but I'm afraid looking won't make me feel much better."

Clear, ice-gray eyes glanced briefly at Diana, then resumed watching the rough road.

"What would make you feel better, professor?"

"Being called something else, *ramrod*," she shot back before she could think better of it.

The corner of Ten's mouth tugged up. "I'm not much on formality. Call me Ten."

Diana started to reciprocate, then stopped, afraid that Ten would mistake politeness for an entirely different sort of offer.

He shot her another quick glance. "Go ahead, I won't take it as a come-on."

"I beg your pardon?"

"Go ahead and ask me to call you Diana. I'll assume you're being polite, not looking for a little action."

"Let me assure you, I'm not looking for a 'little action.'"

"I figured that out the first time I saw you. So uncramp your hand from the door handle and tell me why you're looking at the countryside like you're saying goodbye to your only friend."

"Are you always this direct?"

"Yes. Are you always this nervous around men or is it me in particular?"

"Does it matter?"

"If I'm the one setting you on edge, I'll get out of your hair as soon as possible," Ten said matter-of-factly. "If it's just men in general you don't like, it won't matter who's on site with you."

Diana was silent.

"Well that tells me," Ten said, shrugging. "As soon as Nevada arrives, I'll turn September Canyon over to him."

"It's not you," Diana said, forcing out each word.

"Did anyone ever mention that you don't lie worth a damn? You've been terrified of me ever since I came over the corral fence and taught Baker what his horse already knew—in a fight, smart goes farther than big."

Diana closed her eyes, seeing again the blows landing too quickly to be believed. "Fast, strong and lethal count, too. Baker never had a chance, did he?"

"Only a fool, a horse or a woman would give a man like Baker a chance."

"Are you calling me a fool?"

"No. I'm not calling you a horse, either."

She made a strangled sound that was close to laughter, surprising herself.

A quick, sideways glance told Ten that Diana's grip on the door handle had eased. It also told him that her eyes were an even deeper, more brilliant blue than he had thought, and that the curve of her mouth was made to be traced by a man's tongue.

The shadow of another small canyon opening up off the road caught Diana's attention. The hint of laughter that had curved her mouth faded, leaving behind a yearning line.

"What is it that you see?" Ten asked softly.

The words slid past Diana's reflexive defenses and touched the one thing she permitted herself to love, the Anasazi homeland with its mixture of mountains and mesas and canyons, sandstone and shale, its violent summer storms, and the massive silence that made her feel as though time itself flowed through the ancient canyons.

"That canyon off to the right," Diana said, pointing to a place where a crease opened up at the base of a mesa. "Does it have a name?"

"Not that I know of."

"That's what I thought. There are hundreds of canyons like it on the Colorado Plateau. Thousands. And in each one, it would be unusual to walk more than a mile along the mesa top or the canyon bottom without finding some legacy of the Anasazi, such as broken pots or masonry or ruined stone walls."

Ten made a startled sound and glanced quickly at Diana.

"It's true," she said, turning to face him. "The Colorado Plateau is one of the richest archaeological areas of the world. Some experts say that there are a hundred archaeological sites per square mile. Others say a hundred and twenty sites. Naturally, all of the sites aren't important enough to excavate, but the sheer number of them is amazing. For instance, in Montezuma County alone, there are probably one hundred *thousand* archaeological sites."

Ten whistled through his teeth. The boyish gesture both startled and intrigued Diana, for it was so much at odds with the fierce man who had fought Baker and the quiet man who had treated a sick kitten with such care.

"How many Anasazi lived around here, anyway?" Ten asked.

"Here? I don't know. But over in Montezuma Valley there were about thirty thousand people. That's greater than the population today. It's the same for the rest of the Colorado Plateau. At the height of the Anasazi culture, the land supported more people than it does today with twentieth-century technology.

"And up every nameless canyon," Diana continued, her voice husky with emotion, "there's a chance of finding the one extraordinary ruin that will explain why the Anasazi culture thrived in this area for more than ten centuries and then simply vanished without warning, as though the people picked up in the middle of a meal and left, taking nothing with them."

"That's what you're looking for? The answer to an old mystery?"

She nodded.

"Why?"

The question startled Diana. "What do you mean?"

"What is it you really want?" Ten asked. "Glory? Wealth? A tenured job at an eastern university? Classrooms full of students who think you're smarter than God?"

"Is it academia in general you dislike or me in particular?"

Ten heard the echo of his own previous question and smiled to himself. "I don't know you well enough to dislike you. I'm just curious."

"So am I," Diana said tightly. "That's why I want to know about the Anasazi. Their abrupt disappearance from the cliff houses at the height of their cultural success is as big a mystery as what really caused the extinction of dinosaurs."

She glanced covertly at Ten. Though he was watching the rough, difficult road, she sensed that he was listening closely to her words. Despite her usual reticence on the subject of herself, there was something about Ten that made her want to keep talking, if only to give him a better opinion of her than he obviously had. Not that she could really blame him for being cool toward her; she had done everything but crawl under the table to avoid him at dinner.

The contrasts and contradictions of the man called Tennessee Blackthorn both intrigued and irritated Diana. A man who could fight with such savage efficiency shouldn't also care about sick kittens. A man who could handle the physical demands of the big truck and the rotten road with such effortless skill shouldn't be so interested in something as abstract and intangible as the vanished Anasazi, yet he had shown obvious interest every time the subject had come up.

But most of all, a man who was so abrasively masculine shouldn't have been perceptive enough to notice her silent yearning after unexplored canyons. Nor should she be noticing right now the clean line of his profile, the high forehead and thick, faintly curling pelt of black hair, the luxuriant black eyelashes and crystal clarity of his eyes, the subdued sensuality of his mouth.

The direction of Diana's thoughts made her distinctly uneasy. She turned and looked out the window again, yet it was impossible for her to go back to the long silences of the previous hours in the truck when she had tried to shut out the presence of everything except the land.

"As for prestige or a tenured teaching position," Diana continued, looking out the window, "I'm not a great candidate for any university, especially an eastern one. I love the Colorado Plateau country too much to live anywhere else. I stand in front of classrooms full of students—worshipful or otherwise—because teaching gives me the money and time to explore the Anasazi culture in the very places where the Ancient Ones once lived, and then make what I've seen and learned come alive in drawings."

"You're an artist?"

Short, golden brown hair rippled and shone in the sun as Diana shook her head in a silent negative. "At best, I'm an illustrator. I take the site photographer's pictures, read the archaeological summaries of the site and study the artifacts that have been excavated. Then I combine everything with my own knowledge of the Anasazi and make a series of drawings of the site as it probably looked when it was inhabited."

"Sounds like more than illustration to me."

"I assure you, it's less than art. My mother is an artist, so I know the difference."

"Do your parents live in Colorado?"

"My mother lives in Arizona."

Normally Ten would have let the matter of parents drop, especially since Diana's voice had planted warning flags around the subject, but his curiosity about Diana Saxton wasn't normal. She showed flashes of passion coupled with unusual reserve. And it was reserve rather than shyness. Ten had known more than a few shy cowboys. Not one of them would have been able to get up in front of a room full of people and say a single word, much less teach a whole course.

Diana wasn't shy of people. She was shy of men. Ten had immediately figured out that she didn't much care for the male half of the human race. What he hadn't figured out was why.

"What about your father?" Ten asked.

"What about him?"

Though Diana's voice was casual, Ten noted the subtle tightening of her body.

"Where does he live?" Ten asked.

"I don't know."

"Is he why you don't like men?"

"Frankly, it's none of your business."

"Of course it is. I'm a man."

"Mr. Blackthorn—"

"Ten," he interrupted.

"—whether I hate or love men is irrelevant to you or any other man I meet."

"I'll agree about the other men, but not me."

"Why?"

"I'm the man you're going to spend the next five days alone with."

"What?" Diana asked, staring at Ten.

"One of the grad students broke his ankle climbing up a canyon wall," Ten said. Without pausing in his explanations, he whipped the truck around a washout on one side of the road and then a landslide ten yards farther down. "Another one got a job in Illinois working on Indian mounds. The other three can come out only on the weekends because they work during the week."

"So?"

"So I'm staying at the September Canyon site with you."

"That's not necessary. I've been alone at remote digs before."

"Not on the Rocking M you haven't. There will be an armed guard on the site at all times." Without altering his tone at all he said, "Hang on, this will get greasy."

The relaxed lines on Ten's body didn't change as he held the truck on a slippery segment of road where sandstone gave way to thin layers of shale that were so loosely bonded they washed away in even a gentle rain. During the summer season of cloudbursts, the parts of the road that crossed shale formations became impassable for hours or days. Nor was the sandstone itself any treat for driving. Wet sandstone was surprisingly slick.

"There are professional pothunters in the area," Ten continued. "They've worked over a lot of sites. If someone objects, they work them over, too. Luke and I decided that no one goes to September Canyon without a guard."

"Why wasn't I told this before I was hired?" Diana asked tightly.

"Because the sheriff didn't tell us until last night."

Diana said something beneath her breath.

Ten glanced sideways at her. "If you can't handle it, tell me now. We'll be back at the ranch in time for dinner."

She said nothing, still trying to cope with her seething feelings at the thought of being alone with Ten in a remote canyon for five days.

"If I thought it would do any good," Ten said, "I'd give you my word that I won't touch you. But you don't know me well enough to believe me, so there's not much point in making any promises, is there?"

Diana didn't answer.

Without warning Ten brought the truck to a stop in the center of a wide spot in the road. He set the brake and turned to face his unhappy passenger.

"What will it be?" he asked. "September Canyon or back to the ranch house?"

Almost wildly Diana glanced around the countryside. She had been so excited when Carla had offered employment for the summer. The salary was minimal, but the opportunity to study newly discovered ruins was unparalleled.

And now it was all vanishing like rain in the desert.

She looked at Ten. Part of her was frankly terrified at the prospect of being alone with him for days on end. Part of her was not—and in some ways, that was most terrifying of all.

Shutting out everything, Diana closed her eyes. *What am I going to do?*

The image of Ten's powerful hands holding the kitten with such care condensed in her mind.

Surely Carla wouldn't send me out here alone with a man she didn't trust. After that thought came another. *My father was never that gentle with anything. Nor was Steve.*

The ingrained habit of years made Diana's mind veer away from the bleak night when she had learned once and forever to distrust men and her own judgment. Yet she had been luckier than many of the women she had talked with since. Her scars were all on the inside.

Unbidden came a thought that made Diana tremble with

a tangle of emotions she refused to name and a question she shouldn't ask, even in the silence of her own mind.

Would Ten be as gentle with a woman as he was with that kitten?

CHAPTER FIVE

TEN SAT AND WATCHED THE emotions fighting within Diana—anger, fear, hope, confusion, curiosity, longing. The extent of Diana's reluctance to go on to September Canyon surprised him. He had glimpsed the depth of her passion for the Anasazi; if she were considering turning and walking away from September Canyon, she must be in the grip of a fear that was very real to her, despite the fact that Ten knew of no reason for that fear. While most women might have been initially uneasy at spending time alone with a stranger in a remote place, their instinctive wariness would have been balanced by the knowledge that their unexpected companion was a man who had the respect and trust of the people he lived among.

That fact, however, didn't seem to make much difference to Diana.

"Can you talk about it?" Ten asked finally.

"What?"

"Why you're afraid of men. Is it your father?"

Diana looked at Ten's searching, intent eyes, sensing the intelligence and the strength of will in him reaching out to her, asking her to trust him.

Abruptly she felt hemmed in, required to do something for which she was unprepared.

"Stop hounding me," Diana said through clenched teeth. "You have no right to my secrets any more than any man has a right to my body!"

For an instant there was an electric silence stretching tightly between Ten and Diana; then he turned away from her to look out over the land. The silence lengthened until the idling of the truck's engine was as loud as thunder. When Ten finally turned back toward Diana his face was expressionless, his eyes were hooded, and his voice held none of the mixture of emotions it had before.

"In an hour or less those clouds will get together and rain very hard. Then Picture Wash will become impassable. Anyone who is at the September Canyon site will be forced to stay there. Which will it be, Dr. Saxton? Forward to the dig or back to the ranch?"

Ten's voice was even, uninflected, polite. It was like having a stranger ask her for the time of day.

Bitterly Diana reminded herself that Ten was a stranger. Yet somehow he hadn't seemed like one until just now. From the moment Ten had held out the injured kitten to Diana, he had treated her as though she were an old friend newly discovered. She hadn't even realized the…warmth…of his presence until it had been withdrawn.

Now she had an absurd impulse to reach out and touch Ten, to protest the appearance of the handsome, self-contained stranger who waited for her answer with cool attention, his whole attitude telling her that whether she chose to go forward or back, it made no personal difference to him.

"September Canyon," Diana said after a minute. Although she tried, her voice wasn't as controlled as his had been.

Ten took off the brake and resumed driving.

Eventually the silence, which Diana had welcomed before, began to eat at her nerves. She looked out the window but found herself glancing again and again toward Ten. She told herself that it was only his casual skill with the truck that fascinated her. She had done enough rough-country travel in the past to admire his expertise. And it was his expertise she was admiring, not the subtle flex and play of his muscles beneath the faded black work shirt he wore.

"You're a very good driver," she said.

Ten nodded indifferently.

Silence returned, lengthened, filling the cab until Diana rolled down the window just to hear the whistle of wind. She told herself the lack of conversation didn't bother her. After all, she had been the one to resist talk during the long hours since dawn. When Ten had pointed out something along the road or asked about her work, she had nodded or answered briefly and had no questions of her own to offer.

But now that she thought about it, she had a perfect right to ask a few businesslike questions of Ten and get a few businesslike answers.

"Will it distract you to talk?" she asked finally.

"No."

Brief and to the point. Very businesslike. Irritating, too. Silently Diana asked herself if her earlier, brief, impersonal answers had seemed cool and clipped to Ten.

"I didn't mean to be rude earlier," she said.

"You weren't."

Diana waited.

Ten said nothing more.

"How much farther is it to September Canyon?" she asked after a few minutes.

"An hour."

Diana looked up toward the mesa top where piñon and juniper and cedar grew, punctuated by pointed sprays of yucca plants. The clouds had become a solid mass whose bottom was a blue color so deep it was nearly black.

"Looks like rain," she said.

Ten nodded.

More silence, more bumps, more growling sounds from the laboring four-wheel-drive truck.

"Why is it called Picture Wash?" Diana asked in a combination of irritation and determination.

"There are pictographs on the cliffs."

Six whole words. Incredible.

"Anasazi?" she asked.

Ten shrugged.

"Did other Indians live here when the white man came?" Diana asked, knowing very well that they had.

Ten nodded.

"Mountain Utes?" she asked, again knowing the answer.

"Yes," he said as he swerved around a mass of shale that had extended a slippery tongue onto the roadway.

Diana hardly noticed the evasive maneuver. She was intent on drawing out the suddenly laconic Ten. Obviously that would require a question that couldn't be answered by yes, no or a shrug. Inspiration came.

"Why are you called Tennessee?"

"I was the oldest."

"I don't understand."

"Neither did Dad."

Diana gave up the word game and concentrated on the land.

The truck kicked and twitched and skidded around a series of steep, uphill curves, climbing up a mesa spur and onto the top. There was a long, reasonably straight run across the spur. Piñon and juniper whipped by, interspersed with a handful of big sage and other drought-adapted shrubs.

Abruptly there was an opening in the piñon and juniper. Though the ground looked no different, big sagebrush grew head-high and higher. Their silver-gray, twisting branches were thicker than a strong man's arm.

"Stop!" Diana said urgently.

The truck shuddered to a halt. Before the pebbles scattered by the tires finished rolling, Diana had her seat belt off and was jumping down from the cab.

"What's wrong?" Ten asked, climbing out of the truck.

Diana didn't answer. Watching the ground with intent, narrowed eyes, she quartered the stand of big sage, twisting and turning, zigzagging across the open areas in the manner of someone searching for something. She was so involved in her quest that she didn't seem to notice the scrapes and scratches the rough brush delivered to her unprotected arms.

Ten hesitated at the edge of the road, wondering if Diana was looking for a little privacy. It had been a long drive from the ranch, and there were no amenities such as gas stations or public restrooms along the way. Yet Diana seemed more interested in the open areas between clumps of big sage than in the thicker growths that would have offered more privacy.

Without warning Diana went down on her knees and began digging hurriedly in the rocky ground. Ten started toward her, ignoring the slap and drag of brush over his clothes. When he was within ten feet of her, she gave a cry of triumph and lifted a squarish rock in both hands. Dirt clung to the edges and dappled light fell across the stone's surface, camouflaging its oddly regular shape.

"Look!" she cried, holding up her prize to Ten.

He eased forward until he was close to her, ducked a branch that had been going after his eyes, straightened and looked.

"A stone," Ten said neutrally.

Diana didn't notice his lack of enthusiasm. She had enough for both of them and the truck, as well. Nor did she notice the dirty streaks left on her jeans when she rubbed the rock back and forth, cleaning the part of the stone that had been buried beneath the dirt. After a few moments she held the rock in a patch of sunlight coming through the open branches of the sage.

"Beautiful," she crooned, running her fingertips delicately along the stone, absorbing the subtle variations in the surface, marks that were the result of applied intelligence rather than random weathering. "Just...beautiful."

The throaty timbre of Diana's voice lured Ten as no stone could have. He sat on his heels next to her and looked closely at the rock that she was continuing to stroke as though it were alive.

The contours of the stone were too even, its edges too angular to be the result of chance. When the light touched the rock just right, tiny dimples could be seen, marks left by countless patient blows from a stone ax held in the hands of an Anasazi stone mason. Seeing those tangible marks of a long-dead man made the skin on Ten's skull tighten in a primal reflex that was far older than the civilized artifact Diana was cherishing in her hands.

Without realizing it, Ten stretched out his own hand,

feeling a need to confirm the stone's reality through touch. The rock had the texture of medium sandpaper. The dimples were shallow, more a vague pattern than true pockmarks. Cold from the ground on one end, sun warmed on the other, bearing the marks of man all over its surface, the stone was enduring testimony to a culture that was known only by its fragmentary ruins.

"How did you know this was here?" Ten asked.

"No juniper or piñon," Diana said absently as she turned the relic of the past over and over in her hands.

Ten glanced around. She was right. Despite the luxuriant growth of big sage on the ground, there were no junipers or piñons for fifty yards in any direction.

"They don't grow on ground that has been disturbed," Diana continued, measuring the area of the big sage with her eyes. "When you see a place like this, there's a very good chance that Anasazi ruins lie beneath the surface, covered by the debris of time and rain and wind."

Gray eyes narrowed while Ten silently reviewed his knowledge of the surrounding countryside.

"There are a lot of patches of big sage on Wind Mesa," he said after a minute. "My God, there must be hundreds of places like this on both sides of Picture Wash. That and the presence of year-round water is why the MacKenzies bought rights to this land more than a century ago."

"It was the water and the presence of game that attracted the Anasazi a thousand years ago. Human needs never change. All that changes is how we express those needs."

With the care of a mother returning a baby to its cradle, Diana replaced the rock in its hollow and smoothed dirt back in place.

"That's what is so exciting about the whole area of Wind

Mesa," she said as she worked. "For a long time we believed that the Durango River was the farthest northern reach of the Anasazi in Colorado. September Canyon proved that we were wrong."

"Not all that wrong," Ten said dryly. "You talk as though we're a hundred miles from the river. We're not. It just seems like it by the time you loop around mountains and canyons on these rough roads."

Absently, Diana nodded. When she stood up, she was quite close to Ten. She didn't even notice. Her attention was on the area defined by the silvery big sage, and she was looking at her surroundings with an almost tangible hunger.

"This could have been a field tended by a family and watered by spreader dams and ditches built by the Anasazi," she said. "Or it could have been a small community built near a source of good water and food. It could have been the Anasazi equivalent of a church or a convent or a men's club. It could have been so many things…and I doubt if we'll ever know exactly what."

"Why not?"

Diana turned and focused on Ten with blue eyes that were as dark and as deep as the storm condensing across the western sky.

"This is Rocking M land," Diana said simply. "Private land. Luke MacKenzie is already bearing the cost of excavating and protecting the September Canyon ruins. I doubt that he can afford to make a habit of that kind of generosity."

"Luke's partner is absorbing the cost, but you're right. Ranching doesn't pay worth a damn as it is. The cost of protecting the whole of Wind Mesa…" Ten lifted his Stetson and resettled it with a jerk. "We'd do it if we could, but we can't. It would bankrupt us."

The sad understanding in Diana's smile said more about regret and acceptance than any words could have.

"Even the government can't afford it," she agreed, rubbing her hands absently on her jeans. "County, state, federal, it doesn't matter which level of government you appeal to. There just isn't enough money. Even at Mesa Verde, which is designed to be a public showcase of the whole range of Anasazi culture, archaeologists have uncovered ruins, measured them, then backfilled them with dirt. It was the only way to protect them from wind, rain and pothunters."

Ten looked around the rugged mesa top and said quietly, "Maybe that's best. Whatever is beneath the earth has been buried for centuries. A few more centuries won't make any difference."

"Here, probably not," Diana said, gesturing to the big sage. "But on the cliffs or on the edges of the mesa, the ruins that aren't buried are disintegrating or being dismantled by pothunters. That's why the work in September Canyon is so important. What we don't learn from it now probably won't be available to learn later. The ruins will have been picked over, packed up and shipped out to private collections all over the world."

The passion and regret in Diana's voice riveted Ten. He was reaching out to touch her in silent comfort when he caught himself. A touch from a man she feared would hardly be a comfort.

"Don't sell this countryside short when it comes to protecting its own," Ten said. "The big sage may be a giveaway on Wind Mesa, but this is a damned inconvenient place to get to. There's only one road and half the time it's impassable. There's a horse trail through the mountains that drops down to September Mesa, but only a few Rocking M riders even know about it and no one has used it in years."

Slowly, almost unwillingly, Diana focused on Ten, sensing his desire to comfort her as clearly as the kitten had sensed its safety within Ten's hands.

"As for the scores of little canyons that might hold cliff ruins," Ten said, watching Diana, sensing the soft uncurling of her tightly held trust, "most of those canyons haven't seen a man since the Anasazi left. Any man. The Utes avoided the ruins as spirit places. Cows avoid the small canyons because the going is too rough, so cowhands don't go there, either. What's hidden stays hidden."

Ten's deep voice with its subtle velvet rasp swirled around Diana, holding her still even as it caressed her. She stared at the clear depths of his eyes and felt a curious mix of hunger and wariness, yearning and...familiarity.

"And if some of those ruins are never found, is that so bad?" Ten asked softly. He spoke slowly, watching Diana's eyes, trying to explain something he had never put into words. "Like the Anasazi, the ruins came from time and the land. It's only right that some of them return to their beginnings untouched by any but Anasazi hands."

A throaty muttering of thunder rode the freshening wind. The sound seeped into Diana's awareness, bringing with it a dizzying feeling of déjà vu; of overlapping realities; of time, like a deck of cards, being reshuffled, and the sound of that shuffling was muted thunder. Her breathing slowed and then stopped as an eerie certainty condensed within her: *she had known Ten before, had stood on a mesa top with him before, had walked with him through piñon and sun and silence, had slept next to his warmth while lightning and rain renewed the land....*

The feeling passed, leaving Diana shaken, disoriented, staring at a man who should have been a stranger and was not. Thunder came again, closer, insistent. She took a deep breath, infusing herself with the elemental, unforgettable pungency of sage and piñon, juniper and storm. And time. That most of all. The scent of time and a storm coming down.

Closing her eyes, Diana breathed deeply, filling herself with the storm wind, feeling it touch parts of her that had been curled tightly shut for too many years. The sensation of freedom and vulnerability that followed was frightening and exhilarating at the same time, like swimming nude in a midnight lake.

"Storm coming," Ten said, looking away from Diana because if he watched her drink the wind any longer he wouldn't be able to stop himself from touching her. "If we're going to cross Picture Wash, we have to hurry. Unless you've changed your mind?"

Diana's eyes opened. She saw a powerful man standing motionless, silhouetted against sunlight and thunderheads, his head turned away from her. Then he looked back at her, and his eyes were like cut crystal against the darkness of his face.

"Diana?"

The sound of her name on Ten's lips made sensations glitter through her body from breastbone to knees.

"Yes," she said, trying to sound businesslike and failing. "I'm coming."

CHAPTER SIX

THERE WAS SOME WATER RUNNING in Picture Wash, but the big ranch truck crossed without difficulty. Splash marks on the other side of the ford told Ten that he wasn't the only person who had driven toward September Canyon today. Ten glanced quickly around but saw nothing. They had passed no one the entire length of the one-lane dirt road, which meant that the other vehicle was still in front of them.

Frowning, Ten turned right and drove along the edge of the broad wash. There was no real road to follow, simply a suggestion of tire tracks where other vehicles had gone before. Tributary canyons opened up on the left of the wash, and more were visible across the thin ribbon of water, but Ten made no attempt to explore those openings. After three miles he turned left into the mouth of a side canyon.

Diana looked at him questioningly.

"September Canyon," Ten said. "The mesa it's eaten out

of didn't really have a name, but we've started calling it September Mesa since we've been working on the site. Wind
Mesa is behind us now, across the wash."

"What's upstream?"

"More canyons. Smaller. If you follow the wash upstream
long enough, it finally narrows into a crack and disappears
against a wall of stone, which is the body of the mesa itself.
Almost all the canyons are blind. Only one or two have an
outlet on top of the mesa. Other than that, the canyons are
a maze. Even with a compass, it's hard not to get lost."

Diana turned around, trying to orient herself. "Where is
the Rocking M?"

Ten gestured with his head because he needed both hands
for the wheel. "North and east, on top of the big mesa."

"It is? I thought the ranch was on the edge of a broad valley."

He smiled slightly. "So do most people who come on the
Rocking M from the north. You don't know the valley is
really a mesa until you drive off the edge. The mountains
confuse you. All of the Colorado Plateau is like that."

Diana reached into her back jeans pocket, pulled out a
United States Geological Survey map and began searching for
the vague line that represented the ranch road they were on.
The bouncing of the truck made map reading impossible.

"Perspective is a funny thing," Ten said, glancing at the
map for an instant. "Coming in from the south and east, you
see the wall of the mesa, the cliffs and gorges and canyons.
That's where the explorers were when they started naming
things—at the bottom looking up. You can't see the Fire
Mountains from that angle, and everything looks dark and
jumbled at a distance, so the whole area was once called
Black Plateau or Fire Mountain Plateau, depending on which
old-timer you talk to."

Diana folded up the map and put it away.

"On the other hand," Ten continued, "if you're coming in from the mountain end of the territory, you see a mesa top as more of a broad valley, and you name it accordingly."

"Is that what happened on the Rocking M?"

Ten nodded. "Case MacKenzie started out with a ranch at the base of what became known as MacKenzie Ridge, which is a foothill of the Fire Mountains. From his perspective, the mesa top is a broad, winding valley. But history named the hunk of land for a hundred miles in all directions Black Plateau, even though it's more like a mesa than a plateau. Then you add a hundred years of Spanish and American cowboys translating Indian names and adding their own to the mix, and you have a mapmaker's nightmare."

"You also have a lot of lost tourists."

The left corner of Ten's mouth lifted slightly. "Just remember that September Mesa and Wind Mesa and all the nameless mesas are nothing but narrow fingers stretching out from the huge hand known as Black Plateau or MacKenzie Valley, depending on which direction your mapmaker came from."

"I'm beginning to understand why men invented satellite photos. It's the only way to see how the pieces all fit together."

Ten shot Diana an amused, approving glance, but only for an instant. The truck, moving at barely five miles an hour, bumped and thumped over the rock-strewn, narrowing canyon bottom. To Diana's eyes there was nothing to distinguish the cliff-rimmed canyon they had entered from the many other tributary canyons that emptied into Picture Wash. The mouth of September Canyon was perhaps eighty yards across, marked by nothing but a faint suggestion of tire tracks in the sand. The cliffs were of a vaguely ruddy, vaguely gold sandstone that overlay narrower beds of shale.

The shale crumbled readily, forming steep, slippery talus slopes at the base of the sandstone cliffs.

Scattered on the surface of the gray-brown shale debris were huge, erratic piles of sandstone rubble that were formed when the shale crumbled and washed away faster than the more durable cliffs above, leaving the sandstone cliffs without support at their base. Then great sheets of sandstone peeled away from the overhanging cliffs and fell to the earth below, shattering into rubble and leaving behind arches and alcoves and deeper overhangs—and, sometimes, filling pre-existing alcoves.

In many cases the shale had been eroded by the seeping of groundwater between layers of sandstone and shale. When the water eventually reached the edge of a cliff or a ravine, it became a spring, a source of clean, year-round water for the people who eventually sought shelter in the arching over-hangs that the springs had helped to create. Without the water there would have been no cliff-hanging alcoves for men to take shelter within, no easily defended villages set into sheer stone. Without the very special circumstances of sand-stone, shale and water, the Anasazi civilization would have developed very differently, if it developed at all.

That interlocking of Anasazi and the land had always fas-cinated Diana. The fact that their cliff houses were found in some of the most remote, starkly beautiful landscapes in America simply added to her fascination.

"Does the Rocking M run cattle here?" Diana asked.

"Not for several years."

"Then how were the ruins discovered?"

"Carla was returning a potsherd that Luke had found years ago in the mouth of September Canyon and given to her. She drove out from Boulder alone and spent several hours walking the canyon floor. There had been a storm recently and a tree had fallen. She came around a bend and there the ruins were."

"That must have been incredible," Diana said, her voice throaty with longing.

"I doubt that Carla was in a mood to appreciate it. She had come here to say goodbye to everything she had ever wanted—the land, the ranch, and most of all the man."

"Luke?"

Ten nodded.

"What changed her mind?"

"Luke. He finally got it through his hard head that Carla was the one woman in a million who could live on an isolated ranch and not go sour."

Diana's mouth turned down in a sad curve. "I was ranch-raised. It's not for everyone, man or woman."

"You didn't like it?"

"I loved it. No matter how bad things at home got, the land was always waiting, always beautiful, always there. I could walk away from the buildings and the land would…" Her voice shivered into silence as she realized what she had almost revealed.

"Heal you?" Ten suggested softly.

Diana's eyes closed and a tiny shudder went through her. Ten was too perceptive. He saw things with danger-ous clarity.

"The land was here long before a primate climbed down out of a tree and put a kink in his back trying to see over the grass," Ten said matter-of-factly. "The land will be here long after we're gone. That frightens some people because it makes them feel small and worthless. But some people are made whole by touching something that's bigger than they are, something enduring, something that lives on a different time scale than man."

The words slid past Diana's defenses, making her realize that Ten was one of those who had come to the land to be healed.

"What hurt you?" she asked before she could stop herself.

The lines of Ten's face shifted, reminding Diana of the cold, deadly fighter who had come over the corral fence and flattened a larger, whip-wielding opponent in a matter of seconds.

"I'm sorry," Diana said quickly. "I had no right to ask."

Ten nodded curtly, either agreeing with her or accepting her apology, she wasn't certain which.

It was silent in the truck for a few moments before Ten said, "We're coming up on the base camp. It's beneath that big overhang on the left."

Diana heard more than the words; she heard what wasn't said, as well. Gone was the subtle emotion that had made Ten's voice like black velvet when he talked about the land. His tone was neither reserved nor outgoing, simply neutral. Polite.

Telling herself that Ten's withdrawal didn't matter, Diana looked beyond his handsome, unyielding profile to the smooth cliff wall rising above scattered piñons. The sandstone gleamed against the thunderheads that had consumed the sky. Something bright flickered at the edge of her vision. A few seconds later thunder pealed through the narrow canyon, shaking the ground. Spectral light flickered and danced again, and again thunder reverberated between stone walls.

Diana closed her eyes and breathed in deeply, savoring the pungent, suddenly cool wind. Soon it would begin to rain. She could feel it. She could smell it in the air, the unique blend of heat and dust rising up from the ground and countless water drops reaching down to caress the dry land.

Thunder belled again and then again. A gust of wind

came through the open truck window, pouring over Diana. She laughed softly, wishing she were alone so that she could hold out her arms and embrace the wild summer storm.

The subdued music of Diana's laughter drew Ten's attention. He looked at her for only an instant, but it was enough. He knew he would never forget the picture she made with her head thrown back and her hair tousled as though by a lover's hands, her cheeks flushed with excitement and her lips parted as she gave herself to the storm wind.

The persistent male curiosity Ten had felt at his first sight of Diana retreating from the skirmish at the corral became a torrent of desire pouring through him, hardening him with a speed he hadn't known since he was a teenager. Cursing silently, he forced his attention away from his quickened body and onto the demands of the terrain. The last quarter of a mile to the ruins was tricky, because most of it was over greasy shale slopes studded with house-size boulders of sandstone that had fallen from the thick, cliff-forming layer of rock. The truck bucked and tires spun in protest at the slippery going as the vehicle groaned up the final hill.

"Wouldn't it have been better to walk from the base camp?" Diana asked, bracing herself against the dashboard.

"I was in a hurry."

"Why?" she asked, looking toward him as the truck bucked over the ridge and stopped abruptly.

"That's why."

The flat, predatory quality of Ten's voice froze Diana's breath. Slowly she followed his glance.

A dirty Range Rover was parked among the rubble at the base of the cliff. Beyond the vehicle, lightweight aluminum ladders extended up the twenty feet of massive sandstone that separated the ruins from the rubble below.

Ten reached over, unlocked the gun rack that hung over the rear window and chose the shotgun, leaving the rifle in place. He checked the shotgun's load, racked a shell into the chamber, then got out of the truck and closed the door before he turned to look at Diana through the open window.

"Stay here."

Thunder belled harshly, followed by a cannonade of rain sweeping in shining veils over the ground. Holding the shotgun muzzle down, Ten ignored the rain that quickly soaked through his clothing. There was a muffled shout from the ruins. He ignored that, too. The Range Rover was unlocked. He went through the vehicle quickly, finding and unloading a pistol and a rifle. A quick motion of his wrist sent bullets arcing out into the rain. The weapons he put way in the back of the Rover, next to a big carton. With one eye on the pothunters who were scrambling down the rain-slick ladders, Ten ripped open the box.

It was filled with Anasazi pots, their bold geometries and corrugated finish unmistakable in the watery light. Bits of turquoise and shell gleamed in the bottom of one bowl. Ten lifted the carton out, set it on the ground and returned to the interior of the Rover. It stank of cigarette smoke and gasoline that was evaporating from a five-gallon container with a faulty seal.

As the pothunters hit the bottom of the ladder and started running toward him, Ten opened the container and pushed it over inside the car. The stench of raw gas swirled up, overpowering.

"Hey!" hollered the first man. "Get the hell out of there! That car's private property!"

The Rover was between Ten and the pothunters. When he stepped out around the rear of the Rover, the men could see the shotgun held with professional ease in Ten's hands, muzzle slanted down, neither pointing toward nor away from the men.

The first man slowed his reckless pace to a wary walk. He was in his mid-twenties and carried himself as though he had spent time in the military. He was big, hard-shouldered, used to intimidating people with his sheer size.

"You're trespassing on Rocking M land," Ten said.

"I didn't see any signs."

The line of Ten's mouth lifted in a sardonic curl. "Too bad. Get in your Rover and drive out of here."

The other two men caught up with the first just as he shouted, "You'll be hearing from me, cowboy. You're threatening private citizens. We were just traveling around in the backcountry and made a wrong turn somewhere. It could have happened to anyone—and that's what I'll tell the sheriff when I file a complaint!"

"The only wrong turn you made was in thinking all you'd find out here were pots and a few grad students even younger than you."

"Think you're a big man with that shotgun, don't you?"

"You sure didn't learn much in the marines before they threw you out."

"How did you know I was…" The man's voice faded even as angry color rose in his face. He jerked his head toward the Rover. The other two men reached for the door handles.

Ten watched with an air of shuttered expectancy. He wasn't disappointed. No sooner did the two men open the Rover's doors than there were simultaneous shouts of outrage.

"He poured gas all over the damn car!"

"Milt, the pots are gone!"

Then one of the men noticed the guns. He slammed the door and said in disgust, "Pack it in, Milt. He got to the guns."

Milt's face flattened into mean lines as he measured the cowboy standing at ease in front of him.

"You heard them," Ten said. "Pack it in." He raised his voice slightly and said to the other two men, "Get in the Rover and shut the doors."

The younger man colored with frustration and anger when his two companions obediently climbed into the Rover, slamming both doors hard behind them.

"Those are my pots," Milt said angrily. "If they're not in the Rover when I leave, I'll sue your smart ass for theft."

"Go home, kid. School's out."

As Ten spoke, he casually broke open the shotgun and removed the shell from the firing chamber.

Milt was as foolish as Ten had hoped. The younger man began weaving and feinting, his body held in the stance of someone who had been trained in unarmed combat.

Ten closed the shotgun with a fast snap of his wrist and set the weapon on the Rover's hood before he turned and walked toward the younger man. As though Ten's calm approach unnerved Milt, he attacked. Ten deflected the charge with a deceptively casual motion of his shoulders that sent Milt staggering off balance over the slippery rubble. He went to his hands and knees, then scrambled to his feet and came after Ten again.

One of the Rover's doors opened just behind Ten. He spun around and lashed out with his booted foot, connecting with metal. There was a startled curse, a cry of pain and the sound of the door slamming closed beneath Ten's foot. Before the echo could return from the stone walls, Ten had turned around again.

Milt was more careful in his tactics this time, but the result was still the same. When he lunged for Ten, Milt got nothing but a handful of mud. It happened again, then a fourth time, and each time Milt ended up on his hands and knees.

"Hurry up, kid," Ten said, watching Milt push to his feet for the fifth time. "I'm getting tired of standing around in the rain waiting for you to get smart."

With an inarticulate cry of rage, Milt came to his feet, clawing beneath his windbreaker with his right hand, tearing a hunting knife free of its sheath. This time when Milt charged, Ten made a single swift movement that sent the other man head over heels to land hard and flat on his back, gasping for air. Ten's boot descended on Milt's right wrist. Bending over, Ten took the knife from Milt's hand, tested the edge of the blade and made a disdainful sound.

"You'd be lucky to cut butter with this, boy."

Milt's glazed eyes focused on Ten, who was throwing the knife from hand to hand, flipping it end over end, testing the knife's balance with the expertise of someone thoroughly accustomed to using a knife as a weapon.

"Other than the edge, it's a nice knife," Ten said after a few moments. "Really fine."

There was a brief blur of movement followed by the sound of steel grating through earth. Buried half the length of its blade, the knife gleamed only inches from Milt's shocked face. Ten removed his boot from Milt's wrist.

"Pull the knife out and put it back in your belt."

Milt reached slowly for the knife. For an instant as his fingers closed around the hilt, he thought of throwing the knife at the smaller, rain-soaked man who had humiliated him with such offhanded ease.

Watching with the clear-eyed patience of a predator, Ten waited to see how smart Milt was.

Slowly, reluctantly, Milt returned the knife to its sheath.

"You're learning, kid. Too bad. I was looking forward to watching you eat that knife." Ten bent down and dragged the younger man to his feet with a single powerful motion. "Now here's something else for you to learn. I've been hearing things about a busted-out gyrene pothunter who gets his kicks slapping around teachers whose only crime is wanting to camp in a national park."

For the first time since the fight had started, Milt was close enough to see Ten's eyes beneath the dripping brim of his cowboy hat. The younger man's face paled visibly.

"Hearing things like that makes me real impatient," Ten said matter-of-factly. "When I get impatient, I get clumsy, and when I get clumsy, I break things. My friends are the same way, and I've got friends all over the Four Corners. So if you know any other pothunting cowards, pass the word. Starting now, my friends and I will be damned clumsy. Understand?"

Slowly Milt nodded.

Ten opened his hands and stepped back, his body both relaxed and perfectly balanced. "You're going to start thinking about this, and drinking, and pretty soon you'll be sure you can take me. So think on this. Next time you come after me, I'll strip you, pin a diaper on you, and walk you through town wearing a pink bonnet. Know something else? You won't have a mark on you, but you'll be marching double time just the same." Ten jerked his head toward the Rover. "Make sure I don't hear about you again, kid. I purely despise bullies."

Milt backed away from Ten and reached for the Rover's front door with more eagerness than grace. Ten watched. He was about to congratulate the two men in the Rover on their good sense in staying out of his way when he saw that the reason they had sidelined themselves wasn't good sense.

Diana had stepped down from the truck and was standing in the rain, sighting down a rifle she had braced across the hood of the truck.

CHAPTER SEVEN

WITH OUTWARD CALM DIANA watched the Range Rover slither and slide down the shale, retreating from September Canyon as quickly as the rain and rough terrain allowed.

"You can put it away now. They won't be back."

Ten's voice made Diana realize that she was still crouched over the rifle, sighting down its blue-steel barrel, her hands holding the weapon too tightly. She forced herself to take a deep breath and stand upright.

"May I?" Ten asked, holding out a hand for the rifle.

Diana gave the rifle to him and said faintly, "It will need cleaning. The rain is very...wet."

Ten didn't smile, simply nodded his head in agreement. "I'll take care of it."

"Thank you. It's been years since I cleaned a rifle. I've probably forgotten how."

"You sure didn't forget how to use one," Ten said as he

checked the rifle over with a few swift movements. He noted approvingly that there was a round in the chamber. He removed the bullet and pocketed it. "Thanks."

Diana looked at him and blinked, trying to focus her thoughts.

"For aiming the rifle at them rather than at me," Ten explained, smiling slightly. "It's nice to know you think I'm one of the good guys."

"I—they—you didn't need me," she said, rubbing her hands together.

"Three against one? I needed all the help I could get."

Diana shook her head. "You could have made veal cutlets out of that pothunter before his friends could have taken a single step to stop you. Why didn't you?"

"Never did like veal cutlets," Ten said matter-of-factly, opening the truck door. "Get in, honey. It's wet out here."

"I'm serious," she said, climbing up into the dry cab. "Why did you hold back? You certainly didn't with Baker…did you?"

Ten went around the truck and got in behind the wheel. He sensed Diana's intent, watchful, rather wary eyes. Wondering if Diana were still afraid of him, Ten watched her from the corner of his eye as he began wiping down the rifle and shotgun. Despite the vague trembling of her hands and the paleness of her skin, he began to realize that she wasn't afraid of him; she was simply caught in the backlash of the adrenaline storm that had come from her brush with pothunters.

"Why?" Diana persisted, rubbing her arms as though she were cold.

"Baker is a brute who only understands brute force," Ten said finally. "If I had pulled my punches with him, he would have been back for more. That kid Milt was different. He's a swaggering bully. A coward. So I showed him what a candy ass he really is when it comes to fighting. He'll be a long time forgetting."

"Will he be back?"

"Doubt it." Ten turned around and locked the weapons back into the rack. "But if he does come back, he better pray Nevada isn't on guard."

"Nevada?"

"My kid brother. He would have gutted Milt and never looked back. Hard man, Nevada."

"And you aren't?"

Turning, looking at Diana over his shoulder, Ten smiled slowly. "Honey, haven't you figured it out yet? I'm so tenderhearted a butterfly can walk roughshod all over me."

It was the second time in as many minutes that Ten had called Diana "honey." She knew she should object to the implied intimacy. At the very least she shouldn't encourage him by laughing at the ludicrous image of a butterfly stomping all over Ten's muscular body. So she tried very hard not to laugh, failed, and finally gave into the need, knowing that it was a release for all the emotions seething just beneath her control.

Ten listened, sensing the complex currents of Diana's emotions. He reached for the door before he looked over at her and nodded once, as though agreeing with himself.

"You'll do, Diana Saxton. You'll do just fine."

"For what?" she asked, startled.

"For whatever you want. You've got guts, lady. You'd go to war over a carton of Anasazi artifacts. You stand up for what you believe in. That's too damned rare these days."

Ten was out of the truck and closing the door behind him

before Diana could put into words her first thought: she hadn't stood in the rain with an unfamiliar rifle in her hands to save a few artifacts from pothunters. It had been Ten she was worried about, one man against three.

I didn't need to worry. Ten is a one-man army. Cash was right. Someone taught Ten to play hardball. I wonder who, and where, and what it cost....

The truck's door opened. Ten set the closed carton of artifacts on the seat next to Diana, then swung into the cab with a lithe motion. His masculine grace fascinated her, as did the fact that his rain-soaked shirt clung to every ridge and swell of muscle, emphasizing the width of his shoulders and the strength of his back. If he had wanted to, he could have overpowered her with terrible ease, for he was far stronger than Steve had been; and in the end Steve had been too strong for her.

Grimly Diana turned her thoughts away from a past that was beyond her ability to change or forget. She could only accept what had happened and renew her vow that she would never again put herself in a position where a man thought he had the right to take from her what she was unwilling to give.

"Don't worry," Ten said.

"What?" Diana gave him a startled look, wondering if he had read her mind.

"The artifacts are fine. Milt was an amateur when it came to fighting, but he knew how to pack pots. Nothing was lost."

"Just the history."

His hand on the key, Ten turned to look at Diana, not understanding what she meant.

"The real value of the artifacts for an archaeologist comes from seeing how they relate to each other in situ," she explained. "Unless these artifacts were photographed where they were found, they don't have much to tell us now."

"To a scholar, maybe. But to me, just seeing the artifacts, seeing their shapes and designs, knowing they were made by a people and a culture that lived and died and will never be born again…" Ten shrugged. "I'd go to war to save a piece of that. Hell, I have more than once."

Again, Ten had surprised Diana. She hadn't expected a nonprofessional to understand the intellectual and emotional fascination of fragments from the past. His response threw her off balance, leaving her teetering between her ingrained fear of men and her equally deep desire to be close to the contradictory, complex man called Tennessee Blackthorn.

Ten eased the big truck down the slippery shoulder of shale and headed back for the big overhang that served as a base camp for the dig. By the time they had unloaded their gear, set up sleeping bags at the opposite ends of the overhang's broad base and changed into dry clothes behind the canvas privacy screen that had been erected for just such emergencies, the rain was becoming less a torrent.

Neither Diana nor Ten noticed the improving weather at first. They had gravitated toward the sherd-sorting area that the graduate students had set up. Numbered cartons held remnants of pottery that had been taken from specific areas of the site. The sherds themselves were also numbered according to the place where they had been unearthed. Whoever had the time or the desire was invited to try piecing together the three-dimensional puzzles before they were removed to the old ranch house.

Ten showed a marked flair for resurrecting whole artifacts from scattered, broken fragments. In fact, more than once Diana was astonished at the ease with which he reached into one carton, then another, and came out with interlocking sherds. There was something uncanny about how pieces of history became whole in his hands. His concentration on the task made casual conversation unnecessary, which relieved Diana. Soon she was sorting sherds, trying out pieces together, bending over Ten to reach into cartons, muttering phrases about gray ware with three black lines and an acute angle versus corrugated ware with a curve and a bite out of one side. Ten answered with similar phrases, handing her whatever he had that matched her description of missing sherds.

After the first half hour Diana forgot that she was alone with a man in an isolated canyon. She forgot to be afraid that something she might say or do would trigger in Ten the certainty that she wanted him sexually despite whatever objections she might make to his advances. For the first time in years she enjoyed the company of a man as a person, another adult with whom she could be at ease.

When the rain finally stopped completely, Diana stood, stretched cramped leg muscles and went to the edge of the overhang to look out across the newly washed land. Although no ruins were visible from the overhang itself, excitement simmered suddenly in her blood. Hundreds of years ago the Anasazi had looked out on the same land, smelled the same scent of wet earth and piñon, seen the glittering beauty of sunlight captured in a billion drops of water clinging to needles and boughs and the sheer face of the cliff itself. For this instant she and the Anasazi were one.

That was what she wanted to capture in her illustrations—the continuity of life, of human experience, a continuity that existed through time regardless of the outward diversity of human cultures.

"I'm going to the site," Diana said, picking up her backpack.

Ten looked up from the potsherds he was assembling. "I'll be along as soon as I get these numbered. Don't go up those ladders until they're dry. And stick to the part of the ruins that has a grid. Some of that rubble isn't stable, and some of the walls are worse."

"Don't worry. I'm not exploring anything alone. Too many of those ruins are traps waiting to be sprung. With the Anasazi, you never know when the ground is a ceiling covering a sunken kiva. I'll stay on the well-beaten paths until there are more people on site."

A long look assured Ten that Diana meant what she said. He nodded. "Thanks."

"For what?" she asked.

"Not getting your back up at my suggestions."

"I have nothing against common sense. Besides, you're the ramrod on this site. If I don't like your, er, 'suggestions,' that's my hard luck, right? You'll enforce your orders any way you have to."

Ten thought of putting it less bluntly, then shrugged. Diana was right, and it would save a lot of grief if she knew it.

"That's my job."

"I'll remember it."

What Diana said was the simple truth. She would remember. The thought of going against Ten's *suggestions* was frankly intimidating. He had the power to enforce his will and she knew it as well as he did. Better. She had been taught by her father and her fiancé just how little a woman's protests mattered to men whose physical superiority was a fact of life.

"If you hear the truck's horn beep three times, or three shots from the rifle," Ten said, "it means come back here on the double."

Diana nodded, checked her watch and said, "I'll be back before sundown."

"Damn straight you will be." He held two pieces of pottery up against the sunlight streaming into the overhang, frowned and set one piece aside before he said, "Only a fool or a pothunter would go feeling around in the ruins after dark."

Diana didn't bother to answer. Ten wasn't really listening anyway. He was holding another piece of pottery against the sunlight, visually comparing edges. They must have fit, because he grunted and wrote on the inside of both pieces. After they were cleaned they would be glued together, but the equipment for that operation was back at the old ranch house.

Beyond the overhang the land was damp and glistening from the recent rain. The short-lived waterfalls that had made lacy veils over the cliff faces were already diminishing to silver tendrils. Before she left the overhang, Diana glanced back at Ten, only to find him engrossed in his three-dimensional puzzle. She should have been relieved at the silent evidence that she didn't have to worry about fielding any unwanted advances from Ten. Quite obviously she wasn't the focus of his masculine attention.

But Diana wasn't relieved. She was a bit irked that he found it so easy to ignore her.

The realization disconcerted her, so she shoved the thought aside and concentrated on the increasingly rugged terrain as she began to climb from September Canyon's floor up to the base of the steep cliffs, following whatever truck tracks the rain hadn't washed away.

Summer thunder muttered through September Canyon, followed by a gust of rain-scented wind that made piñons moan. From the vantage point where the Rover had been parked, the ruins beckoned. Partial walls were scalloped raggedly by time and falling masonry. Some of the walls were barely ankle-high, others reached nearly twenty-five feet in height, broken only by the protruding cedar beams that had once supported floors. Cedar that was still protected by stone remained strong and hard. Exposed beams weathered with the excruciating slowness of rock itself.

Using a trick that an old archaeologist had taught her, Diana let her eyes become unfocused while she was looking at the ruins. Details blurred and faded, leaving only larger relationships visible, weights and masses, symmetry and balance, subtle uses of force and counterforce that had to be conceived in the human mind before they were built because they did not occur in nature. The multistoried wall with its T-shaped doors no longer looked like a chimney with bricks fallen out, nor did the roofless kivas look like too-wide wells. The relationship of roof to floor to ceiling, the geometries of shared-wall apartment living, became clearer to unfocused modern eyes.

The archaeologist who first examined September Canyon estimated that the canyon's alcove had held between nineteen and twenty-six rooms, including the ubiquitous circular kivas. The height of the building varied from less than four feet to three stories, depending on the height of the overhang itself.

The kivas were rather like basements set off from the larger grouping of rooms. The kivas' flat roofs were actually the floor of the town meeting area where children played and women ground corn, where dogs barked and chased foolish turkeys. The balcony of a third-story room was the ceiling of an adjacent two-story apartment. Cedar ladders reached to cistlike granaries built into lateral cracks too small to accommodate even a tiny room. And the Anasazi used rooms so tiny they were unthinkable to modern people, even taking into account the Anasazi's smaller stature.

Diana opened the outer pocket of her backpack and pulled out a lightweight, powerful pair of binoculars. As always, the patience of the Anasazi stonemasons fascinated her. Lacking metal of any kind, they shaped stone by using stone itself. Hand axes weighing several pounds were used to hammer rough squares or rectangles from shapeless slabs of rock. Then the imagined geometry was carefully tap-tap-tapped onto the rough block, thousands upon thousands of strokes, stone pecking at stone until the rock was of the proper shape and size.

The alcove's left side ended in sheer rock wall. A crack angled up the face of the cliff. At no point was the crack wider than a few inches, yet Diana could see places where natural foot- or handholds had been added. Every Anasazi who went up on the mesa to tend crops had to climb up the cliff with no more help than they could get out of the crack. The thought of making such a climb herself didn't appeal. The thought of children or old people making the climb in all kinds of weather was appalling, as was the thought of toddlers playing along the alcove's sheer drop.

Inevitably, people must have slipped and fallen. Even for an alcove that had a southern exposure protected from all but the worst storms, the kind of daily risking of life and limb represented by that trail seemed a terrible price to pay.

Diana lowered the glasses, looked at the ruins with her unaided eyes and frowned. The angle wasn't quite right for what she wanted to accomplish. Farther up the canyon, where the rubble slopes rose to the point that an agile climber could reach the ruins without a ladder, the angle would be no better. What she needed was a good spot from which to sketch an overview of the countryside with an inset detailing the structure and placement of the ruins themselves. The surrounding country could be sketched almost anytime. The ruins, however, were best sketched in slanting, late-afternoon light, when all the irregularities and angles of masonry leaped into high relief. That "sweet light" was rapidly developing as the day advanced.

With measuring eyes, Diana scanned her surroundings before she decided to sketch from the opposite side of the canyon. She shrugged her backpack into a more comfortable position and set off. The rains had been light enough that September Creek was a ribbon she could jump over without much danger of getting her feet wet. She worked her way up the canyon until she was half a mile above the ruins on the opposite side. Only then did she climb up the talus slope at the base of the canyon's stone walls.

When Diana could climb no higher without encountering solid rock, she began scrambling parallel to the base of the cliff that formed the canyon wall. Every few minutes she paused to look at the ruins across the canyon, checking the changing angles until she found one she liked. Her strategy meant a hard scramble across the debris slope at the base of the canyon's wall, but she had made similar scrambles at other sites in order to find just the right place to sit and sketch.

Finally Diana stopped at the top of a particularly steep scramble where a section of the sandstone cliff had sloughed away, burying everything beneath in chunks of stone as big as a truck. She wiped her forehead, checked the angle of the ruins and sighed.

"Close, but not good enough." She looked at the debris slope ahead, then at the ruins again. "Just a bit farther. I hope."

Climbing carefully, scrambling much of the time, her hands and clothes redolent of the evergreens she had grabbed to pull herself along the steepest parts, Diana moved along the cliff base. Suddenly she saw a curving something on the ground that was the wrong color and shape to be a stone. She walked eagerly forward, bending to pick up the potsherd, which glowed an unusual red in the slanting sunlight. No sooner had her fingers curled around the sherd than the ground gave way beneath her feet, sending her down in a torrent of dirt and stone.

Clutching at air, screaming, she plunged into darkness, and the name she screamed was Ten's.

CHAPTER EIGHT

TEN WAS RUNNING BEFORE Diana's scream ended abruptly, leaving silence and echoes in its wake. He raced away from the ruins at full speed, not needing to follow Diana's tracks in order to find her. In the first instant of her scream he had seen her red windbreaker vividly against the creamy wall of stone on the opposite side of the canyon.

And then the red had vanished.

"Diana! *Diana!*"

No one answered Ten's shout. He saved his breath for running across the canyon bottom and scrambling up the steep slope. As soon as he saw the black shadow of the new hole in the ground he realized what had happened. Diana had stepped onto the concealed roof of a kiva and it had given way beneath her weight. Some of the kivas were only a few feet deep. Others were deeper than a man was tall. He was afraid that Diana had found one of the deep ones.

Moving slowly, ready to throw himself aside at the first hint of uncertain footing, Ten crept close to the hole that had appeared in the rubble slope.

"Diana, can you hear me?"

A sound that might have been his name came from the hole.

"Don't move," he said. "If you've hurt your spine, you could make it worse by thrashing around. I'll get to you as soon as I can."

This time Ten was certain that the sound Diana made was his name.

"Just lie still and close your eyes in case I knock some more dirt loose."

On his stomach, Ten inched closer to the hole. At the far side he saw stubs of the cedar poles that had once supported a segment of the ceiling. In front of him was an open slot where Diana had gone through about a third of the way across the circular ceiling. Parallel, intact cedar poles crossed the opening Diana had accidentally made.

Ten pulled himself to the edge of the hole and peered over. Eight feet down Diana lay half-buried in rubble, surrounded by a circle of carefully fitted masonry wall.

"I'm coming down now. Just lie still."

Ten tested the cedar poles as best he could. They held. Bracing himself between two poles, praying that the tough cedar would hold under his weight, he slipped through the ceiling and landed lightly on his feet next to Diana. Instinctively she tried to sit up.

"Don't move!"

"Can't—breathe."

The ragged gasps told Ten that she was breathing more effectively than she knew.

"It's all right. You had the wind knocked out by the fall,

but you're getting it back now. Does any place in particular hurt?"

"No—"

Ten went down on his knees next to Diana's head. Her eyes went wide and she dragged raggedly at air when he reached for her.

"Easy now, honey," he murmured. "I've got to check you for injuries. Just lie still. I won't hurt you. Be still now. It's all right."

Dazed, helpless, Diana fought her fear and held on to the black velvet of Ten's voice, remembering the moments when he had soothed the panicked horse and held the injured kitten so gently. It was the same now, hands both strong and gentle probing her scalp, her neck, her shoulders, his voice soothing, directing, explaining; and all the while debris was being pushed away, revealing more of her body to Ten's thorough touch, his hands moving over her with an intimacy that she had never willingly allowed any man. All that kept her from panicking was the realization that his hands were as impersonal as they were careful.

"I can't feel anything broken and you didn't flinch anywhere when I touched you," Ten said finally. "Any numb spots?"

"No—I felt—" Diana sucked in air as much from the emotional shock of being touched as from the force of her recent fall. "Everywhere—you touched—I felt."

"Good. Wiggle your fingers and toes for me."

Diana did.

"Hurt?"

"No."

"I'm going to check your neck again. If it hurts, even a little, you tell me quick."

Long fingers eased once more around Diana's neck,

working their way through her hair, taking the weight of her head so slowly that she hardly realized when she was no longer supporting it herself.

"Hurt?"

"N-no."

Ten's fingers spread, surrounding the back of her head, and his thumbs glided gently over the line of her jaw. Diana's breath came in and stayed, trapped by the sensations shivering through her. So slowly that she realized it only after the fact, Ten began to turn her head to the right.

"Hurt?"

She tried to speak, couldn't, and shook her head instead. His smile flashed for an instant in the gloom.

"If shaking your head didn't hurt, you're okay. Let's see how you do sitting up. We'll take it slow. If your back hurts at any time, tell me. Ready?"

Diana didn't need Ten's assistance to sit up, but she got it anyway. His left arm was a hard, warm, resilient bar supporting her shoulders and his right arm rested across her chest, preventing her from pitching forward if she fainted, which she nearly did at the pressure of his forearm across her suddenly sensitive breasts.

"I'm fine," Diana said in a breathless rush.

"So far so good," agreed Ten. "Dizzy?"

She was, but it had nothing to do with her recent fall and everything to do with the powerful man kneeling next to her in the shadows of an ancient kiva, his arms supporting her, his face so close to hers that she tasted his very breath.

"I'm not—dizzy."

"Good. We'll just sit here for a minute and make sure."

While Ten studied the broken ceiling overhead, Diana studied him. For the first time she was struck by how truly handsome he was with his black, slightly curling hair, broad forehead, widely spaced gray eyes, thick lashes, straight nose, high cheekbones and a beard shadow that heightened the intensely male line of his jaw.

It was more than the regularity of Ten's features that appealed to Diana so vividly at the moment; it was the certainty that his abundant masculine strength wasn't going to be used against her. The relief was dizzying, telling her how much of her energy had been locked up in controlling her fear of men.

Then Diana realized that Ten was looking at her. The clarity of his gray eyes was extraordinary. The clean curves and angles of his mouth made her think of touching him, of finding out if his lips tasted as good as his breath.

"Are you all right?" he asked. "You look a little dazed."

"I am." Diana took a ragged breath, then another. "Having the world jerked out from under your feet does that."

Ten's smile flashed again. "Yeah, I guess so. Ready to try standing up?"

"Um."

"We'll take it nice and easy. Just onto your knees at first. Here we go."

With an ease that would have terrified Diana only yesterday, Ten lifted her into a kneeling position. His eyes measured her response, his hands felt the continued coordination of her body as she took her own weight on her knees, and he nodded.

"Ready to try standing? I don't want to rush you, but I'll feel a lot better once we're out of this kiva."

For the first time the nature of her surroundings sank into Diana.

"A kiva! I fell through the ceiling of a kiva?"

"You sure did, honey."

"We have to mark the site and be careful not to do any more damage and—"

"First," Ten interrupted smoothly, "we have to get the hell out of here. It's dangerous."

The voice was still black velvet, but there was the cool reality of steel beneath.

"Ramrod," she breathed.

"Ready?" was all Ten said.

Ready or not, Diana was on her feet a few seconds later, put there by Ten's easy strength. She braced herself momentarily on his hard forearms, feeling the vital heat of his body radiating through cloth. She snatched back her hands as though she had been burned.

"I'm fine," she said quickly. "Really. I can stand alone."

Ten heard Diana's uneasiness in the sudden tumble of words and released her. He didn't step back, for he wanted to be able to catch her if her knees gave way.

"No dizziness?" he asked.

There was, but it came from Ten's closeness rather than from any injury she might have received in the fall. Diana had no intention of saying anything about that fact, however.

"No," she said firmly. "I'm not dizzy."

"Sure?"

"Where have I heard that question before?"

A smile flashed in the gloom, Ten's smile, warm against the hard lines of his face.

"Feeling feisty, are you?" he asked.

Diana looked away from Ten, afraid her approval of him would be much too clear. She didn't want that. She didn't want to give him any reason to expect anything from her as a woman. With narrowed eyes, she examined the hole in the ceiling that was their only exit from the kiva. If she stretched up all the way on her tiptoes she might be able to brush her fingertips close to a cedar beam. And then again, she might not.

"Actually, I'm feeling rather intimidated," she admitted. "Some women would be able to get out of this hole alone, but not me. In gym classes I was a total disaster at chinning myself on the high bar."

Ten measured the distance to the ceiling and the cedar beams. "No problem. God made men with that in mind."

"He did?"

Ten nodded and kicked aside a bit of loose rubble, giving himself stable footing beneath the hole. He braced his legs and held out his arms to Diana.

"Okay, honey. Up you go."

She looked at him as though he had just suggested that she teleport herself out of the hole.

"Don't worry, I won't drop you," Ten said. "I handle heavier things every day. I'll lift you up. You balance yourself on the cedar poles until you can scramble from my shoulders to the ground."

"What about you?"

"That's where God's design comes in. He made men stronger than women." The smile faded, leaving only the hard male lines of Ten's face. "It's all right, Diana. I won't hurt you. Trust me."

"I—" Her voice broke. She swallowed and forced herself to take the two steps toward Ten. "I'll—try. What do I have to do?"

"First, put your hands on my shoulders."

For a few moments Diana was afraid she wouldn't be able to force herself to do it. Silently, fiercely, she closed her eyes and fought old fears.

Ten watched with narrowed eyes, feeling Diana's fear as clearly as he had the soft feminine curves of her body while he checked her for injury.

"Diana. Put your hands on my shoulders."

Her eyelids snapped open. Gone was the velvet reassurance of Ten's voice. In its place was a steel reality: she could help Ten get her out of the kiva or she could fight him; either way, she was going up through that hole in the ceiling. Diana didn't know how he would manage the feat without her cooperation, but she had no doubt that he would.

Diana lifted her hands to Ten's shoulders. She knew he felt her trembling but was unable to stop it.

"Are you afraid of falling again?" he asked.

"I—"

Her hands clenched around the hard resilience of Ten's shoulder muscles. He was so strong. Much too strong. She was as helpless as a kitten against his power.

Remember that tiger-striped kitten cuddled in Ten's hands. The kitten was relaxed, purring, trusting. Ten didn't hurt that sick kitten. He won't hurt me.

"What d-do you want me to do?" Diana asked, forgetting everything except the need to hold on to her belief that Ten wouldn't hurt her.

"Brace yourself on my shoulders. I'm going to lift you until you can grab a cedar pole. Use it to help you kneel on my shoulders, then stand on them. From there you should be able to get out of the kiva without much problem. Okay?"

She nodded, gripped his shoulders more tightly and braced herself for whatever might come.

"Not yet," Ten said, stroking Diana's back slowly. "You're shaking too much. Slow down, honey. You're all right."

"Being p-petted is just going to make me m-more nervous."

One black eyebrow lifted, but Ten said nothing except "Hang on. Here we go. And keep your back straight."

Diana didn't understand the last instruction until she felt the brush of Ten's body over hers as he bent his knees, wrapped his arms around her thighs and straightened, lifting her within reach of the cedar poles. He need not have worried about her back being straight—her whole body went rigid at the intimacy of his powerful arms locked around her thighs and his head pressed against her abdomen.

"Ten!"

"It's okay, honey. I've got you."

That's the whole problem! But Diana had just enough control left not to blurt out her thought.

"Can you grab one of the poles yet?" Ten asked.

Diana pulled her scattering thoughts together, lifted one hand from the corded muscle of Ten's shoulder and grabbed a cedar pole. It was as hard as Ten but not nearly so warm.

"Got it," she said breathlessly.

"Good. Now grab the other pole."

A few seconds, then, "Okay. I've got that one, too."

"Hang on."

Ten moved so quickly that Diana was never sure how he had managed it, but within seconds she was kneeling on his shoulders, using her grip on the poles for balance. His hands on her hips were holding her firmly and his face was—

Don't think about it or you'll fall.

"Steady, honey," Ten said in a muffled voice.

"Easy for you to say," Diana muttered through clenched teeth.

He laughed softly.

She felt the intimate heat of his breath.

"Oh, God."

"What's wrong?" Ten asked. "Is one of the beams rotten?"

Diana didn't answer. She pulled herself up and out of the kiva before she had a chance to question the shivering sensations that cascaded throughout her body. She scrambled back from the edge and sat hugging herself, feeling flushed in the most unnerving places.

"Everything okay?" Ten called.

"Yes. No. I—" She clenched her teeth. "Fine. Just fine."

"Get back. I'm coming out."

Diana scooted back away from the hole, wondering how Ten was planning to get out. A few seconds later, two hands closed around a cedar pole. With a grace that startled her, Ten chinned himself, held himself one-handed while he grabbed the second pole with his other hand, swung his legs up and levered himself out of the hole with the ease of a gymnast at work on a set of parallel bars.

"Where did you learn how to do that?" Diana asked.

"Same place I learned to patch up kittens."

"Where was that?"

"Long ago, far away, in another country."

"But where?" she persisted. "Why?"

"Commando training."

Diana opened her mouth but no words came out.

Commando training.

Ten held out his hand to help Diana to her feet. "Let's go, honey. The sun will be setting soon."

A wild glance at the sky told Diana that Ten was right. The sun would soon slip beneath the horizon, leaving her alone in the dark at the ends of the earth with a man who was not only far more powerful than she but who was trained to be a killer, as well.

"You sure you're all right?" Ten asked, sitting on his heels next to Diana. "If you can't walk, I'll carry you."

She flinched away from him before she could grab her unraveling courage in both hands. She gave Ten a searching look but saw no triumph in his expression, no malice, no brute hunger, nothing but polite concern for her welfare.

"I can—" Diana's voice broke. She swallowed. "I can walk."

Ten started to reach for her, saw her flinch away and dropped his hand. He stood and moved a pace back from her.

"Get up. We'll drive back to the ranch after we eat," he said matter-of-factly.

"What? Why?"

"You know why," Ten said, turning away from Diana. "Every time I come close to you, you cringe. You'll feel more at ease with one of the other men."

"No!"

The stark emotion in Diana's voice stopped Ten. He looked back at her.

"Please stay," she said quickly. "I trust you more than I've trusted any man since—since I—since he— Ten, please! It's nothing you've done. It's nothing personal. Please believe me."

"It's hard to," he said bluntly.

"Then believe this. You're the first man who's touched me in any way for years and it scares me to death because I'm not scared and you're so damned *male*."

Ten's eyes narrowed. "You're not making much sense."

"I know. I'll get better. I promise."

For a moment Ten looked at Diana. Then he nodded slowly and held out his hand. If she stretched she could take it and help herself up. She looked at the lean hand and remembered the strength and lethal skill of the man behind it.

Then Diana took Ten's hand in both of hers and pulled herself to her feet.

CHAPTER NINE

WHILE THE NIGHT WIND BLEW outside, Diana sat in the old ranch house, staring at a potsherd in her palm, remembering the incident two weeks ago when Ten had dropped down into the darkness beside her and lifted her to the solid ground above. The tactile memories had haunted her…his hands searching carefully over her body, his easy strength when he lifted her, his face pressed so intimately against her while she climbed back into sunshine.

Shivering, remembering, Diana saw nothing of the sherd in her palm. The memories resonated in her body as much as in her mind, sending sensations rippling through her, heat and cold, uneasiness and curiosity, a strange hunger to touch Ten in return, to know his masculine textures as well as he knew her feminine ones.

I'm going crazy.

Once more Diana tried to concentrate on the sherd lying

across her palm, but all she could think about was the instant when she had taken Ten's hand between her own and pulled herself to her feet. She thought she had felt his fingers caressing her in the very act of releasing her, but the touch had stopped before she could be certain.

And since then Ten had been the heart, soul and body of asexual politeness. At the site he treated her with the casual camaraderie of an older brother. It was the same at the ranch. At night they sorted sherds together, spoke in broken phrases about missing angles and notched curves, discussed the weather or the ranch or the progress of the dig in slightly more complete sentences—and he never touched her, even when he seated her at the dinner table or passed a box of sherds to her or looked over her shoulder to offer advice about a missing piece of a pot. He had every excuse to crowd her personal space from time to time, but he didn't.

For the first few days Ten's distance had reassured Diana. Then it had piqued her interest. By the fourteenth day it outright annoyed her.

You'd think I didn't shower often enough.

"Did you say something?" Ten asked from across the table.

Appalled, Diana realized that she had muttered her thought aloud.

"Nothing," she said quickly.

A few moments later she put the sherd aside and stood up, feeling restless. As it often did, her glance strayed to the man who had shared so many days and evenings and nights with her.

The nights were perfectly proper, of course. Some outlaw. The Rocking M's ramrod is nothing if not proper.

Broodingly Diana watched Ten's long fingers turning potsherds over and over, handling the fragile pottery deftly, running his fingertips over the edges as though to learn the tiniest contours by touch alone. She did the same thing when she worked, a kind of tactile exploration that was as much a part of her nature as her expressive eyes and her fear of men.

But she no longer feared men. At least, not all men. Luke still startled her from time to time with his sheer size, yet she had no doubt that Carla was perfectly safe with her chosen man, as was little Logan with his father, a father chosen by fate rather than by the baby. Not all children were that lucky in their parents. Diana hadn't been. Nor were all wives as fortunate in their husbands. Diana's mother certainly had not been safe or cherished with her man.

Restlessly, Diana ran her fingertips over the tabletop, feeling the grit that rubbed off the sherds no matter how carefully they were handled. She smoothed her fingers over the table's surface again and again, watching Ten's hands, fascinated by their combination of power and precision.

What would it feel like to be touched with such care?

The glittering sensation that shivered through Diana at her silent question made her feel almost weak. She wanted to be touched by Ten, but it was impossible. He was a man. He would want more than touching, gentleness, cherishing, holding.

With a small sound Diana looked away from Ten. She didn't notice the sudden intensity in his eyes as he watched her over the pot he was assembling from ancient sherds.

"Mmrreeow?"

The polite query was followed by another, less polite one. Diana hurried to the window, grateful to have a distraction from her unexpected, unnerving attraction to Ten.

"Hello, you old reprobate," she said, opening the window and holding out her arms.

On a gust of air, the tiger-striped cat flowed into Diana's arms. Pounce's fur smelled cool, fresh, washed by the clean wind. Smiling, rubbing her face against the cat's sleek head, she settled back into her chair. Pounce's rumbling, vibrating approval rippled out, blending with the fitful sound of the wind.

"King of the Rocking M, aren't you?" she asked, smiling. "Think you can trade a few dead mice for some time in my lap, hmm?"

Ten looked up again. Diana was kneading gently down the cat's big back, rubbing her cheek against Pounce's head while he rubbed his head against her in turn. The old mouser's purring was like continuous, distant thunder, but it was Diana's clear enjoyment of the cat's textures and responses that brought every one of Ten's masculine senses alert. He had kept his distance from her very carefully since the first day at the site; he would never forget the raw terror that he had seen in her eyes the first time he had reached for her in the gloom of the ancient kiva.

No matter how carefully Diana tried to conceal it, Ten sensed that she was still afraid of him. Perhaps it was because the first time she had seen him, he was the victor in a brief, brutal fight. Perhaps it was the way he had handled the pothunters. Perhaps it was his commando training. Perhaps it was simply himself, Tennessee Blackthorn, a man who never had worn well on women—and vice versa. An outlaw, not a lover or a husband.

Pounce purred loudly from Diana's lap, proclaiming his satisfaction with life, himself and the woman who was stroking his sleek body.

"If I thought you'd give me a rubdown like that, I'd go out and catch mice, too."

Diana gave Ten a startled look.

"Don't know that I'd eat them, though," Ten added blandly, measuring a sherd against the bright lamplight. "A man has to draw the line somewhere."

Uncertainly Diana laughed. The idea of Ten purring beneath her hands made odd sensations shiver through her. Surely he was joking. But if he weren't...

Shadows of old fear rose in Diana. When she spoke her voice was tight and the words came out in a torrent, for she was afraid of being interrupted before she got everything said that had to be said.

"You'd be better off eating Carla's wonderful chicken than trading dead mice for a pat from me. I'm not the sensual type. Sex is for men, not women. In the jargon, I'm frigid, if frigid defines a woman who can live very well without sex."

Ten looked up sharply, caught as much by the palpable resonances of fear in Diana's voice as he was by her words. He started to speak but she was still talking, words spilling out like water from a river finally freed of its lid of winter ice.

"A man must have thought up the word *frigid*," Diana continued quickly. "A woman would just say she isn't a masochist, that she feels no need of pain, self-inflicted or otherwise. But no matter what label you put on it—and me—the result is the same. Thanks but no thanks."

The words echoed in the quiet room. Their defensiveness made Diana cringe inside, but she wouldn't have taken back a single blunt syllable. Ten had to know.

"I don't recall asking you for sex," Ten said.

For a long minute Diana's hands kneaded through Pounce's fur, soothing the cat and herself at the same time, drawing forth a lifting and falling rumble of purrs.

"No, you haven't," she said finally, sighing, feeling herself relax now that the worst of it was over. Ten knew. He could never accuse her now. "But I've learned the hard way that it's better to be honest than to be quiet and then be accused of being a tease."

"Don't worry, Diana. Like the moon goddess you're named after, you've got No Trespassing signs posted all over you. Any man who doesn't see them would have to be as blind as you are."

"What?"

Ten looked up from the sherds he had assembled. "You're stone-blind to your own basic nature. You're not frigid. You have a rare sensuality. You drink storm winds and nuzzle Logan's tiny hands and touch pieces of pottery with fingertips that are so sensitive you don't even have to look to tell what kind of edge there is. You rub that old tomcat until he's a vibrating pudding of pleasure, and you enjoy it just as much as he does. That's all sensuality is—taking pleasure in your own senses. And sex, good sex, is the most pleasure your senses can stand."

Diana sat transfixed, caught within the diamond clarity of Ten's eyes watching her, the black velvet certainty of his voice caressing her. Then he looked back to the sherds, releasing her.

"Did a new box come in from the site?" Ten asked in a calm voice, as though they had never discussed anything more personal than potsherds. "I've been waiting for one from 10-B. I think part of this red pot might have washed down to that spot on the grid. A long time ago, of course."

Her mind in turmoil, Diana grabbed the question, grateful to have something neutral to talk about. "Yes, it's over there. I'll get it."

If Ten noticed the rapid-fire style of Diana's speech, he didn't comment.

Releasing a reluctant Pounce, Diana went to the corner of the room where recently cleaned, permanently numbered sherds were stored in hope of future assembling. The carton collected from 10-B on the site grid was on top of the pile. She brought the box to the long table where Ten worked by the light of a powerful gooseneck lamp.

"Thanks," he said absently. "I don't suppose there's a piece lying around on top with two obtuse angles and a ragged bite out of the third side?"

"Gray? Corrugated? Black on white?"

"Red."

"Really?" she asked, excited. Redware was the most unusual of all the Anasazi pottery. It also came from the last period when they inhabited the northern reaches of their homeland. "Do you think we have enough sherds to make a whole pot?"

Ten made a rumble that sounded suspiciously like Pounce at his most satisfied. He leaned over, pulled a large carton from beneath the table and folded back the flaps. With gentle care he lifted pieces of an ancient bowl onto the table. The background color of the pot was brick red. Designs in white and black covered the surface, careful geometrics that spoke of a painstaking artist working patiently over the pot.

A feeling of awe expanded through Diana as she saw the pot lying half-mended on the table. Ten had been as patient and painstaking as the original potter; the fine lines where he had glued sherds together were almost invisible.

"You never did tell me why this kind of pot is so rare," Ten said, turning aside to the carton of unmatched sherds.

"Polychrome pots are usually found south of here," Diana said absently. Her hands closed delicately around the base and a curving side of the red pot. "Either the potter was an immigrant or the pot was a piece of trade goods. But this pot, plus the surface and regular shape of the sandstone masonry in September Canyon, make it certain that the site is from the Pueblo III period of the Anasazi. Or nearly certain. Since we don't have a time machine, we'll never be one hundred percent positive that we have the true story."

"We know the most important thing."

Diana looked up from the fragment of the past held between her hands.

"They were people like us," Ten said simply. "They built, laughed, wept, fought, raised children and died. Most of all, they knew fear."

"Actually," Diana said, frowning over the box of sherds, "the most recent theory states that the Anasazi moved into their cliff houses for reasons other than fear."

Ten's left eyebrow arched skeptically. "They just liked the view halfway up the cliff, huh?"

"Um, no one said anything about that. The theory just states that we were premature in attributing a fortress mentality to the Anasazi. They could just have been preserving the top of the mesa for crops and didn't build on the canyon bottom because of floods. That left the cliffs themselves for housing."

Ten grunted. "What did the professorial types say about the signal towers on top of Mesa Verde? They were used to pass the news of births, right?"

Diana gave Ten a sideways look, but he appeared to be engrossed in the red potsherds she was finding and carefully placing in front of him. Already he had found two to glue together and was positioning a third.

"The towers could have been used to welcome visitors," Diana said neutrally, "or to show the way up onto the mesa for people who were from other areas."

"People from other areas tend to be strangers and strangers tend to be unfriendly."

"Perhaps the Anasazi believed that strangers were simply friends they hadn't met yet."

"That would certainly explain how the Anasazi died out so fast," Ten said sardonically.

"In some academic circles, your point of view would be considered philosophically and politically retrograde," Diana said without heat. One of the most pleasurable things about her time with Ten was the discovery of his agile, wide-ranging mind. She had come to look forward to the hours spent sorting sherds and talking about the Anasazi almost as much as she enjoyed working on the site itself. "Here's the sherd that goes in the middle."

"Thanks," Ten said. "Hang on to it until the glue dries on these two. Whatever made the professors give up on good old common sense to explain the Anasazi cliff dwellings?"

"Such as?"

"Birds don't fly because they like the view up there. Birds fly because cats can't."

Diana smiled. "Don't tell Pounce."

"I don't have to. He figured that one out all by himself, which is more than I can say for whoever dreamed up that New Age fertilizer about cliff houses being invented for any reason other than self-defense. In a word, fear."

"Logical, but it doesn't explain why there was no increase in burials about the time the Anasazi abandoned the mesa tops and took up living in the cliffs."

"Burials?"

"Self-defense indicates war," Diana explained. "War indicates wounding and death. Death—"

"Leads to burials," Ten interrupted.

"Right. Even around the time the Anasazi disappeared altogether, there was no increase in burials. Therefore, the theory that hostile tribes forced the Anasazi into cliff houses has a big flaw. No extra deaths, no war. Simple."

"More like simpleminded. Those theorists ought to pull their heads out of their, er, books and have a reality check."

"What do you mean?"

"Only winners bury their dead."

The flatness in Ten's voice made a chill move over Diana's skin.

"You sound very certain," she said.

"I've been there. That's as certain as it gets."

"There?"

"On the losing side. It hasn't changed all that much over the centuries. I doubt that it ever will. Pain, fear, death and not enough people left to mourn or bury the dead. But there are always enough vultures."

Ten's narrowed eyes were like splinters of clear glass. Diana could not bear to look at them and think of what they had seen.

He turned and searched through the box of potsherds. When he looked up again, his expression was once more relaxed.

"In any case," Ten continued, "anybody who's read a little biology could tell your fancy theorists that building Stone Age apartment houses halfway up sheer cliffs took an immense amount of time and energy, which meant that the need driving the society also had to be immense. Survival is the most likely explanation, and the only animal that threatens man's survival is man himself." Ten smiled grimly. "That hasn't changed, either."

"Fear."

"Don't knock it. No animal would survive without it, including man." Ten held a sherd up to the light, shrugged and tried it anyway. It fit. "Maybe the Anasazi were no longer actively involved in war. Maybe they just feared it to the point that they retreated to a hole in the cliffs and pulled the hole in after them." Ten looked up. "You can understand that kind of fear, can't you? It's what drew you to the Anasazi in the first place. Like you, they built a shell around themselves to wall out the world. And then they began to shrink and die inside that shell."

Diana concentrated on two sherds that had no chance of fitting.

Ten waited a few moments, sighed and continued. "When you retreat to a stone cliff that's accessible only by one or two eyelash trails that a nine-year-old with a sharp stick could defend, it's probably because you don't have much more than nine-year-olds left to defend the village."

"But there's no hard evidence of repeated encounters with a warlike tribe," she said coolly.

"Isn't there? What does Anasazi mean?"

"It's a Navajo word meaning Ancient Ones, or Those Who Came Before."

Ten smiled thinly. "It also means Enemy Ancestor." He picked up an oddly shaped sherd and stared at it without really seeing it. "I suspect that at the end of a long, hard period, during which they'd had to cope with war or drought or disease or all three, a kind of madness overtook the northern Anasazi."

The quality of Ten's voice, rippling with something unspoken, caught Diana's attention.

"What do you mean?"

"I think a dark kind of shaman cult overtook them, using up everything the society had and demanding even more.

Maybe the fears the shaman cult played on had some basis in reality, or maybe they lived only in the Anasazi's own nightmares." Ten shook his head. "Either way, fear ruled the society. The people retreated to the most impossible places they could reach and walled themselves in with rooms and held ceremonies in buried kivas. When they ran out of space in the alcoves, they built bigger and bigger kivas along the base of the cliff."

Ten's voice shifted, becoming subtly different, more resonant yet softer.

"Their rituals became more and more elaborate," he continued quietly, "more demanding of the people's mental and physical resources. Darker. It's possible for a culture to exist like that, but not for long. It goes against the deepest grain of survival to huddle in a stone crypt."

"Is that what you think happened? The Anasazi died in the city crypts they built for themselves?"

"Some did. Some escaped."

The odd timbre of Ten's voice made the hair on Diana's scalp stir in primal response, the same stirring she had felt with Ten once before, when she had stood on a desolate mesa top and felt centuries like cards being shuffled, revealing glimpses of a time when reality had been very different, and so had she and Ten.

"How did they escape?" Diana asked, her voice strange even to her own ears.

For a long time there was only silence punctuated by the sounds of the wind sweeping over the ancient land. Just when Diana had decided that Ten wasn't going to say any more, he began speaking again.

"Another shaman came down from the north, an outlaw shaman with a vision that swept through the Anasazi, a vision that spoke of light as well as darkness, life as well as death." Ten looked up suddenly, catching and holding Diana with eyes as clear as rain. "The Anasazi who believed the outlaw shaman climbed down out of their beautiful, dangerous, futile cliff cities and never went back again."

CHAPTER TEN

LUKE LEANED TOWARD LITTLE Logan, smiling, speaking in a deep, gentle voice to the baby who studied him so intently.

"Definitely your eyes, Carla," Luke said, running his fingertip over his wife's cheek.

"The mouth is yours, though," she said, smoothing her cheek over his hand.

"We're in trouble then. He'll have half the state mad at him as soon as he learns to talk."

Carla laughed softly, brushed her lips over Luke's palm and settled back against his chest. The nursing shawl slipped to one side, revealing the milk-swollen curve of her breast. With a slow caress Luke adjusted the shawl, then resumed the gentle back-and-forth motion of the big rocking chair he had made before Logan had been born.

Despite its size, the chair was still a snug fit for the three of them—Logan, Carla and Luke—but no one had any intention of giving it up for the couch. The quiet evenings when Carla nursed the baby while sitting in Luke's lap had become the highlight of the day for everyone involved.

"Hi," Carla said, looking up as Diana came from the kitchen into the living room. "Ten was asking about you a few minutes ago. Something about a box from 11-C?"

"More red sherds. He hopes. He has this theory about where the rest of the red pot is. So far he has been right."

A night of broken sleep and restless dreams had convinced Diana that Ten had been right about more than the pot, but she didn't know how to reopen the subject with him, any more than she had known how to respond last night, when he had spoken about fear and the Anasazi and one Diana Saxton. Instead of speaking then, she had handed him another sherd and the conversation had disintegrated into elliptical phrases describing pieces of broken pots.

"Is Ten in the bunkhouse?" Diana asked.

"He's in the barn checking on a lame horse."

Diana hid her feeling of disappointment. Whether in September Canyon or at the ranch headquarters, she looked forward to the evenings with Ten despite the tension that came from her increasing awareness of him as a man. She noticed him in ways that she had never noticed any man at all. The dense black of his eyelashes, the equally dense beard shadow that lay beneath his skin no matter how recently he had shaved, the springy thatch of hair that showed beneath his open collar, the endless flex and play of muscles beneath his skin, the easy stride of a man who was at home in and confident of his body.

But most of all, Diana noticed the frank masculinity of Ten, the male sensuality that was both subtle and pervasive. It compelled her senses in the same way that his intelligence compelled her mind.

"If you see Ten," Diana said to Carla, "tell him I've cleaned the calcium deposits from the 11-C sherds, given them permanent labels, and they're ready for his magic touch."

"Sure. Want to stay for pie? We're having some as soon as we put our greedy son to bed."

"No thanks. Your cooking is straining the seams of my jeans as it is. It's getting indecent."

"Haven't heard any of the men complaining about the fit of your jeans," Luke drawled.

"Luke!" Carla said, laughing.

"Well, have you heard them complaining?" he asked innocently before switching his attention to Logan. "Hurry up, son. Your old man is ready for dessert."

Carla laughed and murmured something Diana couldn't hear. Silently she retreated from the living room doorway, heading for the kitchen. It wasn't that she felt unwelcome, for she knew that the opposite was the case. Carla and Luke loved to question Diana about the progress of the dig and the pots that Ten and she together had proven to be so adept at assembling from sherds. It was just that she wasn't sure she could look at Luke and Carla and their baby without letting her own hunger show.

What a pity it takes a man to make a baby.

It wasn't the first time the thought had occurred to Diana, but the strength of her yearning for a baby was growing. Tonight it had shaken her, making it hard for her to think.

But then, that wasn't new, either. Diana hadn't been thinking too well around Ten lately. A look from him, a phrase, a slight lift of the corner of his mouth, and she would begin thinking all over again about how gentle he had been with the kitten, how patient he was with the fragile, brittle sherds, how easy and yet how exciting he was to be with.

Stop it. Next thing you know you'll be asking him to kiss you.

A curious sensation prickled through Diana, making her shiver lightly. She wasn't sure what it was that had caused her reaction. She knew what it wasn't, however.

It wasn't fear.

Diana let herself out into the night. Overhead the Milky Way was a river of light flowing silently across the sky. There was no moon to pale the glitter of the stars, no clouds to blur the razor edges of MacKenzie Ridge's silhouette. Nothing moved but the wind. It infused the night, filling it with whispers that could have been her own thoughts or echoes of ancient Anasazi prayers chanted to unknown gods.

When Diana opened the door to the old ranch house, Pounce materialized from the nearby bushes and slipped into the house ahead of her. She closed the door, bent down and lifted the big tomcat into her arms.

"Hello, Pounce. How was mouse hunting tonight?"

The cat purred and began kneading Diana's chest.

"That good, hmm?" Diana murmured, rubbing the supple body and sleek fur. "Then I won't bother putting out that dry cat food Carla gave me yesterday."

Pounce purred his agreement.

"Yeah, that's what she said. You only eat the dry stuff when nothing else is available."

Sure enough, Pounce ignored the kibble that Diana prepared with one hand while she held on to the cat with the other. Even a saucer of milk didn't interest him. All he wanted was what he was getting—a chance to snuggle with his favorite human being.

Carrying Pounce, Diana walked through the workroom to her bedroom. The carefully made bed looked uninviting.

It was too early to sleep. Even if the hour had been right, her frame of mind was not. She was too restless to sleep.

Unfortunately she was also too restless to work on the sherds. She tried, but for once the lure of putting together an ancient puzzle couldn't hold her attention. After fitting a few pieces together, she turned off the big gooseneck lamp and sat at the work table with no more illumination than that provided by the lamp in the far corner of the room. The shadows cast by that lamp were soft and inviting, making velvet distinctions between light and dark.

Pounce leaped into Diana's lap and *yeowed* in soft demand. Absently she stroked the cat, drawing forth a ripple of purrs. For a long time there was no other sound. Then a knock came on the front door and Ten called out. Hearing Ten's deep voice sent another curious frisson through Diana.

"I'm in the workroom," she answered.

Her voice was unusually husky, but the words carried well enough. The door opened and closed and Ten walked into the room. With a gesture that had become familiar to her, he removed his hat and set it on the small table beneath the lamp.

"That old mouser must think he's died and gone to heaven," Ten said.

The corner of his mouth tugged up, sending another glimmer of heat through Diana.

"Did you mean what you said?" she asked before she could think of all the reasons to be silent.

"I always mean what I say. When it comes to you and that cat, I'm damned certain."

Diana took a deep breath. "Would you really trade places with Pounce?"

This time the curve at the corner of Ten's mouth expanded

into a true smile. "Why? You have some mice that he's too lazy to catch?"

Her lips tried to smile but were trembling too hard. She could barely find the courage to force out her next question.

"Would you really like to be touched by me?" she asked. "I mean, do I...attract you?"

"Sure," Ten said offhandedly, reaching for the switch on the gooseneck lamp.

"Would you...kiss me?"

Ten's hand froze in midair. Amusement vanished from his expression. His eyes narrowed until there was little left but a silver glitter as he turned and looked at the woman who was only a few feet away.

"You're serious, aren't you," he said.

She nodded because her throat was too tight for words.

"What happened to all the No Trespassing signs?"

Diana opened her mouth. No words came from her constricted throat. She licked her lips. Ten watched the motion with a heavy-lidded, sensual intensity that would have frightened her once. Now it came as a relief. It gave her the courage to put into words the realization that had been growing in her mind for a long time.

"Watching Carla and Luke and their baby has made me understand that I'm missing something wonderful and—and vital." Diana's voice shifted, becoming even lower, more husky. She spoke swiftly, as though afraid of being interrupted and then not having the courage to continue. "But until I get over being afraid of men, I won't have a chance for the kind of life I want. Men want sex. I have to be able to give a man what he wants in order to get what I really want—a baby of my own."

Ten's left eyebrow rose in a wicked black arch. "Honey,

you don't need a man to get a baby." His mouth tugged up at the corner in response to Diana's shocked look. "If you don't believe me, ask any veterinarian."

Silky hair flew as Diana shook her head vigorously. "No. That's not what I want. Too cold. I want my baby to be conceived in warmth, in a—a joining of two people. Not a doctor's office. That wouldn't—I just—no." She took a fast, harsh breath, trying to control her nervousness. "So I have to start somewhere. A kiss seems a logical beginning."

"Why me?"

Diana looked away, unable to bear the diamond clarity of Ten's eyes.

"Because I—I trust you," she said, her voice uneven. "I've seen you handle kittens and delicate pieces of pottery. You're as gentle as you are strong. When I was trapped in the kiva, I was helpless, completely at your mercy. You could have done anything, but what you did was pull me out, comfort me, take care of me. Never once did you so much as hint that I owed you thanks, much less the use of my body for sex."

Unwavering gray eyes watched Diana. "And now you want me to kiss you?"

Closing her eyes, she nodded.

"Despite your fear of men," Ten added.

Again, she nodded. Then, in a whispered rush, she said, "I like you, Ten. I know I could bear being kissed by you, but the thought of any other man makes me—cold."

A visible shudder of fear and revulsion went through Diana. Ten saw it but said nothing.

"Anyway," she added with desperate calm, "if you know going in that all it's going to be is a kiss, you won't push for more, will you? If I'm honest?" Diana opened her eyes and looked at Ten with unconscious pleading. "I'm not a tease. Truly. It's just that I can't bear being touched by men."

"What happened?" Ten asked calmly. "Why do you have such a poor opinion of sex in general and men in particular? What makes you afraid that every man you kiss will demand sex?"

"Because it's true."

"You don't believe that."

"The hell I don't," she said, her voice low and flat.

Ten stared at Diana. All her softness and unconscious pleading was gone, all hope, all color; and what was left was a bleak acceptance that made her voice as flat as the line of her mouth.

"Look," Ten said reasonably, "no man worthy of the name is going to share a few kisses with a woman and then demand a turn in the sack."

Diana shrugged. The movement was tight, jerky, saying more than words about the tension within her, a tension that had been pulling her apart for too many years.

"Maybe you're right," she said. Then she made an angry, anguished sound. Years of bitterness burst out in a torrent of words. "But the only way to find out which men are decent is to try the kisses, all the while praying very hard that when the time comes he'll take no for an answer, because if he doesn't, he's bigger than you are, stronger, and you've been dating him for months and no one on earth will believe that he forced you."

"You're acting as though all men—"

"Not *all* men," she interrupted savagely. "But too damned many! If you don't believe me, ask the psychologist who did a study for UCLA. The statistics are illuminating. More than a third of all women have their first sexual experience as the result of rape."

"*What?*"

"Rape," Diana said savagely. "I'm not talking about being beaten senseless or having a knife at your throat until the rapist is finished, although God knows I talked to too many girls who got initiated that way, in outright violence."

Diana's breath came in harshly, but she gave Ten no chance to speak. "I'm not even talking about incest. I'm talking about the dumb middle-class bunnies who believe that no means no, who believe that the boy they've been dating for three months won't use his strength against his girlfriend, won't keep pushing and pushing and pushing her for sex, taking off her clothes while she says no, putting his hand between her legs even when she tries to push it away, and each time they're alone he pushes harder and harder until finally he was holding me down, telling me all the while how it was okay, nice girls did it all the time, he'd still love me in the morning, in fact he'd love me more than ever—"

"Diana," Ten said, his voice low, shocked.

She didn't even hear him. "—and I was too well brought up to claw and scream and kick, and above all *I couldn't believe Steve wouldn't stop.* Nice middle-class girls don't get raped by nice middle-class boys. He had stopped the times before. He would stop this time. He had to. He simply had to. God help me, I still didn't believe it when he was finished and I was bleeding and he was zipping up his pants suggesting we have a burger and some fries before we went to his apartment and did it some more."

Diana blinked, shuddered again and made a broken sound. "To this day Steve doesn't know why I broke our engagement. The last time I talked to him, he got mad and said if I didn't want sex, I shouldn't ask for it by wearing heels and sexy hairstyles and perfume and I shouldn't make out at all. I was a good middle-class girl, so I believed him. I believed it had been my fault."

Diana's hands clenched until her nails dug into her palms, but her voice remained the same, flat and without warmth. "When I could bring myself to date again—it took more than a year—I was very careful not to lead a man on. No makeup. No perfume. No skirts. A few kisses, that was all, and then only after several dates. It didn't matter. Two of my dates called me a tease. Some called me worse."

Pounce made a soft sound of complaint and leaped to the floor, sensing the tension in Diana. She didn't notice the cat's absence.

Neither did Ten. He was still caught in the moment of shock and rage when he had realized why Diana feared men. He heard her words only at a distance. His hands clenched and unclenched reflexively as he tried to reason with himself, to drain off the useless rage that was consuming him. What had happened to Diana had taken place a long time ago. Years.

But for Ten, it had happened just a few seconds ago.

"Only one of the men came back for more than a few dates," Diana continued tonelessly, determined to tell Ten everything so that no more questions would have to be asked or answered. "Don never pushed me. Not once. Not in any way. Eight months later he asked me to marry him, and he told me about how perfect it would be, two virgins learning together the ultimate mystery of sex on their marriage night." She made a helpless gesture with her right hand. "He was a kind, decent man. I couldn't lie to him. So I told him."

When Ten spoke, his voice was as carefully controlled as the coiled strength of his body. "What happened?"

"He tried to believe it wasn't my fault, but when he found out I hadn't gone to the police..." The downward curve of Diana's mouth became more pronounced. "We saw each other a few more times after that, but it was over."

"Did you love him?"

Slowly Diana shook her head. "I didn't love Steve, either. I just wanted to believe it was possible for a man and a woman to share something beautiful, that a man can be decent and civilized with a woman who is weaker than himself."

"I take it your father wasn't."

"My father was a soldier. A commando."

Ten's eyes widened but he said nothing.

"Dad was short-tempered when he was sober. When he drank, he was violent. The older I got, the more he drank. He and Mom..." Diana's voice died. "I never understood why she stayed with him. But she did."

"He's dead?"

"Yes." Diana looked up at Ten for the first time since she had begun talking about her past. "Steve was a jet jockey for the air force. I haven't had very good luck with soldiers. Any more questions?"

"Just one."

Diana braced herself. "Go on."

"Do you still want me to kiss you?"

Nervously Diana smoothed the soft folds of her oversize cotton sweater. She tried to speak, decided she didn't trust her voice, and nodded her head.

"You're sure?" Ten asked.

There was no emotion in his voice, no expression on his face, nothing to tell Diana what he was thinking. He was as dark and enigmatic as the windswept night, and like the stars, his eyes were a glittering silver.

"Yes," she whispered. "I'm sure."

Ten held out his hand. "Then come to me, Diana."

CHAPTER ELEVEN

DIANA TREMBLED AT THE SOUND OF Ten's voice, a gentle velvet rasp, like a cat's tongue stroking her. For an instant she didn't know if she would have the strength to walk. But even as the thought came she was standing up, walking, closing the small distance that separated her from Ten. She put her hand in his. The warmth of his hard palm was like a flame against fingers chilled by nervousness.

Ten held out his other hand. A moment later, small cool fingers nestled against the cupped heat of his palm. He lifted Diana's hands to his mouth and breathed warmth over her skin before kissing her palms gently. The unexpected caress made Diana's breath break. Before the sweet sensations had run their course through her body, Ten was lowering her hands, releasing her from his warmth.

Diana had asked to be kissed. He had kissed her. She

made a questioning sound that had more disappointment in it than she realized.

"Ten?"

"What?" he asked softly.

"Would you kiss me again?" she whispered.

Ten's smile made Diana want to curl up in his arms like a cat.

He held out his hands and once more felt her smooth, cool fingers come to rest within the curve of his palms.

"You're so warm," Diana said. She closed her eyes and let out her breath in a long sigh, openly savoring the simple touch of her skin against Ten's.

Diana's unguarded, sensual response sent a shock wave of heat through Ten. He hoped she had no idea how fiercely she aroused him with her unknowing sensuality and haunted eyes, her womanly curves badly concealed beneath a sweater big enough for him to wear, and her slender hands lying so trustingly within his.

Ten brought Diana's hands to his mouth and brushed a kiss into first one of her palms, then the other. The tiny sound she made at the touch of his lips was as much a reward as the warmth he could feel stealing softly beneath her skin. He lifted his head and looked at her. She was watching him with eyes that were luminous, approving. Then her dark lashes lowered and she returned the kisses he had given her, breathing a caress into the center of his palm.

"Thank you," Diana whispered.

"My pleasure."

She searched Ten's face with wide indigo eyes, hardly able to believe what her senses were telling her. He had enjoyed the undemanding caresses as much as she had.

"You mean that, don't you," she said finally.

Ten nodded.

"It's a relief to find a man who doesn't want… everything."

An odd smile haunted Ten's lips for a moment. "Don't fool yourself, Diana. I want everything, but I'll never *take* any more than you give me. And I mean give willingly, not because I push you so hard on so many fronts at once that you don't know where to fight first."

Diana smiled uncertainly. "Does that mean you'll kiss me again?"

"I'll kiss you as many times as you want me to."

"And you won't push for more?"

"No."

"Even if you get aroused?" The stark question shocked Diana when she heard her own words, but it was too late to call them back.

"Honey," Ten said, his voice rich with rueful laughter, "if you were standing about two inches closer to me, you'd have the answer to your question."

Confusion showed on Diana's face. Without thinking, she looked down Ten's body. The evidence of his arousal was unmistakable and frankly intimidating. She looked up again, her face suddenly pale.

"Don't worry, honey," Ten said matter-of-factly. "I've been that way every night we've sat around talking and sorting through pieces of the past, and more often than not during the days, too."

"You have?" she asked faintly. "I didn't know."

"I did my best to make sure of that," Ten said dryly. "I'm only pointing it out now so that you'll know you don't have to be afraid of me when I'm aroused."

"But I didn't mean to. Believe me, Ten. I didn't mean anything of the sort!"

"I know. I can't keep myself from responding to you, but I can make damn sure I don't act on it."

"But if I didn't mean to, why…" Her voice faded. "Has it been so long since you've had a woman?"

Ten looked at Diana's confusion and didn't know whether to laugh or swear. Very lightly he stroked his index finger over the inside of her wrist. The touch was gentle but hardly soothing. He felt her pulse rate accelerate, which made his own quicken in response.

"Diana, I could have had a woman five seconds before I walk into a room where you are and I'd still want you. I admire courage, intelligence and a sense of humor. It didn't take long for me to find out that you've got plenty of all three, as well as a fine body you do your best to hide."

Color crept up Diana's cheeks, but she made no move to separate her hands from Ten's while he continued talking in the velvet tones that made her weak.

"I've wanted you since the first day you were here, when you put your own uneasiness aside and helped me with that kitten."

Diana's eyes widened in surprise.

"I respect a woman's right to choose or refuse a man," Ten continued. "You made it clear that you were refusing. You're still making it clear. You're as safe as you want to be with me, no matter what kind of kissing or petting we do."

She barely heard what Ten was saying. She was still trying to absorb the realization that he was more aroused than Steve had ever been, yet Ten had made no move toward easing himself at her expense. Nor had he berated her for teasing him into such an uncomfortable state and then refusing to follow through.

Then the rest of what Ten was saying sank in: *You're as safe as you want to be with me, no matter what kind of kissing or petting we do.*

She didn't doubt it. Despite the provocation Baker had given—and the pothunters—Ten had never lost control over his own actions.

"Where did you learn such self-control?" Diana asked, watching Ten with dark, curious eyes.

"The same place I learned how to fight."

"That kind of training didn't do my father any good. Or Steve."

Ten banked the rage that came to him whenever he thought of a man hurting Diana. "They weren't men, honey. They were boys who never learned the most important part of a warrior's training—self-control. If a man doesn't control himself, someone else will. There are times and places where being out of control can cost a man his life. Your father was lucky. He was never in one of those places. As for Steve, if that fly-boy's luck holds, I'll never meet him."

Ten's voice was so caressing that for an instant the meaning of what he was saying didn't make any impact. When it did, Diana looked quickly at Ten's eyes. There was nothing of amusement or indulgence there, only the icy promise of retribution she had seen twice before in Ten's eyes—and each time a man had ended up flat on the ground with Ten towering over him.

"Now I've frightened you," Ten said, stepping back, releasing Diana. "I'd never hurt you, but after your experiences with the male of the species, I don't expect you to believe that." He turned toward the gooseneck lamp, reaching for the switch. "Let's take a look at those new red sherds you got out of the carton." Ten hesitated, glancing at Diana over his shoulder. "Or would you feel more at ease if I left you to work alone?"

Diana's hand went to Ten's, covering his fingers, preventing him from turning on the harsh light. She tugged lightly. He let go of the switch, allowing her to control his hand. She lifted it to her face. Closing her eyes, she stroked his hard palm with her cheek.

"Diana?"

"It's all right."

"Is it? Your hands are trembling."

Helplessly she smiled. "I don't know why they are, but I know it's not fear."

"Are you sure, honey?"

"I know what being afraid of a man feels like. I'm not afraid of you, Ten."

He searched Diana's eyes for a long moment, then gave her a slow smile that did nothing to steady her heartbeat or her hands. Watching him, trying to smile in return even though her lips were trembling, she found Ten's other hand and brought it to her mouth for a quick brush of her lips. Then she turned her other cheek into his palm, framing her face in his warmth, holding his hands against her skin.

"Ten," Diana said huskily, closing her eyes, savoring the slow caress of his fingers, "will you share a few kisses with me until I ask you to stop? I know this isn't fair to you, but—"

"It's all right," he said, interrupting, his lips against Diana's, feeling them tremble against his own. "Life is never fair. You of all people should know that."

"But—"

"Shh," Ten said, sealing her lips with a tender stroking of his thumb. "It's all right, baby."

Diana's eyes opened. Indigo depths shimmered with the possibilities that were unfolding within her, possibilities that existed because of the powerful man who was holding her with such care.

"Kiss me," she whispered.

"How?" he asked in a velvet voice. "Hard or gentle? Deep or cool? Fast or so long that you can't remember a time when we weren't kissing? I've never had that kind of kiss, but looking at you, I believe it exists."

Diana's eyes widened and she shivered lightly at the thought of trying each and every way of kissing Ten.

"How do you want to kiss me?" she asked.

"Every way there is."

"Yes," she sighed.

Ten's breath came out in a husky rush that Diana felt an instant before his lips touched hers. His lips were smooth and incredibly soft, fitting over hers tenderly yet completely. He brushed against her mouth again and again, letting her become accustomed to his textures, enjoying hers in return, and what he enjoyed most of all was the way her lips began to follow his, silently asking for more.

Smiling, ignoring the heavy beat of his own blood, Ten gave Diana more of the undemanding caresses. Her mouth relaxed and softened and her breath sighed between her slightly parted lips. The tip of his tongue touched the sensitive peak of her upper lip, then withdrew, only to return and touch her again. She made a murmurous sound and tilted her face more fully up to his. Her reward was a warm, gliding caress that went from corner to corner of her smile. She made another low sound that became a tiny cry of surprise when his teeth closed tenderly on her lower lip, holding it captive. Instantly he released her and began the elusive, gliding kisses all over again.

"Ten," Diana said, the word more a sigh than his name.

"Too much?"

"No." Her teeth closed a little less than gently on Ten's

lower lip. She heard his breath break and released him, whispering, "Not enough."

"Does that mean you won't run if I taste that beautiful mouth?"

"Yes."

"The way you were hanging on to my hands, I wasn't sure."

Belatedly, Diana realized that she was imprisoning Ten's hands against her face, holding him hard enough to leave marks on his tanned skin.

"I'm sorry," she said quickly, releasing his hands. "When you started kissing me I forgot everything else."

Ten bent and touched a corner of her mouth with his tongue. "That's all right, honey. I just thought you might be worried that I'd start straying out of bounds if you let go of my hands."

"What?"

"Don't you remember high school? Nothing below the collarbone in front or the waist in back."

Diana started to laugh, but the look in Ten's eyes took her breath away. His words were light, his voice was velvet, but his eyes were a smoldering gray that made her knees weak.

"I remember."

"That's the way it will be for us. If you want my hands anywhere else, you'll have to put them there."

"But then you would—you would expect more."

"I expect to spend this night like I've spent every night since I pulled you out of that kiva—hungry as hell. That's my problem, not yours. You've done nothing to encourage me."

"Nothing? What about right now?"

"This isn't encouraging." Ten lowered his mouth another fraction of an inch. His teeth closed tenderly on Diana's lower lip. The tip of his tongue caressed her captive flesh until she made a small sound at the back of her throat. He released her, gave her a quick, biting kiss and looked at her flushed lips with hunger. "This is pleasure, honey, pure and simple."

"Steve always—he said it hurt him."

Ten's answer was another brush of his lips against Diana's, but this time there was no lifting, no gliding, no teasing. His fingers eased into her hair, rubbing her scalp, holding her with gentle care while he joined their mouths in a different kind of kiss. The caressing pressure of his lips increased, tilting her head back, yet still she felt no uneasiness.

Slender fingers threaded into the thick pelt of Ten's hair, holding him even closer, wanting the kiss not to end. When Diana murmured his name, he accepted the invitation of her parted lips. His tongue glided between her teeth, seeking the moist heat beyond, finding it in a slow, deep tasting that was like nothing she had ever known. He memorized the contours of her mouth with teasing, sliding touches, caressing her, enjoying her, cherishing her. Only when she whimpered and pressed even closer to his body did he complete the seduction of her mouth.

Diana had never realized just how sensitive her tongue was, how it could discriminate so vividly between the satin smoothness and intriguing serrations of Ten's teeth, the silken texture and beguiling heat of his mouth, the nubby velvet enticement of his tongue sliding against hers in a dance of penetration and retreat that made her forget who was stronger, who was weaker, who was frightened and who was not. Tender and sweet, hot and wild, the kiss shimmered with both restraint and the sensuous consummation of two mouths completely joined.

Diana was never certain who ended the kiss or if it had truly ended at all. Slowly she realized that her arms were around Ten's neck, his arms were around her, supporting her and arching her into his body at the same time, and he was looking at her mouth as though he had just discovered fire.

"Ten?"

The huskiness of Diana's voice made his whole body tighten. Her heavy-lidded, luminous eyes told him that she had been as deeply involved in the kiss as he had. When she looked at his mouth and her own lips parted in unconscious invitation, Ten made a sound that was part laugh, part groan and all male.

"Do you want to taste me again?" he asked.

The shiver of response that went through Diana was clearly felt by Ten.

"Then take me," he said huskily.

Indigo eyes widened for a startled moment, then her lashes swept down as she looked at Ten's mouth. Her breath rushed out in a sigh that he tasted in the instant before she took his mouth, relearning his textures in a sharing of tongues that had neither beginning nor end, simply the hushed intimacy of their quickened breaths intermingling with the night.

Diana's last thought before the kiss ended was wonder that she could tremble and yet know not the least bit of fear. She had never felt so safe in her life...or so sweetly threatened.

CHAPTER TWELVE

"NOT A CHANCE," TEN SAID flatly. "If you think I'm letting you excavate that kiva, you're crazy." He pulled Diana out of the truck and shut the door hard behind her. "You're not going anywhere near that hole."

Diana blinked and stared at the man who had suddenly become every inch the ramrod of the Rocking M rather than the restrained lover who last night had taught her the pleasure of being kissed. Just kissed. All through the long drive to September Canyon, memories had come at odd times, making her shiver; then she would look over at Ten and he would smile at her, knowing what she was thinking.

He wasn't smiling now. Neither his stance nor the taut power of his body suggested that there was a bit of gentleness in him.

"I want your promise on that, Diana."

She waited for the fear that had always come to her in the

past when a man had stood hard-shouldered in front of her, his very size a threat that didn't have to be spoken aloud.

"Or else?" she asked tightly.

"Or else we've had a long drive out here for nothing, because we're going back."

"And if I refuse to go back?"

"You'll go anyway."

Diana looked at Ten's gray eyes and wondered how she had ever thought of them as warm, much less hot enough to set fires.

"Ramrod. It does suit you."

He waited.

"I'll stay on this side of the canyon," Diana said angrily. "You have my word on it. Not that you need it. You could enforce your edict and you damn well know it."

"Could I?" Ten asked in a cool voice. "You're smart and quick. You could find a way to go exploring before I could stop you. But now that you've given your word, I won't wake up in a cold sweat, seeing you lying beneath stone, only this time you aren't moving, this time you don't get up and walk away."

Diana felt the blood leave her face. She made a small sound and reached for him.

"Ten?" she whispered, touching his face.

He closed his eyes for an instant. When they opened again, they were alive once more. He bent and kissed Diana's upturned mouth quickly, then more slowly. When he lifted his mouth he whispered, "I'm glad you weren't afraid of me just now."

"I wasn't?"

Ten framed Diana's face between his large hands. "You dug in and gave as good as you got. Then you decided that it wasn't worth a long drive back to the ranch, so you agreed. That's not fear, honey. That's common sense. Me, now. I was scared."

Diana laughed in his face.

"It's true," he said. "I was afraid you'd be frightened of me and then you wouldn't let me kiss you again."

Memories of the previous night rose up in Diana, sending heat glittering from her breasts to her knees.

"What sweet sounds you make," Ten murmured, listening to the soft breaking of her breath. "Will you panic if I put my arms around you and give you the kind of kiss I wanted to give you this morning?"

Her breath came out in a long rush. "I've been hoping you would. I know it sounds crazy, but I feel like it's been forever since I kissed you. I miss your taste, Ten. I miss it until I ache."

"Open your mouth for me, honey," he whispered. "I missed you the same way, aching with it."

The heat and sweetness of Ten's mouth locked with Diana's. His taste swept through her, stealing her breath, her thoughts. Her arms tightened around his neck as she sought to get closer to him, then closer still. Soft sounds came from her throat as she gave in to a sweeping need to hold him so fiercely that he couldn't let go of her until his kiss had soothed the aching that had made sleep elude her through the long hours of the night.

Gravity slipped, then vanished, leaving Diana suspended within the hard warmth of Ten's arms. With catlike pleasure she kneaded the flexed muscles of his arms and shoulders, urging him to hold her more tightly, not caring if she could breathe. She felt no fear at the blunt reality of Ten's strength closing around her in a hot, sensual vise, for that was what she wanted, what she had ached for without knowing why or how.

Not until Diana was dizzy from lack of air did she permit the kiss to end, and even then she clung to Ten, her face against the sultry skin of his neck, her body shaking with each breath.

"Oh, baby," Ten said, shuddering with the force of his violent self-restraint. "There's a fire in you that could make stone burn. If you ever want more than kissing from a man, come to me."

Diana made an inarticulate sound and pressed her mouth against the corded tension of Ten's neck. The touch of her tongue on his skin went through him like lightning.

"You taste good," she said slowly, touching him again with her tongue. "Salty. Does your skin taste like that everywhere, or just on your neck?"

Desire ripped through Ten as he thought of his whole body being tasted by Diana's innocent, incendiary tongue. Very carefully he lowered her until she could stand on her own feet. He forced himself not to look at her reddened lips and cheeks flushed by desire. He wanted her until he was shaking with it. He had never wanted a woman like that. And that, too, shook him.

"Ten?"

"If you want to get any sketching done, we'd better unload the truck. You'll lose the best light."

"Sweet light."

Ten lifted a single dark eyebrow.

"That's what photographers call late-afternoon light," Diana explained. "Sweet light."

An image came to Ten of Diana wearing only slanting gold light, the womanly curves of her body glowing and her husky voice asking him to touch her. With an effort he banished the image, forcing himself to concentrate on what must be done.

"Where do you want to sketch first?" he asked. His voice was too thick, but he could do nothing about that for a few minutes, any more than he could quickly banish the hard proof of his hunger for her.

"I've done all the close-ups of the ruins I can do until the grads clear out more rubble and excavate to a new level," Diana said. "I need to do some perspective sketches, showing the ruins in relation to their natural environment, but to do that, I've got to be on the opposite side of the canyon."

Shrugging, Diana said nothing more. She had agreed not to cross over to the other side of the canyon, which meant that she had no sketches to do at the moment.

Silently Ten swore, knowing his reluctance to let her near the kiva was irrational.

"Get your sketching gear together. I'll go over the area myself. If nothing else gives way, you can sketch anywhere you like. Just make sure I'm within calling distance. And don't go near that damned kiva."

Fifteen minutes later Ten and Diana had unloaded the truck and were ready to go. He set out for the ruins at a pace that made her work hard to keep up. She didn't complain. One look at the line of Ten's jaw told her that he wasn't pleased to be leading her back toward the kiva.

Within a few minutes Diana was tasting the same kind of dread that had haunted Ten. Watching him quarter the area at the bottom of the cliff where she had fallen through, waiting for him to stumble into an ancient trap, standing with breath held until she ached; it was all Diana could do not to call Ten back even though she knew that the chance of his finding another intact kiva was so small as to be insignificant.

The chance had been equally small for her, and she had stepped through the roof of a kiva anyway.

Half an hour passed before Ten was satisfied that the terrain concealed no more traps. If there were any other kivas, they had been filled in by dirt long ago or their ceilings were still strong enough to carry his one hundred and eighty pounds. Either way, Diana should be safe. The kiva she had fallen into on her first day was a hundred feet distant, clearly marked by stakes.

Ten signaled for Diana to join him. She scrambled up the rugged slope with the offhanded grace of a deer. Very quickly she was standing close enough for Ten to sense the heat of her body.

"Find anything?" she asked breathlessly.

"Potsherds, masonry rubble and that."

Diana followed the direction of Ten's thumb. It took her a moment to realize what she was seeing. Sometime in the past five to eight hundred years, a piece of the cliff had fallen, all but filling the alcove below. Once the opening had held rooms. Now it held only an immense mound of cracked, broken sandstone. Water seeped in tiny rivulets from beneath the stone, telling of a spring hidden beneath. Her trained eye quickly picked out the angular stones and random potsherds that marked an Anasazi site.

"I hope they were already gone when the cliff came down," Diana said in a low voice, remembering what Ten had said.

...lying beneath stone, only this time you aren't moving, this time you don't get up and walk away.

Ten's big hand stroked her head from crown to neck. "Somehow," he said slowly, "I don't think they were. In fact, I'm...certain." He caressed her sensitive nape with the ball of his thumb before he lifted his hand and stepped away. "Better get sketching, honey. Even stone doesn't last forever."

Intent and relaxed at the same time, Diana sketched quickly, not wanting to lose the effect of slanting afternoon light on the ruins across the canyon. At her urging, Ten had crossed the small creek again and stood looking toward the ruins, giving scale to the cliff and the ragged lines of once whole rooms.

"Just a few more minutes," she called.

Ten waved his understanding. Diana's pencil flew over the paper as she added texture and definition to cliffs and canyon bottom, cottonwood and brush. The heightened contrast gave an almost eerie depth to the sketch.

The drawings she had made before had been accurate representations of the ruins as they were today. The drawing she was working on now was a re-creation of the ruins as they had looked long ago, when the sound of barking dogs, domesticated turkeys and children's laughter had echoed through the canyon, a time when women ground corn in stone metates or painted intricate designs on pottery while their men discussed the weather or the gods or the latest rumor of raids from the north. The narrow canyon would have been alive with voices then, especially on a day like today, when the sun was hot and vital, pouring light and life over the land.

Yet today, despite Diana's usual custom, she wasn't sketching people among the buildings. Nor was she sketching the burning blue radiance of the sky. There were heavy clouds surrounding the sole figure in her drawing, a man standing on the margin of the creek. The man was both dark and compelling, black hair lifting on a storm wind, an outlaw shaman calling to his brother the storm.

The power of the man was revealed in the taut male lines of shoulder and waist, buttocks and legs, a strength that was rooted in the center of the earth and in a past when the lives of humans and spirits had been intertwined. Standing with his back to the collapsed alcove, the shaman was a still center in the swirling violence of the wind. His brother the storm had answered the shaman's call.

The shaman turned around and looked at Diana with

eyes the color of rain, eyes that saw past the surface of reality to the soul beneath.

Diana shivered, blinked, and realized that she had been staring at the finished drawing so intently that her body was cramped in protest. Automatically she flipped the sketch tablet closed, both protecting and concealing the drawing. She slipped the tablet into its carrying case and stood up. Moments later she was hurrying down the slope toward Ten.

He turned at the sound of her approach, watching her with eyes the color of rain.

"Finished already?" Ten asked, holding out his hand to take Diana's pack.

She gave him her hand instead. Slowly he laced their fingers together until their hands were palm to palm. The sensitive inner skin of her fingers felt the hard pressure of him everywhere. The slow, complete interlocking was as intimate as a kiss. His palm was warm and hardened by work, making her wonder how it would feel on her skin if he were given the freedom of her body.

The thought haunted Diana while she and Ten went through their normal end-of-the-day chores—a basin bath behind the screen, then preparing dinner and cleaning up the campsite. Although the sun had vanished behind stone cliffs, true sunset was still an hour away. Shadows flowing out from the rocks had taken the edge off the unusual heat of the day, but the canyon walls still radiated the captured warmth of the sun.

Diana felt no need to pull her customary loose sweater over the sleeveless cotton blouse she was wearing. In fact, after her camp bath she had substituted sandals and shorts for hiking boots and jeans. Ten was feeling the heat, too. After his bath he hadn't bothered to put on a shirt or socks and boots. At the moment he was stretched out on his bedroll, which he had moved to the edge of the overhang, hoping to catch a vagrant breeze.

"Too bad we're not camping at Black Springs," Ten said, stretching slowly, fully. "There are pools big enough to cool off in."

"Sounds like heaven. Not that I'm complaining," Diana added, frowning over a handful of sherds. "I've been at sites where the only water we had was strictly for drinking."

She turned away from the sherds she had been sorting, saw Ten sprawled with feline ease across his bedroll and felt an increasingly familiar glittering sensation from her breasts to her knees. Without stopping to think, she walked over and sat next to him.

"Ten?"

His eyes opened. They were a burning silver.

Diana's thoughts scattered, and with them her ability to speak coherently. "Can I—that is, would you—could we—?"

"I thought you'd never ask."

Large hands closed around Diana's face, bringing her closer. Their mouths fitted together smoothly, seamlessly, and at the first taste of each other they both made low sounds of pleasure. Ten's hands shifted, lifting Diana, easing her across his chest until most of her weight was pressed against him. The shiver that went through her was as clear as lightning at midnight. He groaned and released her.

"Damn it, honey," Ten said heavily. "I didn't mean to frighten you. I didn't think how you would feel being on a man's bed again, and me half-naked at that."

Diana shook her head. "It wasn't in a bed. It was the front seat of a car. That's why I always sit so far away in the truck. And he never—never completely took off his clothes. Or mine."

Ten closed his eyes so that she wouldn't see the rage tugging against his control. He held her gently against his chest, stroking her head and back, kissing her hair, wishing that he could change the past.

But he could not. He could only hold Diana and want her until it was a kind of agony.

The slow stroking of Ten's hand sent currents of pleasure through Diana, making her breath sigh out. She smoothed her cheek against his chest, encountered a resilient cushion of hair instead of cloth, and made a murmurous sound of discovery. Ten's hand hesitated, then continued its languid journey from the silky hair of her head to the intriguing line of her back. Though the pressure was unchanged, the caress was different, sensual rather than soothing, enticing rather than calming. He felt the heat of her breath on his breast-bone as she kissed him lingeringly. Then he felt her lips open. She hesitated.

"Go ahead," Ten said. "Find out if I taste the same there as I did on my neck."

Diana lifted her head until she could see his eyes. "You won't mind?"

His smile was slow, hot, infinitely male. "Baby, you can put that sweet mouth anywhere on me that you want."

Deep blue eyes widened in shock and...curiosity. The shock he had expected. The curiosity made him want to pull her hard against his body and show her just how much he wouldn't mind any damn thing she wanted to do to him.

The first, exploring touch of Diana's tongue made Ten's breath stick in his throat. He had expected a darting taste followed by a smart comment about the limitations of camp baths. He hadn't expected a sleek, hot foray through the thicket of his chest hair. He hadn't expected her purring sounds of pleasure as she tasted him. Most of all, he hadn't expected her nipples to harden against him when she found and caressed his own nipple to a tiny, aching point.

Ten lay rigidly, fighting his own arousal and the sudden, violent need to touch Diana, to hold the sweet weight of her breasts in his hands, to taste and suckle and tease her until she writhed in an agony of pleasure. But all he permitted himself to do was slide the fingers of his left hand deeply into Diana's hair, holding her mouth against him while his right hand kneaded her back from nape to waist, pressing her even closer to the growing heat of his body. When he could bear no more he eased her mouth back up his chest until he could slide his tongue between her teeth, kissing her deeply, drinking her, mating with her in the only way she would allow.

By the time Ten released Diana's mouth she could barely think, much less speak. Her lips felt flushed, full, sated, but the rest of her body ached.

"I want—more than kissing," she said. "But I don't know how much more."

"It's all right," Ten said, kissing Diana's lips gently. "We'll take it slow and easy. The only rule will be the oldest and best one of all. Anytime I do something you don't want, tell me. I'll stop."

"That isn't fair to you. Yes, I know," she said quickly, before Ten could speak. "Life isn't fair. But I don't want to make it any harder on you."

The left corner of Ten's mouth tugged up. "Honey, it can't get any harder than it already is." He brushed another kiss over Diana's mouth, scattering her objections. Moving slowly, he lifted her from his body and stretched her out on her side with her back to him. "You'll feel safer this way, nothing in front of you, nothing holding you down, nothing trapping you. Just me behind you, and you know I'd never take you by surprise, don't you?"

"Y-yes," Diana said. It was the truth. If she hadn't trusted Ten at an instinctive level, she wouldn't even be in September Canyon with him, much less still shivering from his kisses. She let out a long breath that she hadn't been aware of holding and realized that Ten had been right about another thing. She did feel safer lying on her side with nothing in front of her but the view of a canyon slowly succumbing to the embrace of twilight. The setting couldn't have been farther from her memories of being wedged between cold machinery and Steve's relentless body. "Ten?"

"Hmm?"

"You're right. I feel safer this way."

"Good," Ten murmured, glad that Diana's back was to him, for it gave him the freedom to look at the line of her waist flaring into her rounded hips and then tapering slowly to her ankles. If she had seen the hunger and male approval in his eyes as he looked at her, she might have felt less relaxed with her back to him.

Ten's long index finger traced the line of Diana's body from the crown of her head, over her right ear, down her neck, over her right shoulder, down her ribs to her waist, up the rise of her hips, then down every bit of her right leg to her ankle. The primal ripple of her response followed his caress, telling Ten that her whole body had become sensitized to passion.

"That," he said, kissing the nape of Diana's neck, "broke every one of the high school rules about collarbones and waist. Feel like bolting yet?"

CHAPTER THIRTEEN

DIANA LAUGHED SHAKILY, wondering at the curious weakness that had followed Ten's caress. He had broken the rules, but in such a way as not to touch any of the forbidden areas.

"Does that little laugh mean I can do it again?" Ten asked.

The subdued humor in Ten's voice was another kind of reassurance to Diana. Steve had been deadly serious whenever they had been alone, intent on getting as much from her sexually as he could, as quickly as he could.

"Yes," Diana whispered.

A shiver of response followed the seductive movement of Ten's fingertip from Diana's head to her heels. This time he slid beneath her arm, as well, caressing the sensitive skin.

"You're a pleasure to touch," Ten said, kissing Diana's nape again. "Soft, resilient, alive." His tongue traced the line of her scalp to her ear. He smiled to hear the sudden intake of her breath. "You have the sweetest curves. Here," he said, biting her ear gently. "And here." His fingers curled around her arm caressingly. When his fingers moved on, his mouth lingered. He kissed the bare skin of her arm, biting softly, drawing tiny sounds from her. "And here."

Ten's hand shaped the tightly drawn line of her waist, kneading lightly, then more firmly. Slowly, inevitably, his palm moved over the full curve of Diana's hip. "And here." His fingers fanned out, shaping her. As his teeth closed over her nape, his hand flexed into her resilient flesh, luxuriating in the feel of her.

The unexpected caress drew a ragged sound from Diana. Currents of sensation rippled through her, making her want to shift restlessly. She stirred, and her movements acted to increase the pressure of Ten's hand. When his palm smoothed down her bare thigh, she forgot to be worried that he would slide his fingers between her legs. Only when his hand had stroked over her calves to her ankles did she realize that the danger zone had been bypassed once more.

Ten continued the slow, undemanding sweeps of his hand up and down Diana's body. The long caresses were punctuated by his teeth biting gently at her nape, her shoulder, the elegant line of her back; and each time his hand traveled back up her body, he skimmed closer to the shadowed secrets between her thighs and the fullness of her breasts. He explored the smooth curve of her belly with slow pressures that eased her hips back into the muscular cradle of his legs. The pressure of her against his fiercely aroused flesh was a sweet fire that made his hands shake.

Breath held against a groan, Ten waited for Diana to retreat. When she didn't, he pressed her even closer, savoring the pleasure-pain of his own need for a moment before he released her, not wanting to frighten her. His hand shifted, stroking slowly up the center line of her body, giving her every chance to refuse the growing intimacy of his touch.

Buttons caught and tugged against Ten's hand. He made no move to undo them despite his aching desire to touch Diana without the barrier of cloth. He simply caressed her from navel to breastbone to neck and back again, following the center of her body, knowing only a hint of the womanly curves that were calling to him.

"Wait," she said huskily.

Immediately Ten's hand stopped, then withdrew. Before he could retreat farther, slender fingers covered his, holding his hand against her belly. Her shoulders moved, her fingers urged his—and suddenly Ten found his hand inside Diana's blouse, cupping the lush weight of her breast. A groan was pulled from his throat, a low sound of desire that mingled with the one she made as her nipple peaked in a rush of sensation that left her weak.

Diana's breath unraveled into broken sighs as Ten's hand moved slowly from one breast to the other, caressing her, cherishing her. When his finger slid beneath the thin fabric of her bra and circled the tip of one breast, she gasped at the unexpected pleasure. He teased her nipple again, then withdrew, leaving her aching for more.

"Ten?"

He made a sound that could have been "More?"

"Yes," she sighed.

A long finger skimmed over Diana's nipple again, but the sensation was much less acute, because there was cloth between them this time. Without stopping to think, she released the front fastening of her bra, baring herself to Ten's touch.

A hammer blow of desire went through Ten, making his

hands shake. He eased one long arm beneath Diana's head, cradling her and at the same time giving both hands the freedom to caress her. He caught her nipples between his fingers and squeezed gently, smiling at the rippling cry of pleasure he drew from her lips. The sight of her rose-tipped, creamy curves nestled in his darker hands made fire pool urgently in his body, swelling him against his jeans until he could count each heartbeat as a separate surge of blood. He caressed her hard nipples again, wishing he could take the responsive flesh into his mouth.

Diana's breath fragmented into a low cry as Ten tugged rhythmically on her breasts, soothing and teasing her in the same skilled motions. He squeezed again, harder, knowing that she was now too aroused to feel a lighter touch. Her back arched in a passionate reflex that pressed her breasts against his hands. He rubbed slowly in return and was rewarded by a shivering cry of pleasure.

Deliberately Ten's hands retreated from Diana's breasts to her ribs, dragging slowly across her body, peeling away her bra and blouse. She made no objection, simply moved her shoulders sinuously, helping him. Her reward was the return of his hands to her breasts in a slow loving that drew ragged sighs from her lips; and then she felt the heat of his mouth going down her spine in a sensual glide that made her shiver repeatedly. Each restrained bite was a separate burst of pleasure sending glittering needles of sensation throughout her body. When his tongue traced her spine all the way up to her nape, she called out his name in a throaty voice she didn't recognize as her own.

"I'm right here, baby," Ten said, biting Diana's nape with enough force to leave small marks, tugging at the full breasts that lay within his cupped hands. "And so are you."

Slowly Ten released one breast and sent his hand down the front of her body again. "There is so much of you to enjoy," he said in a low voice. This time he didn't turn aside from the soft mound at the apex of her thighs. Nor did he linger. "Not just the obvious places, the battlegrounds of school kids," Ten continued, smoothing his hand over Diana's hip to the small of her back. "I like touching the rest of you, too." He traced the swell of her hip down to the back of her thighs, and from there to her firm calves and delicate ankles. "Smooth, firm…"

Ten's hand caressed higher, finding and stroking the inside of Diana's thighs as far as he could without seeming to pressure her for more than she was willing to give. His caress went from the back of her knee to the small of her back. He stroked first one hip, then the other, cupping and squeezing, drawing a surprised gasp of pleasure from her. She shifted almost restlessly, giving Ten's hand greater freedom. He moved his hand farther down, curling around her, holding her intimately. Heat burst through her, changing her gasp to a moan.

"Would you like lying just as you are now, but with no clothes to dull your pleasure?" Ten asked softly, kissing Diana's nape, her shoulder, her vulnerable spine. His hand tightened against her, subtly caressing her. "It's your choice, honey. You're as safe as you want to be."

"That's not…fair." The last word came out in a rippling sigh as Ten's hand flexed once more against her softness and heat.

"I thought you liked being teased," Ten said, smiling against Diana's spine despite the sudden, savage clenching of his own need.

"You're not teasing me," she whispered.

"I'm not?" Ten's hand flexed again and he groaned quietly

at Diana's helpless response to his touch. "Baby, I'm sure as hell teasing one of us."

He felt her hand moving, heard the soft slide of a zipper and sensed the sudden looseness of her shorts. His hand bunched, catching cloth between his fingers, pulling it away from the hot secrets he longed to explore.

When Diana felt her remaining clothes being tugged down her legs, felt the powerful, cloth-covered male legs rubbing against hers, a shaft of panic went through her, memories of another time, another place, pain. Her legs clamped together and her body jackknifed in an instinctive effort to protect herself.

Instantly Ten let go, leaving Diana's shorts and panties around her knees. Grateful that she couldn't see the tension in his body, Ten brushed a butterfly kiss on her shoulder.

"It's all right, Diana. It stops right here."

Gently Ten began to ease his left arm from beneath Diana's head. She grabbed his left hand and held it against her breast once more.

"Don't leave," she said raggedly. "I didn't mean to react like that. It was just when I felt the zipper scrape down my leg and felt your legs and you were still dressed—but it's all right now. I know where I am, who I'm with."

Ten kissed Diana's shoulder again but made no move to reclaim the soft curves he had already made his own, much less the shadowed heat that lay newly revealed to his touch.

"Would it make you feel better if I weren't wearing my jeans?" Ten asked.

She laughed a little wildly. "Yes. I know it sounds crazy but—yes."

With a silent prayer that his self-control was as good as he thought it was, Ten rolled over, removed his clothes and returned to his former spoon position with Diana. The feel of her bare bottom nestled deeply into his lap made him clench against a savage thrust of need.

Diana and I could be dead naked together and she could still say no and that would be that. So cool off, cowboy. This one is for Diana, not me. As much as she wants, when she wants it, however she wants it. That's what I promised.

I must have been out of my mind.

The sweet heat and feminine curves of Diana's body called out to Ten in a siren song as old as man and woman and desire, making Ten want to curse his stupidity for promising not to coax or beg or demand from Diana what he had never needed so much before in his life.

He lay motionless, his left arm pillowing Diana's head, his right hand clenched into a fist that rested on his equally clenched thigh.

"Ten," Diana whispered. "Please touch me again. It's all right. I trust you. I won't panic again. And I like—I like the feel of you without your jeans."

Slowly Ten's right hand loosened. He took a deep, secret breath, then another, relaxing himself in a ritual that was almost as old as desire itself.

"Are you sure?" he asked, not knowing of whom he asked the question.

Diana answered it for both of them. Without warning she took both of Ten's hands and rubbed her breasts against his palms, letting him feel the hardness of her nipples and at the same time easing some of the wild ache in her body. His strong fingers closed around her, plucking at the tight velvet peaks, coaxing a ripple of sound from her. After a moment the smooth heat of his right hand caressed her belly, her waist, the small of her back; then a single finger traced the shadow cleft between her hips.

If Diana had thought to conceal herself by locking her knees together and jackknifing her body, she had failed. Ten found her softness unshielded, defenseless, and he traced it lovingly. A sudden shudder took her whole body, surprising her. Her husky cry was matched by Ten's groan of discovery as her heat and pleasure spilled over him.

"Ten," Diana cried, feeling another of the strange, tiny convulsions building in her. "I—"

The word became a gasp and another shudder and then another as she felt his touch glide into her body, retreat, return, only to retreat once more, leaving her dazed and empty, aching. He skimmed the edges of her softness, probing sweetly, discovering the aching nub hidden between sleek, silken folds, rubbing it slowly, hotly, stripping away her breath, her thoughts, her restraint.

Diana twisted sinuously, trying to know more of the pleasure that was greater than any she had ever felt but still not enough; it was driving her mad. *Ten* was driving her mad, stealing into her so gently, retreating, always retreating when what she wanted, what she must have, was his own flesh filling the emptiness she had never known existed within her own body.

"So soft," Ten said, his deep voice a rumbling purr. He teased Diana slowly, loving the wild tremors of her response when he slid unerringly into her softness, groaning as he touched as much of her as he could. "So damned hot."

Ten's name broke on Diana's lips, a strained sound that could have been either fear or passion. Slowly, reluctantly, he began withdrawing from her body. Her hand locked over his, holding him in place.

"Are you sure you want this?" Ten said hoarsely, rubbing his cheek along her bare hip.

"Yes."

"And this? Do you want this, too?"

His hand shifted. The sensuous pressure within Diana increased. The glittering sensation that had haunted her body condensed into a network of wild lightning. The sound she made was as involuntary as the tightening of her body around him. Afraid that he had hurt her, Ten withdrew before she could stop him.

"Baby? Was that pleasure or pain? You're so tight…"

Diana looked over her shoulder at Ten with sapphire eyes that burned in the aftermath of sensual lightning. Slowly she turned her whole body until she was facing him. When she spoke, her voice was low, smoky, as helplessly sensual as her response to him. She guided his hand from her shoulder to the dark triangle at the base of her torso. When he accepted her wordless invitation and returned to her body, a shaft of pleasure made her gasp and tremble even as she instinctively sought more of Ten's touch. His hand shifted and she felt herself gently stretched. Sensual lightning came again, as unexpected and ravishing as it had been the first time.

"You were right," Diana said when she could speak.

"About what?"

"This. It's as much pleasure as your senses can stand."

Ten laughed softly, then groaned as Diana's mouth caressed his bare chest. "We've just skimmed the surface," he said, bringing her mouth up to his. "But I'm glad you're enjoying it."

She smiled hesitantly. "Are you enjoying it, too?"

"Baby, I'd have to be dead and buried not to enjoy touching you."

Ten felt Diana's slender fingers searching restlessly over his chest, pausing to tease the flat male nipples, then moving on to his back. She probed the line of his spine between ridges of muscle, stroking him, learning what it felt like to hold a man in her arms. Closing her eyes, sighing, half-smiling, she kneaded the long, heavy muscles of Ten's back, openly savoring the heat and power of his body.

Seeing Diana's enjoyment at touching him was as arousing as anything a woman had ever done to Ten. The tips of Diana's breasts were like tight pink rosebuds pressing against him with each movement of her hands. When he could no longer bear looking at her breasts without caressing them, he bent his head to her. A startled gasp became a moan as he circled one bud with his tongue, then took her deeply into his mouth, tasting her, tugging softly on her, making her shudder with each soft stab of his tongue, each exquisitely restrained caress of his teeth, each movement of his fingers within the clinging heat of her body.

Sounds rippled from Diana, the elemental huskiness of passion combined with rising notes of feminine surprise. The hot movements of Ten's mouth and hands increased, deepened, quickened, and she called his name with every rapid breath she took, every stroke of sweet lightning scoring her, shaking her, until finally she shimmered and burned in his arms, her body consumed by the pleasure he had given to her.

Ten held Diana as close as he dared, stroking her trembling body with hands that also trembled, kissing her flushed cheeks, her eyelids, her reddened lips, until finally her breath came more evenly. Her lashes stirred and lifted, revealing eyes more blue than any gems Ten had ever seen.

"How can I...what do I say?" Diana whispered.

"Whatever you want."

"I love you, Ten."

The line of Ten's lips shifted into a bittersweet smile. Before she could say any more, he kissed her gently. "I'm glad you enjoyed it, baby. Damned glad."

Diana opened her mouth to object that what she felt was more than the aftermath of physical pleasure, but Ten's tongue slid between her lips. Without thinking she closed her teeth, lightly raking his tongue, then soothing it with slow motions of her own in a pattern he had taught her. The tightening of his body in response and the sweet friction of his own tongue made her nerve endings shimmer again, echoes of lightning from her breasts to her knees. Her breath caught, broke, caught again.

"Ten?"

He closed his eyes, trying to ignore both the soft heat of Diana's body and the hard heat of his own.

"I want more of you," Diana said huskily, sweeping her hands from his shoulders to his waist. "I want all of you. If you—do you want me, too?"

"Move your hands down a little more and tell me what you think," Ten said hoarsely.

She had moved her hands barely at all when she discovered precisely what he meant. The sound he made while she measured his arousal with a slow pressure of her palm could have been pain, but she was looking at his eyes and she knew it wasn't. She repeated the caress again, drawing another hoarse, low sound.

"Baby, you'll…"

Ten's breath hissed between his clenched teeth. His hand slid from Diana's knee to the apex of her thighs as he sought the secret well of her femininity. It was even hotter and softer than his memories. She whimpered and moved with his touch. Her response and her hands searching over his hard, eager flesh nearly undid him.

Very carefully Ten eased Diana's hands up his body, kissed her fingertips and palms and held them hard against his chest while he caught his breath.

"Ten? What's wrong?"

"Hush, baby. Nothing's wrong."

Ten turned away and took a packet from his jeans pocket. With the swift, sure motions of a man performing an accustomed task, he opened the packet. When he turned back to Diana he wasn't completely naked. He saw her rather startled, somewhat dismayed look. With a calm that was exactly opposite to what he was feeling, he put his finger under her chin and tilted her face up to his own.

"Want to change your mind?" Ten asked.

Rather tentatively, Diana ran her fingertips over Ten's tightly sheathed flesh. "It felt better…without."

He clenched his teeth against agreeing with her. It had felt one hell of a lot better to be completely naked. Just as she, now, felt exquisite to his bare fingers as he once more slid into her, testing her readiness to receive him and simultaneously drawing a low sound of pleasure from her as she melted at his touch.

"Sex is temporary," Ten said tightly. "Children aren't. It's a small price to pay for a big amount of protection."

Diana's head snapped up, surprise clear on her face. At that moment Ten realized she hadn't even considered the fact that she might become pregnant. He wanted to swear and laugh and then swear some more at her trust, but most of all he wanted to plumb the depths of her heat with the very flesh that she was once again caressing tentatively. Though her touch was muffled by the price of protecting himself against the lifetime complications of fatherhood, the feel of her hand was nonetheless driving him to the edge of his control.

"Baby?" Ten said.

The aching restraint in his voice made Diana's heart turn over. "Yes," she whispered. "Whatever you want, just show me."

"The first time, it would be easier if...will it bother you to be beneath me?"

"No."

"Are you sure?"

Holding Ten's eyes with her own, Diana lay back and opened herself to him. Her complete trust pierced Ten, making him tremble with an emotion that was deeper and more devastating than desire. Slowly he settled between her legs, watching her for any sign of fear or pain. He saw only blue eyes that widened slightly at the gently probing pressure between her legs, then her eyes closed and she unraveled in a long, shivering acceptance of him within her body.

The ease with which Ten became a part of Diana was another instant of piercing emotion deep within him...and then he was moving and she was clinging to him, measuring him in a new way, moving with him, loving him as she had never loved another man.

Fire swept through Ten's restraint, burning him, burning her, each wanting more and yet more. Instinctively Diana's legs shifted, wrapping around his lean hips, luring and demanding with the same motions. He answered with hard, sweeping movements, driving into her, filling her, drinking from her sweet mouth until he felt his self-control slipping away. He fought against ecstasy, not wanting it to come to him so soon, not wanting to end the burning arousal that was in itself a savage pleasure; then it was too late, the pleasure was too piercing, too overwhelming.

Ten took her one final time, all of her, and held himself there while ecstasy stripped everything away but Diana and the deep, endless pulses of his own release.

CHAPTER FOURTEEN

TEN SAT IN THE ROCKING CHAIR, moving it with a gentle rhythm, looking down into Logan's turquoise eyes. The baby stared with absolute seriousness back into Ten's eyes.

"I know, old man," Ten said, smiling. "I don't look like your momma. What's worse, I'm not built like her and you're getting too hungry to be pacified by a rocking chair and a soothing voice much longer. But I'm afraid you'll just have to lump it for a while. Luke has been trying to show Carla that new colt all day, and this is the first chance they've had. You don't begrudge your parents a few minutes alone together, do you?"

Ten smiled to himself as he spoke. He suspected the new colt wasn't all that was keeping Luke and Carla away from the house. The men were scattered all over the ranch, Diana was working on sketches at the old house, Ten had promised to watch Logan, and the barn was empty of all but a few horses. Ten wouldn't have blamed Luke for taking advantage of the opportunity to steal a few kisses or even the whole woman.

The thought of enjoying a similar opportunity to have Diana alone within the twilight silence of the barn had a rapid and very pronounced effect on Ten's body.

"Damn," he muttered softly. "It's not like I've been exactly deprived in that department, except for the weekends."

When they were away from September Canyon, Ten was careful not to show any difference in his treatment of Diana. Some women could have laughed off or ignored the cowhands' brand of humor with regard to "unwed marriage" or "riding double" or the like, but Ten didn't think Diana was one of them. When the hands discovered, as they quickly would, that no marriage was planned, the humor would degenerate into sidelong looks and blunt male speculations. Diana's trust and uninhibited sensuality deserved better than that. She was very different from the kind of women the cowboys associated with summer flings.

The only time Ten allowed himself to be alone with Diana was in the old house, in the workroom, sorting sherds after dinner, the curtains open and both people plainly in view to anyone who cared enough to glance in. Outwardly, as long as anyone was around, nothing had changed since Diana had become his lover.

As much as Ten was tempted by proximity, he didn't so much as kiss Diana when they were at the ranch house. He didn't trust himself to stop with a kiss or two. On Friday, the drive back from September Canyon had taken so long that dinner was over hours before Ten and Diana made it to the ranch house. Part of the trouble had been a rain-slicked road. The other part had been Diana; Ten hadn't been able to keep his hands off her. What had started as a quick kiss had ended with both of them breathing too hard, too fast, their breath as steamy as their bodies had become.

All that had prevented Ten from taking Diana right there was the fact that her first, unhappy experience with sex had been in the front seat of a vehicle. So he had put the truck back in gear and driven to the ranch with the weekend stretching like eternity in front of him. But it had been a near thing. He had never been like that with a woman, riding the eroding edge of his own self-control until he wanted to put his fist through a window in sheer frustration.

Two nights in the bunkhouse did nothing to make him feel better. No matter how hard Ten tried not to, he kept seeing Diana holding out her arms, opening herself to him. The memory made heat and heaviness pool thickly between his thighs, a reaction that had become uncomfortably familiar since he had first seen Diana.

Becoming her lover had meant only a temporary improvement in the condition, followed all too soon by an even more pronounced return of the problem. Knowing the passion that lay behind Diana's smile didn't help to cool Ten's response. He wanted to make love to her after an evening of conversation and laughter, and then again in the middle of the night, and then he wanted to kiss her slowly awake in the morning, bringing her from dreams to passion, watching the pleasure in her eyes when she woke up and found him inside her. But he couldn't do that on the weekends, when they returned to the ranch house.

Logan bunched up his little fists and cried.

Ten sighed. "I know how you feel, nubbin. I know how you feel."

He shifted the baby and stroked the tiny cheek with his

fingertip. Logan's hands flailed with excitement until more by chance than anything else he connected with Ten's left index finger, bringing it to his mouth. Instantly the baby began sucking on Ten's callused fingertip.

"Uh, old man, I don't know how to break this to you, but...oh, the hell with it. You'll figure it out for yourself soon enough."

The controlled, throaty rumble of a powerful car engine distracted Ten. He looked out through the window into the last light of evening. The paint job on the car was a dirt-streaked, sun-faded black, but everything that affected the car's function was in top shape. The tires were new, the lights were bright and hard, and the engine purred like a well-fed cougar.

Even before the driver got out and stretched, Ten knew that Nevada Blackthorn had come back to the Rocking M.

Smiling with anticipation, Ten watched his younger brother climb the front steps with the lithe, coordinated motions of an athlete or a highly trained warrior. The knock on the door was distinct, staccato without being impatient. Ten's smile widened. There had been a time when his brother would have driven up in a cloud of dust and knocked on the door hard enough to rattle the hinges.

"Come on in, Nevada."

The door opened and shut without noise. Nevada crossed the room the same way. Without noise. Tall, wide-shouldered, his thick black hair two inches long and his dense beard half that length, Nevada looked as hard as he was. Even as his pale, ice-green eyes took in the room with its multiple doorways, his unnaturally acute hearing noted the near-silent approach of someone coming toward the living room through the kitchen.

Knowing that Ten was baby-sitting Logan, Diana had been all but tiptoeing across the kitchen as she headed for the living room. She didn't get that far. Two steps from the doorway she froze at the sight of the lean, long-boned, broad-shouldered stranger who moved like Ten when he was fighting.

Ten held Logan and watched Nevada cross the floor toward the rocking chair. Rain-colored eyes measured the changes in Nevada—the brackets of anger or pain around his flat, unsmiling mouth, the razor-fine physical edge, his muscular weight always poised on the balls of his feet because he had to be ready to throw himself into flight or battle at every instant. For Ten, looking at Nevada was like going back in time, seeing himself years ago, youthful dreams and emotions burned out by the timeless cruelty of war.

Silently Nevada stood in front of the rocking chair, staring down at his brother and the baby.

"I will be damned. Yours?"

Ten shook his head. "Not a chance. I know what kind of husband I make. I'm definitely a short-term man. Marriage should be a long-term affair."

Nevada grunted. "The bitch you married didn't make much of a wife, long or short."

The corner of Ten's mouth curled sardonically. "It wasn't all her fault. Women aren't interested in me for more than a few weeks."

"The way I remember it, you weren't real interested yourself after a few weeks. Two months was your limit. Then you were tugging at the bit, looking for new worlds to conquer."

"The curse of the Blackthorns," Ten agreed, his voice casual. "Warriors, not husbands."

Diana stood motionless, her throat clenched around a cry

of protest and pain, realizing that she had lost a gamble she hadn't even understood she was taking. She had understood the risk of physical injury she took in trusting Ten, and she had been lucky; Ten had given her extraordinary physical pleasure and no pain at all.

But she hadn't understood that she was risking her emotions and unborn dreams. Now she felt as she had the instant the kiva ceiling had given way beneath her feet.

No wonder Ten has been so careful not to touch me when other people are around. He doesn't want them to know we're lovers. They might assume something more, something that has to do with shared lives, shared promises, shared love. But he doesn't see us that way.

I didn't know I saw us that way until now, just now, when a dream I didn't even know I had burst and I fell through to reality.

God, I hope the landing is easier than the fall.

Diana clenched her teeth and forced herself to let out the breath she had instinctively held at the first instant of tearing pain. Silently, gradually, she took in air and let it out again, bringing strength back to her body. After a few aching breaths, her ears stopped ringing. The words from the other room began to have meaning again, Nevada speaking in tones that were like Ten's but without the emotion.

"Heard anything from Utah?"

"He's tired of jungles," Ten said.

Nevada grunted. "Anytime he wants to swap sea-level tropics for Afghanistan's high passes, he can have at it."

"Thought the country calmed down after the Russians left." Ten gave Nevada a measuring, gray-eyed glance. "Thought that was why you decided to come home."

"The Afghani tribesmen have been killing each other for

a thousand years. They'll be killing each other a thousand years from now. They're fighting men. They'd take on Satan for the pure hell of it."

"So would you."

Nevada's pale green eyes locked with Ten's. "I did. I lost."

Ten held out his right hand. "I don't know of any man who ever won. Welcome back, brother. You've been a long time coming home."

The deep affection in Ten's voice went through Diana, shaking her all over again, telling her that she was jealous of Ten's brother. The realization appalled her, and the pain.

All the old wives' tales are true: the landing is worse than the fall.

Diana looked around almost wildly. She had to leave, and leave quickly, before she was discovered. She couldn't face Ten with jealousy and despair and pain shaking her.

"Never thought I'd say it," Nevada said quietly, "but it's good to see your ugly face again. Now maybe you'll introduce me to the lady standing behind me."

Ten leaned sideways, looking around his brother's body toward the front door.

"Kitchen door," Nevada said, stepping aside.

Diana heard the words but took another step backward anyway, wondering bitterly how Nevada had known she was behind him. She hadn't made a sound. In fact, she had barely breathed, especially after hearing Ten's matter-of-fact summation of his lack of enduring appeal to women.

And theirs to him.

"Diana? Is that you? Come on in, honey. I want you to meet my brother Nevada. Nevada, this is Diana Saxton."

Nevada turned around and Diana knew she couldn't flee. The pale green eyes that were examining her were as passionless as Nevada's voice. She had an unnerving sense of looking into the eyes of a wolf or a cougar.

"How did you know I was here?" Diana asked almost angrily.

"Your scent."

Nevada's neutral tone did nothing to calm Diana. The man's unsmiling, measuring aloofness overwhelmed all other impressions she had of him, even the obvious one of his dark, hard, male appeal.

Nevada looked from Diana to the baby sucking industriously on Ten's finger. "Yours?"

"No," she said in a strained voice. "That's Logan MacKenzie."

"Luke's baby?" Nevada asked, looking at Ten.

Ten nodded.

"You mean that long-legged little girl you told me about finally ran him to ground?"

"She sure did. Then she let him go. He decided he didn't want to go anywhere without her."

Nevada shrugged. "To each his own. For the Blackthorns, that means single harness, not double."

Ten looked at Diana's tight, pale face and at his brother, who was a younger, harder reflection of himself. Ten looked down for a long moment at the baby in his lap, then he met again the unsmiling eyes of a warrior who had fought too long.

"Hope you haven't lost your taste for sleeping out," Ten said. "Jervis is getting damned tired of weekends in September Canyon."

"I don't sleep much, so it doesn't matter where I lie down."

Ten's eyes narrowed as he remembered the years he had spent relearning how to sleep like a civilized man instead of a wild animal, coming alert with every unusual noise, waking up in a single rush with a knife in one hand and a man's throat in the other.

"It will pass," Ten said quietly.

Nevada said nothing.

Logan began to fret, no longer pacified by Ten's unyielding fingertip.

Nevada watched the baby for a moment, then said, "Company coming from the barn. Man and a woman."

Ten shook his head at the acuity of Nevada's senses. "I'm glad I don't have to live like that anymore, every sense peeled to maximum alertness."

"Beats dying."

The very faint sound of a woman's laughter floated into the living room. Logan's fretfulness increased in volume.

"Honey," Ten said to Diana without looking away from the baby, "go tell Carla to get a move on it. Logan is getting set to cloud up and rain all over me."

There was no answer. Ten glanced up from Logan's rapidly reddening face. Diana was gone.

"How long was she standing there?" Ten said, his voice as hard as Nevada's.

"Long enough to know you're not interested in marrying her."

Ten closed his eyes and hissed a single, savage word. It would be a long drive to September Canyon tomorrow, and all the way Diana would be tight, angry, thinking of a thousand reasons why she shouldn't melt and run like hot, wild honey at his touch.

Logan began to cry in earnest, gulping in air and letting it out in jerky squalls.

"That's a strong baby you have there," Nevada said. He bent down. A long, scarred finger traced Logan's hairline with surprising delicacy. "It's good to hear a baby cry and know its distress is only temporary, that food and love are on the way."

"Less volume would be nice."

Nevada shook his head and said in a low voice, "The ones who are too weak to cry are the hardest to take."

Ten looked up quickly. His brother's eyes were hooded, unreadable. The front door opened and Carla rushed in.

"I'm sorry, I thought Logan would be all right for a few more minutes." She saw Nevada, noted the similarity to Ten in build and stance and smiled. "Nevada Blackthorn, right?" she asked, reaching past the bearded man for her hollering baby. "I'm Carla. Welcome to the Rocking M. We've never met but I've heard a lot about you." As she hurried from the room with Logan in her arms, she called over her shoulder, "Luke, look who finally got here. Now Jervis can go back to chasing cows."

Soon after Carla disappeared into the next room, the sound of the baby's crying ended abruptly, telling the men that Logan had found something more satisfactory to suckle than a man's callused fingertip.

Luke shut the door and walked across the living room. For a few seconds there was silence while Nevada and Luke measured each other. Then Luke nodded and held out his hand.

"Welcome back, Nevada. The Rocking M is your home for as long as you want it."

After a moment Nevada took the hand that was offered. "Thanks, MacKenzie. You won't regret it."

Luke turned to Ten, measured the expression on his face and asked rather warily, "Something wrong, ramrod?"

"Not one damn thing." Ten stood and crossed the room in long strides. "Come on, Nevada. I'll show you where you'll be sleeping."

The front door closed behind Ten.

Luke looked questioningly at Nevada.

"Woman trouble," Nevada said succinctly.

"What?"

"Five foot three, blue eyes, a fine body she tries to hide underneath a man's sweater."

"Diana?"

Nevada nodded.

"Did you say Ten's *woman?*"

Nevada shrugged. "She will be until she tries to put a permanent brand on him. Then she'll be looking for another stud to ride. Blackthorns don't brand worth a damn."

CHAPTER FIFTEEN

TEN WAS RIGHT ABOUT THE LENGTH of the drive to September Canyon. And the silence. Diana slept most of the way despite the roughness of the road, telling Ten two things. The first was that she trusted his driving skills, but he already knew that. The second was that she must have slept damned little the night before to be able to sleep so soundly now in the rolling front seat of the pickup truck.

When Ten could take it no longer, he said, "Diana."

Her eyes opened. They were dark, clear, and their color was an indigo as bottomless as twilight.

"Pounce's purring must have kept you up all night," Ten said, watching the road. One look at Diana's eyes had been enough.

"Pounce hunts at night." The thought of the cat gliding through darkness in search of prey reminded Diana of Nevada. "Like Nevada."

"He lived as a warrior too long. Like me. And like me,

Nevada will heal," Ten said matter-of-factly. "It just takes time."

Diana made a sound that could have meant anything.

Ten waited.

No more sounds came from the other side of the truck.

"I was glad to see that Nevada and Luke didn't have to sort things out the hard way," Ten continued. "They'll get along fine now that life has knocked some sense into both of their hard heads."

Diana said nothing.

With a hunger Ten wasn't aware of, he watched her for a few instants before the road claimed his attention again. Telling himself to be patient, he waited for her to speak. And he waited.

And waited.

Ten was still waiting when they forded Picture Wash and bumped up September Canyon to the overhang. It wasn't the first time he and Diana had gone for hours without conversation, but it was the first time the silence hadn't been comfortable. Getting out of the truck didn't increase Diana's desire to talk. They unloaded supplies with a minimum of words, each doing his or her accustomed part around the camp.

Without a word Ten carried the two bedrolls to the edge of the overhang, dragged two camp mattresses over and began making up the single, oversize bedroll he and Diana would share. He sensed her watching him, but she said nothing. When he straightened and looked around, he saw Diana shrugging into her backpack, clearly preparing to go out and sketch in the rapidly failing light. His arm shot out and his fingers curled hard around her wrist.

"Damn it!" Ten said. "You were the one who came to me! I never promised you anything!"

Diana's eyes were wide and dark against her pale face. For

a long, stretching moment she looked at Ten, letting the truth echo around her like thunder while painful lightning searched through her body and soul.

"Yes," she said huskily. "I know."

Ten's hands tightened. Her agreement should have made him feel better, but it didn't. He kept remembering the moment when she had looked at him with eyes still dazed by her first taste of sexual pleasure and whispered that she loved him.

Now her eyes were filled with pain. He had never felt another person's pain so clearly, as clearly as his own.

"Listen to me," Ten said roughly. "The pleasure you feel when we have sex—that isn't love. It will wear off. It always does. But until it does, there's no reason you shouldn't enjoy it to the fullest."

The slight flinching of Diana's eyelids was the only betrayal of her emotions. "That's very kind of you, Tennessee."

Her soft, even voice scored Ten like a whip.

"*Kind?* I'm not some damn charity worker. I'm a man and I enjoy sex with you a hell of a lot more than I've ever enjoyed it with any woman. What we have in bed is damned rare and I know it even if you don't!"

Diana looked up into the blazing clarity of Ten's eyes. She didn't doubt that he meant exactly what he had said. She drew a deep breath, drinking his complex truth to the last bittersweet drop. Pleasure, not love. But a rare pleasure, one he valued.

"I'm glad," she said finally.

And that, too, was a complex, bittersweet truth.

Ten should have been relieved at Diana's acknowledgment that what they shared in bed wasn't love. But he wasn't relieved. She understood, she agreed—and somehow she had never been farther away from him, even the first day when she had turned and run from him.

Swearing beneath his breath, Ten stood with his fingers locked around Diana's wrist and wondered savagely how he and she could be so painfully honest with each other and yet somehow allow an important truth to slide through their fingers like rain through sand, sinking down and down and down, farther out of reach with every second.

"To hell with talking," he said savagely.

Ten bent his arm, bringing Diana hard against his body. His tongue searched the surprised softness of her mouth with urgent movements. The hunger that had been just beneath his surface blazed up, shortening his breath, making his blood run heavily, hardening his body in a rushing instant that he felt all the way to his heels; but Diana was stiff in his arms, vibrating with emotions that had little to do with desire.

"Don't fight me, baby," Ten said heavily against Diana's mouth, his voice as dark and hot as his kiss had been. "What we have is too rare and too good to waste on anger."

Ten probed the center of Diana's ear with the hot tip of his tongue, feeling her shiver helplessly in response. He probed again and was rewarded by another sensuous shiver. With a low sound of triumph, he caught the rim of her ear between his teeth and bit delicately, repeatedly, demanding and also pleading for her response.

The intensity and need within Ten reached past Diana's pain to the love beneath. She tried to speak, didn't trust her uncertain hold on her emotions and slid her arms around Ten's lean waist instead. His breath came out in a barely audible sigh of relief when he felt her soften against him.

"Diana," Ten whispered, hugging her in return, "baby, I don't want to hurt you. When you gave yourself to me that first time, looking right at me, knowing to the last quarter inch how much I wanted you..." Memory lanced through

Ten, making him shudder. "Yet you held out your arms to me. No one has ever trusted me like that. I was so afraid of hurting you I almost didn't go through with it."

She looked at him with startled blue eyes.

"It's true," Ten said, easing his fingers into Diana's cool, soft hair. "I was arguing with myself all the way down into your arms. Then you took me so perfectly and I knew I wouldn't hurt you. Your body was made for mine. And somehow you knew it, too, didn't you? That's why you watched me with such curiosity and hunger, day after day, until I thought I would go crazy. Then you asked me to kiss you and I was sure I would go crazy. You fit my hands perfectly, my arms, my mouth, my body. I knew it was going to be so damned *good*. I was right. It was good then and it's even better now, each time better than the last."

The words caressed Diana even more than the heat of Ten's body or the pressure of his fingers rubbing slowly down her spine.

"Is it that way for you, too?" Ten asked. "Tell me it's that way for you, too."

He bent to kiss Diana's neck with barely restrained force, arching her against his body, letting her feel his strength and what she had done to him.

"Baby?"

"Yes," she said as she gave herself to his power. "You must know it is, Ten. Don't you know?"

"I do now," he whispered against her hair, and then he whispered it again.

Slowly Ten straightened. He held Diana gently against his chest, just held her, as though he were afraid to ask for any more than she had already given.

And he was.

"Go ahead and sketch while you still have light," Ten said finally, kissing Diana's eyelids, brushing his lips gently across her mouth, caresses without demand. "I'll open the new box of sherds and see what the grads found over the weekend."

Shaking, feeling like crying in protest when Ten turned away, hungry for him in a way that eclipsed anything she had ever felt before, Diana looked blindly out over September Canyon. She couldn't force herself to walk away from the overhang and the man she loved more with every day.

And with every day she was closer to losing him.

The pleasure you feel when we have sex—that isn't love. It will wear off. It always does.

But it wouldn't for her. Diana knew that as surely as she had known she could trust Ten not to force anything more from her than she wanted to give. She had been right. He had taken nothing from her that she hadn't given willingly.

It wasn't Ten's fault that he didn't want everything she had to give to a man.

Though Diana knew sketching would be impossible, she took off her backpack, brought out her pad, opened it and sat down on the bedroll she would share that night with Ten. Adrift on the cool wind flowing down from the mesa top, she looked out over the canyon she loved. She saw neither trees nor cliffs nor even the wild beauty of the setting sun, only the image of the man she had come to love even more than the land.

In her mind she saw Ten's face with eerie precision, each line that sun and wind had etched around his eyes, eyes whose probing clarity had first unnerved, then fascinated her. The same was true of Ten's powerful, unmistakably male body; first it had frightened and then finally it had fascinated her.

Now, in the clear light of pain, Diana acknowledged

what she had previously been too caught up within her own fears and needs to see—the shadows that lay beneath the clarity of Ten's eyes, the reserve that lay beneath his passion, the internal walls he had built as carefully as an Anasazi cliff fortress, walls keeping her out, his own words describing solitude.

He lived as a warrior too long. Like me. And like me, Nevada will heal. It just takes time.

But Ten hadn't healed. Not wholly.

She wanted to heal him. She needed to. But there were so few weeks left to remove scars that were years deep, a wounding so old, so accustomed a part of the man she loved, that Ten himself didn't even realize that he hadn't healed. He had scarred over, which wasn't the same thing at all.

"Such a pensive look," Ten said. Sitting down next to Diana, he glanced at the drawing in her lap. It was a close-up of September Canyon's ruins, detailing the precarious eyelash of a trail that led from the cliff dwellings up the face of the cliff to the mesa above. "Are you thinking about the Anasazi again, trapped within their own creation?"

"And time," Diana said, her voice husky, aching as she flipped slowly through the sketchbook. "Time is another kind of trap."

"Why? Are you getting behind in your sketching?"

"No. I'll be finished well within the deadline."

"Deadline?"

"The middle of August. That's when my contract with the Rocking M ends."

Ten looked deeply into Diana's eyes, wanting to protest what lay beneath her quiet words: when the contract ended, she would leave the Rocking M and Tennessee Blackthorn.

Diana looked only at the sketch in her lap, praying that Ten would reach past the wall he had built and ask her to stay without the pretense of archaeological work between them.

Ask me to stay, Ten. Ask me as a man asks a woman he wants and needs and might someday love. Please, love, ask me.

Silently, Ten's fingertips traced the line of Diana's chin, tilting her face up to his lips. He kissed her slowly, seducing her mouth for long moments before accepting the invitation of her parted lips and warm tongue. With controlled urgency he began undressing her, only to discover that he was being undressed, as well. Relief coursed through him almost as violently as desire. He kissed her again, drinking deeply, urgently, from the woman who haunted his sleep even when she was lying by his side.

By the time the kiss ended, their breathing was ragged and their clothes were scattered randomly around the bedroll. Ten's hand slid from Diana's ankle to the apex of her thighs. The deep, sultry welcome of her body made blood hammer in his veins until he could hardly breathe.

"It's a little soon to be mentally packing your gear, isn't it?" Ten asked in a low, rough voice as he caressed Diana, calling forth a husky moan and a tiny, searing melting. "A lot could happen in the next few weeks."

"Could it?" Diana asked, hope leaping even more hotly than desire within her body.

"Sure. The Rocking M is going to need some expert advice on excavating the kiva you discovered. Who better than you to give it?"

Before Diana could speak, Ten took her mouth. The slowly building pressure of his kiss arched her across his hard forearm. She gave herself to the kiss and to the man, feeling desire and regret, caring and hunger, passion and restraint in Ten's embrace, every emotion except the love that filled her until she ached.

When the long kiss ended, Ten lifted his mouth with tangible reluctance.

"There's no reason not to extend your contract."

"Luke might see it differently."

"September Canyon is my land. The dig is being underwritten by my money. If I want it to go beyond the middle of August, it will."

Diana shuddered from desire and grief mixed together, feeling as though she had been turned inside out until everything she was and could be lay exposed to the cool sunset light. Bittersweet understanding of the difference between her own needs and Ten's knifed through her, and in its wake an anguished acceptance.

She wanted his laughter, his grief, his victories, his defeats, his silence, his conversations. She wanted his body, his mind, his children and a lifetime of tomorrows. He wanted the passion that ran like invisible lightning between them, and he wanted every bit of it for as long as it lasted.

She loved him. He did not love her. But she could take from him one of the things she wanted and give him the only thing he wanted in return.

Diana rolled onto her side and began running her hands down Ten's muscular torso, caressing and inciting him with the same motions.

"No, there's no reason at all not to extend the contract," Diana said, finding and teasing a flat male nipple with her teeth, "except common sense."

"What does that mean?"

"Simple. As simple as this."

Her hands closed around the thick evidence of Ten's desire and he groaned with leaping need. She continued talking as she caressed the length of his body, scattering his thoughts, taking away everything but the heat of her mouth.

"The Rocking M—" Diana's tongue probed Ten's navel "—can't afford to pay me." She closed her teeth on the tightly flexed muscles that joined neck and shoulder. A shudder moved the length of his body. "Not as much as I earn being an assistant professor at the university."

"We could—work something out. Weekends. Vacations." Ten's breath came in with a hissing sound as Diana nuzzled his ear, teasing, biting. "Part-time work. Something."

Diana's eyes closed against a wave of pain, but her mouth and hands remained gentle, loving Ten, sharing with and returning to him the gift of passion he had given so generously to her. After a few moments she could trust herself to speak again.

"You don't have to pay me to come to the Rocking M." She bit the hard muscle of Ten's biceps in a sensual punishment that was just short of pain. "All you have to do is ask. Or you can come to Boulder when you feel like it."

"Diana…"

She waited, hope penned within her acceptance like a wild animal.

Ten made a half-angry, half-helpless sound.

She let out her breath in a long, soundless sigh, knowing acceptance had been right and hope had been wrong.

"I agree," Diana said softly. "It's better to keep it just a summer affair."

"That's not what I said."

"No. It's what you meant."

"Damn it," Ten said roughly, "I learned long ago that I'm piss-poor husband material."

"Did you?" Diana asked, lifting her head, looking into

Ten's narrowed eyes. "Or did you just decide sex isn't worth all the inconvenience of marriage?"

Bleak gray eyes searched Diana's face.

Smiling sadly, she turned away and let her mouth slide down the warm, muscular tension of his abdomen. "It's all right, Tennessee. I learned something long ago, too. Then you came along and taught me that I hadn't learned everything."

Diana's cheek rested for a moment on a dense cushion of black, curly hair. Her lips brushed flesh that was hot, smooth, hard, pulsing with the swift beat of Ten's life. When she moved her head to test the resilience of his thigh with her teeth, Ten made a deep sound. When her head turned again and the tip of her tongue touched him curiously, his breath came out in a low groan that was also her name.

"If I made you a promise," Diana said, biting Ten lightly once more, stroking the thick muscles of his thighs, skimming over without ever really touching the hard, violently sensitive flesh that she had aroused, "would you trust me to keep it? Would you trust me not to ask you for anything more, ever?"

Blindly Ten reached for his jeans, his fingers seeking the familiar packet, finding it.

"Tennessee," Diana whispered, brushing her lips over the musky cushion of hair, touching his hot flesh with the tip of her tongue. "Do you trust my promise?"

He groaned as a fine sheen of passion broke over his skin. His right hand clenched, crumpling the packet. "Baby, it's damned hard to think when you're doing that."

"Then don't think. Just answer from the instinctive part of you. Do you trust me to keep my promise about never asking for one more thing from you?"

"Yes," Ten said hoarsely, knowing as he spoke that it was true. He could trust Diana's word. "What do you—want?"

"This."

The sound Ten made was a combination of surprise and searing pleasure as Diana's mouth tasted him with lingering sensual curiosity.

"When I first asked you to kiss me," she whispered against his hot skin, "it was because I wanted to be able to lead a normal life, and that meant responding to men the way other women did. And it worked, up to a point. But then I began trying to imagine other men touching me the way you had, and I knew I wouldn't be able to go through with it."

"Fear?" Ten asked, the only word he could force past the passionate constriction in his throat.

Diana shook her head. Tendrils of silky hair brushed over Ten's skin in the instant before her mouth circled him in a caress that took what little breath he had remaining, tasting him, loving him as she never had before. When the caress deepened, Ten's whole body flushed with wild heat. She held him for long moments, savoring him, loving the wildness coursing through him at her caress. Slowly, reluctantly, she released him from tender captivity.

She lifted her head and met the smoldering brilliance of Ten's eyes. The look in them made her body melt. He felt it, knew that she wanted him as wildly as he wanted her, and had to close his eyes against the force of the need twisting through his body.

"It's not fear that will keep me away from other men," Diana said finally, biting Ten with great gentleness, feeling the wave of desire that swept through him almost as clearly as he did. "It's the fact that I don't want them. Other men wouldn't have rain-colored eyes that blaze with desire. Other men wouldn't have a scar below their jawline or one on their shoulder, their hip, the inside of their left thigh. Other men wouldn't be able to handle a brute and a kitten with the same ease. Other men wouldn't look like you, feel like you…taste like you."

Ten made a hoarse sound of intense pleasure as the moist heat of Diana's mouth caressed him again. He called her name roughly, feeling the world being stripped away with each silky movement of her tongue.

"Make love without barriers for the weeks I have left on the Rocking M," she said. "Be completely naked inside me. No matter what happens afterward, there won't be any demands, any regrets." Slowly Diana slid up Ten's body until the thick length of his arousal skimmed her softness, making her breath break. "Ten?"

His own breath came in with a harsh, ripping sound as she melted over him. "I'm not sure I can hold back with you, baby," he said roughly. "You could get pregnant. Have you thought of that?"

"Yes," Diana said, shivering, melting, searing him with her need. "Many times."

Ten's right hand opened with a savage movement, sending the small packet tumbling onto the ground. He lay still but for the elemental tremors of desire coursing through his hard body.

"Last chance," he said thickly.

Her hips moved. Sultry fire licked over Ten. Shaking with a hunger he had never felt before, Ten knew he was going to take what he must have, what she was asking him for, what they both wanted until it was agony not to have it; but he had never taken a woman like this before, no barriers, nothing except violently sensitive skin and a need so great it kept him on the breaking edge of self-control.

When Ten's aroused flesh found the incredible softness and heat waiting for him, the sensation was so intense he couldn't breathe. He felt each separate pulse of Diana's response as he parted the soft flesh, sheathing himself within her slowly, deliberately, deeply, sharing her body and his own in an exquisite intimacy that was just short of anguish.

"I've never—been like this—before," Ten said thickly, his breath breaking. "Naked. Nothing held back. It's—I can't—"

He went utterly still, fighting desperately not to lose control.

"Tennessee," Diana whispered, looking into the silver blaze of his eyes, feeling the first waves of pleasure ravish her. "Give me your baby, Tennessee."

A sound of hunger and ecstasy was torn from Ten's throat, and then ecstasy alone, Diana's name repeated in shattered syllables as he gave himself again and again to the sweet violence of a union unlike any he had ever known.

CHAPTER SIXTEEN

THUNDER CRACKED WITH A NOISE like rock shearing away from tall cliff faces, a naked violence of sound that made September Canyon tremble in the night.

Ten eased out of the blankets he shared with Diana and went to stand at the edge of the overhang. The chilly air took the heat from his body, but he barely noticed the temperature. The smell, taste and sound of the wind told him all that he needed to know. He and Diana would have to pack up and cross Picture Wash before dawn.

And Ten had counted on spending the hour before dawn quite differently.

"Damn."

"What's wrong?" Diana asked sleepily.

"Storm coming on. A big one."

By memory alone Ten went to the camp table, struck a match and lit the Coleman stove. The golden glow of naked flame danced in graceful reflections over the pale sandstone. He made coffee with the swift, economical motions of a man very familiar with the task. Then he walked to the warm blankets where Diana lay, grabbed his clothes and began dressing.

"Ten...?"

It was only a single word, but he understood all that she wasn't saying. Reluctantly he shook his head.

"Sorry, honey," Ten said, his voice gritty with hunger and regret. "We've got a lot of packing to do and not much time to do it."

Diana bit back her protest even as it formed. The storm didn't care if it were cutting short her last hours with Ten in September Canyon.

Silently she kicked off the blankets and began pulling on clothes, shivering as the cold wind washed over her body. Working by the light of a gas lantern, she packed quickly, forcing herself not to think how this day was different from any day that had come before or would come after.

As soon as Diana's personal gear was packed, she began working on the artifacts that were to be taken back to the ranch. She packed slowly, carefully, saying goodbye with her fingertips to the ancient pots and stone axes, fiber sandals and bone implements that she had come to know as well as she knew the less textured camping equipment of her own time and culture.

When each box was ready, she set it aside for Ten to carry to the truck. Periodic lightning shattered the black sky. Thunder rang repeatedly, a barrage that deafened. She ignored it, working steadily, thinking only of the task at hand. As she reached for another empty box, she found Ten's hand instead. Startled, she looked up.

"Leave it for the grads," he said in a clipped voice. "We have to cross while we can. It's raining like hell up on September Mesa."

She looked out into the encompassing blackness and saw nothing at all. "How can you tell?"

"Listen."

At first Diana thought what she heard was the wind, a low, muttering kind of sound. Then she realized that she was hearing water. September Wash was filling.

"Is it still safe to cross?" she asked, unable to suppress the hope in her voice. If the wash weren't safe, they would be forced to stay on this side until the water went down.

As though Diana had spoken her hope aloud, Ten shook his head. "This is a big storm. Carla will fret and then Luke will send men out in hell's own rain to look for us. I don't want anyone getting hurt looking for people who could have and should have gotten back."

The sky exploded into twisting, wildly writhing forks of lightning. Barely four seconds later, thunder hammered down.

"Time to go, honey."

Diana closed her eyes against the pain that was lancing through her as surely as lightning lanced through the clouds.

Thunder filled September Canyon, followed by a gust of rain-scented wind that made piñons moan. No rain was falling, but there was no doubt that it would. Soon.

Ten opened the passenger door for Diana and helped her up into the cab. Her breast pressed against the lean male hand that was wrapped around her upper arm. Though the contact was accidental, it made every one of Diana's nerve endings shimmer. When she tried to fasten her seat belt, her hands were clumsy with the sudden rush of her blood.

Ten climbed in, saw Diana's difficulty and said, "Let me.

That belt mechanism is getting kind of cranky. First you have to slack off and let it retract all the way. Like this."

He took the metal tongue from Diana's fingers, then followed the retreat of the harness across her lap. The sound of her indrawn breath was as much an inadvertent caress as his hand skimming across her body in the wake of the buckle's metal tongue. When he pulled the harness across her lap once more, his hand skimmed, hesitated for a breathless instant, then moved on. He inserted the metal tongue slowly into the locking mechanism. A subdued *click* broke the taut silence.

"See? Perfect fit." Ten's voice was low, gritty.

He touched Diana's mouth with his thumb and swore softly, wanting her. And she wanted him. It was in her eyes, in the tightness of her body, in the huskiness of the few words she had spoken. He gave her a quick, hard kiss and forced himself to concentrate on other things.

Ten drove to the wash, studied the roiling water carefully and bit off a vicious curse. There was no doubt about it, no ignoring it. The wash was definitely still safe to cross.

He put the truck in gear and drove into the water. As soon as he reached the other side he spoke without looking at Diana.

"Hang on. I'm going to drive hard to get ahead of the storm."

The road was dry and familiar, its occasional vagaries and hazards well-known to Ten. He held the big truck to a punishing pace, boring through the predawn darkness, outrunning the storm outside the truck, ignoring the one within as long as he could.

Finally the truck climbed up for the long run across Wind Mesa. For a time the road snaked along the very edge of the highland, giving a breathtaking vista of predawn light locked in luminous embrace with a high, slowly seething lid of clouds. The tenuous light was eerie, astonishing, flawless, utterly without color.

Ten stopped the truck at a point where the road gave an uninterrupted view of the dark land below.

"We're at least an hour ahead of the rain," Ten said, releasing his seat belt. "Want some coffee?"

Diana made a murmurous sound of approval that could have meant the view, the idea of coffee or both.

By the dim illumination of the dashboard lights, Ten opened a thermos and poured coffee. A clean, rich fragrance filled the cab. He handed the half-full cup to Diana, who refused it with a shake of her head.

"You first," he insisted.

"Afraid of poison?" Diana asked huskily. She forced herself to smile, concealing the sadness that had grown greater with each mile flying beneath the truck's broad tires.

Ten's own smile flashed briefly. "No, but I've discovered that coffee tastes sweeter if you drink out of my cup before I do."

Diana said his name softly, then bent her head and sipped the hot liquid. Ten flicked off the lights, killed the engine and rolled down his window. Cool air breathed across the cab, air redolent of distance and unfettered land. In silence they passed the cup of coffee between them while spectral light slowly filled the space between clouds and earth, transforming everything, infusing the very air with radiance.

"Spirit light," Ten said finally.

Diana looked up at him questioningly.

"That's what Bends-Like-the-Willow, my grandmother, called it. The kind of light that enables you to see right through to the soul of everything."

"She was Indian?" Diana asked.

Ten's smile was a thin, hard slice of white in the truck's

interior twilight. "Honey, there aren't many families that were in America before the Civil War that don't have Indian blood in them. The first Blackthorns came over from Scotland more than two hundred years ago."

"Did they marry Indians?"

"Sometimes. Sometimes they just slept with them. Sometimes they fought with them. Sometimes Blackthorn women or children were taken in raids." Ten shrugged. "There has been a lot of mixing and matching of bloodlines, one way or another. If children were the result of a town marriage, they were raised white. If children were the result of no marriage, they were raised Indian."

Ten sipped coffee from the shared cup before he resumed talking about the past, because anything was better than talking about the unshed tears in Diana's eyes and the turmoil in his own mind.

"By now there's no way to tell who got which genes, native or white or everything in between. Nevada and I have black hair and a copper tone to our skin. Utah has skin like ours, but he has blond hair and black eyes." Ten shrugged. "In the end, it's the quality of the person that matters, not the rest. That's what Bends-Like-the-Willow had. Quality."

"Was it a 'town marriage'?"

He shook his head and smiled oddly. "The Blackthorns were warriors. They leaned toward informal marriages. Up until the last generation, we were raised mostly in Indian ways. Bends-Like-the-Willow was quite a woman. Her father was a MacKenzie."

"As in the Rocking M MacKenzies?"

Thunder belled again, filling the canyon.

"Probably," Ten said. "Her mother was Ute. Her father was a wild young white who rode out one night and never came back. Luke has a few like that in his family tree. One of them disappeared at about the right time and place."

"Is that how you came to own part of the Rocking M?"

Smiling sardonically, Ten shook his head. "Honey, a hundred years back, nobody gave a damn about part-Indian kids born on the wrong side of the blanket. It's only in the last generation people have started to get all puffed up and sentimental over Indian ancestors whose skeletons have been rattling in white closets for a long, long time."

"Then how did you end up here?"

"When I got out of the warrior business, I was like Nevada. Hurting and not knowing what to do about it. Needing a home and not knowing how to get one. Luke's father was selling off chunks of the Rocking M to pay for his drinking. I bought in. The ranch has been my home ever since."

Diana waited, but Ten said no more. She followed his glance out the windshield. The land lay beneath the storm like a woman waiting for a lover. Though no rain had fallen, the storm had brought an eerie glow to the air, a timeless gloaming that made all distances equal. There were no shadows to define near and far, no sun's passage to mark hours across the sky, no waxing or waning moon to measure weeks, nothing but the eye and mind of man to draw distinctions.

"Spirit light," Ten said, his voice harsh. "When you see everything too damn clearly."

He looked at Diana and saw too much, his own hunger clawing at him, telling him that he would remember her too long, too well.

Diana looked away from the eerie clarity of the land and saw Ten watching her with silver eyes that burned.

"What are you thinking?" she asked before she could stop herself.

"I'm remembering."

"What?"

"How you look when your skin is flushed with heat and you're as hungry for me as I am for you."

Knowing he shouldn't, unable to stop himself, Ten slid partway across the big seat, took the coffee cup from Diana and set it on the dashboard. Her dark blue glance went from his eyes to the clean, distinct line of his mouth. Even as she leaned toward him, he pulled her close, lifting her, turning her so that she was half-lying across his lap. His mouth came down over her parted lips, filling her with his taste and his hunger, wordlessly telling her about the need that would make the coming days restless and the nights endless.

Diana gave back the kiss without restraint, loving the taste of Ten, coffee and man and passion. The kiss deepened even more, becoming an urgent mating of mouths. When she felt the hard warmth of his palms sliding beneath her sweater, she twisted sinuously, bringing her breasts into his hands. His fingers stroked, caressed, teased until exquisite sensations radiated from her breasts to the secret core of her, melting her in a few shuddering moments.

With a soft whimper Diana began to move against Ten's body. She felt rather than heard the rasping groan he gave when his hands released the catch on her bra, allowing him the freedom of her breasts. He pushed up her loose sweater and bra and looked at her. Flushed by passion, soft, creamy, resilient, tipped with tight pink buds of desire, her breasts begged for his mouth.

"Baby?"

"Yes," Diana whispered huskily, raising her arms and arching her back as she reached to remove her sweater.

Ten didn't wait for her to finish. He kissed one peak,

licked it with catlike delicacy, then gave in to the need driving him. His mouth opened over her in a caress that sent sensual lightning glittering through her. With a ragged cry she threw off the sweater and held his head against her breast, asking for and receiving a different, harder caress.

Even as Ten's mouth sent forerunners of ecstasy shimmering through Diana, his hands closed on her hips, shifting her until she was sitting astride his lap. One hard palm slid between her legs, cupping her, stroking her, making her burn. Sweet cries rippled from her, cries like fire consuming Ten, cries that made him wild with need. He unfastened the front of Diana's jeans and pushed his hand into the scant space between denim and her body. Hungrily he forced aside cloth until he could search through the warm nest to find the sultry woman-heat he needed to touch more than he needed air to breathe.

And then Ten found what he sought. He took as much as he could of Diana's softness and wanted more, much more, his body straining and his breath a groan.

The hoarse sound Diana made and the feel of her struggling against his hand brought Ten to his senses. He closed his eyes and took a tearing breath, afraid to look at her, afraid to see the fear and horror in her eyes as she remembered another out-of-control man, the front seat of another vehicle.

"God, baby, I'm sorry," Ten said hoarsely. "I've never lost control like that."

He heard Diana take a broken breath, then another, and felt her incredible softness pressing intimately against the hand that was still tangled in her jeans. Very carefully he dragged his hand free. Another broken sound from her scored him.

"Baby, I'm sorry," Ten whispered, looking at Diana's wide

eyes, wanting to cradle her and yet afraid to touch her. "I didn't mean to frighten you."

"You—didn't."

The words were like Diana's breathing—ragged. Ten shook his head slowly, not believing her.

"I heard you," he said flatly.

"I wanted you—so much—it hurt. I didn't know—it could be like that."

The last word was spoken against Ten's lips just before he brought Diana's mouth over his own. The kiss was deep, searching, wild. She returned it with a hunger that made both of them shake.

"If you kiss me like that again," Ten said finally, breathing hard, "I'm going to start taking off those boots you're wearing."

"My boots?"

"And then your jeans," Ten said, sliding his hand inside denim once more, searching for Diana's softness, finding it, drawing liquid fire and a ripping sound of pleasure from her. "I want you. Right here. Right now. Do you want me like that?"

With fingers that trembled, Diana reached blindly for her bootlaces. Ten made a low sound as his hand slid more deeply into her jeans. He smiled almost savagely, savoring her heat and the ragged breaking of her breath. Each movement she made as she worked over her laces increased the effect of his hidden caress. Ten made no move to help with the boots, for his other hand was too busy stroking the firm curves of her breasts to be bothered with such unrewarding objects as boots and socks.

One boot, then the other, fell to the floor of the truck, followed by the rustling whisper of socks. Slowly Diana shifted her body to the side, not wanting to end the wild, secret seduction of Ten's hand, but at the same time wanting to be free of the confinement of her jeans.

This time Ten helped, lifting Diana and peeling the rest of her clothes away, letting them fall to the floor. She shivered with heat rather than cold as she sat astride Ten once more. He looked down at his lap and the woman whose body was flushed with the passion he had aroused.

Slender hands reached for Ten's belt buckle.

"Baby, if you start there, that's where you'll finish. I want you like hell burning."

Diana looked into the hot silver of Ten's eyes and knew if she didn't take his boots off first, they wouldn't get taken off at all. His hand slid up her thigh, touched, tested deeply, knew the scalding need of her body.

"Yes," she whispered. "Like hell burning."

Watching Ten's face, Diana opened the buckle. Leather pulled free of the loops with a sliding, whispering noise. Metal buttons gave way in a muted rush of sound. She reached down only to find that he was there before her, his hard flesh parting her as he watched her take him, and he was filling her even as she watched. Her breath unraveled into a low moan as she was hurled into ecstasy. He drove into her again, burying himself in the clinging, generous heat that had haunted his dreams, and then ecstasy convulsed him and he held her hard, deep inside her, his mouth against her hot skin and her cries washing over him, echoing the sweet lightning of his own release.

Locked within ecstasy, surrounded by the cruel clarity of spirit light, Ten knew this was the way he would always remember Diana, and the realization was a knife turning, teaching him more about pain than he wanted to know.

CHAPTER SEVENTEEN

THE KNOCK ON THE DOOR WAS BOTH unexpected and the answer to Diana's secret hopes. Even as her heartbeat doubled, she told herself that she was being foolish.

It isn't Ten. He hasn't so much as telephoned in the weeks since I left the Rocking M, so what makes me think that he would waste a Friday driving all the way to Boulder to see me?

The cold, rational thoughts didn't diminish the fierce, hopeful beat of Diana's heart. She pushed away from her drawing table, took a deep, steadying breath and walked the few steps to her studio apartment's front door.

"Who is it?" she asked.

"Cash McQueen. Carla MacKenzie's brother."

With hands that weren't quite steady, Diana unlocked the door and opened it. Once she would have been unnerved at the sight of the big man who almost filled her doorway. Now the only emotion she felt was a disappointment so numbing that it was all she could do to speak. She forced her lips into the semblance of a smile.

"Hi. I thought you were in…South America, wasn't that it?"

"It was. I got back last week."

"Oh. Did you find what you were looking for?"

Cash smiled slowly, transforming his face from austere to handsome. His eyes lit with a rueful inner laughter. "No, but not many of us do."

Diana felt a flash of kinship with the big man. "No, not many of us do."

"May I come in?"

"Of course," she said, automatically backing away from the door, allowing Cash to enter. "Would you like some coffee? Or perhaps a beer? I think one of the grads left some here last night."

"Thanks, but I'll have coffee. Party last night?" he asked, looking around with veiled curiosity.

Diana's mouth curved in something less than a smile. "Depends on your definition of party. If it includes chasing elusive potsherds through mismarked cartons, we had one hell of a party here last night."

"I thought all the September Canyon stuff was staying at the Rocking M."

"It is. This is from a different site. Still Anasazi, though, as you can see. They're my first love."

While Diana disappeared into the kitchen, Cash walked carefully around the apartment. It was in a state of casual disarray that resembled an academic office more than living quarters. Scholarly periodicals, books and photos covered most flat surfaces, except for a worktable. There, potsherds and partially reconstructed pots reigned supreme. Photos and sketches were tacked to the walls. A bin full of sketches stored in protective transparent sleeves stood in a corner.

"Cream or sugar?" Diana called from the kitchen alcove.

"Black."

Cash walked over to the bin and began flipping slowly through the contents, studying various drawings. When Diana returned, he looked up.

"These are very good."

"Thank you." Diana set a mug of coffee on a table near Cash and cleared periodicals from a chair. "But photos are preferred by most scholars, unless they're trying to illustrate a point from their pet theory. Then they're delighted to have me draw what no one has yet had the good sense to discover in situ."

Male laughter filled the small room. Diana looked startled, then smiled self-consciously.

"I didn't mean that quite as peevishly as it came out," she said, clearing away a second stack of periodicals and sitting down. With a casualness that cost a great deal, she asked, "How's everything on the Rocking M?"

"That's why I'm here."

Diana's head turned quickly toward Cash. "Is something wrong?"

"You took the words right out of my mouth."

"I don't understand."

"Neither does Carla."

"Mr. McQueen," began Diana.

"Cash."

"Cash," she said distractedly. "You came here for a reason. What is it?"

With a characteristic gesture of unease, Cash jammed his hands in the back pockets of his jeans, palms out. He looked at the small woman with the haunted indigo eyes and lines of strain around her full mouth. Cash didn't know what was wrong, but he was certain that something was.

Carla, what the hell have you gotten me into this time? You know better than to try and set me up with another female in a jam.

Cash looked closely at Diana. Despite her abundant femininity, she wasn't sending out the signals that an available woman did. She had smiled at the sound of his laughter, but then, a lot of people did. They hadn't learned that laughter was a perfect camouflage for his view of people in general and women in particular. One woman, however, was exempt from Cash's distrust—Carla.

"My sister would like to see you again," Cash said, "but apparently you're angry with her."

Diana started to speak. No words came out. All she could do was shake her head.

"Does that mean Carla has it all wrong and you'd be glad to come out to the Rocking M next weekend?" Cash asked smoothly.

"No." The stark refusal was out before Diana could prevent it.

Not that it mattered. She wasn't going back to the Rocking M. Not this weekend. Not the weekend after. Not ever. She couldn't bear seeing Ten again and pretending that nothing had ever happened between them in September Canyon. Nor could she pretend that his baby wasn't growing day by day within the loving warmth of her womb.

"Carla's right," Cash said. "You're angry with her."

"No."

"With Luke?"

"No," Diana said quickly. "It's nothing personal." She licked her lips with a tongue that was dry. "I'm—I'm very busy. The school year is just getting rolling. There are a lot of things I have to do."

Cash's eyes narrowed to brilliant blue slits. "I see." And he did. He saw that Diana lied very badly. "Surely you'll have everything under control by, say, November?"

"I don't know."

"Probably?"

She gave him a dark look. "I don't know!"

"Well, I know that Carla will have a strip off my hide if you don't turn up for Thanksgiving. Now I can probably finesse my little sister, but I'd hate like hell to try finessing the Rocking M's ramrod with anything less than a bulldozer."

Color drained from Diana's face, silently telling Cash that Carla's guess had been correct: it was Tennessee Blackthorn who was keeping Diana away from the ranch.

"I can't see that the…" Diana's voice dried up. She swallowed painfully and continued. "What does Ten have to do with this?"

"You tell me."

"Nothing."

"Whatever you say," Cash muttered, not believing Diana and not bothering to disguise it. "Ten has developed a passion for all things Anasazi. If the recent past is any example, he's going to be a miserable son to live with until that kiva gets excavated."

Diana's eyelids flinched, but her voice was under control when she spoke. "Then by all means he should have the kiva excavated as soon as possible."

"Amen. How long will it take you to pack?"

"I'm not going anywhere."

"You're not making any sense, either."

"Mr. McQueen—"

"Cash."

"—the kiva can be excavated by any number of qualified archaeologists. I'm sure Ten knows it. If not, he'll know it as soon as you go back and tell him."

"I already have. He almost tore off my head. Either you excavate that kiva or it doesn't get done."

"Then it doesn't get done."

"Why?"

"Would you like more coffee before you leave?"

"None of my business, is that it?"

"That's it."

"Would it make any difference if Carla dragged the baby all the way out here to talk to you?"

"I'd love to see Carla and Logan, but they would be going home alone."

"What if Ten asked you to excavate his damned kiva?"

Diana's eyes darkened and her tone became as bittersweet as the line of her mouth. "He already did."

For the first time Cash showed surprise. "You refused?"

"Yes."

"Why?"

"Ask Ten."

"No thanks. I like my head just where it is. Lately that boy has a fuse that's permanently lit. The only one willing to take him on is Nevada. They had hell's own brawl a week ago. Never seen anything quite like it. A miracle no one was killed."

Diana remembered Nevada's dark, cold power. She closed her eyes and fought against showing her fear and love and despair. It was useless. When she opened her eyes she saw that Cash knew exactly how she felt.

"Is he all right?" Diana asked tightly.

"Nevada's a little chewed up, but otherwise fine."

"Ten," she said urgently. "Is Ten all right?"

Cash shrugged. "Same as Nevada."

Diana hesitated for a moment, then went to the bin and withdrew a two-by-three-foot folder. She opened it and silently looked at the drawing. Within the borders of the paper, September Canyon lived as it had once in the past, stone walls intact, houses and kivas filling the alcove. But the people were no longer walled off within their beautifully wrought prisons. They were responding to the call of an outlaw shaman who had seen a vision filled with light.

Women, children, warriors, every Anasazi was pouring out of the cliff dwelling, walking out of the alcove's eternal twilight and into a dawn that blazed with promise. Their path took them past the shaman, who stood in the foreground within the shadow of the cliff, watching with haunted eyes, his outstretched arm pointing the way for the stragglers as they filed past below. Something in the shaman's position, his eyes holding both light and darkness, his body removed from the other Anasazi, stated that he was not walking out of darkness with his people.

The face, the lithe and muscular body, the stance, the haunted crystalline eyes were those of Tennessee Blackthorn.

"I sketched this for the owner of September Canyon," Diana said, closing the folder and holding it out to Cash. "It's a bit awkward to mail. Would you take it to the Rocking M for me?"

"Sure." Cash looked at the folder and then at Diana. "You do know that Ten owns September Canyon, don't you?"

"Thank you for taking the sketch." Diana went to the front door and opened it. "Say hello to Carla and Luke for me."

"Should I say hello to Ten, too?" asked Cash on his way out.

Diana's only answer was silence followed by the door shutting firmly behind Cash. He raised his fist to knock on the door again but thought better of it when he heard the broken, unmistakable sounds of someone who was trying not to cry. Swearing silently about the futility of trying to talk rationally to a woman, he turned away and went toward his beat-up Jeep with long, loping strides. If he hurried, he would be at the ranch house before the afternoon thunderstorms turned the road to gumbo.

The next night, barely fifteen minutes after the last grad student left, Diana spotted the scruffy knapsack slumped in a corner. Bill usually remembered halfway home, turned around and came back. It had become a ritual—the knock on the door, the knapsack extended through the half-open door and the embarrassed apologies. Tonight, however, she wondered whether the knapsack would be an overnight resident. Bill had left with Melanie, and the look in his eyes had nothing to do with unimportant details such as knapsacks.

Diana glanced at the clock. Midnight—if Bill were going to retrieve his property, he would be back soon. With a shrug, she sat down at the table full of sherds and picked up two. The edges didn't match, but that didn't matter. Diana wasn't seeing them. She was seeing other sherds, other shapes and a matching that had been superb.

At least for her.

I've got to stop thinking about it. I've got to stop asking where I went wrong and why I wasn't the woman for Ten when he was the man for me. I've got to stop thinking about the past and start planning for the future. He trusted me enough to give me his baby. That has to be enough.

The sound of knuckles meeting the apartment door was a welcome break from Diana's bleak thoughts.

"Hang on. I'm coming," Diana called out.

She snagged the knapsack by its strap, opened the front door without looking, held out the knapsack at arm's length and waited for Bill to take it.

The door opened fully, pushing Diana back into the living room. The knapsack hit the floor with a soft thump, falling from her nerveless fingers.

Ten walked into the room and shut the door behind himself, watching Diana with hooded eyes that missed none of the subtle signs of stress—the brackets at the side of her mouth, the circles beneath her eyes, the body that was too thin. And most of all the eyes, too bleak, too dark.

Ten didn't know what he had expected Diana to do when he walked back into her life, but shutting down like a flower at sunset wasn't one of the things he had imagined. He kept remembering the moment when she had looked at him with eyes still dazed by pleasure and whispered that she loved him. She must have accepted his explanation that what she felt was temporary rather than lasting, for she had never mentioned love again. Yet the moment and the words had haunted him at odd moments ever since, tearing at his emotions without warning, making it painful to breathe.

But nothing had prepared him for the cruel talons sinking into him when he had opened the folder and seen himself standing alone, watching life pass by in a shimmering parade while he stood lost in shadow.

"You look tired," Diana said tonelessly. "Is the ranch still shorthanded?"

Ten made a dismissing motion. "I didn't come here to talk about the Rocking M's personnel problems."

Diana waited, asking in silence what she didn't trust herself to put into words. *Why are you here?*

"I came here to find out why you won't come back and excavate the kiva," Ten said bluntly.

"I have enough work to do in Boulder," she said, lacing her fingers together, trying to conceal their fine tremors.

"Bull."

Her hands clenched. "Why do you want me to excavate the kiva? Why not some other archaeologist?"

"You know why."

"Yes." Her lips curved down. "Sex."

Ten flinched but said nothing.

Diana turned away, knowing that she couldn't conceal her feelings any longer if she kept looking at him. When she spoke, her voice was desperately reasonable. "Don't you think that's rather a long drive just to get laid?"

Ten hissed a vicious word. "That's not what I meant and you know it!"

"Then what did you mean?"

"Are you pregnant?"

The bald question seemed to hang in the stillness like a wire being pulled tighter and tighter until it hummed just above the threshold of hearing.

"Don't worry, Tennessee," Diana said. "I keep my promises and I know you made none. Whether or not I'm pregnant, you're free."

"Damn it, Diana, *are you pregnant?*"

She let out a long, soundless breath. "You aren't listening. If I'm pregnant, I continue teaching. If I'm not pregnant, I continue teaching. Either way, I'm not going to excavate that kiva, so it makes no difference to you."

"No difference? What do you take me for!"

"A man who prefers living alone."

In the silence, the sound of Ten's sudden intake of breath

was appallingly clear. Anger and the cold fear that had driven Ten since he had looked at the sketch exploded soundlessly inside him.

"You said you loved me."

More accusation than anything else, the words scored Diana. "And you told me I didn't know what love was. You told me what we had was sex. Sex doesn't last."

The bleakness of his own words coming back to him cut into Ten more deeply than any intentional insult could have. Like the sketch, the words were a wounding that sliced through old scars to the living flesh beneath.

"My God, how you must hate me," he whispered. "That's why you sketched me as an outlaw too cruel to be part of his people's freedom."

The pain beneath Ten's words shattered the last of Diana's control. She spun around, her face white. "That's not what I sketched!"

Ten's breath came in hard when he saw the tears glittering on Diana's pale cheeks. He started to speak but she was already talking, words tumbling out, her voice shaking with her need to make him understand.

"I saw a man who turned away from the possibility of love even as he freed me to love for the first time in my life, a love that you didn't believe in. But that's not the point. The point is that you gave me a great deal that is of lasting value and took as much as you wanted from me in return, and what you wanted wasn't lasting. It was a very beautiful, very passionate, very brief affair. I don't hate you. End of story."

Long, lean hands framed Diana's face. Ten bent and kissed away her tears as delicately, as thoroughly, as he had once kissed away her fear of him.

"Ten," she whispered, "don't. Please don't."

"Why? If our affair was that good," he asked in a dark velvet voice, "why can't it go on?"

"What if I—" Diana's voice broke. "Oh, Ten, don't you see? What would happen if there were a child?"

Ten bent again, taking her mouth, making it impossible for her to do anything but kiss him in return. Diana made an odd, broken sound and held on to him, taking and giving and trembling. By the time the kiss ended, she was crying wildly.

"Shh, don't cry," he said repeatedly, trying to kiss away the tears again, but there were too many this time. "Don't cry, baby. It tears me apart. I never wanted to hurt you like this. Everything is all right, baby. Don't cry."

Diana thought of the child growing inside her and felt a dizzying combination of love and despair. Ten was back, but only for a night or two. A week. Maybe even a few months.

And then he would leave again. *What we have isn't love. It passes.*

"I'm sorry—I can't stop crying and I—I can't—I can't continue our affair."

Ten made a hoarse sound that could have been Diana's name and tried without success to stem the hot silver flood with his thumbs. He kissed her gently, then kissed her again and again, breathing his words over her lips as though wanting to be certain that she absorbed his words physically as well as mentally, that she believed him all the way to her soul.

"Listen to me, Diana. You're the only woman I've ever been completely naked with." His lips brushed hers slowly. "You're the only woman I've ever trusted enough to have my child." His tongue traced her lips. "You're the only woman I've ever wanted so much it haunted me to the point that I couldn't sleep. Not just your beautiful body, but your quick-silver mind and your laughter and your quiet times and even the anger that makes your eyes almost black. I want all of you. Don't turn away from me. Please. I can't bear losing you. Tell me I haven't lost you. Tell me that you still love me."

The dark, ragged velvet of Ten's voice wrapped around Diana, stripping away her defenses, leaving only the truth of her love.

"I'll always love you," Diana said, her voice breaking. "That won't change. But other—other things will. You—I—"

Ten's mouth closed over hers in a kiss that was a promise as well as a caress, a yearning hope as well as a burning hunger, a need and a sharing as complex as love itself. When he finally lifted his mouth he was trembling with more than desire.

"I love you, Diana. It's the last damn thing in the world I expected to happen. But it did and I'm not going to fight it any longer. Don't cry, love," Ten whispered, rocking Diana against his chest. "Don't cry. Just hold on to me and let me hold on to you. I've never been in love before. I've never wanted to live with a woman, to have children with her, to build a life around something other than silence." He looked down at Diana with hungry silver eyes. "Will you marry me? Will you have my children?"

Diana tried to speak but couldn't. She took Ten's hand in hers, kissed his hard palm and silently put it over the soft curve of her body where his baby was growing. She watched his eyes widen, felt his hand probe gently, heard the sudden raggedness of his breathing.

"Diana?"

"Yes," she said, laughing and crying at once. "Oh, yes!"

Ten's arms closed around the woman he loved and he lifted her off the floor in a huge hug, laughing with a joy he had never thought to feel—an outlaw walking out of the shadowed past into a future filled with light.